The Cooking Class in Kuala Lumpur

BY KAREN TRIPSON

Chapter 1

Amy pulled the cashmere blanket up to her chin, nestling her head into the down pillow. She kept her eyes closed and her back to the silk curtains that hid the French doors to a small porch just in case a sliver of light was coming through. The overhead fan made a soft whirring noise and a cool breeze on her face. The caress of the cotton sheets was another enticing reason for her to stay put. Her cocker spaniel lay on top of the bedspread, pressed against her in his favorite spot for nighttime companionship. She wanted to go back to sleep. She thought the dog agreed with her as he burrowed into her more firmly.

She heard footsteps coming up the stairs. The dog stirred again, listening with her. They both smelled the coffee. Kevin put *The Seattle Times* and a still-steaming cup on her bedside table. She turned over to embrace the dark roasted aroma intertwined with kisses and sweet nothings.

"Oh, honey, come back to bed. It's too luscious in here right now to give up." She reached over the dog and held up the covers to make an entrance for him.

He got in between the sheets, getting comfortably settled on his side, propped up on his elbow with his head in his hand cradling the dog between them. Thor rolled onto his back with a big, upside-down gravity grin, exposing his teeth as though this situation was hilarious, with all four legs askew. His tail quivered, legs shook, and his head went side to side to share his smile while Kevin rubbed his stomach. After a few minutes, he rolled back over, and stood up to lick Kevin's chin and then Amy's chin before jumping to the floor.

"Is it time to get up?"

Kevin closed the distance between them and kissed her forehead. "It's not exactly the crack of dawn. Some people have been up for hours."

"Oh, no. I'm not ready to get up yet." She put her head on his shoulder and his arms held her close to him. "I have a great idea. I know you don't want to have this party tonight."

"You have my attention."

"Let's cancel the party and stay in bed all day."

"I'd love to cancel the party, believe me, but if the price is an all day marathon, I'm happy to report that you are not the only one aging around here. I wish I could bargain in good faith with you about this, but if this is a negotiation, my opening offer is dinner at Rover's."

"No."

"A red leather jacket?"

"No."

"How about something gold in a small box?"

"A week in Paris."

"You're killing me."

"I want my party. But you look so good and feel so good. Why don't you ravish me just once then for fun?"

"What do you think this is, Saturday morning, with all the time in the world?"

"Yes, that's what I was thinking." She kissed him. He kissed her back.

"Your coffee will get cold."

"Who cares? You can warm it up again."

"You are so high maintenance."

"But totally worth it, right?"

"Yes."

When she finally was ready to get up, she couldn't resist repeating one of her favorite titles to an as yet unwritten poem, "*I Wish Every Morning Was Saturday Morning*."

Kevin said, "I know, and you *Wish Every Night Was Friday Night*. Aren't you glad I don't feel that way? Who would make the coffee or bring home the foie gras?"

"You're right. Someone's got to do all that stuff. Lucky for me, it isn't me. Let's have one round of 'Oh, poor Kevin' and then I'll make you some breakfast."

"Actually, I already had breakfast, but I'll be glad to sit with you."

Standing in front of the open refrigerator, Amy slowly surveyed the crowded shelves from top to bottom for a breakfast idea. She knew she was wasting electricity as the thermometer ticked upwards from thirty-nine to forty degrees, but she was hungry and wanted to make the best choice. Lunch would likely be later than usual due to errands for the party. The cold air from the fridge felt good on her face. The shelves were so crowded it was hard to see the possibilities and the storage drawers were full of fruits and vegetables. She didn't want to take the time to make bacon and eggs. She thought carefully about what she would eat that night, selected a few items that weren't on the party menu, and placed them on the counter beside the refrigerator. She dropped a slice of whole-wheat bread in the toaster and began slicing an avocado in half and then each half in four sections. When the toast popped, she spread a little pesto on it and topped it with a slice of low-fat Swiss cheese. Carefully pressing the avocado out of the shell on top of the cheese, contemplating whether to add salt and pepper, she felt Kevin pressing against her back with his chin on her head to observe the process. She pressed back. What nice, warm feelings were in the air this morning.

"I love watching you treat yourself. What are you eating?" Kevin asked.

"I'm on the verge of something amazing here, a good breakfast for a busy hostess. I wish I could say I invented it, but that Parisian baker, Eric Kayser, inspires this. I served it at a wine tasting recently and you enjoyed the leftovers. He uses a lovely smoked mozzarella, which really adds something this fake cheese does not, but it will work. There's avocado and pesto to spare. Want some?"

"Sure, I'll have a piece of toast garnished with all that Parisian stuff. My cereal with a banana seemed very l-i-t-e."

She put another slice of bread in the toaster. "Next time try a few cashews or dried apricots on the Kashi to give it some extra weight and texture. It might make it last longer. Would you mind giving Thor his breakfast while I do this?"

"Sure." He opened the refrigerator to get a big plastic container out of the pull out drawer for oversized items containing some very special raw dog food. Created by a local company, the food was delivered to the door every month in sixty small frozen packages inside a Styrofoam cooler, two for each day, with beef, chicken, turkey, or duck mixed with vegetables. With the easy peel off lid, it took ten seconds to feed the dog. He still wasn't sure about the economics of this monthly expense compared to home-made mixtures, but Thor, the previously finicky eater, wolfed it down every time, just as he was doing right now. It didn't even seem like he chewed it; he just inhaled it.

"Damn, he really likes this food. Are your feelings hurt?" Kevin stood over Thor, watching him licking the bottom of the stainless steel bowl so hard he was making a racket as it rolled around and around the rim of the wrought-iron stand that elevated it off the floor.

Amy put Kevin's plate down on his placemat and looked over at him still surveying Thor's activity. "I'm getting over it. Can we talk about today?" Amy put her plate down next to the laptop, which was open to a spreadsheet, and the newspaper folded open to the Business/Technology section. She sat down, took a small bite of her toast, and glanced at the headlines.

4

"Do I need to make a list?"

"Yes. When you're ready, let me know."

Kevin looked around for a pen and notepad in the junk drawer and sat down at the table next to her. "Okay. Fire away." He ate half of the toast she had made him in one bite.

Amy raised her eyebrows, resisted saying, "Chew!" and refreshed her laptop screen. "The top priority is vodka, Absolut, Grey Goose or better—a big jug, since Alan will make big martinis and inspire everyone to have two. Nice French vermouth, please, or one of the fancy ones from Oregon."

"Why aren't we serving those fancy cocktails everyone seems to like so much?"

"Because I don't want to let craft cocktails distract from the food. I want one simple cocktail option and get to the table promptly."

"What else?" Kevin asked impatiently.

Amy looked at him and smiled. "A quick sweep of the front steps and sidewalk. A playlist. Background music but with a variety of energy, new and old. I want to show my slideshow on the laptop during cocktails, and you remember the music I have for that. My show is fast, about two minutes. You can show your photos after that while I do the last-minute serving things."

"I'd rather show mine after dinner," he said, looking down at his list.

"It will never happen if you don't do it before. Don't be shy. Your pictures are great and everyone will love hearing you talk about them."

"I hate showing my pictures to anyone. It bores people and makes me look stupid."

She could see and hear that his previous good humor had evaporated. "Sweetheart, I don't think that at all. It's entertainment. We're getting them out of the house and into another world for a few hours. It's

5

supposed to be fun and different than staying at home watching TV."

"What else?"

"They are *your* friends. They are interested in your thoughts. They will be interested in your excellent photos. It will take five minutes max."

"I meant what else do you want me to do."

She smiled at him. "Ah, how about two more leaves for the table, and if you would bring them up now, that would be great so we can put them in together. I want to set the table soon."

Kevin got up and walked toward the steps to the basement where the extra leaves for the table were stored with the winter coats. Amy put the last bite of toast in her mouth as she took her dishes to the kitchen sink. She began moving the laptop, newspapers, and all the condiments from the table to the nearby chest of drawers so she'd be ready when he returned with the leaves.

Amy was standing by the table lost in thoughts of table linens when he leaned the leaves up against the wall behind her. Together they inserted them and repositioned the table to be centered on the carpet.

Kevin looked at the table and said, "What are you serving with the drinks?"

He seemed so cranky now. Amy wondered what was really on his mind and hiding behind all these questions about the menu, but she didn't want to indulge his bad mood by asking.

"Crab in butter lettuce cups and those crispy rice snack things."

"Is that enough? Aren't those crackers Japanese?" Kevin looked at her.

Ooh. He *was* cranky. And his hair was getting so gray around the sides of his face. She couldn't bear the idea of his beautiful reddish-brown hair going gray. "Yes, it's enough. I don't care if they are Japanese. They are the new potato chip. It's perfect with the martinis and the crab, all that crunch and salt. We have so much food at the table. I want people to be hungry." She looked at him but he didn't say anything.

"I don't know if you've thought about dessert since we last talked about it, but I still like your idea of a tropical fruit sherbet from Ken's Market. That would be easy for you to buy today and to serve. We don't need any death by chocolate from Macrina Bakery, and we've given everyone the lemon tart several times. Whatever flavor Ken's has that looks good to you would be great. We have some toasted grated coconut and mint leaves for garnish to give it a little Asian spin."

"Jeez, this is a long list. Whatever happened to relaxing on Saturday after a brutal week helping conglomerates oppressed by taxes?"

"Hey, life sucks, but you get to sleep with me. Lighten up." Amy put her arms around his waist and hugged him, pulling him close, willing his bad mood to go away. She looked up at him and grinned with mischief in her eyes. "Why don't you live dangerously and let me give you a few golden brown highlights around your face. It would blend naturally into your red and look great!"

He stepped back from her, "No way! My hair is not a creative project! Gray is what happens to everyone—except you."

She chuckled at him as he turned and walked away from her into the living room. He didn't think she was funny, but she had distracted him and gotten his mind off the menu. He didn't need to concern himself with that.

He turned back to look at her before he went upstairs. "Marrying you was the best thing I ever did, but if I'd known how many parties we were having, I might not have."

"Thanks." She smiled at his humor and puckered an air kiss. She loved hearing those words and accepted all compliments happily, believing every word. It wasn't in him to idly flatter anyone, including her. Compliments made him uneasy, but there were never too many for her. They calmed her anxiety about her sagging face and figure. He made it seem like he didn't see what she saw or didn't think it was bad. She wished she were not so worried about what she saw in the mirror. How shallow was that? She tried to only look once a day in her 8X magnifying mirror, just for a minute to assess the status of existing imperfections, and that was in the morning after a good sleep, when the benefits of the powerful double layer of nighttime emollients should be evident. If she looked any longer than that, she might see another age spot materialize before her eyes. Now that dark spot under her eye was the first one she looked at every day trying to gauge if it was bigger than the day before. She was terrified it was not a freckle but the beginning of something that might grow to be as big as a dime like the one on her jaw. The morning inspection guaranteed that she would not ever skip the anti-aging serum, daytime moisturizer with 30 SPF and the B&B cream for her daytime appearance.

"Are you leaving soon?" she said, wishing he would stay and chat some more.

"As soon as I shower. I'll be back by four or so to do my party chores because I know there is more than this list."

"Thanks for being so helpful and for making me feel wanton."

He shook his head at her and smiled, "You're hard to say no to."

Amy was excited. They were having a party tonight with dear friends. She was cooking Malaysian recipes she had learned on vacation at a fabulous cooking class in Kuala Lumpur. Her spreadsheet's completed column had lots of checks on it. What was left to do was very manageable this afternoon. Nothing was more fun than having company, except being invited to someone else's party, but that didn't last as long.

Ben and Alexis were coming, which was special because she and Kevin always had so much fun with them and they didn't get together that often. She and Alexis had been on the same product team in the dot-com days and had stayed in touch, unlike so many other co-workers from times past who seemed like friends until they didn't work together any more. Ben and Alexis were great cooks and eaters, not shy about trying anything. Alan, their oldest friend from college, was coming. He was always charming and a wonderful cook who took his dining very seriously. He was bringing a young friend she'd heard about but never met. Alan's young friends, who were always twenty-something, usually (and unintentionally) provided some big laughs in an all fifty-something crowd at Amy's. A self-assured, young beauty at the table would be fun for everyone, particularly Kevin, Ben, and Alan.

That made four people from the A-list. Two more would be perfect for good conversation and being able to listen to everyone. She had also invited another couple, Julie and Drew, somewhat new friends and brave consumers, with whom they'd had fun a few times, but they couldn't come. Other candidates for the last two chairs had been much discussed with Kevin. Amy's first choices were unavailable. He didn't agree with the second choices. Spontaneously, she had invited Laurence, an interesting old man she spoke with every week at the library where she volunteered. They talked about science and cooking. She loved his quiet confidence, no swagger. Of all the old dudes who flirted with her at the library, he was her favorite. He was tall and thin like Kevin, but his hair was pure white and he had the neatly trimmed white beard popular with many of the older guys. The invitation had just fallen out of her mouth as she was telling him about the recipes. She was surprised that she had done it and so was he, but he immediately said he could not come and walked away. She felt badly that her invitation seemed inappropriate to him.

Amy had even broached the topic of inviting some friends from the old neighborhood whom they hadn't seen in a few years, Natalie and Sam. Amy couldn't remember if they owed her an invitation or if she owed them. It became awkward when so much time had gone by to figure out how to reopen the door. Everyone else had met them at least once at other parties. Natalie and Sam were always fun but weren't that much on exotic travel or exotic food. Amy decided that a better fit for starting over with them would be a bigger event, a casual barbecue with more traditional dishes.

She wasn't going to buy any flowers because it didn't seem very creative. She liked to make her own centerpiece with props from her cabinets, greens from the yard, or potted herbs. She had two long thin oval mirrors that looked stunning in the center of the table reflecting whatever she chose to put on top of them. She might wrap some gold or red beads around the mirrors for extra sparkle. And it was inevitable that someone would bring a giant mixed-color bouquet, available at all the markets, too large for any of her vases, that wouldn't match the table settings or the color scheme of the house. It made such a mess to split up the bunch of flowers to fit in two or three vases, cut the stems because they would be too tall for the vases, and dispose of the wet newsprint wrapped around the stems underneath the decorative paper. Why didn't she just buy a giant vase for these occasions? The end tables in the living room were all small and already crowded with books and magazines. She just didn't have a good place for a dramatic bouquet. This was a small, single-flower house.

The only things she was serving that weren't from Malaysia would be the appetizer and the dessert. Cold Dungeness crab salad with cocktails was her favorite thing to serve to people she really liked. *Nothing says I love you like crab.* She would put a little Pacific Rim spin on it with some fresh-pressed ginger juice for aroma and flavor in addition to the mayonnaise, lemon juice, sea salt, and cayenne. She felt a little guilty for not taking more time to make an authentic Malaysian appetizer and dessert, but not enough to start more projects. It wouldn't be fun if she had too much to do.

The first course at the table would be a savory fish custard, called otak-otak. A rich, thick curry sauce with chicken, called rendang, served with rice and lacey, thin crepes, called roti jala, would follow. The crepes ensured not a drop of rendang sauce would be left on the plate. Those three recipes were from her cooking class in Kuala Lumpur. Amy was looking forward to showing everyone the darling copper roti jala cup that created the lace pattern in the crepes. Her cooking teacher had given it to her as a souvenir. Since she got back she'd been enjoying looking at it every day on her kitchen window sill next to the orchids.

Instead of a hot vegetable side dish, she choose a popular street vendor dish with fresh fruit and vegetables in a tangy fish sauce dressing, called rojak, that would be on at the table to be eaten whenever anyone wanted it. She wanted the contrast in temperature and texture with the otak-otak and rendang. This was going to be such a great meal! She was so excited.

FRUIT ROJAK by Rohani Jelani

Dressing

1 teaspoon pre-roasted Belacan shrimp paste *

2 bird chilies, finely sliced (or serrano chilies or cayenne)

2 tablespoons chopped palm sugar (or soft brown sugar)

3 tablespoons Kicap Manis (thick, sweet Indonesian soy sauce)

3 - 4 tablespoons finely chopped roasted peanuts

Salad Fruit and Vegetables

1/4 small peeled pineapple, cut into small slices (about 1 cup, prepared)

1 unripe green mango (or Granny Smith apple), peeled and cut into small chunks

1/2 small jicama, cut into small, irregular pieces (about 1 cup, prepared)

1 small green guava (or unripe papaya), cut into small irregular pieces (about 1 cup, prepared)

1/2 small cucumber, cut into small irregular pieces (about 1 cup)

Crush shrimp paste and chilies together finely in a mortar and pestle (or crush as best as you can in a small bowl with the back of a wooden spoon). Stir in sugar and sweet soy sauce and mix well until sauce is well combined and sugar is dissolved. Transfer mixture into a small bowl.

Prepare fruit and vegetables and place in a bowl or serving platter. When ready to serve toss with the dressing until well mixed, garnish with peanuts.

* To pre-roast the shrimp paste, turn the exhaust fan on high, as the pungent aroma is intense. In a small dry frying pan over medium heat, cook thinly sliced shrimp paste until crisp and browned on both sides about 2-3 minutes. Cool before using.

Chapter 2

Laurence woke up with a start that found him sitting upright when he opened his eyes. The top sheet was bunched, wrinkled, and lying beside him in a heap. The soft light framing the metal blinds told him it was still early. Day was just beginning. Thank god it was morning and he was free once again of the night. Laurence didn't particularly look forward to his days, but at least then he had more control over his activities. He was helpless at night, first waiting for sleep and then being tortured by his dreams. A dreamless night would be a gift. When had he been dreamless? Maybe never, but the nightmares seemed to have gone on for years.

He punched up his hot, compacted pillows to make a mound to rest his head on and lay staring at the ceiling, trying to ready his body and mind for the day. He started with bending his toes back and forth, then flexing his feet and rotating his ankles. Bending his knees, he progressed methodically toward his head, stretching and moving all the joints and muscles so they would work efficiently together when he stood up.

The ceiling looked gray in the early morning light. Later, it would become more of a dusty white, like the walls. He'd read there were hundreds of hues of white created by paint manufacturers. This one should be named "neutral." It was the color of nothing, no inspiration or activity. It was not warm or cold. It was likely sold in huge vats for refilling commercial spraying machines efficiently and purchased by landlords like his so every property under their management could benefit from the bottom line economy of dollars saved per gallon. Once, Laurence had been interested in color and affected by it. Thinking about color now seemed a waste of time and energy. The green escalators at the downtown library were a superficial aesthetic by an artistic ego, Koolhaas, who was talented no doubt, but surely wasted some of his resources creating theories for architectural students to learn. Green was not the color of motion, and it didn't matter what color the escalators were; people would use them. The color didn't encourage people to use them nor make them go any faster. His hip flexors were ready. The joints felt fluid without a hint of pain. The morning stretching ritual performed like high-quality jet engine oil, lubricating every joint and muscle.

As Laurence continued stretching, he heard the typical early morning traffic straining as it began the climb up Queen Anne Avenue North. The metro buses' transmissions heaved at the small plateaus of bus stops and intersections at Aloha, Prospect, and Highland before reaching the summit at Galer. The avenue was lined on both sides with apartment buildings, mostly brick and stucco, nothing very tall, built between the turn of the twentieth century and the 1960s. Poorly maintained cars struggled in second gear. New SUVs revved at high RPMs with their gas gauges ticking downward. His neighbors were still mostly quiet, a few steps in the hallway, someone taking a shower, but no voices yet to mar his morning ritual.

Laurence stared at the ceiling but tried to keep his focus on each muscle. Focus was important. Visualize. Concentrate. Keep the mind clear. When he had completed the routine on his back, he engaged his abs and sat up with his hands over his head, arms pressing against his ears, then leaned over to touch his toes in a ten-second stretch. He swung his legs over the side of the bed and rotated the ankles a few times more before touching his feet to the floor. Then he stood and stretched carefully and slowly with his arms straight up over his head. Then he leaned left and right several times, engaging his lats. Finally he rotated his neck slowly left and right and up and down. Feeling fully functional, he dropped to the floor in front of the bed and did ten push-ups. He caught his breath and did ten more. He stood up and felt his pulse in his wrist. Not bad for a seventy-five-year-old. In fact, some charts showed this to be a good rate for a sixty-five-year-old.

The next step was to reassemble his bed. He shook the top sheet out, made square corners on each end at the foot of the bed, and carefully tucked it in under the mattress. Then he spread the cotton blanket on top as the bedspread. Surveying the cover for unevenness and finding none, he walked into the kitchen to start the coffee pot. Later he would walk the interior stairs of his building, ten flights total, to complete his cardiovascular work.

While the cold water ran to clear out any stale water in the pipes, he carefully measured two tablespoons of Folgers regular grind for the gold filter, added one cup of water to the pot, and hit the button for the coffee maker to begin its process. He had been a widower for five years, and it still felt like a mistake to make one cup of coffee. Despite knowing exactly what he would find, he studied each shelf in the refrigerator, hoping for an error in his memory.

The centerpiece of the first shelf was a butterflied roast chicken still in the baking pan with one leg and breast missing. Surrounding the chicken were a few small red potatoes, green beans, and carrots. Two Pence peaches and two Cameo apples occupied the fruit storage drawer along with a half-pound block of sharp white cheddar wrapped in a cotton dishtowel. Would it be cheese and fruit, or cereal? He decided that cereal with a banana from the bowl on the counter was the better choice. He would save the cheese and apple for tonight after dinner. The cheese was so sharp and dry it almost burnt his tongue, and he liked to alternate bites of cheese with bites of crisp apple. The big finale of his day and the last grasp for pleasure was always the apple. Planning dessert before eating breakfast might be over-regimenting his day, but the alternative was to add some new ingredients to change the routine and he doubted he would do that.

Laurence closed the refrigerator door and opened a cupboard to grab the All-Bran Buds. By the time he had assembled the cereal and banana in a bowl, the coffee was ready. Settling in with his cup and bowl at the table for two, he opened the book about computer hacking still lying there from last night's dinner. When he had started studying the subject, he had been amazed how much of the defense against hackers was nontechnical, a lot of common sense about managing employees, security habits, and guarding the physical plant from intruders. On the other side of the hack was old-fashioned research into the fundamentals of the company. Learn the key employee names and then search for filenames and text such as "password," which were easily found once you were searching inside the network! Of course, he had no network to protect, but he looked forward to trying to breach one, just to see if he could. It was the challenge that made it all worthwhile. He wasn't planning to be malicious. He just wanted to be a voyeur of company secrets to know what was considered worth hiding.

Once you understood all the ways hackers could come at you and how to defend against an attack, you were then armed enough to hack those who weren't prepared or not prepared enough. He would soon be ready for a more advanced title. *Hacking* was no longer a compliment for innovation as in the early days of computing. Now it meant something else, more like a name for a cyber-thief, sometimes in the spirit of Robin Hood but mostly not. Terrorists and criminals were

17

hacking around the world making ordinary people and big corporations afraid. Some of the material he was interested in from studying the card catalogue was only available in digital format, which would make progress slow with the ninety minutes per day online allowed at the library. The inconvenience in some ways was better, because once he had breached a network, if his activity was noticed, the trail inside the public library back to him would be more difficult to trace than on a personal computer at home.

The hot coffee cleared his sinuses. He liked it black, the simplest way. He liked to streamline things as much as possible. Even the cereal was streamlined—high quality, high fiber, and acceptable vitamins and minerals, so no vitamin supplement was required. No milk. Milk could go bad before you drank it. Milk made the cereal soggy if you didn't eat quickly enough. He liked to eat slowly, chewing his food carefully. People who didn't chew their food properly suffered for it with no appreciation for the flavor and poor digestion. Food should be savored, however humble it might be, and each bite deserved focus. Focus gave the meal meaning. He was sure the body processed food eaten properly more efficiently than food eaten carelessly. Laurence was appalled at the people he saw on the street and inside the bus wolfing down fast food without a thought but speed, without any thought for quality or nutritional value. Food was fuel for the engine and required respect for the quality, quantity, and the timing. It was another lesson to be learned from jet engines.

Laurence finished his breakfast and completed the page he was reading, closing the book on the folded piece of paper he used for a bookmark and notes. Out the picture window of his studio-plus-dressing-room apartment, the layout that was so popular when the building was built in 1910, blue skies and the big brick Bayview Retirement building filled his view. It was the most massive structure on Queen Anne Avenue and much newer. The small, modest rooms facing the avenue and Aloha Street had a view of his humble building. The independent-living apartments with views of Elliott Bay were on the other side out of his sight. His view was Aloha living. Hello and goodbye. They might call it assisted living, but he could see into the windows of its residents. He could see the beds always occupied and not too much traffic in or out of the always-open doors. Aloha. Hello and goodbye. They should call it the Aloha Arms, not the Bayview Retirement Community. Aloha Arms would be a very efficient name for the place. Laurence wasn't going there even if he could afford it. He'd take a big jump off the Aurora Bridge before the nursing home that he could afford was his only option. The one he could afford would be worse than any other option.

Laurence feared a slow death from cancer like his wife had suffered. If it should happen to him at home, alone, he would die much faster than she had with a fleet of healthcare workers and him trying to keep her alive. He feared becoming homeless. But the odds were against either of those. His personal horror was an endless calendar of bare-bone days, like the non-color paint on the walls, enlivened only by his daily bus ride to the library and reading, and of course, his two meals each day, All-Bran Buds and later, chicken garnished with fruit and vegetables. The end most likely would be ignominious; he would fall down, break a hip, and starve to death lying on the floor by the refrigerator. But he would not violate his first rule: Never dial 911. That would keep him out of the hospital and out of the hypothetical Aloha Arms. To ensure he stuck to his guns, Laurence had no phone. That was no hardship. There wasn't anybody he wanted to talk to.

Laurence continued to imagine the grisly scenario. Quite some time would go by before the neighbors complained of the bad odors emanating from under his door. The management company employees would be annoyed for sure. But this option might be above and beyond the call for difficulty to him personally. There were better ways to put oneself out of misery. Yes, he knew the choices. He didn't have a gun or a car, but he could hang himself or drink poison or jump off a bridge.

Logically, one had to ask why not jump today? He needed to return his library books. Why not tonight? His dinner was already cooked. Why not tonight after dinner? He probably had five years left in these hips and knees. Those noisy joints would be the cause of his demise. Why put it off until he fell down? That would limit his choices further. Trying to guess the best time was probably like stock market timing. He hadn't been good at that either. He might wait too long to be able to do the job. That was the downside risk of waiting. After carefully reviewing this circular argument for 1825 days, he had not yet found a better way out of the labyrinth of *why not today*, but he was very tired of the argument. Freedom was so close. If all went well today, tonight would be the perfect night. Tonight after dinner he would wait until it got dark and he wouldn't attract any attention.

With that resolved, Laurence washed the cereal bowl, spoon, and coffee cup in the sink, leaving them to dry on a dishtowel.

His completed books were stacked, ready to go back to the library. As for the two unfinished ones, the one on learning to hack was on the dining table where he would look at it while he ate dinner. The Scottish mystery was still on the bedside table, with very few pages left to read. He would finish it on the bus today and return it. He was losing patience with the poor inspector who was at yet another crossroads, where everyone seemed to wish he would retire or disappear but he couldn't. Police work was all he had and only a few people were of interest, *not importance*, to him and they felt the same way about him.

Laurence identified with the inspector's narrow world but was frustrated with him for not realizing how lucky he was that he was only sixty years old. *That's still young,* Laurence thought. *They can't make you quit then, no matter how much they want you to or fiddle with your pension.*

Too bad there weren't more books featuring seniors as heroes. Older people like himself got tired of reading about young people. Books with old heroes would also be an education for younger people who thought they knew so much but didn't.

Taking a seat at his desk, Laurence surveyed the papers he had carefully arranged last night. He wanted to review the budget report one more time to be sure he hadn't missed anything. Highly unlikely, but errors could be discovered on the third or fourth review. Being meticulous was his habit, an attitude toward life, a philosophy he couldn't change if he wanted to. He felt he had done all he could do to be prepared for this day. His checklist entitled "Before I Croak" was almost complete. He would get rid of an old item today that had been languishing for years, waiting for the appropriate time. He was ready for it to be off his list. He was going to meet an old ex-friend from the Boeing days and apologize for crossing the picket line ten years ago. If all went well, they would exchange information about what had happened since they last spoke to each other. Then his history would be complete. His friend would not be able to contain the information even a day. He would be on his cell phone on the drive home calling people with the giant news of this meeting. After that, there was only one item left on the list that he could do whenever he decided the time was right, and that very likely might be tonight.

His schedule for today, as every Saturday, included walking on the Ship Canal in Fremont before catching up on some magazine reading at the Ballard Library. He hoped *Popular Science* and *Scientific American* would be on the magazine rack when he arrived. He

21

would take the #30 Sandpoint bus departing 9:39 AM from Mercer and Warren Avenue North. After his walk, he would take the #28 Broadview from Fremont to Ballard at 11:43 AM and walk across Market Street. He would go home after the library closed on the #18 Downtown at 5:55 PM or at 6:36 PM, depending on if he felt like strolling Market Street or Ballard Avenue. The thermometer outside his window showed the temperature was currently sixty-seven degrees, normal for the season, so he would walk down the hill from Aloha to the stop at Mercer Street and Warren Avenue North. Depending on how the day went and if he decided tonight was not the night, he might even check out a new book to read tonight or tomorrow morning. None of his Sunday branches opened until 1 PM. He didn't schedule Sunday. That was a wild-card day that might include the Capital Hill or Greenwood branch. He thought it was good for his brain to have an open day to consider and make decisions about. The schedule was about discipline and knowledge. Making decisions was a muscle that required flexing.

Seattle was his hometown. He'd never lived any other place. He'd watched it grow and make mistakes and have moments of grandeur. It had spawned Boeing, which once was the joy of his life, aside from his wife. These days he felt Seattle's finest achievement was the public library system. It was a complicated system that was well designed and ran efficiently.

For Laurence, it was a lifestyle. No, it was a lifesaver. The library was much more than just a place to spend the day studying any of his chosen topics. It featured aesthetically pleasing architecture, well-stocked shelves, and was equipped with computers, good databases, and reference librarians who knew how to find the obscure and elusive details he craved. The staff was service oriented and efficient, never cranky with an old man trying to learn something new.

Downtown on Mondays, for the last few years anyway, the spunky welcome desk woman had greeted everyone with a smile, even the ones like him who didn't want one. She was part of his Monday routine. He never smiled back or waved; he nodded. He approached the desk but kept his distance so he could slide away easily if real tourist business presented itself to her for help. He didn't discuss the personal things that he overheard other people telling her about their new teeth or thrift shop purchases. When he felt like talking, he spoke with her about something from *The New York Times* Science section, which they both read every week, or something from the cooking section. That seemed to be a big interest of hers. When he didn't feel like opening a conversation, he would linger farther away, long enough to nod hello, and she might ask him what he read over the weekend to draw him up to the desk. She was pretty, maybe fifty years old, which seemed quite young to him. He could tell by the consistency in her presentation that she was exactly what she appeared to be, a fortunate human being trying to give a little back to the community. Volunteering was a good thing to do. He had done it himself when he was younger and his wife thought it was important.

On the #2 bus, where he saw her frequently, he acknowledged her only with a glance and a nod that telegraphed *I see you, now leave me alone.* He hated people who chatted on the bus almost as much as the people blathering away on the cell phones. They never sat together. She liked to sit in the back on the left side by the exit door. Since her stop was the first one, she always got the same seat. When he got on the bus, he took the first available seat on the right.

When the Libraries for All renovations were complete, Laurence had toured the city to see all twenty-seven branches to inspect the architecture and the engineering. Every one of the branches' renovations

23

displayed intelligent design. The $290.7 million project, launched by the voters in 1998 and not completed until 2008, was quite impressive. Without question, it was the best achievement of the dot-com boom. The city and the library had raised the money when people were flush and willing to share the wealth. Nobody gave a thought then to what could happen if the bubble burst. It was a remarkable achievement in raising money and hiring good architects for each building. Several stock market corrections later in 2011, with the economy lackluster and budget cuts city wide, the libraries were struggling to keep the doors open thirty-five hours a week. He felt very lucky to have had the Seattle Public Library at his back. As some of his daily companions liked to joke, *The only good news, other than I woke up today, is that the library will not run out of books to read before I die.*

Laurence locked his door and headed to the stairwell for a quick walk up and down the five flights of stairs before he left for the day. Cardio sessions always made him feel stronger afterwards. Today some extra strength could be helpful.

Chapter 3

Kevin liked thinking about the trip to Malaysia. Amy had been thrilled by everything. He had thoroughly enjoyed himself, which surprised him. He liked traveling because everything was new, but it didn't always please him or amuse him as much as Malaysia had. The sights and the crowds were stimulating. Strolling the back alleys of Chinatown in Georgetown, the capital of Penang, one of his favorite stops during the trip, provided a jolt to the senses every few feet. He loved the sensation of being shocked and confused. What was it he was looking at? Having to dissect the scene to explain it to himself was a cerebral experience he longed for at home.

One of his favorite photos that he wasn't going to show anyone (in fact, he had decided he wasn't showing any photos at the party tonight), was a small motorcycle with a padded plastic seat that would fit two skinny teenagers comfortably in America but was used in Asia for families of five or six, including infants and toddlers, all without helmets. Attached to the seat was a flat metal rack that might have held textbooks with a bungee cord but held instead two stacks of brown eggs on papier-mâché trays about one foot square that each held thirty eggs. With ten trays right behind the driver and seven trays behind that stack, Kevin did the math several times to be sure of what he was seeing. He was good at math. But he was still awed by the result. The driver was departing with nothing more than two pieces of ordinary white kitchen string to secure the cargo of 510 eggs to the rack. Kevin watched him drive away until the motorcycle rounded a corner and was out of his sight to see if any eggs jounced out onto the paved, but certainly not perfectly flat, street. He wished he had seen the stacking procedure. Weeks later, he still marveled about the egg driver. That was one small event in long days of unusual sights and sounds.

The whole experience of eating in Malaysia was also captivating to him and Amy, creating conversation about what, where, and when it would occur. More conversation during the meal and afterwards might be accompanied by note taking or research. The food was phenomenal. Eating was a big deal, all day long. The big hotel breakfast buffets were elaborate and catered to international diversity with stations spread out in the room for traffic flow—and probably to give extra room or imagined privacy to each group. The Arab visitors lined up with plates in hand in front of the Muslim station on one side of the room, the Chinese in another area, and the Indians in yet another. Kevin felt like a man of the world standing in every line and sampling the most interesting of the hot choices from each station. Even a simple buffet in a small hotel would have the oatmeal of Asia, rice in chicken broth, curried meat in gravy with those thin crepes he liked so much, and always some fresh fruit choices, pineapples and melons, white, green, or orange. He really enjoyed how substantial the breakfast meal could be and realized how tired he was of eating cold cereal at home. The Malaysians were so accommodating to all the tourists. Kevin developed a respect for this trait and added it to his list of things he liked about the country.

"Amy, we need to have curry for breakfast. I love this and I am not even sure what it is. Here take a bite."

She took the offered bite and agreed it was good, with quite a bit of heat for first thing in the morning. She looked at his overflowing plate and said, "Honey, we only eat meat at lunch so you stay svelte with a healthy heart, so enjoy it while it lasts." She returned her attention to her mango and yogurt with coconut on top. She was glad he was relishing every meal like she was, but knew that readjusting to eating lightly at home would be painful. "Which buffet line did you get it from?"

"The Indian."

"It's probably vegetarian then! Good for you."

"I don't believe this is vegetarian. It tastes too good."

Lunch was the next eating adventure after touring in the morning. Kevin maintained lists in his notebook of recommendations from the guidebook, bartenders, hotel staff, and taxi drivers, or spotting a place that looked appealing to him. He liked to ask everyone they dealt with, "Where's your favorite place to eat?" There were so many options in Malaysia, not just restaurants, but carts, stalls, windows, food courts, and night markets. There were no worries for the tourists about eating anything either, as the vendors were regulated and the water was good, unlike some places they'd been where you had to be very careful not to eat anything that might have been washed. Kevin didn't want to waste time with the ordinary or the most popular spots. They were trying to eat only three or four times a day, but it wouldn't have been hard to add on a few extra bites, as there was so much to try.

Ordering was easy. The hawker stalls, carts, and walk-up window vendors were specialists at the item they sold, some for generations with the same recipe, and typically had signs in English, Malay, and Chinese. Establishments big enough to have a chalkboard or printed menu listed the English below the Malaysian, but the descriptions could be extremely basic at smaller places, more like translations, such as shrimp or beef.

Sometimes there were photographs of dishes near the ordering station. In the rare circumstances where there was no English spoken or a photo, Amy had been successful pointing to a nearby plate that looked good, hopeful her gesture was a polite *what he's having* and not a terrible tourist gaffe.

They felt like very tall white world travelers, the only non-Chinese perched on tiny metal stools around a tiny metal table in an open-air Chinese restaurant eating hot, spicy barbecued pork and greens. The clerk was right; this was not a place tourists went. That made it extra special to them.

When uncertain about what the etiquette was, he could count on Amy to embrace the moment, advance into the bustle, and figure out how and what to order. This was a good job for a bon vivant.

In small Muslim establishments, they knew to look for the sink where everyone washed their hands. They decided that there were certain times, no matter how much they wanted to, it was inappropriate to bring out the hand sanitizer that was always in her handbag.

The first time they had tried to observe and imitate the utensil-free eating of the Malays, the real challenge was the food was too hot to handle. The people around them had quit eating to stare at them. Amy grinned at the closest table and made a motion with her hand to her mouth, and they started eating again so she could see how they were balling up the rice with their fingertips and dipping it in the mounds. The rice, as it turned out, prevented burns on fingers, but they also learned that following the proper order of the dipping was essential to tempering the burns inside the mouth from the spices. The authentic dishes could be insanely hot even to chili heads like them. It wasn't just the sinuses that cleared. Eating an aptly named devil curry, Amy said she felt her whole head from the neck up was clearing, getting lighter through the steam releasing out her ears and the top of her head expanding upward, like a *Saturday Night Live* Conehead, finally to open up and let her brains slowly float out in a cloud of steam. She was so delighted with the whole experience. "Remember that time in LA we went to the Tunisian place and they brought out a whole roasted chicken that was so hot you did burn your fingers? This is much easier to eat because it's chopped up, but wow is it spicy! Give it a ten."

Then they felt like diplomats on a successful goodwill mission in international relations. Maybe they were glorifying a small event that didn't mean much but a good laugh for the locals, but they enjoyed the hunt for meals off the main path as well as the interaction.

If there was a night market open, that's where they ate dinner. The big cities had markets in several locations every night. Smaller towns had markets on Friday night or over the weekend. Multigenerational families squeezed in as many plastic chairs as possible around plastic tables. Sitting together with empty chairs at their table, Kevin and Amy attracted attention. They were both taller than the average European tourists, and their pasty Seattle complexions made them stand out from the Scandinavians who shared the height but were bronze sun lovers.

Sometimes people wanted to borrow the extra chairs or practice speaking English. Anybody who asked them anything was invited to sit down, of course. Mostly they were just curious about where Amy and Kevin were from, why they had come to Malaysia, and where the rest of the family was. Everybody was friendly and polite. No one had a clue about what or where Seattle was, but they all knew Microsoft.

Kevin's first pleasure in the night market experience was walking the perimeter of the food vendors studying what each one offered, discussing the options with Amy and then walking back around again ordering what had looked best, trying to be somewhat reasonable about quantities. It was easy to end up with food for four people and to eat it! Turning dinner into a tasting menu by ordering much more than they could eat just to be able to taste more dishes seemed wasteful and obnoxious when everyone else was eating family style and cleaning their plates. They always said they would stop ordering separate dinners and share like everyone else, but they never did.

Sweating cooks in front of woks on hot burners and deep-fat fryers were in constant motion, stirring, turning, shaking, and piling up food on plates. Frequently a front counter man took the order, collected the money, and gave the customer a cardboard number on a stand to use to mark the table with the order. A runner delivered the food to the table when it was ready. Kevin felt that five-star restaurants couldn't get food to the table any faster, fresher, or as hot as these night market vendors, and all without a word from the waiter!

Kevin's first Malaysian words were ikan panggang, which means grilled fish. Under that sign he might find mackerel, snapper, sea bass, stingray, prawns, crabs, or squid that could be grilled, sometimes wrapped in a banana leaf, making a concise package to slice open at the table and release steam and intoxicating aromas. The mackerel often was very simply prepped with lime juice and salt and pepper before grilling over charcoal but served with a big spoonful of chili sambal on the side. Every time, the fish was so moist and hot from the grill it didn't need anything else to improve it, but he was acquiring a taste for the sambal. Hotter than Sriracha or Tabasco, a minimalist salsa he thought, with chopped red chilies, lime juice, salt, and a pinch of sugar. The Malaysians seemed to be able to successfully work a pinch of sugar into many things. To merely dab a bite of white fish on the red sambal transferred a unique fiery accent that made a mouthful of the juicy fish with a crisp skin surrounded by lime, chili, and smoke from the grill. Impressive, yes!

Fried Black Pepper Prawns and Fried Black Pepper Crab were specialty preparations he also enjoyed, as were Chile Crabs. Kevin thought a big, cold bottle of Tiger beer was essential to accompany all this fish. Every bite of this food was pleasing to him. He thought it was the freshest fish he'd ever eaten. The heat from the grill and the spice made his whole mouth warm. Eating with his hands seemed efficient, almost sensual. Sucking the sweet meat out of the cracked crab claws and leaving no trace of the black pepper coating the shells was satisfying in a visceral way. He stopped peeling the prawns and ate the whole thing as he observed others doing so as not to miss any of the black spiced crunchy coating. Succulent! Eating with a knife and fork at home would seem cold and sterile. He would also miss selecting his fish while it was still swimming in a bucket.

The second day in Georgetown, they had started out after breakfast and consulted their notebooks with lists of sights to see in a walking tour of Chinatown and ideas of where to eat lunch and dinner. After touring the impressive Khoo Kongsi clan house with elaborate gold ornamentation, Amy said, "It's too hot for me today. I'm wilting. Walking around is not going to be fun. Maybe I should go back to the hotel."

Kevin looked seriously at her. "Do you need a cold drink? Want to go swimming in the hotel pool?"

"With a hundred kids on vacation in the pool the last time I looked? There's not enough room for me and the pee would probably melt my nail polish."

"Okay, I'm getting it now. The princess needs some A/C and a taxi. Can do." He turned to face the oncoming traffic and held out his hand to flag one down.

"My, you are so gallant. What a great idea."

Within a minute, a battered black taxi had pulled into the curb to chat with Kevin about the destination and the price. Kevin said, "How about a drive, a small tour of the island?"

The response from the driver was enthusiastic. "I'm a professional tour guide. I know everything about the island and its history. I have lived here all my life. How many hours would you like?"

After learning they had focused on the sites of Little India and Fort Cornwallis the day before and executed a strategic eating plan to hit a few of the well-known Indian specialties, he asked what they had eaten. Kevin didn't even need to look it up in his notebook. They had managed, with no trouble whatsoever, to snack on fried curry puffs, spicy noodles, and shrimp in red sauce called mee goreng, as well as a hot and sour fish stew with mackerel and okra called asam pedas in the daylight hours. After dark, they had attacked a fiery lamb korma with lime pickle on the side, sautéed cabbage, and memorable flatbread hot out of the oven. He agreed they had done pretty well and maybe Chinese would be a good change today. Why not drive down to the Chinese fishing villages at the end of the island, which you could only see by private car, and eat seafood? With that excellent salesmanship, Amy settled herself in the seat behind the driver, while he and Kevin agreed to a half-day tour including a very special lunch stop they would never find on their own. (The exclusivity of the tour turned out not to be exactly the truth. They later learned there was regular bus service, but they weren't mad.)

Amy seemed relaxed with her eyes closed, enjoying the ride in the air-conditioned car driving along a coast highway. It was a pleasant change from walking. The driver relayed important events in the history of Penang to Kevin as they passed landmarks. He had a British accent and was pleasant to listen to although Amy didn't seem to be paying attention.

"Snakes?"

Amy was startled out of her daydream and horrified to see the driver looking over his shoulder at her instead of the highway traffic.

"Snakes! Where's a snake?" She looked around the floor of the taxi and at Kevin.

"Amy, wake up. He wants to know if you want to see snakes and a Snake Temple? It's a photo op we'll be passing by in just a moment."

She looked at Kevin incredulously. "Of course not. Snakes come right after rats and vacuuming. Why did you even bother to ask me?"

Amy seemed to perk up after her little rest. She sat up straighter and paid attention now to the conversation. They both thought the driver turned out to be a real charmer. He looked incredibly like Omar Sharif, except he was much darker, almost black. He told them about his family, his arranged marriage, and hopes for his twenty-something-year-old kids. He didn't care if they didn't want an arranged marriage, but his wife had already been to see the matchmaker. He drove them up to a cliff to see the view of the deep-water harbor from the War Museum in Batu Maung. They walked around a bit to absorb the details of the view below them but declined to tour the museum. Kevin felt he knew enough about the activities of the Japanese prisoner of war camp from other sources. Amy was relieved he felt that way and thanked him again for the luxury of the taxi tour where you could decline all the shopping opportunities as well as the horrors of war.

The taxi drove them around the Chinese fishing village of Batu Maung as a historical point of reference because after hundreds of years of being what it was, it was soon to disappear and become something else entirely due to a bridge to be built linking it to the mainland. Ramshackle piers, brightly painted fishing boats, and a beach comprised the appeal of Batu Maung. After parking the taxi in the shade, the driver encouraged them to try a few hawker stands before they went on to the next village for lunch. Ah, a man who understood eating! They walked among the hawker stalls and finally decided on an order of crispy squid and one of sweet and sour crab. They bought two bottles of cold water to beat the heat and the spice.

The little morsels of fried squid in the paper cone were hot, crunchy, and succulent. The sweet chili sauce on the side was a surprise after so many hot, hot dipping sauces. They traded a few bites, but Kevin wasn't feeling that generous about sharing his crab.

"Kevin, I think there are people in North Carolina that would say, 'Hey, that's my BBQ sauce on that crab.' I love the vinegar edge to it. What do you think?"

Kevin was sucking his fingers to clean the red sauce off. "I give the Chinese credit. They were here first and smart about so many things. Those wily Carolina dudes will steal any recipe and call it an old family recipe. Look at my shirt! You can't even tell this is my second meal of the day. My technique is improving."

It was so nice to see their man waiting for them in the shade. Amy patted Kevin on the shoulder and said, "Honey, you are making me so happy today. I had no idea a private car and driver would appeal to me so much. It's not elitist, it's efficient."

"I'm glad it's working for you, but he's not coming home with us. In fact, you aren't going to see him tomorrow either, so enjoy."

"Oh, but he's so perfect, handsome and smart."

Kevin shook his head no but made a note to himself about the success of this idea. Points! He would hire some more taxis.

The next village, Teluk Kumbar, had prettier beaches and nice restaurants that served dinner only. One that was hard to get a reservation for, the driver told them, served at tables on the beach. But knowing Malaysia as they were beginning to, no doubt a fabulous lunch spot was just around the corner. The specialty of the house was also sort of the specialty of the town, Mee Udang. The house recipe had been within the family for years and featured more than sixty spices, according to the driver.

When he stopped the taxi in front of the restaurant and looked over the seat at them to indicate this was the place, Amy said, "Won't you join us? Please be our guest for lunch. We'd love to hear more about your family immigrating from India."

"Thank you, but I will visit with some friends while you eat."

"What are you having for lunch? Are you eating Indian food or Chinese?"

"I don't like Chinese food," he said with a big grin.

As they walked away from the taxi toward the restaurant, Kevin said, "Honey, I know you are sincere when you ask him to eat lunch with us, but do you ever stop to think that these spontaneous invitations of yours are very odd to someone like a taxi driver? Please try to think of it from his point of view."

"Well, I hope he's flattered that I think he is so charming I want him to join us."

"We're all having fun here, but I bet he thinks it's inappropriate of you to be so familiar. Would you ask a taxi driver at home to lunch?"

"He's not a taxi driver; he's our tour guide. They eat breakfast, lunch, and dinner with their clients."

"He's an educated taxi driver who has been hustling the tourists for twenty years. We're spending a few hours with him and it's his lucky day that we are."

"Okay. I'll try to remember to keep people in the proper slot, but I don't think I've done any harm here today in world relations."

"I am not saying you are being an ugly American. You are a vivacious American woman enjoying your vacation. Everyone can see that. I'm glad you are. But I'm sure your invitation will be a topic of conversation at his lunch and dinner."

"What's wrong with that?"

"You take everyone on as an equal and that's not how the world works."

"I think I'm a good tourist and everyone I meet is glad I am in their country spending money."

"No doubt about that."

She smiled at him. "It's one of my special talents."

The restaurant had a metal roof but was open air with striped cloth awnings to keep the sun off so it seemed shady and cool inside. Mee Udang turned out to be prawns and noodles with green onions and green peppers in a fish stock with a bittersweet aftertaste. Amy and Kevin both thought the sour note was special and stood out, as the other prawn dish they had enjoyed the day before, Mee Goreng, was spicy and not served in a broth. It was also Indian! Who ever heard of an Indian dish with noodles?

The prawns today were giant, bright pink, perfectly cooked, tender, and sweet. The broth would have been delicious all by itself. The fish flavor was so intense she could guess the stock had been made with a luxurious quantity, pounds and pounds of fish heads and bones, delicately simmered with onions and cilantro before the shrimp had been added for one minute. Guessing what other ingredients created the unusual flavor profile and had been strained out for a clear, pale red result was beyond her abilities, but had to include some lemongrass and galangal for the aromatics and delicate lemon flavor. Could it be tamarind paste creating the base sour note complemented by the top sweet citrus note of Calamansi lime? It was Chinese but like no Chinese they had ever had before. They lingered over the Tiger beer after slurping the last bit of the noodles and broth in a haze of well-being, affection, and feeling exceptionally lucky to be where they were. They resolved to solve the mysteries of the Malaysian fusion cuisines by buying a cookbook.

On the way back to Georgetown, Kevin quizzed the driver and took notes about more Indian food, hotels, and nightclubs. All the insider information gave him that feeling of getting more than his money's worth that makes a satisfied customer. Call it *lagniappe* or freebies, he believed in it as a business tool. After he dropped them back at their hotel, Kevin called a beach resort the driver recommended. The next day they took another taxi down the opposite coast road to Batu Feringghi and spent three nights that were memorable for several reasons.

When the bellhop opened the door for them, Amy practically swooned over the big room with a king-size bed with layers of pillows, white cotton sheets, and a textured white coverlet draped with a floor-length fringed piece of orange silk. Beyond the regal bed was a balcony overlooking hundreds of palm trees around an S-shaped pool and a big beach and the ocean beyond that.

"Honey, you're making my heart pound with these textiles and the view. Who will want to leave the room? Let's pop a cork and sit on the porch and then test the thread count in those sheets. I want to wrap myself in that silk throw. What a color!"

Kevin agreed to all of that, silently giving himself points. They didn't venture down to explore the new neighborhood, hotel, and pool area until it was almost dark and they were starving again.

Relocating to a higher-priced location on the ocean surrounded them with a more affluent crowd than they had run into in Georgetown and the business hotel. The bartender at a nearby restaurant could have been a barman in New York or London. The white tablecloth dinner experience seemed from another country compared with the street hawkers a few blocks away. They toasted Malaysia with gin and tonics for providing so many pleasurable contrasts.

After the first night at the swank restaurant, they chose to eat at the night market where the crowd seemed a mixed bag of locals and tourists but none of the finely dressed Arabs from the hotel. To get to the food court, they had to inch their way through a gauntlet of vendors on both sides of a narrow sidewalk crowded with shoppers perusing jewelry, knockoff designer bags, and crafts. Suddenly a narrow opening between vendors revealed a big concrete square full of tables lined on three sides with hawker stalls selling all the classics of Penang. It was a dazzling display of red paper lantern lights, people, food, and the best smells of cooking and grilling. Amy felt like Alice falling down the rabbit hole to find herself in Wonderland.

Kevin shook his head at her and said, "You're not enjoying yourself too much are you?"

"Impossible!"

He laughed and said, "Here, have some more of my crab."

They spent a few hours day and night on the balcony overlooking the pool enjoying the view, the breeze, and justifying the expense of the room. They ended up agreeing that luxury isolates itself behind walls and becomes monotonous. It could be a beautiful beach anywhere they were staring at, and, meanwhile, Malaysia was continuing outside these walls and they were missing it. They were happy to move on after a few days and see something new.

Seattle would seem dull and drab when they returned. That was exactly why he went on vacation, to experience something completely new and stimulating. He knew he would slowly shut down all the extrasensory receptors needed to comprehend the scenery here. After a while, he would be back to his quiet, low-key existence, his weekday schedule and his weekend schedule. The monotone of life, when not on vacation, was not bad; it was just different. What he and Amy needed was to go on vacation more often to keep those receptors operational, which was impractical for his work and retirement savings. He tried to convince himself that not going on vacation very often is what made it exhilarating.

The real carrot for continuing to work diligently was to sock away as much as possible so that when he couldn't work anymore, for whatever reason, there would be plenty of money. He was not going to be old and poor. Old was inevitable. Poor was in his control. The stock market collapses in the 2001 and 2008 had made him a conservative investor and ratchet up his final number goal. He wasn't counting on the past performance of anything or Social Security. So a vacation not taken was one in the bank for future pleasure. He would look forward to the next and preserve the memorable moments of the recent trip.

But, he didn't really see the need to tell everyone all about it tonight the way Amy did. He didn't want to be a complete curmudgeon about her excitement for the trip because he shared it, but it felt too personal to him to be broadcasting the details. It wasn't anybody's business what he did or didn't do on vacation. It was the absence of people he knew that made it a vacation. He preferred to keep his shirt buttoned up in front of friends and his tie on at the office. His carefully cultivated reserve that was essential in business to inspire confidence and respect from clients and competitors would be undermined if photographic proof of clowning and romance were to be distributed. He made a note to be sure to permanently delete that photo of him pretending to answer a call in a red pay phone booth marked with a big white "Helo." It looked like a Three Stooges sketch. She thought he was hilarious when he did it—and he was—but no one else needed to share that moment. Thank god there were no photos to worry about of him lounging in the bed built for sultans.

The focus of the night should not be the vacation, but rather that Amy had learned some new recipes overseas. Cooking was her passion. There was nothing she enjoyed as much. He appreciated it every day. He was sure he knew no one who ate as well as he did. She planned and packed lunches he looked forward to eating at his desk and something lighter, but equally anticipated, for dinner at home. When she worked full time, she thought nothing of spending an hour preparing dinner. She said it was relaxing! He knew she had had a bad day at the office when she arrived home and said, "I'm making a pot of black bean soup tonight." What that meant was she was needed several hours in the kitchen in order to relax. When her work days ended at midnight for months on end, she cooked on Sundays for the whole week so he never missed a lunch or dinner. Good food was a pillar of her philosophy of life. He had quickly come to embrace her concept.

Amy loved creating a party, too. That was a separate obsession from cooking but related to it. When Amy was excited about cooking and connecting with people, she was being herself. He had to stand back and let her go full force. There was no point in trying to slow her down or deviate from the course she had plotted.

She spent hours on the spreadsheets with lists of ideas and recipe cross-references. Afterwards, she carefully recorded in the hostess notes column what recipes people liked, failures, suggestions for next time, and her opinion of the evening or the people. He had advised her it was dangerous to be so honest on a wireless network. They could be hacked. Guests gathered around the bar area where the laptop was always open might happen to view a document in error or in curiosity. He hoped no one ever got hold of those spreadsheets. No one needed to know how shocked she was at personal preferences different from her own.

"Oh, my god! They don't eat crab!"

"Thank god, we're never having them again."

"He's drinking again—gin and red wine."

"She brought an expensive bottle of wine!"

The planning that went into parties always astonished him. What was it about planning that was so intriguing to her? If only she would be so meticulous about her checkbook.

Kevin couldn't believe how adept he had become at helping with her parties. He hated parties. He hated going to parties. He hated giving parties. Parties were an element of the marriage that was hard on him. Relaxing evenings in front of the fire with a good book were squandered away being social here or at someone else's house or worse, a restaurant where the food was never as good as it was at home. Why couldn't everybody stay home? For every invitation she received with glee, he shook his head and thought, that's one more party we're having here. The women she knew kept perfect records on whose turn it was. Only a disaster could knock someone off the roster not to be invited again or accepted again. Sometimes he hoped for crude, rude, obnoxious behavior that would guarantee this was his last sighting of these people.

Despite his complete lack of interest in entertaining, he *would* do whatever it was she wanted him to do to show he was participating, and earning his points. He wanted her to feel supported in her hobby even though the only pleasure in it for him was showing off the house.

Kevin loved his house. He was proud of it. He thought it was beautiful. He happily spent money on maintenance and any decorative things she wanted. Kevin imagined that anyone who came to their house looked around and thought, *This is a fabulous house, not big or luxurious, but very inviting. Every room welcomes you with a comfortable place to sit down to read or chat or study a painting that attracts your attention.* Kevin accepted all these imagined reactions as a reflection on him, a compliment to his hard work to pay for them and his good taste.

And the food was always good. That made entertaining a little less painful. This photo deal tonight made him nervous though. This would be a disaster. The pictures would be embarrassing. He pictured the crowd rolling their eyes behind his back. Making the playlist for this crowd was a pain, too; it was a lot of trouble for what would be background music no one noticed unless a song they hated popped up. Then someone would pounce on him. Kevin enjoyed being with Alan and Ben—they were his favorite guys to hang with—but Alan had no taste in music and would be the most opinionated about it. Alan excelled in making provocative conversation about world events and Ben would spur him on by knowing the details about everything else. Kevin looked forward to that part.

Hopefully, the monkeys in Congress would be the topic, not Malaysia. Kevin reconfirmed his resolution to skip the photos and move on to politicians on the hot seat. There were so many to choose from. That would be the topic for the night. And of course, there were the usual plethora of wars going on around the globe that would make good conversation about the different politicians.

Kevin had his newspaper to read over lunch and after he finished the paper, his book about meth labs in the Midwest as the new regional cottage industry. He was looking forward to eating quietly as a reward for his errands. Ballard would be the place to go for the vodka with good parking and good lunch venues to choose from. Lunch would seem appealing in a few hours after only eating healthy bran cereal for breakfast. A chicken sandwich would be tasty, maybe a Reuben as a reward for not eating bacon and eggs. A steak sandwich would be good, too. No harm in a little beef after a week of white meat, or no meat and staying with the exercise program. Every day this week his weight had been right on the number he wanted. No fries, though. He'd ask for Caesar salad on the side.

He would drop by his tax law office to research an angle that had come to him in the night. No one would be there. He didn't expect the admin, the paralegal, the associate lawyer, or his partner to work weekends because he didn't like to work weekends unless absolutely necessary. The quiet would be helpful to the research he planned to do that might be the solution to a problem that had been eluding him all week since this special referral from an old client had dropped on his desk. He counted the work as a windfall and doubted he would be able to retain the account but he wanted to demonstrate acumen and speed. It would be sweet to be able to call today, bonus points for it being Saturday and say, "I have an idea that may work for you to file for a refund of taxes paid by the ownership entity before the default. I'll research it and run the numbers. We can get together Monday afternoon to review them. I think it might really improve the current cash situation and get you out of the hole." Kevin would plant the hopeful outcome in the words *refund* and *improve* and get the guy thinking all weekend that this was going to work out and how lucky he was to have a creative tax guy, who so valued his business, he was working on Saturday. True creativity, according to Kevin, was creating a billable on a Monday with a happy client who will pay promptly. If his idea worked, it would definitely be an event worthy of celebrating tonight.

If his idea didn't pan out, the logistics of new filing deadlines needed to be outlined for the accountants. He might be able to buy them some time to work another angle. He'd cover his own bases by reviewing his current list of work in progress and reprioritize by shortest amount of time to complete rather than by the start dates. There's always a way to keep the work moving efficiently if you actively manage it. Score! This day was looking up.

"Honey, I'm leaving now. See you later," he said to no one as he passed through the foyer. She must be upstairs.

He inspected the narrow lawn on his way down the steps and shook his head. If he mowed it once a week, that northwest trinity of moss, clover, and dandelions could be construed as grass. Right now, it looked as though he hadn't mowed in a month. The median strip between the sidewalk and the street looked like a dandelion farm ready to be harvested. He put deadheading the dandelions with his push mower on his list for later today.

His car was parked at the beginning of a tight line of cars that extended to the other end of the block. The advantage of getting the end parking space was being able to back up around the corner and not having to drive around the block. It was a good thing traffic enforcement didn't come by too often to measure the fifteen feet from the fire hydrant. His interpretation had been very liberal the last time he parked. He frowned at the peeling paint on the fender. The car would look perfect if it hadn't been for that replacement fender being shoddy. He cursed the idiot who had run into him fifteen years ago. Backing up slowly around the corner, he got headed in the right direction, and drove up West McGraw Street past Ken's Market, the #2 bus stop, and the Macrina Bakery to turn toward downtown on 10th Avenue West for his office on 4th Avenue. He was glad to be driving instead of taking the bus. He'd had enough of his bus friends this week, what with having to be civil at the bus stop while not being inclined to go into detail about anything *and* walking home up the hill for exercise. Today already had enough aggravation built into it to waste any precious moments he might carve out for himself.

Chapter 4

Amy was self-taught but well-armed and fearless in the kitchen. The only good thing she could think of about being her age was that she had participated in every cooking, restaurant and travel trend over the last thirty years *in real time* as a loyal subscriber to *Gourmet* magazine. She still hated Ruth Reichl for killing that golden goose of entertainment with lots of new recipes to try from every issue. Amy had trusted the editors there to keep her informed of what was important around the world in food. None of the other cuisine magazines could hold her attention. She absolutely did not trust many of the online resources. She saw too many inaccuracies and poorly written recipes. Her cookbook collection was extensive but carefully selected and occasionally edited to make shelf space for more useful books or new interests. She read her books cover to cover, flagged recipes to try, cooked from them, and used them frequently for research. Often after consulting a few of her heroes on a topic, she put the books away and proceeded with her own version. Her books were a valuable asset and some she loved like old friends or family, others had the electricity of new friends or a handsome stranger in a bar, but nothing could replace the thrill of *Gourmet* magazine in the mailbox full of new tastes and ideas.

Beyond the amazing flavors, the allure and challenge of Asian cooking was the ingredients. She had devoted time trying to learn Thai and Chinese cooking over the years. So many vegetables, herbs, and spices were still unfamiliar to her despite reading recipes, researching the unknown items in an encyclopedic reference book that covered all the Asian cuisines, and looking for them at Uwajamaya. One of her goals in Malaysia was to learn new ingredients firsthand, rather than studying pictures in a book.

Amy had a good scale for weighing one gram to two pounds, imperial or metric measurements with the push of a button. She had a spice grinder, a mandolin, a food processor, a rice cooker, a good-size wok, and a fifteen-gallon pot with a lid for big jobs. Other than a sharp knife, that's all she felt she needed to handle the cuisines of Asia. She felt ready to take on Malaysia.

It had only been a few weeks since they got back from Malaysia, but the afterglow of the trip was starting to diminish. She hoped to revive and maintain the emotions with this party and then another and another. She might have a party a month for a while to practice all the things she had experienced and wanted to be able to make herself. Amy felt there was magic in the Malaysian food that made her happy. She was going to re-create the delightful sights on the plate and sensations on the palate that she and Kevin had both enjoyed so much and make the feelings go on and on.

Finding the cooking class had taken hours of looking online. She was motivated to learn new ingredients and dishes, but her hidden agenda was to be independent from Kevin for a day or two and satisfy an old dream of taking the cooking class at the Oriental Hotel in Bangkok. Kevin had an annoying habit of announcing he wanted to take some time to himself. She could count on it happening over the weekend when she least expected it, when there was a warm and fuzzy feeling in the air, after a lazy morning reading in front of the fire, or after the last bite of a good lunch. Why interrupt this rosy glow? She was all for his solo time because he returned relaxed and refreshed, but the abruptness bothered her and left her having a hard time making up her mind how to use the unexpected free time. Sometimes she tried to manage her time by saying in the morning, "Why don't you plan to take some time off this afternoon? I want to go look at something that would bore you to death." He would be so surprised he'd say, "I didn't have any thoughts of going anywhere today. I want to hang out with you."

When he did it traveling, she usually went back to the hotel to read and take a nap. Signing up for a cooking class was the perfect way to take charge of the schedule and let him figure out something to do with a big block of time. It might satiate his need to be alone. They would plan the trip around the class. She would do something meaningful to her, and he would have his precious time. Why hadn't she thought of this strategy about twenty years ago?

Amy had been so excited about the cooking class she could hardly sleep the night before. She worried she would be a horrible student and the other student would be amazing or that she would sever a finger chopping meat and need to go to a hospital, even though she'd never had a bloody mishap with a knife in her life. She wouldn't have the right shoes. The taxi wouldn't find the right address and she would miss the class. Kevin was encouraging her in the hotel room the morning of the class as if she was a kid afraid to go to the first day of school.

She had no idea what the location might be like, even after studying the map online; it seemed like it might be in a shopping center. She envisioned a fifth-floor walkup tenement with creepy men in the stairwells, screaming kids, and bad smells. Once she got in the taxi, she was more worried about being killed in a traffic accident before she arrived than anything else that might happen that day. When she finally did arrive sweating profusely at the address she had been given, she found herself in the lobby of an upscale apartment building with a luxury food market in the lower floors. She felt she was entering another world, enveloped by something aesthetic and calming. The air inside was cool and refreshing after the humid and hair-raising taxi ride across the chaotic city of Kuala Lumpur.

Rohani Jelani, food stylist, cookbook author, and cooking teacher, was diminutive and stylishly thin with a graying, chin-length bob haircut parted on the side to frame her high forehead and oval Chinese face with a small nose and big, dark eyes. In a sleeveless fitted dress, pearls, and a chef's apron tied around her waist, she looked so chic. Amy felt like a giant American outfitted for a safari and wished she had worn something else. Rohani's posture was perfect. She welcomed Amy and the other student with a cold drink in a tall glass and introduced them to each other and the work area.

The kitchen for the class was beautiful and new. A long, brown granite counter separated the kitchen into two work alleys with a stainless steel counter and sink area against a wall. A textured opaque glass-paneled wall rose above the steel backsplash, and gold textured glass formed the base of the granite counter. Small ivory tiles and robin's egg blue paint covered other parts of walls. The combination was like nothing Amy had ever seen before. It certainly was a contrast to the long side of the L-shaped room, very white with modern art, a long, dark French leather couch with lime green silk throw pillows and two chairs. The dining table was white marble with a dark banquette on one side easily seating four or five people and two mahogany chairs on the other side, plus chairs on either end. The total effect was stunning and so unusual. She had never seen anything like it in any of the shelter magazines she read. Amy kept trying to figure out what made it so different. It had to be the nontraditional combination of textures and surfaces that made it modern but not cold. Was it Asian, Malaysian, or just Rohani's style?

Whether Rohani was sitting, standing, or moving, she made it look effortless. She glided around the kitchen. It was a pleasure to watch her move. She spoke with the same calmness reflected in her body language. Words, too, fell effortlessly out of her mouth without hesitation. She never seemed at a loss or had to search for the right word. This level of articulateness from the multilingual always staggered Amy. *What a pathetically uneducated bunch we Americans must seem to so many people. Her third or fourth language skills are better than my first and only language.*

Rohani wasted no time putting them to work at separate prep stations and launching into a dialogue about her cooking school. "I'm fifty-one and my children are grown. I'm divorced. Make those turmeric slices smaller, the same as the ginger. I bought this place thinking I would spend more time in town. I haven't yet. Then I decided if I was going to keep the cooking school, I needed to remodel and make it bigger and more modern. So we meet here today. I had room for eight students and now I can do fifteen to twenty. I can do corporate classes now. That seems to be the new thing. In the beginning I wanted to help the generation of Malays who didn't learn at home to cook the traditional methods. Their mothers didn't bother to teach them because they were going to have careers, and it is so cheap to have a cook, everyone does." She looked at her assistant washing dishes, who didn't seem to notice the comment. "Amy, I think you forgot to add the water to the spice paste. It should be more liquid than that. We do the classes outdoors in a beautiful garden where you can harvest the herbs as you need them. I call it Bayan Indah."

Afraid to look up and nod for more than a moment while chopping shallots, Amy couldn't believe how easily, even casually, Rohani announced she was fifty-one. Amy was fifty-something and unable to say her age without choking, so she never offered it, even when prompted by other people. When forced, she usually lied by at least three years, even to the treadmill at the gym. Rohani could be telling people she was forty-two and anyone would believe her, if she would cover up the graying hair. It would be so easy and look so much better.

Not only could she share her age, but she completed the profile noting the lack of husband and far away children. This was a confident woman. Rohani was starting a new enterprise all by herself. Amy was so impressed with her calm and competence and couldn't get over how comfortable Rohani was in her fifty-one-year-old skin. Rohani was her new hero. This was a woman to emulate. She was following her dream and investing seriously in the business aspect of it. Amy resolved to try to stop worrying so much about everything and start rethinking her early retirement plans and come up with a new business plan.

Rohani held up a handful of long, thin green leaves that looked sharp on the end and not that pliable. "Let me show you a nifty trick with the pandan leaves. Do you know pandan? I didn't think so. Here, take a handful like this and fold them over three or four times so that you have a bundle like this about eight inches or so. Take the scissors and split one in half to tie the bundle securely. Cut all the leaves on this half into thin strips about five to ten centimeters long. See, now you have a basting tool. Pandan is poor man's vanilla. Make a pan hot with butter and swish your pandan baster all around. Smell that. Yes, vanilla. Anything you cook in this pan will have that flavor and aroma. Great trick, isn't it?"

Clearly Rohani was delighted with this demonstration, and both students were totally charmed. The aromas in the kitchen were heady. Neither of the students had ever seen ginger with a practically translucent skin. It didn't look or smell like the ginger with a tough, thick tan skin Amy had been using for years. They had also never seen fresh turmeric, a thinner relative of ginger, with an exterior tan skin and texture similar to ginger but with a carrot orange interior.

Working off trays with premeasured ingredients in small plastic portion cups, each tray with a copy of a recipe, it seemed easy to process each ingredient as instructed. *How nice to have someone to do all the measuring and washing up.* They plumped up dried chilies in hot water. They cut ginger, galangal, garlic, shallots, and fresh chilies in chunks and then processed it all to a paste. Preparing a paste and then frying it was a familiar technique to Amy from Indian and Mexican cuisines, but the smells were foreign.

Dry roasting coconut in a sauté pan over very low heat was a new technique to Amy and smelled delicious long before it was browned. It started out smelling sweet, although it wasn't artificially sweetened, and then became a nutty aroma as the color suddenly changed from white to golden brown. It stayed white so much longer than you expected it to, but the change in aroma was simultaneous and another cue that the estimated twenty minutes time was almost up. Amy was a big believer in her sense of smell as her most important cooking tool. She believed her nose was more accurate than the timer she always set just in case she got distracted. Standing, stirring the coconut for twenty minutes had a Zen-like calming element to it, but Amy was still connected to every other activity and aroma in the room.

She inhaled citrus oil, squeezing kalamansi limes. The little green balls were the size of a key lime but had a natural sweetness that must be the result of a cross with another citrus fruit that was not tart. Amy felt her loyalty to Meyer lemons wavering. Her nose was aquiver. She felt light as air and like she, too, was hovering above the floor instead of standing. She wanted this fabulous feeling to go on forever.

Amy's classmate was an American man in her age group who revealed early in the session that he cooked for a wife and child that between the two of them ate no garlic, chilies, green pepper, or fish. That was a jaw-dropper for both Amy and Rohani. Despite those limitations, he had great enthusiasm for what they were learning and was very meticulous. He planned to share all the details with a food friend in Connecticut. This was to be the menu he would cook for the annual New Year's Eve dinner with his friends. He planned to practice it several times and make the necessary modifications for his family's preferences.

Rohani kept them busy for hours. Other than pausing to watch demonstrations, everyone chatted while working. Amy was amazed at the conviviality of the group and the complexity of the recipes. This was old-fashioned time-consuming preparation from another era when cooking the main meal was an all-day job for somebody. When they all sat down to eat, it was almost two.

The curry laksa was served first in small white bowls. The golden soup was a sensation in the nose, the mouth, and the brain. Spicy enough to clear the sinuses but not incendiary on the tongue, the soup was creamy with a hearty depth that she could only compare with a Bolognese sauce that had simmered for hours. This laksa recipe was worth traveling thousands of miles for.

Amy marveled at how the ingredients were perfectly balanced as a chorus with no soloist. Sweet, sour, salty, bitter, and umami were in each bite. She wondered about the nasty-smelling Belacan shrimp paste, a Malaysian specialty, as the umami element. There was no trace of that bad odor in the soup bowl. She looked forward to experimenting with it when she got home and trying it in dishes that weren't Asian just to see what happened. She wondered what would result if she added a little to the stock when braising a brisket. She used anchovies as a secret ingredient in many sauces; this Belacan might be her new flavor weapon.

The table settings were austere but elegant, a style Amy had never mastered. But Amy had similar soup bowls at home and vowed to make laksa once a week in the future and set a clean Asian-style table with chopsticks and the white ceramic soupspoons she almost never used. She had bought the spoons to serve appetizer bites in when that was fashionable, but now that seemed like a dated look. When Amy told Rohani the laksa at Wild Ginger in Seattle was a famous hangover cure, Rohani looked stunned. The other student just laughed. Malays apparently were not big drinkers of alcohol. Amy hadn't known. She would try to be more respectful of the local culture.

The tiny roti jala crepes were light and delicate. They could accompany so many dishes with panache. Amy envisioned herself serving them with salmon roe for breakfast or with cocktails. What a great new life she was going to have because of this class.

The otak-otak came next, served in small white ramekins. The fish had miraculously melted into the custard. Julia Child would have liked this bit of magic and chemistry. Yin and yang could be understood in this dish; delicate yet powerful, creamy texture but substantial in the mouth. The aroma was so sea breeze fresh, the flavor was briny blended with curry but the tongue couldn't find the fish. It was like a riddle, an *amuse bouche* Amy would serve sometime as a guessing game.

The beef rendang with "respected" rice was next. Rohani had demonstrated how to rinse the rice gently, by hand, in a bowl of water, stirring it and removing it from the water one handful at a time to put in the rice cooker. It was a quiet exercise in being thankful to have the rice to eat. Did the rice taste different after being gently washed and handled? No, Amy didn't think so, but treating it respectfully made her feel different. Maybe that was the point. All food should be treated respectfully. She would try to remember this approach to handling ingredients when she got home.

The rendang, too, was such a surprise in the mouth. This was the beef stew of Malaysia, tender meat in a rich sauce that was hot, sweet, nuanced, and aromatic. What a crash course in Malaysian ingredients, flavors, and textures the menu was. Amy felt the confusing cacophony of tastes and smells floating around the night markets they had visited since arriving in Malaysia was coming into focus. While chopping the individual ingredients and processing the combinations for the herb pastes that seasoned each dish, her nose was aware of new experiences. When sautéing the pastes in hot oil, she detected more new smells. Now with the finished dish in front of her, when she leaned over to inhale the aroma before she took a bite to encourage the best communication between her mouth and her brain, she could identify the fresh turmeric, galangal, and lemongrass rising as one new powerful aroma above the chilies and shallots. That's why the spice paste was cooked until the oil separated. The heat had transformed the ingredients into something new. It felt like a foreign language she had studied but not mastered suddenly revealing its meaning in a crowded street with a few key words that let you know that woman next to you was going to see her son at the bakery. Three key words—*see, son, bakery*—learned in vocabulary lessons now made sense combined together. Every bite of Malaysian food she and Kevin had eaten so far was accompanied by the question, "What is it?" Their taste buds just hadn't recognized the new ingredients or the result of the combinations. They had to be learned. What an adventure it was going to be to teach themselves the intricate language of the Malaysian cuisine item by item.

The dessert was disturbingly black, a surprising texture and very sweet. It couldn't compete with all the other thoughts and flavors swirling around the room. It reminded Amy of some of the slimy textures Chinese love that Americans find taboo at first like sucking on chicken feet that had been stewed to a rubbery jelly.

Amy was enjoying herself, laughing and talking as though dining with old friends. At the end of the meal when Rohani graciously indicated the session was over, Amy didn't want to leave. She suggested she would go downstairs to the market to buy a bottle of wine so they could all continue talking and sitting on the couch with the lime green pillows. The other two declined her offer, saying they had to get going. Amy was sad to say goodbye to them and leave this wonderful bubble of well-being behind with Rohani in the beautiful apartment. The whole day had been magical to her. Amy felt very fond of her classmate. His sincerity was winning. He was genuinely a nice person and he had shared this experience with her. He was now a witness. She shook his hand goodbye and said, "Please email me your photos and let me know how the New Year's dinner turns out."

When she got back to the hotel, she told Kevin, "I'm going to stop worrying about the world imploding and my face sagging! I am going to be happy and appreciative of everything we have. Life is good."

Chapter 5

Laurence's bus stopped at the traffic light at Westlake and the Fremont Bridge. The span was up, allowing a single-mast pleasure craft to pass through on its way west toward the Puget Sound. The *No Wake* sign in big red letters on a wooden barrier in front of the sea wall marked the beginning of the Ship Canal, which some boaters preferred to call the Fremont Cut. The bench two hundred feet below the Aurora Bridge that he intended to sit on later was positioned on the grass above the sign as though the two went together, the no-wake bench for dreamers and leapers. He looked up at the west railing of the bridge where the suicide prevention fencing might be installed if the proposal for its construction went through. He had been following the controversy over trying to make the Aurora Bridge jump-proof online at the library. The issue was proving to be emotional and many sided. He chuckled at the black humor of the urban poetry posted on the neighborhood blog:

"Oh good god
let them jump
put in an observation platform
bring in some sharks to feed on the bodies…"

He identified with the frustration of the government types who tried unsuccessfully to explain to the whiners and complainers that the gas tax funding for the railing absolutely couldn't leap across budgets and categories to become social prevention programs administered by a different agency.

Laurence pulled the cord to stop the bus at the Fremont Library and got off the bus at Troll Avenue and North 35th Street underneath the Aurora Bridge. He looked back briefly a block away at the big stone sculpture of a troll holding a VW beetle in its hand. Cars full of tourists looking for parking haphazardly stopped, started, backed up, and did U-turns. When they couldn't find parking, they usually abandoned their cars in the middle of the narrow street to jump out for a quick snapshot. He shook his head at their disrespect for the public thoroughfare.

He walked down Troll Avenue toward the greenbelt under the bridge that created a wide-open entrance to the Ship Canal Path. Houseboats were peacefully parked at quiet docks lining the left side. A two-story office building and parking lot for technology companies formed the right border. He waited a bit to be able cross 34th Street as the traffic was zipping along, with bikes trying to share the road with cars, but there were no pedestrians, no sidewalks.

A family with three kids sat on a blanket around an open green and white box of Krispy Kreme doughnuts. Two picnic tables were occupied with young hipsters drinking Peet's coffee and smoking cigarettes. It was hard to tell if they were up early or hadn't been home yet. His bench and the one close to it on the corner now had one man on each, staking out the view of Eastlake and Queen Anne. He wasn't ready to sit yet anyway. He would make the route two or three times before he sat.

The first part of the walking path was paved but around the corner that soon turned into pressed hard clay with patches of green grass on either side, an occasional bench, and landscaping designed to look natural. Next came the private garden with black wrought-iron gates keeping the public out and the employees in. A stroll along the Ship Canal Path cleared his brain more than some of his other walks. He believed it to be because the various widths of the path, the margins, the sky, and the water made parallel lines of different colors, and the perpendicular lines of the bridges were calming like a Mondrian painting. In winter, the canvas was a pleasing monotone of gray that seemed uniquely Seattle to him.

He preferred Saturdays because the crowds were more interesting. The weekday foot traffic on Tuesdays, when he walked there before reading at the Fremont Branch, was usually light with just a few bikers and joggers. Saturday was the full complement of families, baby carriages, and young lovers. Joggers, dog walkers, and jogging dog walkers passed Laurence going in both directions. The freshness in the air was palpable. Serious bicycle riders whizzed by in garish spandex suits. Bikers with helmeted toddlers strapped into baskets went more slowly past couples relaxing on benches.

Where the path became parallel with the canal, the water was only a few feet away. He could look right into boats going west toward the Puget Sound. The eastbound vessels returning from a vacation in the San Juan Islands or a fishing trip were a little too far away to see the details inside. The walkers on the path on the other side of the canal had that option for voyeurism. It was always interesting to him to see the boats of all shapes and sizes with the people of all shapes and sizes out on deck or relaxing below the deck. Vases of roses, beer cans, and magazines were all on view to anyone on the path. The people didn't seem embarrassed to be on display. They looked like they were enjoying being observed. It was the beginning of their day on the water having departed from Lake Washington or Lake Union and the Ballard Locks were almost four miles of slow cruising away. That's where it could be downright entertaining to spend some time watching the same people scurry to tie up their crafts according to the longshoremen's instructions for the ride through the locks that would lower them about twenty feet down to the salty water of the sound. The pecking order of the group was clear by who drove the boat trying to look competent giving instructions and who was on deck trying to look confident as they received the instructions about handling the ropes. Oh, those instructions could be loud and vulgar. Now the audiences' intimate view was not so welcome. Kayaks, canoes, sailboats, and the Argosy cruise ship were all together in one big bathtub for a few minutes.

What a nice life it must be to have a boat and be out on a Saturday with daylight until almost 10 PM. This blue-sky day would entice many who would normally sleep in or stay home and watch TV if the day were overcast.

He wanted to review again how he was going to present himself. He'd planned the conversation many times over the years, but today was finally the day the meeting was going to happen. Laurence wondered how old *he* would look and how old *he* would seem to his ex-friend. They probably both looked a lot older. His hair was now completely white to match the beard that had been white for a long time. He could use a haircut but he kept postponing it in case he needed the money for something more important. Who noticed his hair anymore anyway? Nobody was looking at him. Passersby looked through him. He had become invisible. He tried not to look in mirrors anymore. He didn't recognize himself when he did. Being seventy-five looked like eighty-five to him. Who wanted to think about it?

But the appearance part was not important. The issue was the body diminishing and no longer functioning as a fuel-efficient machine. It wasn't designed for the life span. It should be retired now, before it really broke down, but it clunked on. He wished he had a retirement lot to go to like old elephants and airplanes did. Maybe he should make a farewell visit to the cemetery for planes and just walk out into the desert. That would be more

59

appropriate for him, the aerospace engineer, than jumping off a bridge. However, the bridge was close by, tonight was a good night if the meeting went well, and the plane cemetery was a thousand miles away in Mojave, California.

He felt ready to give it up. His pleasures were few. Reading and eating? Just reading. Eating wasn't that much fun anymore. Fewer things agreed with him. The expense of quality meats was ridiculous. He remembered when a steak was a steak; grilled medium rare with sweet and salty red juices flowing with each cut of the knife—and affordable. Beef these days was frightening to contemplate with all the antibiotics and additives from feedlots and butchering facilities. Salmon and halibut were once so plentiful and practically free. Now the oceans were so polluted that buying sustainable fish was only for the rich. Free-range chicken was all he could afford to eat in good conscience.

Cooking had lost its joy in the process of eliminating so many foods. Preparing the chicken to seem a little different every week had become a challenge he ignored. Usually nothing was different but the vegetables because he'd gotten lazy about complicated recipes, another lost pleasure. Roasting the butterflied bird and three vegetables in one pan for an hour and a half at three hundred degrees was now the default recipe. Sea salt and black peppercorns were the only spices in his kitchen. Occasionally he thought about the roasted squash and mushroom lasagna he used to make with homemade pasta.

Preparing the pasta by hand was a contemplative task he had found relaxing. He hardly needed to watch the process because he could feel in his fingers that the eggs in the well of flour were mixed enough to start accepting the flour and when they had absorbed all they could without becoming dry. Kneading and pressing the dough until smooth didn't require eyes either. When the ball of dough felt just right and he was ready for the rolling pin, he opened his eyes and paid careful attention to turning the dough evenly to make a perfect circle that was uniformly flat and ready to be stretched to make it even thinner, almost transparent, with quick handwork and the rolling pin. The result melted in your mouth and brought to mind a vision of and the aroma of a wheat field on a hot, sunny day. Whatever humble ingredients you might have on hand tasted sublime when paired with homemade pasta. Using expensive veal or beef seemed like gilding to him. A tomato from the garden, chopped with a little olive oil was all that was needed, but this squash recipe combined three humble vegetables, elevating them all into another realm. When the squash cubes were tossed with olive oil and coarse salt and browned by high heat, he thought it was the essence of the sweet and savory gold vegetable with a crisp coating, a buttery smooth inside, and a highlight of crunchy salt. But dealing with peeling and cubing the raw butternut was tedious. Roasting the onions and mushrooms separately from the squash so each had its distinct flavor sealed in and then layering them with a small amount of homemade béchamel sauce and freshly grated Parmesan seemed like a lot of work before parboiling the pasta and assembling the components. Too bad he had become so lazy, or tired, because it was a great meatless meal he had enjoyed for years and would make dinner for a week now that he was only one person. Fresh pasta was a relic of the past. It no longer made sense as an activity or a commodity.

He focused on what he could change. His brain refused to stop assessing all life's problems as solvable if only you kept analyzing, applying basic principles of engineering. What are the processes, what are the consequences? He could save a lot in rent if he would move to Renton. But leaving downtown was not an option. His brain needed the urban stimulation. It was still his best functioning body part and he felt the suburban location would cause rapid atrophy. He'd rather be poor on the #2 bus line than have extra money to spend at South Center or hang out with the Bluebills. He wondered what the union/nonunion breakdown was in that club of retirees and how many of them were still mad about the strike.

The beginning of his problem was the strike in 2000. The strike marked the spot where his life changed and began tumbling out of control. It was only eleven years ago, but it seemed like decades. Everything afterwards seemed much less clear. The strike had been well documented in the press. The cast of characters controlling his destiny seemed almost like those in a stilted Victorian play. Mr. Barnes was the federal mediator and was referred to that way in the newspaper. Laurence still called him Mr. Barnes in his thoughts. The Boeing spokesman and the union spokesman had names but weren't *mister*. Harry Stonecipher and Jim Dagnon, the bad guys from Boeing, weren't *mister*, either. The nuts and bolts of the strike were cuts in life insurance and long-term disability, inadequate wage increases, and a defined bonus. The fuel that kept the dispute white hot was the feeling that the engineers just weren't that important to the company anymore. Morale was horrible. Anyone who could find another job quit. More quit, hoping to find another job by looking harder. No one in management thought the engineers would strike. After all, they were white-collar professionals with no history of strikes except a one-day walkout eight years before. Knowing there would be no strike pay, 17,000 engineers and technical workers had gone on strike and exceeded everyone's expectations for endurance. Laurence wasn't one of the strikers. He crossed the picket line and all his old friends of the last thirty years never spoke to him again. That had surprised him.

Laurence continued walking on the path. The hour or so strolling back and forth had gone quickly, it didn't take that long to walk the most scenic part, which was short. He had stopped a few times to sit on a bench to watch the boat traffic in the Ship Canal. He rehearsed his key points. He tried to think of a joke or two if it turned out to be convivial. That was all he could do to prepare. Now he just had to go do it and count on his old ability to think fast if it began to go awry.

Chapter 6

Amy felt the Ship Canal path was a nice change from the neighborhood sidewalks, easy walking for her, full of exciting smells for Thor, and just a few minutes away down Queen Anne Hill, over either the Aurora or Fremont Bridge.

She and Thor headed west from the grassy entrance to the park below the Aurora Bridge. The houseboats looked chipper in bright colors like a row of birds on a clothesline. The Ship Canal was glassy smooth. The sparkle of sunlight on the water was pleasing and auspicious for the day. Everything was going well for the party. She felt an extra lift from the sunshine.

Thor was working the ground using his nose as a Geiger counter, executing rapid but random angled shifts in position and direction, seemingly covering every quadrant efficiently for evidence of activity by rats, cats, dogs, ducks, and squirrels. She felt she knew when he got a dose of squirrel. His whole body quivered, and he attacked the project with renewed vigor.

The air was that perfect seventy-degree temperature, which was exhilarating to her. That was almost as good as a dose of squirrel to Thor.

Walking by the Google cafeteria always gave Amy a little thrill. Both sides of the canal had low-rise buildings with high-tech innovation going on inside. Built with lots of glass, they sparkled along with the canal on a day with sun. Who knew what all the companies were or what they did. Google seemed to be the only one announcing themselves with their colorful logo letters on the side of the building. They weren't trying to hide. What genius was sitting on the other side of the window in the cafeteria cogitating on an engineering revolution?

Amy admired some of the other dogs and dog walkers coming and going her way. Of course, there were some fashion don'ts on the path today that made her wince. Seattle was famous for muffin-tops, polar-fleece vests and sweats in all seasons. Amy never wore sweats to walk the dog. She always wore mascara. But she did wear a fleece vest sometimes; they were so practical when it was sixty-something degrees. She wondered if that golden retriever was the first or the fifth dog that slim woman with the good haircut had walked over the years.

Nothing had prepared Amy for falling in love with a dog. She had anticipated amusement and affection but not being totally swept off her feet. Thor looked into her eyes and communicated so clearly, "I love you." Even more amazing, it had happened to Kevin, too! Who would have ever thought Mr. Taciturn would be on his knees playing and chuckling at a four-legged shaggy beast? One lick on the chin was all it took to win him over. The money—and devotion—that went into Thor was a substantial, daily joint venture in her marriage. What would she and Kevin be doing if they hadn't adopted Thor? Now that she knew what a money pit he was, she should try to think of a cottage industry involving canines. What irresistible dog treat could she sell or a super-stylish collar and leash? Having her own small business would be divine. She missed working and having money for nonessentials. Mostly she missed the money. The working part really hadn't been fun for a long time. She despised some of her coworkers and was sure the feeling was reciprocated. They were an underhanded, back-biting bunch that cared about nothing but trying to squeeze more stock options out of management. The only sure path to that was to take out the person ahead of you and try to increase your headcount. She looked forward to chatting with Alexis tonight about her job hunt and if she had any optimism about it. Amy had given up her own job hunt and was trying to embrace the concept of being a nonworking spouse. She didn't love it yet, but she was trying to get better at it every day. Filling the day wasn't hard as she was obsessed about her house and it was a guilty pleasure to have all the time in the world to start projects she'd had on her list for a long time, such as making new seat covers for the bar stools, creating a vignette of old family photos in the media room, and planning enhancements to the landscaping around the patio. What was hard was the hole in her identity that the job used to occupy. She was no longer the responsible, dependable, creative problem solver who worked at XYZ Company and earned a salary. She was now something much lighter, almost see-through and inexperienced. She dreaded anyone asking her what she did. That sound bite wasn't quite ready yet.

Thor was happy to be on this terrain, gravel here, grass there, and rugged undergrowth where animals could hide from him. He ran up and down the steep banks to the concrete retaining wall of the canal, doubling and tripling his exercise while she waited at the top for him in the shade of the trees. The *Speed Limit 7 Knots* signs on the opposite retaining wall were mile markers of sorts.

At the end of the grass path, Amy turned around and headed back toward the Fremont Bridge. The marine industrial corridor ahead wasn't fun to walk on. The paved bike path was the only option, and the bikes went too fast in both directions. It wasn't meant for dog walkers. She tried to focus on reviewing the cooking projects for the afternoon to clear her mind and prioritize the tasks. The otak-otak was a fairly simple custard procedure made a little tedious by having to skin the fish before cutting it in equal-size pieces to fit in six small ramekins.

At the cooking class, Rohani made skinning the fish look so quick and easy with the pressure of her bare hand on top of the flesh, sliding the knife a millimeter above the skin against the cutting board. Practice makes perfect, and a really sharp knife makes all the difference. Amy would sharpen the knives first, before anything else. Then just like at the cooking class, she would make a cold drink before beginning to cook.

Rohani had made a beverage by steeping some leaves in hot water and then pouring both over ice. It was refreshing, like limeade with an aromatic garnish of Calamansi lime, the first new ingredient Amy learned that day. Amy wished she had asked her the name of those leaves.

Rohani's assistant had set up white plastic trays with ingredients measured out in various sizes of plastic portion cups; one tray for each recipe. Two workstations were set up, with wooden cutting boards and several knives, one on each side of the granite counter. Amy was dazzled by the whole setup in the kitchen. The recipes had been much discussed in email to create a class that worked for Amy and the other student. It was a special menu pulling items from standard classes, like a full-day laksa Workshop that featured five different laksa recipes. Amy would have loved to take that workshop.

Curry laksa was an important recipe to learn for Amy because she fell in love with it at first slurp at the bar at the old Wild Ginger before it moved up from Western Avenue to the spot across the street from Benaroya Hall, turning the best little Pacific Rim restaurant in Seattle into an expensive, sprawling, top destination joint. Professional basketball players late night at the bar attracted a new high-heeled crowd that wasn't part of the old Benaroya rabble. Those were heady days of start-ups and stock options that seemed to promise everyone a bright future.

Laksa was a happy reminder of those free-spending dot-com days. While she was peeling fresh turmeric in Kuala Lumpur, she had decided when she got back from vacation to have a laksa party with a big platter of the green beans, shrimp, sprouts, fried tofu, mint leaves, and two kinds of noodles in the center of the dining room table so that everyone could garnish the laksa any way they wanted. Golden, with the consistency of a hearty stew, in a white bowl with the green, pink, and white garnishes, what a glorious presentation it would make. Substantial enough to feed a hungry man or please a more delicate eater, laksa was definitely not delicate in flavor. Making a curry paste from fresh ingredients instead of using canned curry powder created a superior vibrancy and complexity that warmed your nose and then your whole mouth. She would plan this laksa extravaganza for a casual late Sunday afternoon dinner party with vodka infused with lemongrass and ginger to accent the flavors in the soup. That would be so easy and fun!

Otak-otak sounded interesting and unique. Rendang, another thing she'd never heard of, was a traditional Malay item. The roti jala, a thin crepe, accompanied many dishes. Rice wasn't a recipe, but they would make it at the class because it was served at most every Malaysian meal. Amy hadn't tried to do any of the recipes at home before the trip. She had wanted the whole experience of cooking and eating these recipes to be fresh in Kuala Lumpur. The cooking class experience had exceeded all her expectations for newness. It had been exhilarating.

The whole trip had been exhilarating. She loved spending all day, every day, with Kevin. At home he often seemed remote; physically present sitting in front of the fire reading but not mentally in the room with her. They got along so well traveling without getting irritable about small things like they did at home. They laughed. It was

68

easy for her to make jokes on vacation and make Kevin laugh. He could always make her laugh. Amy so wished she was funnier. She admired anybody who could make her laugh and wished she could do it more for other people. They also had lots to talk about, as the sites and the culture were so interesting with so many details to absorb. Every day felt like an engrossing advanced course with a great instructor. Traveling in Malaysia raised the bar on other vacation spots. Of course, she wished they could go on vacation more often. That would be great. She hoped the retirement budget would include some nice, long trips.

"Whoa, Thor, dude!"

She looked up, startled to hear someone talking to her dog and saw Alexis' husband, Ben.

"Ben, how are you? What a surprise to see you in the work neighborhood on a Saturday."

"New product coming. I'll be lucky if I get to go home this weekend. I just needed some fresh air and real coffee after being up most of the night. I'm tired of Red Bull."

"Oh, Ben. Aren't you too old for that all-night stuff? That's for the young bucks. You are coming to my party tonight, aren't you?"

"Oh, jeez, is that tonight? I'd forgotten about it. I'm sure Alexis hasn't. She will call me and remind me. I really shouldn't come, but I'll try."

"Vodka and Malaysian food will be good for your brain, maybe even give you new ideas. I'm demonstrating pandan leaf tonight, a new thing to me that's part of the Malaysian mystique. Have you tried it before?"

"Vodka I have tried and I like it for that feeling of temporary amnesia. I can't remember if I had pandan leaf before." With a big grin, he said, "Do you smoke it? Ha! It's probably *pandanus,* a genus of *monocots*."

"You're way ahead of me as usual. I don't know my genus and species."

69

"Whatever, I'll try anything once. Good to see you." He started to walk away.

"Please, before you go, a quick question about the suicide vigil on the Aurora Bridge I read about in the neighborhood blogs. I couldn't believe it because I haven't seen anything in the newspaper about the suicides. Is it really true that a parking lot under the bridge had to be closed to prevent cars and people from being damaged by jumpers?"

"I saw the vigil from an office window, but I haven't read the blogs and the newspapers have a policy of not publicizing suicides. If someone jumps, no one will know except the next of kin. The only details I've read were in *Real Change* newspaper last year about the very sad life of one of the jumpers. It's easy to find online. The office workers around here don't talk about it much because it's too gruesome to believe. It's surreal. Everyone I know, including me, has witnessed a jump or an attempt. I once had to walk around a body. Luckily none have fallen on my car! That would be the end of *it*."

"Like always, it's worse than I thought. Good luck with your project. See you later." Amy watched Ben's rumpled, burly body saunter down the path toward Canal Coffee, pulling a phone out of his pocket to study the display. Amy hoped he would call Alexis right now to say he remembered about the party. She was probably at home fuming about him not coming home last night.

Amy resumed her leisurely pace with Thor leading the way, noting all the important scents as he went. Ben looked terrible beyond the obvious of no sleep and no shave. He'd gained weight since she saw him last. He hadn't seen his barber in ages. The salt had overtaken the pepper in his hair. He wasn't gray; he was white headed. It made him look like he was sixty-something and she knew he wasn't! If he was still looking for another job he better loose weight and color his hair. No one wants to hire an old, fat person.

70

She wasn't worried about Ben not coming to the party. He was used to being tired. All the engineers she knew were always tired from running for days at a time without sleep fueled with Red Bull and often mixed with Jägermeister. Amy had stayed up twice with the all night crowd at her office in sympathy for some beta testing on a product and been appalled at the noisy process. The whole memory was associated with the disgusting Jäger flavor and aroma that combination made—more like industrial floor cleaner than an energy beverage. Being tired was part of the macho ethos of the tech business. They loved bragging about how many nights they had been up straight. Alexis would keep him on schedule for dinner. Ben could be revived. Absolut would jolt him out of his daze and temporarily brighten him up like the runway models gray with fatigue being fed shots of vodka in between walks. The party food would stimulate him, too. When he crashed after that, hopefully he would be in his own bed or at least the backseat of the car on the way home. He was famous for sleeping in the car.

Amy knew how hard it was not to be fat. It got harder every year. When she was young, if she skipped dinner she lost five pounds. Now she'd have to starve herself for a week and exercise like a maniac to lose five pounds. She imagined if she didn't walk the dog two hours a day and go to the gym, she'd have to quit eating and drinking. That was too awful to think about.

Technically, she wasn't even one pound overweight but so many parts jiggled that shouldn't. Amy didn't just feel bad about her neck; she hated her neck. She hated her upper arms, too. She hated the spider veins in her thighs. She hated hot flashes. She hated yoga, which made her angry instead of calming her. She wasn't brave enough, or rich enough, for a neck, face, and arm lift. She couldn't wear turtlenecks all year-round without looking weird, but she could wear long pants and long sleeves. That would have to be the uniform for the rest of

71

her life to hide the flaws. She was starting to notice how many older people wore that uniform. How sad to be broadcasting oldness by clothing long before anyone was close enough to see the wrinkles!

The noise of the Aurora Bridge traffic high overhead distracted her from her rant and made her look up and notice the city view framed by the support columns. It looked a lot taller from the ground looking up than it did driving over it, but that might be because the three southbound lanes were so narrow cars barely fit without scraping and it required complete concentration so she didn't notice the height of the railings. The issue of suicide-prevention railings had been featured in the newspaper that week as part of a discussion about funding for the project. The yellow emergency phones installed a few years ago with autodial 911 and the crisis line number had not reduced the statistics. A few more were jumping every year. In 2009, twenty people killed themselves in Seattle by jumping from a height, but did that mean they all jumped from the Aurora Bridge? It was incredible to her that anyone would be so depressed or oppressed they would choose jumping off that bridge. She had learned it was the second most popular place in the U.S. to jump next to the Golden Gate Bridge in San Francisco, which recorded a jumper every two weeks. *The Seattle Times* said it took three seconds to hit the water or the pavement.

From the welcome desk Amy watched the crowds outside on Fifth Avenue waiting for the library to open, then rushing in competitively to get the seat they wanted for reading or the computer located in a certain spot. She felt she could see who was depressed by their body language. So many were white-haired with little chance that things would change for them. Some of the younger ones would find a job and dig out, but that was unlikely any time soon in this economy. When you're sixty-five or seventy years old with nothing, nowhere to go, with no

72

relief in sight, it must be very depressing. There isn't any cure for that depression, except money, thought Amy. The chronically poor probably couldn't be professionally drugged or talked out of their accurate perception that life is cruel and unfair. Self-medication had definitely been tried and failed. Heroin almost seemed benign next to crack cocaine and other new recreational drugs. What worked?

If the point was to be successful at killing yourself, not to maim yourself, surely there were easier or less painful ways to do it. It was not surprising to her to read in the Seattle news that 20% of the suicides were senior citizens. Not much to be happy about. The teenagers made her sad. They couldn't really know how tough life could be yet, could they? Maybe they could. She felt very far removed from the tough lives of teenagers. The tough life of seniors seemed very close by.

After rounding the corner of the much smaller, lower, reach-out-and-touch-me Fremont Bridge with its big MXVI plaque, she spotted the familiar profile of dear old Alan reading a magazine on a bench facing the water.

"Hello. What a surprise to see you here reading! How often do you do that?"

"This is the first time ever."

"What inspires you to make this historic visit?"

"I'm meeting someone for lunch at the new sandwich place and arrived too early, so as not to be late. With something to read, who cares? So here I am enjoying this spectacular summer day and looking forward to dinner at your place."

"Anybody I know?" Amy looked at him as a co-conspirator.

"You are so nosy! But it's not a secret. I'm lunching with Woody."

"Sorry, I didn't mean to pry. You could just say "*no*" and then I'd know it was one of your secret girlfriends. How's Woody?"

"You aren't good at keeping secrets. No idea about Woody, haven't seen him in ages."

"Well, say hello for me. Thor and I are headed down to Uwajamaya right now for fish and rare herbs. Have you heard of pandan leaf?"

"No, but I look forward to making its acquaintance. How are we imbibing it?"

"In a crepe."

"Undoubtedly from the famous cooking class you mentioned in the invitation. I look forward to all of it. I assume I'll have to work for my supper?"

"Kevin insists on it. Alexis is so happy you're coming."

"The rest will endure me I suppose."

"With pleasure. We have entertainment. The food is dazzling. You will love the photos."

"Do you have time to sit down for a minute? You know, I think I may have seen those photos shortly after you returned when we met for happy hour."

She sat next to him on the bench as a canoe with two rowers went by silently in the water and gave Thor the down command. She smiled at him and mouthed, *good dog*. Turning to look at Alan, she said, "Oh, you're right. You did see a few of my favorites. Kevin has his own show, that's the joy of two cameras. I hope you won't be bored. What are you reading?"

"No worries." He held up the *Traveler* magazine cover for her to see. "This is what the unemployed are obsessed with. I'm planning trips. What are you reading?"

"I'm on an adventure in China with a porcelain expert. She would teach you something about smuggling art. That could turn out to be a handy new skill in this economy."

"I'll put it on my list. I'd like a new industry. I didn't know you walked your dog here."

"Once or twice a month. This is our alternate to Discovery Park or Green Lake or Gasworks—the closest park—because pounding the neighborhood sidewalks is killing my knees."

"Let's not get started on aging aches and pains."

"How are your parents doing?"

"They never complain, but I worry about them; they are on the verge of being ancient."

"Oh, god, I see now how it goes, middle-aged, senior, ancient. Yikes!"

"At least they have each other. So many ancients have to do it alone. I feel like I'm in training already."

"Do you ever think about getting a dog for company? I can't tell you what good company Thor is. Thor, relax. I didn't mean we're done here."

"I'm not lonely, but the dog would be and I'd have to come home before going out. They need kids to play with and a wife to feed them."

"Welcome to my world. I'm the chief walker, personal chef, co-hunter, and playmate."

"The man of the house isn't helping?"

"Ha, in all those years we talked about getting a dog he was going to be the early morning and late night walker. He had a romantic notion about being in the dark and the rain. It fit his image of himself as a brooding, solitary soul. Somehow, the reality is that the best time for him to walk the dog is Saturday morning around ten after a big breakfast. He can't get up any earlier before work and he's too tired after work."

"So, we get back to what are you doing out on Saturday morning walking the dog?"

She laughed. "Well, he has stuff to do, errands and relaxing before this evening's festivities."

"I would have thought you'd have a few things to do to get ready for this evening's festivities."

"You are a genius and a sensitive soul. Intuitive even. I don't know how you stay single! You know me; I do my relaxing while I'm cooking. And I'm organized. Look at the old dude there."

75

"Where?"

"Khaki slacks and jacket, white beard."

"I see him. Who is it?"

"That's one of my library guys. I talk to him every Monday downtown when I'm working the welcome desk and he rides my bus. That's the one I told you about who said he invented the Kindle, or something like it before there was a Kindle."

She waved at Laurence. He did not wave back but nodded his head in recognition.

"He probably did invent it and someone stole his plans or his employer claimed the plans as belonging to the corporation. That's how the bastards get rich, by stealing."

When Laurence was only a few feet away, Amy spoke to him, "Hi. How are you today? Isn't it gorgeous?"

Laurence paused and nodded in agreement.

"This is my brave friend, Alan, who is coming to my party tonight to sample the Malaysian recipes I learned on vacation."

"You're a lucky man. I expect from what I heard about it the food will be quite good." Laurence did not offer his name or his hand. His blue eyes studied Alan.

Alan did not get up and responded with equal reserve, "I couldn't agree more. I am exceedingly lucky in having my old friend here," looking at Amy, "and in having one of her invitations." He looked back at him just as intently. "Have you tried any of her cooking?"

Laurence almost smiled. "Actually, I was invited to this party, but I'm unable to attend."

Alan looked surprised and said, "Well, that's too bad."

Amy nodded. "Yes, it's too bad because I really think it's going to be a great evening! Please, change your mind or your plans and come tonight. There will be another engineer there I know you would enjoy talking to." Amy beamed at Laurence while thinking, *These two are being a little competitive about me aren't they?*

Laurence shook his head. "No, I couldn't possibly come, but you are very generous to ask."

"Thanks. Maybe another time. Are you headed for the Fremont Library?" Amy asked.

"No, just strolling before meeting an old friend in Ballard."

"Well, enjoy the day. Good to see you." Amy watched as he walked on down the path. "He's kind of cool, isn't he?"

"Yes, I'd say so in the one minute that I have known him, but why else would you have invited him? Have you started taking in strays? I'd say he's curious about me."

She smiled at him. "No, I'm not into strays or any kind of social work. He intrigues me. He likes me more than just flirting like all the old dudes do. I think he's considering whether or not to take me to the next level. After all, I invited him to the party a few weeks ago. You're his first glimpse into me beyond the library. Old friends and husbands are a scary and exciting part of that. You'll like his brain, and I suspect he could be wickedly funny if he ever let down his guard. Then he'll remind me of Kevin or you, the two funniest guys I know."

"Maybe meeting me will inspire him to change his mind about tonight."

"Oh, my god, you're feeling powerful today. If he should come, which I doubt, don't you dare try to embarrass me by telling any stories about what a clueless coed I was or about any of my before-Kevin loser boyfriends."

"I guess we can make a pact. I won't tell the funniest episodes if you won't either."

"That's a promise. Sometimes I think we should have a big photo-burning session and rewrite history. I worry about leaving too much evidence of my errors."

"Hum. Who are you worried about? As I recall, Kevin knows those fellows because he was there too, watching you and them, with envy."

"Did you really think that at the time? I didn't notice that. Oh, well, I think our memories play tricks on us. Let's make some plans to do fun things during the day, quickly, before you get employed again."

"I doubt I'll be snapped up that quickly. In fact, I hope to enjoy unemployment for at least three months."

"Three months is a good vacation. Look what time it is! I have got to get going. Kiss, kiss. Come, Thor, let's exercise. See you around seven."

CURRY LAKSA by Rohani Jelani

Stock base

1 chicken leg, skinned

3 small slices ginger

1 teaspoon salt

10.5 ounces medium-sized prawns

1 quart water

Spice paste

1/3 cup shallots, sliced

3 cloves garlic, sliced

1/2 inch slice ginger, thinly sliced

3 chilies, seeded and sliced

2 stalks lemongrass, sliced

1/2 teaspoon Belacan shrimp paste

3 tablespoons "meat" curry powder *

Gravy

3 tablespoons oil

1 quart stock base

1 teaspoon salt

2 teaspoons sugar

3/4 cup thick coconut milk

Noodles & garnishes

3 long green beans, cut into 1 inch pieces

1/4 pound meehoon (fine rice noodles)

1 pound fresh yellow noodles

2 cups bean sprouts

6–8 pieces fried tofu (taufoo pok), cut up

1 cup mint leaves

4 calamansi limes, halved and seeded or Meyer lemons **

Place chicken, ginger, salt, and water in saucepan. Bring to boil, turn down heat, and simmer until chicken is tender, about 20 minutes. Remove chicken, add prawns, and cook till pink and firm, about 3 minutes. Remove from heat. Shell prawns, shred chicken, and return bones and shells to stock. Simmer 15 minutes more, strain stock, and discard solids. Set aside.

Finely grind shallots, garlic, ginger, chilies, lemongrass and Belacan shrimp paste in electric blender, adding 1/2 cup water to enable blades to work. Transfer ground paste into small bowl and stir in curry powder.

Heat oil in a deep saucepan and cook shallot spice paste on low heat until well cooked and oil surfaces. Add stock base, salt, and sugar and simmer 10 minutes. Add coconut milk, boil once, and turn off heat. Taste and adjust seasonings.

Blanch long beans in big pan of lightly salted water for 2 minutes. Remove with slotted spoon.

Add meehoon noodles to the big pan of boiling water, blanch till tender, 1–2 minutes before adding yellow noodles, bean sprouts, and tofu. Swish around for 1/2 minute, then drain.

Divide noodle mix among serving bowls, ladle on hot gravy, and top with prawns, chicken, long beans, and mint.

Serve with squeeze of lime and eat immediately.

* Malaysians frequently make their own curry powder instead of using a commercial brand and have different recipes for meat, fish or poultry dishes. The difference between meat curry powder and a fish curry might be the addition of cinnamon, nutmeg and cloves to the meat blend—and using more fenugreek and mustard for the fish for the desired sour flavor. Use your favorite brand if you don't feel like making or purchasing a special mix. The flavor will still be wonderful and you'll appreciate the difference when you try the recipe again with the fish curry powder.

** Meyer lemons are the most similar flavor and aroma. Key limes are the same size but not as sweet and juicy.

Chapter 7

Alan watched Amy walk away and then turned back to his magazine, but he couldn't keep his focus on the top destinations of the season. Funny, running into Amy in Fremont, especially today. She was always full of surprises. Imagine her inviting the old man from the library to dinner! What was she thinking? Alan couldn't quite picture him sitting at the bar or at the table with Alexis and Ben. He seemed so serious, no frills. Alexis and Ben were smart, but they excelled in getting lively and noisy. They loved to have fun. Why wasn't Amy at home surrounded by boiling pots and dirty dishes? He experienced the miracle of a clean kitchen and the dinner ready every time he walked in her door. How did she do it? His sink was always full and the stove was busy when his guests arrived. She was starting to look older in her face. Maybe she was too thin and needed to gain some weight? Wouldn't she love to hear that she needed to gain weight! In his opinion, the two of them looked better than any of their college chums. He really should say the three of them because Kevin was still as thin as he had always been and had all his hair, just not the same color.

He looked forward to taking the stage tonight with a good crowd that would get the jokes and enjoy the rants. Alexis would drive him home. She was always a pleasure to trade quips with. He was also excited about his lunch date with Woody, an old friend who used to be a major prop in his social life. He didn't get to see him often anymore and he missed him. Woody had recently surprised everyone by getting married for the first time and creating a family right away with a nice enough-looking woman who must have been desperate to have kids before it was too late. Alan still wasn't sure exactly what Woody got from the arrangement. He didn't seem to be passionate about the woman or the kids. Maybe he was tired of living alone. Maybe he was starting over. Woody socialized with different people now, younger couples with children the same age as his.

Alan relished the rare opportunity to lunch with Woody and indulge in good conversation about everything, because time spent with Woody was still superior to time with anyone else he knew. They read many of the same books, liked the same music, and they had closet paramours they never discussed with anyone but each other. All were precious bonds to him, the last remainders of their easy-going years together. Too many people he knew bought into a modern romantic philosophy of marriage that ignored the history of the institution and therefore had no sense of humor about it. Politics and cuisine were his default topics with the rest of the world because anyone could join in on those. Too bad more people didn't read something worth talking about.

He felt very lucky in his friendships on this fine summer day celebrating saying goodbye to twenty years of the mind-numbing quarterly sales cycles of a product manager. The product had been taken off the shelf for good. That was a cause for celebration. To be unemployed was divine. He hoped a few months, but not too many, would go by before he found another job. Time off would be the perfect compensation for the last three years of drudgery. His first move had been to turn off the cell phone and put it in a drawer at home. He was so tired of the twitch at his hip that meant he had to leap to attention and be sharp at any time of the day or night.

It was demeaning like a farm animal responding to the flap of the reins to avoid the whip. He was no longer at anyone's beck and call. He planned to read, relax, maybe do some traveling with his young babes, not too far away as he wanted to be careful with his severance money, just in case. They might love a cruise to Cabo or Alaska. Seven days lounging by the pool and changing clothes three times a day to eat would be perfect fun for them. He would take two of them so they could share a cabin and he could have his own. He was considering a week in the Napa Valley with his favorite widow. He certainly wasn't dipping into savings as the stock market had whacked his account in 2008 like a Silversea's World Cruise with butler service. The stockbroker said so cavalierly, "Don't worry, it will all come back, it just may take a few years!" Well it was a few years and he wasn't that impressed with the recovery. The balance might be back but the missing growth and interest was gone forever. Working ten more years was nothing he liked to think about and any more than that would totally suck. This thought got him up on his feet to walk a bit to get rid of the vision.

Alan arrived at the sandwich shop a few minutes before 12:30 and saw the long line waiting to order and most of the tables already taken. He hated that. You should get a table and then have your order taken! If he'd known, he would have suggested something else on the block. He skipped the line and sat at the last open table for two, putting his magazine on the chair for his friend. Alan hoped Woody wouldn't be too late as he was now marooned in a noisy, small place, hungry, thirsty, and unable to move or lose the spot. *This isn't fun. Maybe I should leave now and wait outside and say it's too busy,* Alan thought. *We can go somewhere with service.*

He kicked himself for leaving the cell phone at home. He hadn't planned to need it for the next few months and here he was already wishing he had it! If he had brought it, he could call Woody right now and tell him to meet elsewhere.

People with sandwiches on plates gave him dirty looks as they wandered in the maze of occupied tables looking for a place to sit or perch. People were eating standing in corners. Oh, crap. To go or stay? A few more minutes would be all he could bear. He had been looking forward to a dining experience and this would simply be eating. He would have to try this place another time, maybe for takeout. He stood up and grabbed his magazine. The chair was pulled away from him immediately and two lucky people sat down before he was two feet away from the table.

Oh, the air seemed fresh outside. The sky was so blue and someone had put tie-dyed shirts on the figures in the sculpture, Waiting for the Interurban, to give them a festive summer look. He stood at the corner watching the cars going both directions on Fremont Avenue and scanning North 34th Street sidewalk traffic for his friend. Which direction would Woody come from? No telling with parking as tight as it was. But Woody would be driving, he felt sure. Alan thought again how much he was looking forward to the day polluting cars were banned from city streets and were left at the county line or someplace far away. He hadn't had a car in years and he loved not owning a car. He loved not paying for it, the gas or the insurance, the parking, the tickets, the fines. Everybody should get rid of their cars. It would make the world a better place and certainly improve the quality of life in this city. How freely and safely the pedestrians and cyclists could move without cars. It would be such a pleasure to walk everywhere without worrying about being run over.

Alan saw Woody from about twenty feet away looking for him. He raised his arm straight up and called out, "Yo, Woody!"

Woody returned the signal, "Yo, Alan!"

When Woody was beside him, Alan said, "You don't know how close you came to lunching by yourself, pal. I'm starving and about to give you up. I couldn't wait inside that zoo any longer. Let's go someplace with service, like the 35th Street Bistro or this marvelous Greek establishment. They appear to be ready to greet us and seat us, offer us a beverage while we peruse the menu. What do you say?"

"I really wanted to try this place. It's supposed to be great. Who minds a little bustle?"

"Another day, okay? They've got all the business they can handle right now."

"The Greek is pretty ordinary," Woody said.

"Who cares? They have a table, a bar, and a waiter, something that place does not."

"All right, you old grouch. You're getting to be so fussy."

They walked into Costas Opa, where cool and quiet greeted them along with a waiter who saw them enter and waved them over to a booth for four by the window overlooking the Fremont Bridge, placing menus over place settings as they approached the table. When they were seated, he filled water glasses from a pitcher of water and stood silently for a moment until they looked up at him.

"I'll start with an ouzo and water," Alan said, nodding to the waiter.

"You unemployed people are hard to lunch with."

"Have some more water if that's what you want."

"I'll have what he's having," Woody said.

"This isn't exactly like dining on the terrace at Milopita Beach but it seems quite civilized. Cheers. It's good to see you. How's the store?"

"I feel like an indentured servant with a lifetime of work required to repay my debt for being given a job. So, no change."

"What's selling well?"

"Nothing, everything. We seem to be trendless at this point. Remarkably well given the economy, but not enough to be really making money. It's worrisome. I hate my job, but I would sure hate to lose my job. How's unemployment treating you?"

"Not working agrees with me. I'm enjoying it. There's no hurt pride in this stupid product being withdrawn from the market or the layoff. My severance is good. Of course, if the holiday lasts too long, that won't be good, but old dogs like me always find something else."

"Ah, yes, the lemon soup and the prawns for me too with vinaigrette on the side of the salad, please."

After the waiter took the order, they exchanged status reports of the people of interest to them both. They agreed they needed to continue to have lunch at least once a year to keep up with marriages, divorces, births, and deaths. Of course, when Woody's kids went to college in about fifteen years they could get together more often. The soup was served with no interruption in the conversation.

"What's fun on your calendar?"

"I have had dinner out almost every night this week to tell the story of the layoff and severance package. Rover's and the Palace were the highlights. Tonight I'm dining with Amy and Kevin."

"Doesn't that sound swell. How are they?"

"They are good these days. They seem upbeat about everything. Not as well read as you are, of course, but she adores me, which makes up for it. He's always up on current events, so the politics will be lively, but he has the worst taste in music! It will be painful to listen to it. And he does it all by hand—no Spotify, Slacker, or any programming, just ridiculous. He could just choose one bad song and be done with it. They're showing off souvenirs and recipes from exotic travel in South East Asia. The travel log may be tedious; the food, however, will probably be good. I expect there will be a couple of other people there, too, that may be amusing. One of the wives has a thing for me, so that adds. I love married women. You know, they are the most appreciative. She will drive me home with him passed out in the backseat. That should be fun."

"It always amazes me the number of people who like to wine and dine you," Woody smirked.

"As you know, I am witty and single, unlike yourself. That keeps the invitations coming."

The waiter who knew they didn't want to be interrupted served the prawns silently. Another round was ordered. They moved on to the much more important business of what they had been listening to and what they had been reading. The conversation turned at last to romance.

"So, who do you have on the side these days?" Alan asked, as though he couldn't wait any longer.

"Same old."

"Really? That's no longer a risky liaison. I call that a risky relationship."

"It's definitely a relationship. I love listening to her complain about that sod of a manager I have and I love thinking about being with her when he's berating me. The circular nature of it is so satisfying. The wheel keeps on spinning. It's my favorite thing about going to work, gloating about my paramour, the manager's wife."

Alan laughed and shook his head. "How stimulating for you. Your smugness must make him want to smack you all the time. What do think of the prawns? Shall we have another round?"

"Yes, to all of the above. It's so refreshing to be out with you. Nothing on my agenda today seems that important any more."

"So are you getting pressure on making the relationship public?"

"No way. I need my job *and* I have kids, you know. These kids keep me independent. I can't get divorced because of my kids and I definitely can't get married because I'm already married! It's all perfect."

"I see, sort of." Alan laughed. "Does that also seem circular to you?" Conversation with Woody was always fascinating. What a great day this was.

Chapter 8

As she was heading south on Highway 99 over the Aurora Bridge, Amy tried to look over the railing at a moment when there weren't cars on either side of her. It was difficult because the railing mostly obscured the ship canal below and she couldn't see the section where the jumpers crawled over the fence. She would have to read the article in *Real Change* and then come back and take a look on foot to understand how it worked. Maybe Kevin would want to come with her and see it, too.

At the moment, just blue sky was visible, which was lovely for driving. The lanes seemed narrower every time she drove over the bridge. When it rained, the congestion, the closeness, and the speed made her nervous. Driving in the rain had joined hot flashes, failing memory, and unwanted fat as the middle-age curses. An absolutely confident, competent driver at home and abroad, she was now worrying about rainy days when she needed to do errands in the car. Ridiculous. She had driven on gravel roads in Turkey for heaven's sake! There, she'd managed narrow mountain roads with no guardrails and plenty of overloaded trucks careening around corners to display the driver's belief in kismet.

Exiting at Safeco Field, she cued up for the left turn on South Royal Brougham Way to wind back to 5th Avenue South and South Jackson Street for the Uwajamaya parking lot. She loved shopping here. She loved the activity, the bustle of people, and the products clamoring for her attention. The smell of roasting chestnuts from the vendor's cart outside the front door began the shopping experience. She knew exactly how she would hit the produce section at the door; grab the pandan, shiso, and kaffir leaves shrink-wrapped on refrigerated shelves filled with vegetables and herbs that lined the wall. She would not take time to tour the perpendicular long rows of fresh vegetables stacked high. The sheer quantity of produce on display was impressive. Mobs of people could shop here and not make a dent in the display. As much as she cooked Asian, there were still so many leaves or bulbs that she hadn't cooked yet. She should just buy a few vegetables she didn't know every time she shopped and then find a recipe at home for each one.

The banana leaves were in the long aisle of frozen items separating the fresh produce from the first aisle of shelves stocked with packages of refrigerated noodles. On the other side of that aisle began the dry goods in cellophane, cans, and bottles. The shelves glittered with shiny jars and cans with brightly colored labels. The selection was so large it could be stupefying if you didn't know what you wanted. What seemed like hundreds of bottles of soy sauce were more daunting than any aisle of cereal she had ever tried to search through. Serving the Japanese cuisine customer was no longer the main intent; Uwajamaya aimed to please Chinese, Koreans, Vietnamese, Malaysian, Filipinos, Indians, and Indonesians with selections that were not common in American supermarkets. Were there more countries she didn't know the names of? Probably.

Amy went straight on through the produce and past the butcher behind the meat counter to the fish counter on the back wall where a dozen workers with sharp eyes and sharp knives were ready to take your order and expected you to speak clearly and promptly when it was your turn.

Rohani had used garoupa fish in the class, a local choice for her, and suggested lemon sole or red snapper if

91

that wasn't available. Dozens of good-looking fish, whole with heads and tails, or cut in fillets and steaks, were displayed on crushed ice in a long display case with a counter top with scales and specific merchandise having to do with cooking or serving fish. In the separate low refrigerated cases behind her where sashimi quality fish wrapped in small packages were kept, it was easy to grab wasabi, nori wrappers, and all the garnishes and accompaniments for making sushi. Amy admired the professionals who selected the goods and assembled them in attractive stacks that helped the shopper get what she needed.

Studying the price per pound, doing the math in her head, Amy decided that snapper was going to be the pick of the day for the otak-otak.

"One pound of snapper fillet and one pound of crab, please." With the five packages in hand, she stood in the express line looking over at the kitchenware section she enjoyed browsing to see the latest in lacquer trays and small ceramic dishes for dim sum. Her rice cooker had come from here, and she adored it every time she used it. What a simple and marvelous machine it was. She was in and out of the massive store in ten minutes total, appreciating the Asian efficiency. It was always a pleasure to do business at Uwajimaya. When she got back in the car, Thor was relaxing on the backseat, seemingly happy about his walk and being included in the ride.

On 4th Avenue heading through town, Amy suddenly had the idea to stop at the Spanish Table on Western Avenue just because she had the car. She usually traveled by bus, which severely limited how many bottles she could easily carry. She had a few minutes and the afternoon cooking was organized. The olive oil was so good there and much cheaper than the grocery store choices. It would be good to have another bottle on hand and maybe there would be some interesting bargain wine in the bins by the door. The allure of the three-minute load and unload parking spot by the front door sealed the deal. She turned left on Madison Street and buzzed right down to Western Avenue. The loading spot was waiting for her. She did a beautiful parking job. She secured Thor with a promise of quickness and a small treat, a partially opened window on both sides, just enough for some air but not wide enough for him to pounce on any strange hand that tried to pet him. Her Maxima still looked good, particularly when washed, not dated or dented or otherwise betraying the fact it was a 1993 model. She noted that it might be due for its annual visit to the Elephant Car Wash.

The Spanish Table was well stocked with imported food, wine, books, music, paella pans, and all sorts of small extras that hung from the shelves and ceiling, which made up for the service in her opinion. The wine and olive oil were stacked waist high in open cartons on the floor. Cans and small jars of imported fish, roasted peppers, olives, beans, and spices with bright yellow, red, and green labels occupied the shelves on the right wall of the store. Handwritten cards about flavors of grass, minerals, jam, and plums hung from every shelf. Red cards with special prices jumped out at her for extra consideration.

One thing Amy always had in the cupboard from this store was the Spanish smoked paprika, pimentón. It came in rectangular red cans, almost the size of Coleman's Dry Mustard, in dulce (sweet), agridulce (bittersweet), and picante (hot) with an intense smoky aroma and flavor accent that was practically magic dust. She liked the sweet and hot more than the bittersweet. It could be used as a dry rub all by itself if she was in a hurry to get a piece of chicken or pork tenderloin cooking right away. She couldn't remember if she needed any, but decided to buy a dulce because she was here and it would be used.

Amy liked to look but seldom bought anything from the deli section at the back of the store, which was jammed with cured meats and cheeses in refrigerated cases.

Padron peppers in net bags were stacked on the deli counter. The cost per pepper was shocking, but they made the most wonderful happy hour treat sautéed in olive oil and sprinkled with a finishing salt. An inch or so long, they were bright green and tough when raw but turned brown, mildly spicy, and meaty when cooked. Even though many Padrons could be eaten, she rationed three each with a martini or a glass of sherry as an indulgence she saved for herself and Kevin. She kept quiet about her *too good for company* list: duck liver pate, foie gras, veal chops, and cèpes risotto.

Spanish extra-virgin olive oil was her favorite all-purpose for sautéing, marinating, and making vinaigrette. The hazelnut nut oil was phenomenal as a salad dressing with shallots over frisee and mushrooms. This store carried no less than twenty varieties of Spanish oil and in many sizes from miniature bottles to three-liter cans. Who knew how many vinegars they stocked. She could go crazy with vinegar but tried to limit herself to a quality red wine, sherry, champagne, and rice vinegar. She adored the fruit vinegars, particularly the fig, which was sweet and tart with a vibrant fig flavor, drizzled over sliced pears, or in vinaigrette over watercress and bleu cheese. Her favorite olives for martinis were here too, colossal size stuffed with garlic, almonds, lemon, or anchovies. Kevin loved the olives stuffed with crunchy almonds best. Conveniently located next to several shelves of olives was another favorite purchase, jars of roasted piquillo peppers. They were bright red and tasted like they had just come off the grill with a meaty, smoky sweetness. An American sweet red bell pepper was a tepid cousin to these powerhouses of flavor. They needed no accompaniment, but if she felt like splurging, she purchased them stuffed with bacalao (salt cod) or tuna, which was a perfect fancy snack to go with cocktails or to make a fast dinner salad. The economical way to have the salty fish and sweet pepper combo was to buy a premium jar of the roasted peppers and a small jar of anchovies in oil. Amy presented them stacked side-by-side in a small divided dish or laid out in alternating slices of red and pink on a lime green plate. Spanish toothpicks or pickle forks for servers made it easy to put a bite right in your mouth or on a small plate. No crackers or bread were necessary.

The wine was a huge draw to her. Amy loved looking at the boxes of bargain wines on the floor underneath the window overlooking Western Avenue that ran the length of the room. Anything less than fifteen bucks was always worth a try. It would probably turn out to be respectable dry table wine to serve any time or the ultimate goal—something that drank like old-world elegance—that tasted like it cost twice as much. She knew she'd found a winner in a red wine when she stuck her nose in the glass and the first whiff was a hot sunny day wandering through the vineyards and the fruit was warm from the sun. That was a good indicator to her that the same fruit, the ripe grapes, would be in the glass and on her tongue but not cloying. It would be simultaneously dry and smooth. That well-balanced flavor and feel in the mouth was harder to come by than it should be.

Tintos, blancos, and rosados, displaying a variety of red, gold, and pink hues inside the clear and green bottles, reflected the sun coming in the window. The colors in the overcrowded room were bouncing around as though a disco ball was rotating from the ceiling. She envisioned the red and gold wines sparkling in wine glasses on her dining room table, adding extra lighting effects to the tabletop setting. She should open a bottle of rosé because it would look so pretty with the pink and purple Malaysian sarong she intended to use as a table decoration. A dry rosé with herbal notes was just as food friendly as sauvignon blanc in her book. She was getting ahead of herself—after careful study a local riesling had already been purchased as the white wine to be served tonight. It smelled and tasted like ripe apricots and peaches with a hint of sweetness that was purported to be the perfect thing to accompany spicy food. She would see tonight if she agreed with the experts. She had selected an Australian grenache-shiraz blend as the red wine on the table for its fruity, soft tannins but had a California zinfandel and a sangiovese backup with more body if the Australian didn't suit someone or sold out too quickly. It was likely every bottle she put out would be consumed anyway. If any interesting wine came in the door as a hostess gift, they would open that, too. Amy felt strongly that a group and several dynamic courses was a great opportunity to open many bottles to taste and see what worked with the individual dishes. Taste buds and pairings were so personal she didn't believe in any hard and fast rules. She tried to keep paper and pen close by to make a note after dinner of a pairing she thought stood out or for her standard wine rankings: #1) okay, #2) buy a case or #3) don't buy this again.

The serious wine out of her price range was racked floor to ceiling along the left wall of the store all the way to the deli with parallel rows of racks filling a third of the room. Styles and regions and countries organized those shelves. She loved Spanish wines in general and thought they represented good value because they matured in oak barrels and in bottles years longer before being offered for sale than winemakers did in the States, which gave the wine complexity and softened the edges. Brand new wine could taste so raw and rough and acidic in a bad way. She was partial to wines from Rioja, the red blends with tempranillo dominating, tasting like a blue-sky day with dried cherry in the nose and more dark cherry and plum flavors in the glass that was so soft around the edges they could be paired with any meat, fish, or fowl. For an aperitif, an albarino gave her the same crisp, mineral and citrus notes as her standby, sauvignon blanc.

Leaving the store with a shopping bag full of olives, oil, peppers, and spice and a man following her with a mixed case of red and white bargain wines to try, she was surprised to see a big crowd walking toward her on Western Avenue. Some cruise ship from Alaska must have just disembarked a few thousand tourists who had time to get to the Pike Market and see the sights for a few hours before jetting home.

With the purchases stored in the trunk and a treat through the open window for Thor who had been very good, she paused by the front car door to look up the avenue at the crowd meandering down the sidewalk. She saw a familiar face in the middle of it: Natalie with her mom about thirty yards away. Amy knew they would bump into each other sometime; the town just wasn't that big. Her dear old friend Natalie, whom she hadn't seen in quite a while, but she had thought of her fondly from time to time and had even thought of inviting her to the party tonight.

Amy had rehearsed the scene of bumping into Natalie as she thought it would take place at a party or at Nordstrom. She'd described her envisioned scenario to Kevin and to Alan. Kevin had his own version if he was there when it happened.

Whenever they met again, Amy anticipated a big, toothy smile and the forced enthusiasm that Natalie had thrown out at her the last time Amy had seen her. Since that night, Amy and Natalie had exchanged a few emails with some idea of going shopping for silk flowers, but it never happened. Amy figured the relationship could use some time to refresh and was sure that Natalie would be in touch for a holiday shopping. When she didn't get a call, she didn't feel as if the distance between her and

Natalie was final. They weren't neighbors anymore. They were both busy with their lives and let each other drift away. After a while, Amy seldom thought of her at all. But she was glad to see her today. She wanted to say "hello" and "let's get together soon."

Natalie looked cute and perky with a retro flip up in her hair, instead of curled under, and a pastel peach skirt and blouse, very summer weekend wear. She recognized the espadrilles as one of Natalie's favorite pairs of shoes that made her taller without killing her feet.

Amy raised her left hand up to wave as they were approaching her car. Natalie gave Amy a long look behind her big sunglasses and then Natalie looked down, took a sip through a straw in a super-size cup, and turned her head toward her mom, making her hair bounce in a move she must have practiced in the mirror as they walked by Amy without another glance or a word.

Amy put her hand down quickly to rest on the roof of the car. She felt odd and it was hard to swallow. Maybe she was having some strange hot flash. She leaned against the side the car, watching them walk away. *Oh, really? So that's how things are with you?*

Amy got in the car and sat for a few minutes, looking up the street at the traffic going both ways past her and thinking about the flip, the flounce, the bounce that said it all: *You're not in my book anymore; you've been deleted.* She could hear the ding, ding, ding of the pinball machine flashing error, error, error. She shook her head and sighed. Thor seemed sympathetic and rubbed his head against her shoulder. Why couldn't Natalie have said hello and kept walking? She could have waved and kept walking. Amy wouldn't have chased her. She could have nodded and kept walking. She would have taken the hint that no conversation was needed. Maybe they were in the middle of something critical, although it didn't look like she was talking to her mom. Why did she just walk on by pretending she didn't see Amy? Amy obviously had missed something. What?

Chapter 9

Kevin drove down Ballard Avenue looking for a parking place not too far away from Hattie's Hat or The Old Town Alehouse. Either one would be cool, dark, and have some hoppy India Pale Ale on tap. Then maybe he'd order a burger or possibly a healthier chicken sandwich. He wished the Noble Fir had more to eat because the beer selection there was better. He needed a few minutes to relax, not think about work, read the newspaper, and not talk to anyone. When he wanted solitude, a bar was the safest place to be. An open newspaper was the signal that he didn't want to engage in conversation. The bartender could be depended on to get it. Any stupid person who ignored the signal would soon understand it when he refused to answer them. If that failed, the iPod earbuds got the message through. Every day needed some peace and quiet and he had a feeling this was his only shot at it today. Saturdays he counted on some hours alone to relax, to be unavailable. He looked forward to it. When it didn't happen, he felt deprived of something essential and deserved.

That might be a parking spot. No, too small. That? Maybe, maybe not. Kevin didn't want to put a lot of effort into parking. He hated parallel parking. There around the corner was one place he could just drive into and maybe back up a bit and it would be okay, not perfect but legal.

Locking the car door, he looked up at an old man waiting at the bus stop watching him park and unable to hide his contempt at Kevin's sloppy parking job. Kevin pretended not to see him. There's always a critic around when you park the car. Was he a client? He didn't look quite prosperous enough to afford Kevin's hourly rate. He saw so many elderly people and they all looked familiar. It was the buses and the bus stops. Bodies wearing down, inside and out, populated the bus stops. He looked at his reflection in the window and immediately straightened up. Round shoulders like his dad. Argh!

He folded his newspaper carefully and put it in his sport coat pocket and walked toward The Old Town Alehouse. The restaurant side was fairly busy with only a few empty tables. Inside the bar area, he choose a stool at the corner end close to the window in a row of three, where no one was likely to sit next to him. Two other men, with four stools between them on the long side, were chatting quietly, the only customers at the bar. He couldn't hear them. That was good. He preferred to sit next to two empty seats on the bench at the back of the bus too, reasoning no one would sit that close, unless they had to.

The bartender read all Kevin's signals correctly, even taking the order with a look instead of a greeting or question and delivered the pint glass of the locally made India Pale Ale promptly. He liked it when the bartender could take the order with their eyes. Good communication. He unfolded *The Seattle Times* and started reading the front page. Everything was going his way. He was so pleased that his middle-of-the-night idea had panned out after quite a bit of research and strategizing about options for the client. He had found a solution that was conceptually simple and clean. He loved it when it worked out like that.

He would look like a hero on Monday and bill it that night after the meeting. In his experience, heroes could expect a prompt payment from a relieved client. At the meeting Monday, he would say, "If you run into someone else with a similar situation, tell him to call me." Kevin sincerely hoped his client would not be able to resist bragging. That was all the advertising Kevin needed.

He had been so pleased with himself he'd made a phone call to his folks just to say hello and see how they were. They were old but still healthy and he hoped that would continue. He was dreading them becoming feeble. It was nice to be able to say that he'd experienced a small windfall and would send them a check. They reacted just as expected: "Oh, you shouldn't, you're too generous, but there is something I have been thinking about. What's Amy going to get?" He could hear the excitement in his mom's voice about a shopping expedition. His dad seemed interested in the situation he was working on and remembered the building when it was under construction. Kevin appreciated his dad following his cases; it was his way of saying he was proud of him.

Most people outside the tax law business didn't want to talk about it. It was a guaranteed conversation stopper when a stranger at a party asked him what he did. They usually grimaced and tried awkwardly to suggest a new topic. They had no idea what he did, but guessed it was something they couldn't understand. The next time someone asked, he would craft a succinct response. What was hard to describe to anyone about tax law was an appealing complexity. The numbers were tangible, reliable, predictable, and sometimes beautiful. The laws meant to encourage business activities were only as logical as the authors who wrote them. One man's idea of motivation was not necessarily another's idea—or effective in practice. Effectiveness also depended on the knowledge of adjoining municipalities, the city, county, state and regional laws. It was that intricate layering of laws he found appealing.

He ordered a grilled turkey sandwich on whole wheat with a salad instead of fries and bleu cheese dressing on the side as his compromise on healthy eating.

He turned his focus to the national and the international news in his paper.

After years of following current events closely as required reading, watching and thinking, he was beginning to feel that it didn't matter at all whether he knew about it or not. He could join the millions that didn't read the news everyday delivered to the doorstep and online. *Washington Week in Review*, a Friday night staple for years, no longer held his attention. In fact, he couldn't stand to watch anything on television anymore. The Sunday *New York Times* seemed like an overwhelming pile of newsprint. The first section and the op-ed was all he could muster. He watched Amy breeze through *The Seattle Times'* funnies, the local news, the business section, the front page, and then start on *The New York Times* Style section and Sunday magazine. It all seemed a waste of time to him. The local news was lame, mostly police blotter which must be the least expensive news to produce. Celebrities weren't interesting. The funnies weren't funny; even Amy didn't laugh most of the time but read them every day anyway, usually first thing and then the horoscope. Please don't read mine out loud to me. Reading the newspaper was an individual ritual. When he finished the front page, he picked up the free weekly paper lying on the bar.

Kevin studied all the venue advertisements and the weekend listings. There were no bands he wanted to see in the few venues he favored. He was all about the venue. It had to be intimate. He liked the Showbox at the Market, not the Showbox Sodo. He liked El Corazon, the Tractor, and the Sunset Tavern. Neumos was good. He wished the Croc, now that it was reopened, would have some bands he liked. The Triple Door was becoming more of a venue for them; another sign of aging and not a good one. The truth was old rockers and bands he'd never heard of were playing his favorite venues because they both had the same miniscule audience.

103

Kevin had once taken pride in knowing all the bands in the ads. He was adventurous and went to see lots of bands that were new and sounded promising. But he knew less and less, and realized he cared less and less. It was no longer critical to him to know it all and to have seen it live. The next surest sign of his aging was that the symphony experience was the one he cared about most. He and Amy had gone from buying a subscription with seven tickets to nine tickets and this year thirteen. Symphony tickets every Sunday afternoon began to seem like a goal. If this was his dotage, it wasn't all bad, was it? He wasn't sure. Would his politics suddenly take a sharp right turn like his dad when he got old? He'd be on the lookout for that and try to fight it.

The sandwich and the beer were gone. He folded up the paper he had hardly read. There was nothing like a little quiet to refresh him and help him prepare for the next part of the day, which would be errands and shopping for the company tonight. He felt relaxed, pleased about his morning's work and ready to move on with the day. He wanted to help Amy with her party and make her happy.

He signaled *I'll take a check* with a gesture of his hand. He consulted his to-do list while he waited for his change. He had plans to be a good husband this afternoon, be helpful, and get points toward tomorrow's free time. There was a documentary he really wanted to see that Amy was not interested in because it was too depressing. It would be cool to leave after lunch and come back at five. That was his reward for good deeds today and tonight. Kevin kept careful records of his points.

He really had nothing to complain about. His life was good. There had been lots of laughs over the years and he felt very lucky about that. He admired how she enjoyed herself and got such pleasure out of so many things. She got his jokes! She thought he was funny. She was fearless when times were tough and made him feel like his back was covered. He was proud of her. He didn't think he deserved her. That still seemed to be the truth almost thirty years later. She was more than he ever thought he could seduce and hang on to.

He thought he put serious effort into trying to keep her happy. Occasionally he worried that he wasn't doing enough. The way she smiled at men, even some of their friends, seemed a bit more than was appropriate to him. She wasn't the straying type, was she? No, he didn't think so. But if she was, he would be as stunned as every man he'd ever known who found out his wife was cheating on him. What could he say to her about it? Nothing. To ask if she really needed to fawn over Ben or Alan as much as she did would be to admit some insecurity. No way was he headed into that slippery conversation that could end up revealing something he preferred to keep private.

He was looking forward to telling her all about his middle-of-the-night idea. She would be thrilled about the unexpected billing. Amy was always prepared to spend a windfall. He had no clue what they desperately needed, but just name an amount, and she knew exactly how it could be spent.

Now his mission was to be helpful with this party of hers and so onward to purchase vodka for the crowd tonight. He wanted everyone well oiled so he could lead the conversation as far away from Malaysia as he could take it. No one needed to see his photographs or hear him tell how much he enjoyed the trip. The only thing they needed to know about Malaysia was that Amy loved the cooking class. She had been walking on air ever since, energetic, upbeat, and pleased with everything. He worried about her anxieties about aging and money. He tried to comfort her with compliments and philosophy. Stop worrying about those things you can't change. Life with a happy wife was all he wanted. He hoped the afterglow of this vacation lasted for a long time for her. He felt he was already shutting down his vacation sensors. He hoped no one would ask him what he liked about the class. A creative alternate answer was necessary. If anyone did ask, he would say, *It's the amazing food that makes Amy so happy.*

The real truth was his favorite part about the class was getting a whole day to himself to wander around Kuala Lumpur. Exploring on his own had made him feel young and adventurous. That was the best day of the entire trip, but no one needed to know that.

As someone who had wandered around Bangkok several different times before he felt like he *got it*, he was excited about exploring Kuala Lumpur. He wanted to own it personally in his mind. On paper it was so much smaller than Bangkok, population wise, but still enormous in its concentration of human beings and urban sprawl. He looked forward to trying it on foot and seeing what he could see and if he could find his way from here to there. He had studied his map so he could shut the door on her taxi and head out for the day. They would have two full days after his expedition to see the sights together, which would refine his first impressions. In the end, he didn't think Kuala Lumpur had much charm, and it certainly was difficult to walk around with highway-like streets creating dead ends for the pedestrians as though they had forgotten to put in overpasses or detour signs. But he had thoroughly enjoyed the time alone wandering.

He was ultimately able to find Chinatown, which wasn't that far away and true to the guidebook's description didn't seem to be big or busy in the morning. Oddly, or not because he was in Malaysia, his first stop in Chinatown was at an opulent Indian temple, Sri Mahamariamman. Kevin was dazzled by the sheer quantity of decorative sculptures on the outside of the structure that surely must be telling an epic story that his guidebook wasn't. He loved the cynical vendor stationed on the sidewalk in front making long yellow strings of flowers to sell for offerings who clearly wanted money for his photo being taken, but Kevin didn't oblige him on that. The interior of the temple didn't disappoint, either, with an eclectic mix of south Asian ornaments, European tiles, and precious stones among other things.

The Central Market seemed too commercial and souvenir oriented to be worth his time. Much more to his liking was the fruit and vegetable market off the main shopping lane, Jalan Petalin, that gave him plenty to look at that was appealing, appalling, or somewhere in between. Part of the charm of these markets was the shock factor. Could you keep looking at it or would you have to turn away? What was it? What would you do with it? What was that on the floor and now on his shoes?

He loved to laugh at Amy, who would eat anything, blanch in horror, and have to leave at the sight of some of the ingredients, which were sometimes still breathing. Barbecued rats with long tails stacked on a platter, dark as Peking ducks, had undone her one day in Thailand, instantly ending that market tour when she raced out to the sunlit street to have heart palpitations. She had a thing about rats, dead or alive. It required a large Tusker beer to calm her down.

The vendors and the shoppers were the other part of the charm. He smiled at the women who stared at him. He knew it was his height they were noticing. Six feet three didn't attract much attention in Seattle, where six feet seven was not uncommon, but in Southeast Asia, he got plenty of stares. He slurped a big bowl of beef and noodles from a small cart with Chinese workers on a break. He and Amy would have to come back together in a taxi at night to see this spectacle at its full roar.

There were two Chinese temples to look at. Sze Ya Temple, the one closer to the fruit market, was older and smaller, so he went there first for a cursory look, as he felt they would be back later to see the other famous clan house with the taxi tour guide they planned to take. It featured a green tile roof, which seemed unusual to him but had lots of ornaments on the roof, which was typical. He learned the story of the two local men who became heroes and then deities who were worshipped there. He was moved by it and would make sure that Amy saw it, too. She would like it.

He was eager to move on to the mosque Masjid Jamek that was close by and then explore Little India. The mosque was impressive in size with regal red-brick Moorish architecture with several big domes and two tall minarets to broadcast the call to prayer. The landscaping around the giant plazas and covered walkways was lush and tropical. Kevin felt small and humble walking around the edifice.

The streets nearby were busy with shoppers for all sorts of South Asian goods. He stopped in a coffee shop for a snack where he ordered pulled tea because he had been fascinated watching the man pouring it back and forth dramatically between two containers to make it frothy. It was too sweet for him. He couldn't finish it, but the curried vegetable fritters still sizzling from the hot oil were so delicious he ate four as a small snack dipped in some yogurt sauce.

Next, he was swept away with the textile displays of fabrics tied in bundles stacked literally to the roof and stacked to be used as lounges for the young women waiting for a customer. The women looked drowsy, but as he photographed them, they became a little coy and playful. He thought they were the best photo of the day. He laughed and gave them money for posing for him.

His last stop may have been more carefully researched than some of the cultural extravaganzas he had seen so far, but it was just as important to him for trying to experience Kuala Lumpur. He headed for the Coliseum Café & Hotel. In the 1920s, it was the value choice. To Kevin, it looked as though nothing had changed since. It was old school all the way in the furniture, tile floors, and ceiling fans. The ancient waiters were all business and no-nonsense. It reminded him of Musso and Franks in Los Angeles, where it seemed all the original employees were still on the premises almost a century later upholding the tradition of the place. He was promptly given a nice table with a white tablecloth and a very cold beer to study the menu with. The café was a Zagat Guide Teflon, a tourist attraction that didn't have to have great food to bring in customers, but he was very pleased he had been able to find it without difficulty. This was a perfect spot to relax and reflect on this very satisfactory day in the tourist business and it wasn't over yet. Malaysia was rewarding them at every step. He hadn't thought about himself, corrupt politicians, or the war in Afghanistan once the entire day! He hoped that Amy had enjoyed her day at the cooking class as much as he had enjoyed his.

Kevin had arranged online for four nights in a business hotel, the Royale Bintang, in a central location, the Bukit Bintang, a busy shopping district, so she could be in position to reach her cooking class by taxi easily early in the morning. (That taxi ride turned out to be a long, expensive scam, he learned when her return ride was much shorter.) The hotel was big but nothing special, a little run-down and surrounded by mega shopping centers selling fashion and electronics from low end to high end. He thought of Bukit Bintang as the Times Square of New York City, the new Times Square with sophisticated commerce and hotels, unlike the old version of seedy movie theatres and delis that he had visited as a young man. Shopping wasn't of that much interest to either of them, but they were excited about being close to a night market called Jalan Alor Food Street. It was about a ten-minute walk from the back of the hotel down a main street, and then off into a small side street were food vendors set up at night in some odd partnership across from a long row of restaurants. There was a lot of fun to be had on Jalan Alor. It was the best of both worlds for tourists like them. The night scene was endlessly fascinating to them to watch and to consume. They chowed down on hot and spicy chili crabs and long green beans one night, grilled stingray, a remarkable new fish to him (ikan pari bakar), and rojak salad another night. The third night they missed a turn and stumbled into the outdoor terrace of a nice-looking restaurant that was occupied by a rowdy ex-patriot group celebrating a big win on the soccer field. Mostly English and Australians, the group welcomed them into the conversation. After a few gin and tonics and the recommended house noodles, Amy and Kevin learned they were partying with people from an infamous insurance company. Amy couldn't stop herself from dropping her jaw and saying, "Really? What's that like these days?" The crowd wasn't as friendly after that.

The last night in Kuala Lumpur, they decided to splurge and took a taxi to The Sky Bar in The Traders Hotel near the Petronas Towers. The elevator ride up to the rooftop bar got your heart rate up with speed and vibrations that in some way prepared you for the stunning entrance into the open-air bar, which featured a long swimming pool and close-up view of the iconic towers. At least you already had an idea of how high up you were before the door opened and you felt you could walk off the edge of the bar and make the return trip even more rapidly than the elevator. They were not insulted to be given a table for two by the door, rather than long couches lining the room. Quite the contrary, it seemed much safer to be sitting back from the short glass walls that effectively gave you the feeling of no walls at all. Fancy (expensive) cocktails, piping hot, tender (expensive) beef, and shrimp satays on bamboo skewers and a chic waitress looking ready for the runways in Paris were soon all upstaged by a dramatic thunder and lightning storm. To be so high in the air overlooking the metropolis was exciting enough, but the storm ratcheted up the experience. The roof protected the room but people sitting at lounges against the security glass edge scrambled for seats away from the rain. Kevin and Amy's little table turned out to be perfect when it started pouring. They didn't have to move. Pleasantly terrified? Thrillingly frightened? Amy wasn't sure what she was feeling, but she wasn't leaving. They had a lively discussion about the engineering of skyscrapers in tropical climates where storms like this were common and lightning rods had to perform perfectly every time. Did lightning rods ever fail?

Chapter 10

It was ridiculous how much money young people made these days, Laurence thought. Yes, Google was a marvelous search engine. Yes, it was lightning fast. But how did that translate into so many new millionaire employees and billionaire founders? He did not understand the business model. The money involved was absurd. Aerospace engineers had lived the good life on $63,000 per year. The new Redmond engineer made $236,000 including stock options. How could it be? He felt sure none of what went on in the manufacturing plants and technology offices today were as brutal as the demise of engineering at Boeing.

Being in the aerospace industry had once been the highest status he could imagine. There was no work as challenging and exciting. Then things changed. What had once been the greatest career in the world was decimated. The company stopped designing new airplanes. There was no more problem solving, because they didn't invent anything new anymore. They stripped the pride out of the job. They stripped out all of the science and art. You might have had a job title that said aerospace engineer, but there wasn't any of that work to be done. How long could you sit at a desk doing menial tasks? It wore you down and made you angry. Engineers started quitting in droves. After the strike, he was too old to get another job and old enough to retire, so he retired. The end was ugly and sad. No one had remained friends.

Laurence breathed deeply and rhythmically, as he walked down Ballard Avenue toward Hattie's Hat. He had to go through with it, no matter that he was feeling nervous. He was surprised at the depth of his emotion. He tried to think about how Steve was feeling and imagined him already calming his nerves with beer. He entered the bar and scanned the crowd for his old friend. He recognized his back immediately. There was no change to those big shoulders and neck. With a bar stool open on either side of Steve, Laurence sat down on his left, meeting the eye of the waiting bartender standing in the middle of the bar.

"I'll have what he's having."

"So, you made it after all." Steve studied him, revealing nothing in his face.

"Am I late? Am I far behind?" Laurence studied him back just as coolly.

"Maybe I was early but you're only one behind."

The bartender put a pint glass of pale ale in front of him and kept moving down the rubber mat toward the next empty glass.

"So, thanks for coming. I wasn't sure if you would," Laurence said.

"Well, I tried to think of a reason not to come and I couldn't. And I had room on my calendar."

"Fair enough. I hoped it would seem that way to you." Laurence nodded his head, agreeing with what Steve was saying.

"Yeah. So, what's so important now that you called me?"

"Simple. I wanted to tell you that I wish I'd done the picket line with you. It wasn't worth $10,000 and a vacation to me to live with it afterwards."

"Well," Steve paused and looked him in the eye, trying to gauge the sincerity of the statement and finally shrugging his shoulders. "Okay. It was a long time ago."

Laurence studied his old friend's face, which looked so much older than he remembered. Steve had put on a lot of weight, and it really showed in his face with big jowls making his eyes seem smaller than they should have been. Laurence couldn't believe Steve was accepting his apology so quickly, without any anger or reciting of grievances. "Thank you for not needing to duke it out or rehash."

"You're welcome. I'm too old and fat to punch you in the nose, though I used to want to. Why now?"

Steve again went straight for it, no beating around the bush, which Laurence had always admired. He tried to answer with equal intent.

"It's been on my list. Yesterday seemed like the last day I could stand to walk around with this task incomplete." Laurence paused and decided not to say, *You know how I like to check things off.* Instead he said, "You doing okay?"

"Okay at this point is overrated. I feel like shit, look like shit, and so do you, by the way. You becoming a hippie in your old age?"

"Thanks. I feel like shit, too. Maybe I should get a medical marijuana prescription. How about Marge?"

"She's okay, too. She's getting to be a real cranky old woman who hates living with a sloppy retired guy who watches television all day and night. How about Ingrid?"

"She's better now. She died about five years ago."

"Sorry, I didn't know."

"There was no obit. She wanted it that way."

"What do you think about the new plant expansion in South Carolina?"

"I guess we didn't know how good we had it then."

"No, we didn't."

"So what do you do for fun?"

"I go to the library."

"Ha, ha." Steve chuckled. "That's a good one."

"It keeps me off the street and out of the bars. It's very stimulating and I occasionally see the old Boeing crowd."

"No shit, you really do go to the library and see engineers there from the old days?"

"We don't talk much, there's nothing to say, but if you see something interesting you want to point out, you can. It's nice to have someone nearby who speaks the language."

"I can't believe it, aerospace engineers at the public library. I thought only homeless people hung out at the library."

"No, that's a common fallacy. The homeless are there every day, but plenty of other people are, too. Boeing sponsored an aviation room that attracted our crowd. That's how I was introduced to the venue. That room is locked now, you have to ask permission to do research, but once you see the whole operation you will see the potential in spending time there."

"What do you do there?"

"Read. Listen to speakers. Take classes. Surf the web. They run a big schedule of events and you might be surprised at how interesting it is."

"I can't even imagine what you're talking about. What speakers?"

"Authors, politicians, music, dancing, adult stories."

"What's an adult story? Pornography? I heard they had porn there." Steve chuckled again.

"Sometimes steamy but not triple X—bleak tales from when times were really tough, you know, noir stuff, some horror, some funny. A man with a great voice reads aloud for an hour. It's at noon every other Monday downtown. It's definitely not for kids." Laurence felt like he was talking too much and too fast. He needed to slow down. Was Steve really listening?

115

"I am astonished. I had no idea. What are you reading?"

Laurence thought for minute about how to answer that as he read so much and wasn't trying to turn this into a bragging session, just I'm still alive and thinking, which he doubted the rest of the old group were doing. Maybe he was thinking too highly of himself. He wanted Steve to report accurately so he chose his best three topics.

"I'm following the microwave bombing technology pretty closely. I like that application. I wish NASA would do something radical with the shuttle. My new hobby is learning to become a hacker."

"Hacking? That seems to be the up-and-coming career for crooks. An old geezer like you is competing with the Russian mobsters or the Chinese freedom fighters? Do you have any tattoos?"

"No tattoos, just trying to learn some new tricks. I'm making new friends. Computer geeks are pretty interesting people. Ethics or morality issues don't slow them down. They seem to have the old frontier spirit. If it's out there and you can grab it, it's yours."

"So, you're swimming with young sharks? This sounds like the movie *War Games*." Steve looked for the cue this was a joke Laurence was setting up.

Laurence read his body language correctly and followed the movie analogy. "You know how the hackers in books or movies sit in front of a keyboard for hours with a clock ticking trying to crack the password? That's Hollywood. In real life, you run some software programs you've downloaded from the Internet and it takes a few seconds to come up with the passwords for a network."

"I'm impressed. Who are you going to hack?"

"No one in particular. I just want to know how to do it. I'm trying to understand the new economy and so far I'm baffled." He sipped his beer and tried to think of a question for Steve to change the focus on him, but Steve beat him to it.

"You still live in Sunset Park?"

"No, I gave up the house for an apartment on Queen Anne. It's a lot less trouble to take care of. I like being in town."

"You put so much work into that house. Must have been tough to give it up."

"Well, you know she was the one who was attached to it because she grew up in it. I commuted all those years for her. After she died, I didn't mind selling it."

"You gave up your woodworking tools?"

"Yep." Laurence wanted to move away from this line of personal questions but he couldn't get a move ahead of Steve's quick new questions.

"I am surprised. You kept the furniture you made?"

"I kept a few things, like my kitchen table, my bed, and a chest of drawers. I've moved on. You must have some new hobbies, too?"

"If you call upgrading my TV every year or two a hobby. Requires quite a bit of reading of *Consumer Reports* and spending time at Fry's and Best Buy. Talk about changes in technology. Let me tell you sometime about all the cable delivery systems I've tested."

"You remember my old idea about the electric book?" Laurence couldn't stop himself from saying it and hated himself instantly for it.

"Sure."

"I'm proud that an idea I had a long time ago has been developed into a phenomenon."

"You mean the Kindle?"

"I do. You own one?"

"I do. My kid gave it to me."

"Like it?"

"Yeah. I've read a few things. It works. I should read more. Why do you think your electric book idea is the Kindle?"

"I've studied my old schematics and what I can learn in public records about the technology of it. There are similarities. One of the key differences has to do with lighting, a problem I was working on. Well, I forgot about it for a while, put it on the shelf before I retired. Things have changed a lot since then."

"You are still thinking big and outside of the box."

"I'm trying to learn how to research things that are hard to find or technically not available to the public, but they exist. That's another way to look at hacking. The e-reader is an interesting example of technology that has been worked on by a lot of different people. I wonder if it will become part of the patent wars like the cell phone industry.

Shaking his head, Steve said, "How do you start hacking?"

"Dumpster diving is a big part of hacking. They call it social engineering, getting out there and asking for the information as though you're entitled to it and taking it if you find it. You start with one piece of the puzzle, a name, a password, a modem number, and you follow the trail into the network. It's more like genealogy. Tombstones and family Bibles lead to deeds and bank accounts."

"Oh, you make it seem retro or slow. When we were young I thought we had unlimited vision of the future and it was all about how fast and far the planes would go, and then without a pilot. But what else were we thinking about?"

Laurence was visualizing the young and dynamic Steve and Laurence with relentless energy and confidence in their ability to design the best in the air. "It wasn't money, was it?"

"No, you are right about that. It was a great business to be in then. It felt like we were rich just to be part of it."

"That's true. These young engineers today seem to be chasing a jackpot; everything is about money. I'm interested in it now too, I would like to develop a new source of income and learning to hack might help that."

"Things are bad, huh?"

"Slim pickings would be about right."

"What happened?"

"The usual. After the strike, not being a union member made the retiring benefits not as good as before. Ingrid was sick for a long time. When the standard protocols didn't work, the experimental treatments were even more expensive. It doesn't take long to blow through the dough. Don't feel sorry for me. There're plenty of people in the same shape, relying on social security. Things happen. I know people whose worthless kids bankrupted them. Some did it to themselves at the casino. You're lucky you stay home and watch television. Makes the pension go further. What kind of television system do you have?" Laurence was at the end of this topic and ready to talk about television technology. He had read about it even though he wasn't planning to own any.

"Satellite HDTV system with an HD receiver, DVR, and a multi-satellite dish antenna. I'm getting almost three hundred digital channels with about one hundred HD programming. I've got the Sony 60-inch screen networked into the house computers. It's a nice picture and so much bigger than the 55-inch."

"Your own personal theater. That's impressive." Laurence hoped his lack of television wouldn't be noticed in this otherwise very interesting conversation. "What are you watching?"

"Everything."

Steve signaled the bartender for another round.

Chapter 11

Amy put the bags of groceries on the counter and looked around the kitchen. What to do first? She couldn't remember. She needed to crank up the laptop and get the spreadsheet out to review very carefully. She put the fish away first before sitting down, deciding the rest could sit out for a while. Maybe she should make some tea or have a glass of wine and chill to regroup. Where was Kevin? She wished he would come home now and hear this shocking tale of old friends meeting on the avenue.

She still couldn't believe Natalie pretended not to see her. Amy knew Natalie had seen her. They had locked eyes before Amy had been dissed with the bounce of the flip and the sip. Natalie could have seen the car from a block away if she had been looking down the avenue. How could she not be looking down the avenue? Natalie had to have seen her standing by the car looking up the avenue at the crowd and had plenty of time to plan her interest in the store windows, the sidewalk, and talking to her mom. She erred only in not being able to resist that one long look, when Amy was close enough to see her eyes.

So that's where it would end. Amy knew they weren't close friends anymore, but she didn't think it was like this. She thought they might be friends again down the road. Occasional friends; someone you see once a year, fun to catch up, but enough.

When they were friends, they had had a lot of fun. They were both obsessed with decorating and cooking. They had shopped for bargains in furniture and accessories for every room in the house. The husbands liked each other. How had she let that slip away? Clearly, she had been stupid and missed the signs along the way. She should have called months ago or invited them for dinner right after they moved to the new house. The truth was she had been too busy in the first year, and after the second year, she had forgotten about them. It was all her fault. Amy felt sick.

Friends were so hard to make and then to casually let one slip away was so stupid. She should have realized she needed to do some extra reach-out to compensate for not being neighbors anymore to stay in Natalie's radar. Natalie was now another failure to add to her long list of errors. She felt like crying. Amy walked into the living room and sat down on the couch facing the fireplace. Thor jumped up beside her and rested his head on his paws philosophically looking up at her. His love and loyalty broke down Amy's last bit of self-control. A few tears ran down her face. She patted his back and began sobbing.

Every sad experience in her memory came pouring out with a tear for each one. It felt like the credits of her life were scrolling in six-point type and each line recounted an event, a poem, a movie, a book that had made her cry. Stupid things she'd said or done as a child, teenager, or adult rolled by with news footage of the starving children in Africa, mistreated animals, and her friends who had died of cancer and in tragic accidents. Her parents and grandparents, who had been dead for years, she still missed every day. She cried for her loss, mourning each death with a new facet of her personal pain and regret for words not spoken. Then she polished that with remorse for her selfishness. Finally, she was exhausted and dry.

Amy tried to list her troubles so she could count them and then deal with each one to deflate it. First, her anxiety about not being young anymore; in fact she was on the verge of being *old*, which caused middle of the day and night panic. How long did middle age last? When did it become senior citizen? What about ancient status? She threw all the solicitations from AARP in the trash without opening them. She was too young for that! Kevin kidded her about giving up discounts, but there was no way she was asking for a *senior* discount for anything.

At three in the morning, almost any ache could be construed as the first sign of a rare and incurable cancer or other debilitating disease that would leave her bedridden. A nuclear holocaust was always possible with the long-term feuds in the Middle East so full of hatred and the mentality of suicide bombers. She envisioned the water wars in the United States when they had sunk to second world status. The Pacific Northwest would be besieged with desperate immigrants thinking there was plentiful water there, which there wasn't. If she lived, her second anxiety was being poor while she was old. If the stock market and sluggish economy didn't revive, being able to travel leisurely at last, after Kevin retired, might be a pipe dream. They could slide into poverty like so many other people had, a victim of changing times. Worse than not being able to travel would be trying to being cheerful and loving through thirty years of retirement without enough money to eat well. They'd probably have to sell the house and move to a small, apartment on lower Queen Anne. That would kill Kevin. He took such pride in being a good provider. The house gave him joy and inspiration every day. Then she would be a widow living alone in a dingy apartment, easy prey for hoodlums of all ages to mug her every time she got out of the elevator. She gulped and sat up straighter, trying to shake off that last image. Here she was terrifying herself in broad daylight!

She stood up, startling Thor. She needed to get a grip on reality, and nothing could do that more efficiently than cooking. That reminded her she had company coming and plenty to do between now and then. Amy went to the kitchen, made a cup of green tea, and studied her spreadsheet with links to the recipes. She put on an apron and began sharpening her favorite all-purpose knife, a 7.5-inch Japanese Kyotsu universal style that had the most comfortable handle in her hands for hours of chopping. Then she sharpened an old steel knife from her mother's kitchen for filleting fish or slicing tomatoes. It was a comfort to have old utensils with lots of history that still performed perfectly. If she ever had to downsize her kitchen, she'd keep the cast-iron skillets that were old when she got them.

The otak-otak recipe began by soaking the almonds she was substituting for the candlenuts (even Uwajamaya didn't have everything). She hadn't been able to confirm it, but she suspected soaking the almonds was a wasted step as the soaking instruction was probably to remove a toxic element from the candlenuts, not change the texture. The dried chilies also needed to be soaked, so she put them and the almonds in glasses of water before she began slicing the shallots, garlic, chili, lemongrass, galangal, and turmeric. Her knife rocked rhythmically on the big white cutting board, creating symmetrical piles of similar-sized slices. Each pile was generating its own personal power statement and role in the recipe. The shallots were acidic and made her eyes run. She loved breathing deeply into the garlic's sharp, therapeutic cloud—what a powerful, pleasing aroma that was. Caesar salad was one of her favorites because of the wallop of fresh garlic. When she licked her finger after chopping the chili, the heat made her head jerk and she decided to go lightly with the chili to keep the custard seasoned but not so fiery as to distract from the creamy texture or fish flavor. The lemongrass required real muscle to slice, as it was so hard inside. She ended up giving it a couple of fierce karate chops to separate the lower third and peel back the other leaves to reveal the root end with all the flavor. It felt good to whack the cutting board and see how strong she was.

The galangal she had purchased at Uwajamaya looked so old and brown compared with the moist pink root in Rohani's kitchen. It was hard and fibrous, which made peeling and slicing difficult. She hoped the less than perfect ingredients weren't going to ruin the balance of flavors in the recipe that had made it seem so yin and yang when she first ate it. Unmistakably curry, but more delicate than any curry she'd ever had with subtle lemon citrus flavor that accented the fish lightly and perfectly.

It was shocking and humbling to learn in the cooking class she didn't recognize fresh galangal or ginger on the ingredients tray. The ginger skin was softer like a white radish and a creamy white, not beige and woody, as she was familiar with. When she described it to Rohani, she learned in Malaysia they would call it "old ginger." She learned also that galangal was used more in Malaysia than ginger and always paired with lemongrass to be the rosy background aroma note to the citrus lemongrass that leads the nose into the dish.

The turmeric, too, looked small, brown, and woody outside; this was very different from Kuala Lumpur, where the skin was so thin you could see the bright orange flesh through it. Slicing it released a floral note that surprised her because it tasted bitter when she tried a small piece. Prior to taking the class, she would never have cut things up so small and uniformly before processing, but it did make a uniform paste, without odd chunks, lumps, or fibers. She would enjoy using this technique to improve her cooking results and say, "thank you, Rohani every time." Everything went into the food processor bowl and was pulsed a few times. She added a little water and the dried shrimp paste, which stunk like something that had been dead for weeks in a wet basement, processed for about thirty seconds, and then pulsed again. She hated taking the lid off to let more of the vile smell out to scrape the sides of the processor bowl to make sure no ingredients were stuck or dry. She hated that half a teaspoon was all that was required from a half-pound bar in the pretty blue and white Belacan wrapper. Someone said it lasted forever if kept airtight in the freezer, which was good when you owned a lifetime supply.

She added the coconut milk, eggs, sugar, and kaffir lime leaves and pulsed a few times to combine the liquids with the paste, double-checking the sides and the bottom of the bowl with the white scraper.

Now that the ingredients were combined, a new aroma was rising in the air dominated by the fresh eggs and cream seasoned with an incense of clove and lime from the kaffir leaves. The custard was ready. She felt competent and proud of the work. Her life and marriage were pleasing, inspiring even. She was a long way from old and poor. She really had nothing to worry about. That miraculous change in attitude in a short period of time was the magic of cooking. To lose herself in the process and come out with a tangible, successful product that could be enjoyed and shared always made her feel that cooking was consistently her favorite activity. Nothing compared with it. It worked for her every time. She never had a bad day cooking.

"Thor, you see what a difference a few minutes in the kitchen makes? The world may be collapsing, but you and I are both very lucky." He looked up at her from the rug in front of the stove, not nodding in agreement exactly, but in recognition of being spoken to.

Next, she would dance with the fish and the sharpest knife. Amy tried to replicate the hand positions Rohani showed her. The left hand gently pressed the fillet, skin side down, on the cutting board. The right hand with the knife came smoothly between the flesh and the skin. Rohani had made it look so easy. Amy's technique was better this time but still not perfect as a little flesh stuck to the skin, which she tossed in the bowl of food scraps for the food waste bin outside. Her frugalness made her pull it back on the cutting board to remove the fish meat and put that in Thor's bowl, which he ate in one bite. Slicing the fillet into somewhat even, small pieces went very quickly.

If she'd been thinking properly, she would have already prepared the ramekins with washed spinach leaves and one pandan leaf, her extra touch to the recipe for aroma and flavor. But she had neglected the *mis en place* in her hurry to get started, so she had to stop, wash her hands, and then wash the spinach leaves and get the ramekins out of the cabinet.

Lining the small ramekins with the leaves was easy because the spinach leaves were almost as big as the ramekins. The pandan leaf needed to be cut in four or six pieces to drape over the spinach leaves. She paused for a moment, looking at the long, narrow, green pandan leaves. This idea of hers to add pandan to the otak-otak was crazy. She should stick to the recipe. She would make the basting brush out of pandan leaves to show the crowd and be done with it.

Amy arranged three small pieces of fish in each ramekin and poured the custard over to fill almost to the rim. She placed the ramekins in a deep baking pan covered with a long piece of plastic wrap over all of them and put it on the bottom shelf of the refrigerator, which was the last clear space. A nice check mark on the spreadsheet was so satisfying! Next item: Set the table, which was one of her favorite things to do. She spent hours looking at photos of tabletops in books, magazines, and online. The creativity involved in setting the table was so satisfying. Selecting the china to go with the food, selecting the tablecloth to go with the china, and the right napkins and napkin rings. The most fun of all was creating a centerpiece or decorations to run the length of the table from odds and ends in the china cabinet or

126

around the house. It was too lazy, not creative at all, to just buy flowers and put them in a bowl in the center of the table. Lack of money may have inspired elaborate centerpieces when she was young, but the joy in the process kept her spending time, not money, to make the table beautiful and unique for each occasion. Although she didn't get much credit for it, she really was frugal. She did her own nails. She washed the aluminum foil and resealable plastic bags to use a second time. She almost never let food go bad or threw out scraps that could be used for stock. Who was more frugal than she was?

In the dining room, an old French chest painted high-gloss white with the original ornate brass drawer pulls was full of props for the table. The first drawer stored napkins, napkin rings, and candles. The second drawer was for placemats and more napkins. The bottom drawer was full and heavy with tablecloths. She dug around in a stack of white ones of different sizes for the biggest one. It had been a great bargain with a dozen napkins, from that kitchen shop in Portland. It draped almost to the floor, which was really too long but she didn't feel like going to the basement for another leaf for the table.

Thor sat watching her with disapproval. She knew that the tablecloth was the giveaway to him that company was coming. Amy turned to him. "Oh, lighten up. It's going to be fun and you love the people who are coming. Alexis and Ben and Alan, all good people who will not bother you. They may even bring you treats."

He cocked his head to the side, indicating he was listening and definitely got the key word, *treats*.

She covered the white cloth with a two-yard piece of hand-painted batik fabric bought as a sarong in Malaysia, not because she was ever going to wrap it around her hips to parade down the beach with her navel exposed, but because the colors were to die for. The bright reddish rose background with pink and white flowers and an accent of dark violet sang to her. Centered and flattened on top of the white cloth, it was a riotous flower arrangement.

She counted out four red and four white beaded napkin rings that sparkled in any light, planning to alternate them at each place setting. Whoops, there were six people coming tonight, not eight. Having those two empty seats seemed a waste. Too bad they couldn't come up with someone else to ask. She pushed the extra chairs back against the wall. Having six of each color and no need to use both, Amy tried them around the table a few different ways and decided the red ones were the best accent. Grabbing the center of each napkin, she pulled it slightly through the ring so the two inches above the ring was narrow and the ten inches below was bunched to make a big white flounce that laid at each place setting like a hydrangea bloom.

Plates, which plates? She pulled out dinner plates from four different sets of china and tried them with the tablecloth. She ended up liking a stacked look with a yellow plate on top of a white plate with the napkin and ring on the side. The sterling forks, knives, and spoons were arranged quickly. Red and white wine glasses at each knife point completed the task and added more sparkle. Water glasses on the chest with a pitcher of ice water created extra room on the table. It was practically a Christmas tree with colored lights flashing. No one had ever seen this table before because it had never existed before. It was a temporary art installation, and she felt like an artist in her studio who had just completed a small but perfect painting.

Amy's rush of pleasure in her creation was pierced by a pang about the failed relationship with Natalie. She berated herself for letting go of the creative energy she had generated just moments ago; she was forgetting how lucky she was. She had a nice life, a good marriage, a beautiful house, and a wonderful dog. The wolf was not at the door. She and Kevin were healthy and enjoying life together. Friends would come and go. This was not the end of the world. She needed to stay steady and refuse to be buffeted by this feeling of failure. It was just as useless as feeling guilty for having a nice life. Being anxious about losing her nice life was debilitating. In imagining all the wretched luck that could come her way, poor and homeless was the worst. No, the truth was being sick was the worst. That would be extremely wretched even inside her nice house.

Thor rushed to the front door just before the two-tone ring of the door opening alerted her. Amy rushed up as Kevin came in. "Oh, god, I am so glad you are here! You won't believe what has happened."

"Would you let me come inside before you assault me with information?" he said.

"Alright, alright, sorry, let me help you carry something."

She followed him from the foyer through the living room and dining room into the kitchen. He put his packages on the big counter with the phone and laptop. She sat on a bar chair and sipped the tea now half full and cold.

"So, what horrible thing has happened? Is someone dead or dying?"

"I saw Natalie today on Western Avenue with her mom."

"What did she have to say?"

"Nothing. She looked me right in the eye and walked on by as though she didn't know me."

"Are you sure?"

"Positive. We had solid eye contact. She saw me. I was standing there by my car like a big bullseye with my hand up waving at her. She couldn't have missed me. I could have missed her because there was a big cruise ship crowd on the sidewalk, but I saw her."

"I'm really surprised she did that."

"Thank you. I've been in a state of shock ever since and I still can't believe it. But it happened. Add another name to my list of ex-friends."

"Oh, stop. She's the one who didn't want to be friends anymore. It just happened longer ago then we realized."

"I have been working hard at managing myself. I have been constructive and creative. I've set a beautiful table and got the otak-otak ready. I am starving."

"I am not. I ate out."

"You did! Where did you go?"

"The Old Town Alehouse."

"Oh, you bum. I would have loved to do that. Why didn't you ask me?"

"Well, as I recall there was no mention of us having lunch today. I was to return at 4:00 to do my chores. I'm early! You should have taken yourself out before you came home. You were close to about thirty restaurants and unlimited takeout food."

"Lunch wasn't on my mind at the time. Now I'm hungry and I need to make the rendang with all that stirring to brown the coconut."

"Do you need anything at Ken's Market for the rendang?"

"No, I'm all set for that. Did you remember to get the sherbet? How about an egg salad sandwich for me?"

"I would be happy to do both those things for you right now. I'm sorry this happened to you." He hugged her and kissed her gently on the cheek. "Everything will be okay. The table looks great. Sit down for a minute and relax while I go to Ken's. Are you sure you don't need anything else?"

"A new brain and my twenty-two year old body."

OTAK-OTAK by Rohani Jelani

11 ounces fish, boned and skinned *

6 dried chilies, snipped into 1/2 inch slices

1 fresh chili, cut in 1/2 inch slices

1 stalk lemongrass, cut 3-4 inches from the base, thinly sliced

1/2 inch piece galangal, thinly sliced

1/2 inch piece turmeric, thinly sliced

2 candlenuts (buah keras), roughly chopped, or almonds **

1/2 teaspoon crumbled Belacan shrimp paste

1/4 cup sliced shallots

2 cloves garlic, sliced

1/4 cup water

1/2 cup thick coconut milk

3 eggs, beaten

1 teaspoon sugar

1/2 teaspoon salt

1/4 teaspoon freshly ground black pepper

3 kaffir lime leaves, finely shredded

10–12 'wild betel' leaves (daun kaduk) or spinach or romaine leaves

Cut fish into 1/2 inch slices. Cover and refrigerate until ready to use.

Soak dried chilies in warm water until plump, about 15 minutes. Drain and rinse chilies, leaving most of the seeds behind. Place dried and fresh chilies, lemongrass, galangal, turmeric, candlenuts, shrimp paste, shallots, and garlic in an electric blender/chopper and grind finely, adding 1/4 cup water to allow the blades to work. Combine this paste with the coconut milk, eggs, sugar, salt, pepper, and kaffir lime leaves.

Line the base of a casserole dish or 4 or more ramekins with leaves, place the slices of fish on the leaves, and pour the custard over. Steam over gentle heat for 15–25 minutes, depending on the size/depth of the container. Serve warm. If no steamer, make a bain marie by putting dish or individual dishes in a water bath to keep moist with no crust formed.

* Lemon sole, red snapper, grouper, and Spanish mackerel are all suitable.

** Aleurites moluccanus, looks similar to macadamia nuts with a high oil content but does not taste the same; soak for 1 hour before blending. Substitute almonds, peeled and blanched.

Chapter 12

Ben sat at his desk, looking at the ship canal. It was 3:05 according to his iPhone and his desktop monitor. He should call Alexis back. She would consider it a gift, maybe equal to a bottle of champagne, or an apology to get a call from him saying he remembered the party and would be home in time to go. But he thought she could wait a little longer for his call since she had been so snarky last night. No, not last night. He didn't go home last night. Maybe it was the night before. Did he go home that night? He couldn't remember exactly when he'd been home.

He would let the work sit a little longer. It was lousy work anyway, so why not let it take a little longer. If anyone said anything to him about the deadline, they would be risking one of his favorite rants against the subcontractors in the subcontinent. Low bidders were running and ruining the world.

Alexis was at home not complaining loudly, yet, that he was still at work. Pandanus was starting to come back to him. He remembered something else he wanted to do at home and looked for his checklist. The stacks of paper everywhere hid the surface of the desk and many small items that had been slowly buried. Whoever had thought cutting back on the cleaning crew to twice a week was a reasonable way to save money had never seen engineers at work. His space was a mess. That was the only way to describe it. It even smelled like garbage because of the discarded wrappers from sandwiches, cheeseburgers, and Thai take-out cartons. Empty coffee cups and cans of Red Bull seemed to mark the piles and the overflowing wastebasket and recycle bin. It was a junk food detritus sculpture that could only be created by eating the food randomly over time with no thought whatsoever to where the wrappers flew when thrown. No glue was necessary; the grease did the job. He should photograph it quickly before it collapsed under its own weight. He might title it "Heartburn or Engineering: A Life." However, a truly nice white yacht was cruising by at 7 knots as specified by the channel markers. Maybe it was a two million dollar toy, possibly a bit less, a senior VP model, not a CEO or Chairman model and definitely not a mogul model. Paul Allen's or Larry Ellison's boats wouldn't fit in the ship canal. The mogul models needed special docking outside of typical marinas.

It was a nice Saturday out there. He should not be sitting here. He should be at home welding on the cold smoker exhaust pipe. He should give his mother a call and say they were thinking of coming to see her soon, even though they weren't. He should take a look at his bank balance and see if the last checks he'd written had cleared. He was tired. The last few nights had been late or all night. The solution wasn't in sight. Time was running out. He had tried to explain to his boss again on Thursday afternoon that there was no easy solution. There was no slick fix to slide over the bridges that had collapsed into ravines miles deep. The work was shoddy so far back, it needed to be done again, correctly, and several tiers back. That wasn't going to happen in a few days. That was at least a few weeks' work; maybe a month or more, if they had anyone good do it. That was the problem.

As usual, his boss thought Ben's view was not practical or pragmatic. Ben had jumped into the ring so often since they had started outsourcing the work to much less expensive production facilities his appearance in his boss's cubicle on Thursday was not welcome. This being not welcome all the time was becoming a new irritant to him.

One day soon he would appear at the manager's cubicle and the response would not be *Thanks for the input but this is the way we're doing it*, but *Thanks, security is on the way to help you put your stuff in a box and carry it to the door for you.*

Ben was beginning to look forward to the latter scenario. Unemployment benefits were pretty good if you'd been fired. He'd have time to work on some other projects he thought had merit, maybe do a startup with some buddies. The only reason not to do it was that he knew at his age, fifty-nine, he would never find another engineering job. If the startup failed, which was Plan B with his best buddies, the slide into a "paper or plastic" job at Safeway might be fast indeed. He had discussed the alternatives with Alexis so many times, he wasn't welcome at that portal either. I hate this job, but I'd better not lose it. I better stop complaining and get back to creating a magic solution. The iPhone in his pocket vibrated. He looked at the incoming call number. Oh, shit, Alexis, again.

"Hello. I was just getting ready to call you."

"Liar. This is your last reminder; we have an invitation to dinner tonight that will be fun. I will hate you if you don't come home and go with me. I will go without you. Leave that problem for tomorrow. You can take a nap, have a shower, and be a new man by 7:30. With some sleep, you might be a new engineer tomorrow. If you don't, you're going to be a tired old dude sleeping at his desk again instead of in his bed, while I'm out having fun with friends, dining on fabulous food, and drinking nice wine."

"Good points," Ben said. "I'll be on my way soon."

Chapter 13

Alexis was using her no-nonsense voice instead of her sympathetic voice. Sometimes Ben responded to it. He called it her bitch goddess voice when he was in a good mood and other things when he was not. Her instinct was that this voice would work today and maybe it had. She wanted to go to the party. She wanted to get out of her dirty house and be in someone else's clean house at a table set for company, the dinner prepared, and a handsome bartender at the ready to make drinks and entertain her. Alan would be there tonight she knew from seeing his name on the group email invitation. Alan always made her laugh. She would offer him a ride home. Alan would be grateful for it as sometimes the taxis took forever to come late at night. Ben didn't mind; he would undoubtedly have a nap in the backseat the whole way there and home. Alan and Alexis could then have a private chat about everything. These chats were hysterical. Of course, she would never repeat to anyone what Alan said. Out of context it might be misunderstood as mean, not funny. Dropping him off downtown was not really that much out of the way, a small detour. If Ben didn't go to the party, she might take Alan up on his standing offer to come inside and have a nightcap. She felt like she deserved some quality attention and appreciation. That seemed to be Alan's specialty. Depending on how the evening went, even if Ben did go, she might leave him asleep in the car to squeeze one last bit of pleasure out of the evening and run the risk a thug or a policeman would try to wake him up. He would be so mad at her for abandoning him.

Alan's condo was nicely done, particularly for a bachelor's place, with good furniture and smart arrangements to take advantage of the view of Elliott Bay. He had a bar, of course, which was well stocked and with very comfortable leather bar stools. She imagined he spent plenty of evenings behind the bar making drinks for young women and seducing them quickly with his conversation and décor. The art was well hung, which was hard to do alone. She wondered if he had consulted with a decorator or if one of his women friends had helped. The first time she and Ben were invited by him to dinner at his place, she had asked him if this was where he lived when he was married. He said, "No. This place is all mine, every book and chair," and did not elaborate further. Some people liked to tell you where they purchased every piece and what they paid for it but not Alan. He understood the power of discretion; a little mystery is appealing, too much information is not.

He had invited them to dinner a few times, always with Amy and Kevin, and she had admired the way he handled the gig all by himself with no difficulty. He served a sophisticated hors d'oeuvre he had prepared himself and a three-course dinner, no shortcuts or party platters from the big-box store. His food was good and the wine pleasing but not showy.

She was dying to ask, "So what exactly did you do to convince your wife to leave all this charm and talent behind?" But she didn't and never remembered to ask Amy the next time she saw her what had happened to that marriage. He looked like a good deal to her. He seemed to listen so intently and understand everything. What more could you ask for in a man? At the moment anyway, those seemed like golden qualities.

She thought that putting some festive color in her hair and assembling an outfit with some oomph to go with it would cheer her up. Getting out was good. She hadn't been out in days—it just seemed like too much

137

effort to get dressed properly. She usually got up before 7:30 AM, made coffee, fed the dog, and read the newspapers in the kitchen. She got Ben up at 8:30, and he was usually out the door by 9:00. She would put a cup of coffee in his hand as he passed through the kitchen on his way to the car. He would eat at his desk, when he was hungry. After he left, when she could relax, she made breakfast for herself, a thick slice of good bread, from a bakery, toasted, with European butter from DiLaurenti and French apricot jam. Her policy was no penny pinching when it came to bread and butter; she could find other ways to be frugal if necessary.

It was hard to be calm when Ben was in the house. He was so agitated by things at work that he overreacted about everything at home. He was unhappy, and there was nothing she could do about it. She had tried to distract him with theater or weekend drives or having friends over. He wanted to do none of those things. All those conversations were such failures the concepts would not be brought up again as just mentioning them could create a new ugly scene. In fact, so many topics were off limits, she couldn't really think of anything to say to him anymore. That probably was an exaggeration, but it felt that way.

Even cooking, which used to be a safe topic, now seemed fraught with land mines. One day last week, she'd splurged at the market on a new avant-garde farmer's slab of pork belly, one of his favorite ingredients, thinking it would entice him into researching new recipes and cooking something for fun.

"I'm exhausted and you want a study group before a dinner that takes at least three hours to prepare?"

"I didn't mean it for tonight. I just wanted to show it to you."

"Why didn't you cook it this afternoon?"

"It was a gift for you!"

"A gift for me would be hot and ready right now."

"What a waste of time it is to try to romance a turnip—even harder than wringing blood from one."

"Are you calling me a turnip? Do you mean fat or stupid or both?"

"I didn't call you a turnip!"

"You just did!"

"It's an expression of futility, wringing blood from a turnip. Haven't you heard of it?"

"So I'm stupid in the cliché department? It's true no courses in bad writing were part of my PhD program, but I'm sure they were required in your Fine Arts Master."

"Never mind, you geek. You may be high functioning, but you've lost your right mind, if you ever had one."

"Fuck you, at least I have a left one," he said and then stormed upstairs to his office.

Tiptoeing around his foul humor was a problem, but it wasn't the only one she had. She needed a job and after looking for months, she still hadn't been able to find one. At fifty-five, her options were limited to put it lightly. Looking for work sucked. She felt fat. She had given up looking for jobs that used her best skills in design and packaging. She'd given up looking for jobs with her advanced skills using design software applications. She had applied to so many menial jobs without a single interview that it seemed useless to apply to any more. No one wanted to hire her. Ben technically made enough money to cover the lifestyle, which was a nice one, no complaints from her about that, but they weren't saving any and that made her nervous.

It made her sick to think about how hard she'd worked for years at a tough job to shore up her 401K to comfort her anxiety about finances in the long term. Since the last stock market crash, it appeared retirement wasn't going to be much to look forward to. Everyone said their mutual funds were coming back and were almost where they had been, but not hers. She suspected the fund family was a turkey and would never come back. If it did, how old would she be then? How would she be spending her days? She wished she had insisted on remodeling the kitchen with some of the 401K money while it still existed. At least she would have something to show for that last cruel episode in the web design business. Maybe she should sell the fund, take the loss and start over with another company. Could you declare a loss inside a retirement plan? She'd ask Kevin tonight what the rules were. The whole investment business was too awful to think about.

Depending on Ben for every penny was depressing her, too. The house seemed to be falling down around her, and he didn't notice or share her concern. He didn't think this was a good time to invest in the house, and he had no time to work on any home repair projects. If she had been working, she would have had a plumber out long ago to replace the disposal and that leaking faucet no matter what he said. That was at the top of her long list. She would have hired a fleet of people by now to attend to the details that if left too long got worse and more expensive to fix. He called her a chronic spender and it wasn't true. She was very thoughtful about spending money on the house.

Whereas most of her friends considered their wardrobe the money pit, she was frugal about clothes and preferred a vintage look with lucky finds at Value Village and shops that specialized in period pieces. New clothes seemed so plain she couldn't bear to wear them. The workmanship was so shoddy. The details and the construction of garments of other eras were art and craft. Who wanted man-made fabrics when real cotton and silk felt so sensual on her skin? She felt good when she wore a well-made dress that fit properly and expressed her feelings about the day or the event. Her total presentation made an immediate impression that she was not ordinary

140

in any way. That was very important to her. She did her own hair, which saved a ton of money, as she liked to change the color, but that wasn't really a hardship. She loved doing her hair. The colors she mixed up were fabulous, much better than any commercial colors for sale and a source of satisfaction to her. Her restaurant and bar bills were zero since she had quit going out with friends. That was a hardship. She missed going out. The phone wasn't ringing much anymore. She had said "no" enough times to make it clear she was not interested in going out.

Every week her mom in New York said, "Why don't you come and visit while you're unemployed and can stay longer?" She lied about her job hunt and prospects instead of saying she hated asking Ben to buy the plane tickets. She didn't want to ask her parents, either. It was pathetic to be her age and have to beg a plane ticket like a college kid.

So Alexis and her pride stayed home in her studio painting and tried to limit her path through the house to the kitchen and bedroom, neither of which received much attention from her. In every other room, she saw a mess that needed cleaning up and a home improvement project that lacked funding. It was so frustrating not to have money. Until she did, there was no reason to do anything but paint, which was truly the only thing going well these days. Other than walking the dog, she was standing in front of a canvas. Whole days and sometimes nights, when Ben didn't come home, went by very quickly. She thought the work was good in a strident, bleak way that pleased her. The audio component would feature screeching and clanging. She liked the art the bitch goddess painted much more than the commercial art she produced with designated corporate colors that were considered motivational to make consumers feel upbeat about the product. If the corporate taskmasters had ever unleashed her, she could have showed them some

141

motivational art that would attract attention from consumers. They were such dolts!

Her personal art was about outrage, her own and the human race's. She was currently working on a series of ten pieces that explored the range of emotions women feel because of political processes. *Strangulation* was on her easel right now. This series followed a series of ten on business processes. Nobody would ever know just how emotional she could be because no one was ever going to see it, except occasionally Ben when he was brave enough to come into the studio and feign interest. The private nature of the collection was an essential aspect of her art. She liked having a secret life. She painted because it was her habit and she was miserable if she couldn't. Painting by herself for herself was where she lived freely.

Tonight was going to be a much-needed break in the routine and to get out of the stale air lingering in every room of this house. She was going to Amy and Kevin's with Ben or without him. She would just sit in the pretty dining room, enjoy the wine and the food that she didn't cook, and listen to everyone talk. She was going to be in receptive mode. It was an exercise in opening up to inspiration that began physically by sitting quietly and willing her whole body to notice all the elements and then absorb the ones of interest from the atmosphere and the energy in the room. The air at Amy's would be vibrant, and Alexis would soak it up to use later. She was also looking forward to catching up with Amy to learn how her job search was going. Another goal was to get a company tip or contact from her tonight to pursue with her new inspiration. Hopefully, they would have a chance to chat alone as what Alexis really wanted was to have a good session with her on how to jump-start a reinvention program. Amy had done it before, somehow selling herself as something she'd never been before, and Alexis wanted to borrow her notes.

142

With high hopes for the evening, she got out her box of hair potions and started creating a color she envisioned as the rocket fuel for making changes. It would be practically combustible when combined with a blue silk cocktail dress from the 1950s that was very flattering to her figure. Once she assembled her outfit, she would be mentally open and ready for whatever was coming next.

Chapter 14

Amy was standing in front of the power burner, turned to lowest setting, guiding a wooden spatula with her left hand around and around in a large, dry frying pan slowly browning ground desiccated coconut for the rendang. Switching hands whenever her wrist got tired, she noted the microwave timer keeping track of how time was left. Stirring constantly over low heat could take twenty minutes or more to get the coconut golden brown and couldn't be rushed because it burned easily and then you would have to start over. Oven roasting couldn't duplicate the toasted flavor of the manual labor.

The stirring motion today seemed a silent memorial service for the loss of the friendship, for her failure to maintain it properly. The relationship was over, not taking a break. It was dead. If she had handled this better, if only she had invited them to the party tonight, or some other night, this wouldn't have happened. She had been dismissed as unworthy. She was over the surprise but felt wounded. Maybe tomorrow she would have some semblance of self-respect to overturn the current feeling of rejection into anger or something more benign and see this whole thing as bad behavior on Natalie's part.

With casual friends, Amy had found the easiest way to get rid of people she had lost interest in was just not to contact them again. She was an instigator. People got used to her organizing expeditions and events. She'd been amazed at first that's all it took, and then she realized the feeling must be mutual. That was not a bad

144

ending. If she received a message after that, she ignored it. She'd seldom experienced any follow-up after that. When she felt she was being ditched, she'd write someone twice and if they didn't respond, she added them to her *do not call* list. The drifting away had occurred. If she ran into them a year or ten years later, she could still say hello without any discussion of grievance to retrieve and bandy about.

Amy had a few people on her *do not call* list. Some she missed and some she did not. She wondered how many lists she was on. If they kept lists, there were husbands who had her on their bad list for enabling the wife to do anything the husband didn't want her to, like shopping. It was a black comedy indeed after a big afternoon at the outlet mall when she helped a friend carry shopping bags into the side door of the garage to hide them from the husband. He happened to be in the dark garage doing something very quiet. Everyone screamed. He turned on the overhead lights. Amy laughed so hard she thought she'd split her jeans, but he wasn't amused at all. If the wife had only said something light to deflect the moment like, "Jeez, honey, are you practicing your second coming routine?" But she didn't.

Amy tried to stay reconciled with the notion that there would always be people she wanted who didn't want her. There would always be people smarter and less smart, richer and poorer, more attractive and less attractive, fatter and thinner.

When she thought of people who probably mourned her quietly in the same way she mourned others, Amy particularly admired one friend's pride for not getting in touch with her. If she had called Amy, she would have been warmly received to chat to catch up, but she would get no suggestion from Amy to get together. Amy would have declined any invitation she issued. That relationship had to end, not because she was half crazy but ever so entertaining, but because Amy couldn't stand the woman's husband. He was truly some kind of weird and always seemed to insert himself in their meetings. Someone once said they must be in the witness protection program—that was the only explanation for those two human beings masquerading as a married couple. One of them was the undercover agent guarding the other from certain death. Which one? Probably her.

Sadly, the *awful husbands* category had several women in it who might have been great friends, if they weren't married to that guy. Awful husbands wanted to be included in everything. Why couldn't husbands and wives be more independent? She frequently invited women to go shopping because just mentioning the word shopping usually made the spouse happy to stay home. Once you were out, you could walk, do lunch, happy hour, or many things in addition to poking around stores. Awful husbands always wanted to turn the invitation into something they wanted to do. And she'd never figured out a way to tell a friend, I'm sorry I like spending time with you so much but I can't deal with your husband. So the drifting away on these could be awkward and painful.

The other sad category, the *no way* group, was couples Amy had invested some time in and thought seemed worth trying to get to know better by going out as couples, only to be nixed by Kevin's quick assertion, "There is no fucking way I'm going out for dinner with those people. You be friends with them without me." He had no idea how difficult it was to be friends and exclude the spouse from all events because he had not tried it as many times as she had. After making a bunch of excuses why Kevin couldn't come to whatever was planned, they quit inviting her to do anything. Touché! She got it.

No wonder she felt they had a small group of friends and that it was difficult to try to make new ones.

The spice paste in the processor seemed so similar to the otak-otak she'd made earlier she wondered why it tasted so different in the end. She stuck her nose into the bowl and breathed deeply, trying to get every nuance. The shallots and garlic were pungent, the galangal and lemongrass were soft and floral. It would be cooked with the coconut milk until it thickened and was no longer raw before the toasted coconut and chicken would be added. It must be the browned coconut that had started out smelling sweet like baking pastries but became roasted nuts when the color changed. That was the difference. At the cooking class in Kuala Lumpur, she was assigned the otak-otak and the other student the rendang. She hadn't looked at the recipe since the class, except to make a shopping list, and her memories of the class were supercharged with visuals, aromas, and tastes. She tried tracing back in her memory to the individual experience of tasting the otak-otak for the first time versus tasting the rendang. The otak-otak was briny and tasted of the sea with a light curry flavor. The rendang had been made with beef and simmered slowly to a stew like bolognaise. Sweet red meat, of course, that dramatically altered the flavor of the curry sauce. The chicken version she was making was only simmered a short time to keep the meat tender and moist. Of course it would taste different.

She put the recipes side by side and, indeed, the ingredients were very similar. She shook her head. How had she missed this when making the shopping list? This was a big mistake, a menu flaw. People were going to think she was crazy serving the fish in the same flavored sauce as the chicken that followed. Was it too late to make laksa?

Amy took a few deep breaths. Yes, it was too late to make laksa. That would be crazier. Don't even think about it. Go with the plan. It will all be delicious with similar flavor profiles that seemed planned. No one will complain. She sighed with relief and complimented herself on making a wise decision.

Someone would probably ask her tonight how she happened to take the cooking class and she should be ready with a brief answer. She didn't plan to tell anybody that in the beginning the dream was the cooking school at the Oriental Hotel in Bangkok. Her mom's best friend had been there and raved about it. Amy had also read about it in *Gourmet* magazine when she was twenty-something, knew everything of importance, and sarcasm was funnier than it was today; she used to laugh and say, "Right, when I'm taking cooking classes at the Oriental Hotel and going shopping at the floating markets in the hotel's boat." She loved that line because she thought it achieved the effect she wanted so badly: older, cynical, and knowledgeable about places not everyone knew about. What a silly twenty-two-year-old she had been! All the years she had spent time trying to look older made her cringe. As a teenager she thought eyeliner was the key to sophistication, more was better. Now she thought eyeliner was an essential to appearing alive.

Becoming obsessed with trying to become a professional with a career and a dress-for-success wardrobe with Italian shoes and purses after graduate school made her more serious. Then the new status symbol was to be in therapy. Everyone she knew was in or had been in therapy. It indicated intellectual and philosophical maturity. Incredible, how all her girlfriends, whom she saw several times a week and spoke with daily, knew so much about everything. They had the self-knowledge of what they wanted and why and spoke of it with some reverence. The reverence probably had more to do with the expense of going to therapy. No one was making that much money, despite the navy blue power suits, but status symbols exist at every income level. This phase didn't last that long. Amy lost interest in the subject.

When she became romantically involved with Kevin, who was part of the old college crowd, her lusts changed and they were soon married. Amy was now obsessed with her husband, house and hunting for the right pieces of furniture and accessories at good prices. Kevin was the world. Pantsuits were acceptable at the office. She didn't see her girlfriends much anymore. If anyone called at night to chat, which didn't happen that often, she was getting ready to serve dinner or go to bed. Kevin liked to go to bed early. It occurred to her when she missed seeing them that maybe it was the men all along that undermined the relationship with girlfriends. Looking back, she was revolted at how the preference of a boyfriend took precedence without any thought for the girlfriend, apology or argument from her. *Oh, sorry I can't do it, he wants to do something else.* If the courtship or engagement was long, by the time someone married, their old friends had made new friends to fill up the time slot. Marriage was definitely a killer of friends.

In her forties nothing was black and white any more. World events seemed so convoluted. Office politics were a quagmire. Management decisions about product development made no sense to her. Principles seemed spindly. Were they working for the consumer or the company? She felt she knew less about every thing. Work demanded grueling hours and it was all about stock options or going public. Casual Friday had become jeans every day. Weeknight sex? That was last decade. When she and Kevin finally made Bangkok, a notch in the tourist belt, she hadn't even thought about the cooking class until one afternoon they went for a drink just to see the Oriental Hotel.

Watching the water taxis speed by and the ferries dock and depart below the Oriental's open-air bar overlooking the Chao Phraya River, she tried to savor the moment, but it was depressing to accept that the vast distance had been accomplished and she was no closer to taking a cooking class at the Oriental than she had been at home in Seattle. You had to be a guest of the hotel to take the class. She wasn't going to be a guest this trip or any other trip. Kevin was very practical about vacation spending and felt a five-star hotel was an ostentatious expense. She agreed with him. She couldn't imagine rationalizing the expense for the five-star hotel room, not just one night, but five nights. It was a five-day class with mornings spent shopping with the chef at local markets and afternoons in the kitchen. She realized then she was never going to the cooking class at the Oriental Hotel. This realization felt like a punch in the stomach. She had neglected to research carefully! When she had embraced this cook's dream of Bangkok, she hadn't known what a five-star hotel was. It had been a foolish fantasy, not a goal or a grail. This type of careless oversight on her part confirmed that she was an idiot doomed to failure.

Several ginger martinis later, she made a mental note: Figure out a new grail after the vacation. She would come up with something else that was perfect for her that no one else she knew had done or heard of. There had to be a unique adventure out there for her.

It hadn't taken long after she got back to realize that trying to figure out a new grail was debilitating. Grails descend upon a person uninvited. What descended upon her after her arrival home from glorious Southeast Asia was a short stack of anxiety-producing items concerning career moves and lack of any jobs whatsoever in the traumatized post 9/11 world. The future looked bleak indeed. The best years were definitely behind. She was only forty-something years old and doomed to mediocrity or worse; a bag lady on the street or in a store saying "Paper or plastic?" to customers for the rest of her life. Argh! She was determined she was not ending up like that! But what could she do?

Her marriage was slumping along with her mood. When she felt lackluster, his natural reserve no longer felt strong to her; it felt cold. The longer she was immobile, the more detached from him she felt, which added

150

sadness to her list of worries. When she asked him about his day over dinner, his response seemed minimal. Maybe he was trying not to rub it in that he was working and she was not. Maybe he didn't want to talk about it because it wasn't essential for her to know the details anymore. Not to be emotionally connected to him was unbearable. They had weathered bigger crises and events than unemployment.

"Kevin, I am deeply concerned about us not talking."

"Amy, I am deeply concerned about you being so depressed over not having a job you're almost comatose. It's not worth it. I'll say it again if you want me, too: 'I don't mind if you don't work. I think you're smart, talented, and can be very creative at something other than bringing home a paycheck from an office you hate.' You need to make yourself feel okay about it. I can't do that for you. Believe me, if I could, I would. I'm here for you, waiting for you to wake up and deal with the facts."

"It is all about me, isn't it? It's not about us."

"Yes, it's about you. I'm the same."

It was obviously time to reinvent herself. This was a serious long-term project she dedicated herself to everyday. All her experience with managing big projects taught her that the daily checklist is all that counts. Keep moving toward the goal. Check, check, check, things will get better, the more checks you make. She rebranded herself as a freelancer with specific skills to sell, printed new business cards, made a new website, and found new clients. She was proud of the results. The world seemed lighter and brighter, more possible.

She joined a new volunteer group. She did that twice because the first wasn't rewarding.

After a few years struggling to find and then complete small projects, she got a contract job from a freelance client, which was the hidden agenda, and finally a full-time position where she knocked herself out in a noisy, open-environment office so popular at the time because of the start-ups in garages but so stupid when you have a big building full of employees. She longed for the days of cubicles and could barely remember when she had had offices with doors that closed. Within a year, the stock market crashed and she got laid off in a room full of people the same night there were layoffs all over town. She was offered her old job back within a week as a contractor at half the previous salary, which she took because she knew it was the only gig in town for her then. That lasted until the economy refused to take off again as hoped and the product she was working on was killed.

By then, in her fifties, she knew nothing. All her previous knowledge and expertise evaporated. She felt like a high school student in a PhD program. How did everyone else get so smart and successful? Where had her skills gone? She didn't have the energy to start a new business or create a new career path. She didn't have any good ideas.

She auditioned some new friends. She let some other people drift away. She took golf and bridge lessons. She took up neither.

She decided to make lemonade out of the unlimited free time by adopting the dog she and Kevin had talked about for twenty years. *That* had been wildly successful. Thor made them laugh. The three of them played together in the living room for hours. Kevin took him for a walk on Saturday by himself so they could be manly together. They all walked miles together in the parks on Sunday. Thor gained ten pounds the first month with regular meals, which she cooked for him. She lost ten pounds in the first month from walking him two hours a day during the week. Amy embraced a new world of dog people and activities she never knew existed: dog walking, dog school, and behavior therapists. Thor, although devoted to Amy and Kevin, turned out to be afraid of most other people and ready to bite anyone who reached out to pet his head. He would try to attack UPS deliverymen on the sidewalk delivering packages—or driving their trucks down the street—and young boys on bicycles or skate boards. The first therapist said it was all Amy's fault that she wasn't demonstrating enough leadership for the dog to feel confident she could handle the world, so the dog was trying to take care of things the only way he knew how. *Leadership! Isn't rescuing a dog an exchange of food for companionship?* Amy knew how to handle that. The second therapist said fear biting is common in rescued dogs. Thor probably had bad experiences with deliverymen and boys. Amy was advised she must be vigilant when walking him to protect him from what frightened him. Her dog had a behavior therapist! Wasn't that ridiculous?

Now that she had time, she read all the books about retirement and the small house concept. They were not going to retire to the desert of Arizona, Texas or California with the oppressive heat she couldn't bear. She needed the Pacific Northwest cool, moist air to be able to breathe properly. Amy dreaded every aspect of aging but she was determined to excel at it. She researched neighborhoods on paper and on foot to find the ideal place for their future as active, healthy, independent senior citizens. The right house and neighborhood were key to being successful. They must go there before retirement age to make friends and get involved in the community. They must be able to walk to a good bus stop, shopping and restaurants so they could give up having two cars. They were going to be environmentally correct seniors. Kevin was not quite as sold on this green aspect as she was.

The old house she fell in love with looked small on a narrow lot with two slivers of side yard and a modest front yard of grass to set the house back from the sidewalk. Inside it had been lovingly renovated by an artist with a modern floor plan and exquisite turn of the century details. It was the perfect size for them. The living room made a cozy reading room after dinner in front of the fire. Kevin read his newspaper in the morning there too, in every season. The dining room was big enough for their old table with all the leaves inserted. The kitchen featured a big stone counter for a crowd to gather around, but no room for a table. There was no under utilized space. They would sleep in the big bedroom on the second floor until they couldn't manage the stairs, then they would move into the guest bedroom off the dining room. Kevin agreed that she had picked a beauty. He would be happy to be free of a big yard, a long commute from the east side, and to die here according to her plan, he said, as long as he got to go first. "Honey, the statistics are with you on that wish."

Amy sewed new curtains for the downstairs rooms. The window treatments were always terribly important to her because they created part of the first impression from the street and once inside the front door. The colors and the fabric worked together to make a statement about the home, the use of the room, and the people who lived there. She opened the curtains every morning to let the sun and life in. She closed them at night to secure the family from the world.

Making curtains was her emotional bonding with a new home. It was a process she loved. Fabric shops were dream factories. She brought home lots of fabric samples to hang around the windows and furniture to test the colors in different lights. Making the decision was exciting mental and creative work. She felt sorry for houses that had pillowcases nailed to the window frames or broken, sagging blinds, which meant a lack of time, or money, or caring.

It didn't matter to her if a room didn't get finished, as a house was always a work in progress. This was her personal example of wabi-sabi. Nothing is perfect or complete.

The theory of the house proved itself quickly. They settled into the neighborhood easily, started making friends with the neighbors and enjoying everything about the new situation. Amy's lists for maximizing each room got shorter. She was working on the logistics for a wine tour of Chile when Kevin came home one day all fired up about Malaysia. One of Kevin's clients had succeeded where she never had in getting him jazzed up in an hour to jump on a plane before it all changed. The urgency to go now, not later, because it won't be there if you wait. They knew nothing about the country, but all the city names rang historical and exotic: Kuala Lumpur, Penang, Malacca. The countries of Singapore, Borneo, Indonesia, and Jakarta all seemed close by. What rolls off the tongue more easily than Kuala Lumpur? She didn't know anybody who had been there. Kuala Lumpur was going to be a competitive notch in her tourist belt. Why not go now? She started lists of key cultural sites and looking online for cooking schools all over the county. Finally, she found the school outside of Kuala Lumpur that sounded wonderful with so many classes she wanted to take she could have spent a week there.

Tonight at her party, if asked why she took the class, she decided to say, "The cooking class at the Oriental Hotel in Bangkok had always been on my list—but this class in Kuala Lumpur seemed to choose me."

BEEF RENDANG by Rohani Jelani

Preparations

3/4 cup grated coconut (desiccated or dried in the U.S.)

15 dried red chilies, Chinese or Indian

1/2 cup sliced shallots *

4 cloves garlic, sliced

1 inch slice of ginger, thinly sliced

1 inch slice of galangal, thinly sliced

1 inch slice of turmeric, thinly sliced

2 stalks lemongrass, thinly sliced

4–6 bird chilies, optional

1/2 cup water

Dry fry coconut in wok until golden brown. Cool slightly before grinding finely in mortar and pestle. Set aside for adding at the end of the recipe.

Snip chilies into 1 inch lengths. Soak in warm water till softened. Discard half the chili seeds and place in electric blender jug with the shallots, garlic, ginger, galangal, turmeric, and lemongrass.

If you want a hotter rendang, add the bird chilies. Add 1/2 cup water and grind chilies to a paste, but not too finely.

Cooking

1 pound lean stewing beef, sliced in 1/2 inch pieces

1-1/4 cups thick coconut milk (cream)

3/4 cup water

1 small turmeric leaf, tied into knot (or 1/2 leaf, finely shredded)

2 kaffir lime leaves, torn

1 1/2 teaspoons salt

1 teaspoon sugar

1–2 pieces asam keping (substitute lime or lemon)

Place spice paste, beef, coconut, and water in roomy pan. Bring to boil and simmer on medium heat, stirring now and then until mixture is well reduced and thick and oil surfaces, about 30 minutes.

Add ground toasted coconut (kerisik), turmeric leaf, kaffir lime leaf, seasonings, and asam keping. Cook another 5 minutes, taste and adjust seasonings if necessary, and take pan off the heat.

CHICKEN RENDANG

For chicken rendang, prepare the recipe as above, with the following adjustments:

Use 1 pound of chicken, skinned and cut into 2-3 inch pieces instead of the beef.

Omit the 3/4 cup water (under 'cooking').

Cook spice paste with coconut milk until mixture is thick before adding chicken (as it does not need the long, slow cooking that beef does). Complete the recipe as per beef rendang.

* Note about metric conversions: Asian shallots are tiny compared to typical shallots found in the U.S. The original recipe specified 100 grams of shallots or about 10 Asian shallots or about 3-1/2 ounces.

Chapter 15

Laurence parted company amiably with his old friend, refusing a ride home, because he said he had errands to do. He didn't want to say he was going to the Ballard library to relax before it closed at 6 PM because he really didn't have anything else to do and didn't want to go home early. He stuck to his schedule.

This branch was his Saturday afternoon place because it was not too crowded or noisy as it was in the morning with small kids. The afternoon crowd would be some old farts reading newspapers, students doing homework, and a few teenagers horsing around outside. He liked the demographics. It was only a short walk up to Market Street and then one block up 22nd Avenue to 57th Street. He felt good after the two draft beers, that unusual feeling of well-being. He seldom indulged and remembered why he used to enjoy it. Beer made you feel good but it wasn't in his budget. Today was a special occasion. He had been prepared to pay the bill since he had done the inviting, but Steve insisted on picking up the tab. That was nice. But he did feel a little odd. The meeting had gone better than he could have hoped for. It had felt like old times with an old friend. It was a relief to have it checked off his list.

He thought he had presented himself well, not accurately, but that was the reason for the meeting. Thinking over some of the points he had made about microwave technology and hacking seemed to have hit higher with Steve than he thought they might. Steve had been particularly impressed with the new geek friend and learning hacking. He felt a little guilty about misleading him, not a lie but an exaggeration. He did speak a bit and learn some tricks from an odd young man he saw frequently downtown sitting at the computer on

Mondays, one of those people he knew instinctively to approach only with math. Math people were good people in his book. They weren't engineers, but he respected their turf.

Easily giving up Ingrid's house was a big fat lie. It had killed him to sell it, but he needed the money for hospital bills. She was dead and didn't know about it. Her not knowing was the only easy part.

He felt relieved Steve hadn't questioned him or prolonged the conversation about his motives or the sketchy apology. It wasn't an apology. He hadn't said he was sorry, merely that he wished he hadn't crossed the line. That was a lie, too, but the essential one to accomplish his mission with Steve. That's all that mattered. The last chapter of his story, albeit embellished, would be told to the last people who had really known him, even if they didn't hear about his death. He could be dead for years before the old friends knew he was dead, but they would assume he was spending his days hacking corporate secrets or hearing stories at the library. That was his goal. He had a life of the mind, not a mindless life.

Wasn't it odd, though, Steve asking about a lawsuit? He thought he'd been amusing with his quick-witted response about legal eagles (he meant to be amusing), but really he hadn't thought of a lawsuit at all. It was too long ago. Even that first day several years ago now that he'd researched the news story about the electric reader at the library with the help of the Business, Science, and Technology reference desk, he didn't have a lawsuit on his mind. That had been his first interaction with them and now they were a regular stop on Mondays. It was what he had learned there that led him on to study hacking. He had never known there were so many hidden things that could be discovered by ordinary people.

Steve was going to tell anybody he could think of about this meeting with his old friend. Laurence knew him very well. Steve would not be able to contain himself. He was probably on his cell phone already while driving home.

Laurence hoped he hadn't overdone it, laid it on too thick. He hoped his brief history wouldn't sound like bullshit on the second and third telling in Steve's telephone tree. Laurence wished there had been an opportunity to tell him about the stairs. He'd wanted to work it in because walking ten flights of stairs every day for fitness was one of the things he was proudest of in his schedule. Very few men his age were doing it, judging by the guts around him. Steve for sure wasn't walking any farther than to the refrigerator or his SUV. He was fat. In retrospect, maybe talking about the stairs would have seemed mean to someone who was overweight. So it was better he hadn't mentioned it.

Laurence was pleased to be free of the obligation to apologize. That part had been easier than he thought it would be and very fast. He hadn't expected Steve to be so quick to move on past the strike. Laurence had a bit more groveling planned. Steve really was a good guy. It was regrettable not to have had that feeling of camaraderie in such a long time, and unlikely to have it again. Even if he didn't jump tonight, if they wanted to get together again, the logistics were difficult and he had no money for meeting in bars where they had spent so many after-work hours together. Their lives, such as they were, had a new schedule; it was too hard to make a new pattern.

The easy companionship with Steve reminded him of the odd feeling earlier today of being invited to dinner again by Amy. He was shocked by the initial invitation at the library weeks ago. It was a crazy idea that he would go to the house of someone he knew so casually, even though he enjoyed hearing about the vacation cooking class. He felt sure she was just making polite conversation at the unexpected meeting in the park this morning. She couldn't possibly mean it. He and she

160

were worlds apart in age and experience. He didn't go out to eat with anyone, anywhere.

Despite seeing her once a week at the library and occasionally on the bus for years now, he didn't know much about her personal life. She didn't bring it up in their conversations about cooking and science. Her big engagement ring meant she had a husband with a good job, but she never talked about him, except to say they traveled together on this trip and they had a good time. He did know where she lived because they had talked about Ken's Market and the neighborhood. She was always so smiley. It was pleasant to see that pretty face and smile, but it made him feel she'd had an easy life, like most of the people her age. They never had to do without or grow up fast. They had easy jobs and made a lot of money creating intangibles. She was probably rich, too. That would explain all that pleasantness and the wild idea of inviting him to her house to eat dinner with her friends. The rich could afford to be pleasant, as they didn't have too much to worry about.

Laurence had not sat down to eat at someone else's table since before the strike. What a strange feeling it would be, to be part of a group eating dinner together, talking about engineering or science. She said another engineer was coming, so it must be an intelligent crowd. Of course, she was intelligent, so that made sense they would not be stupid people. The man with her on the bench in the park today had looked reasonable and a little suspicious of him, which was a sign of intelligence. Laurence could tell he was surprised by this invitation. And the food was probably going to be very good. Food was of special interest to her and it used to be with him. He tried to picture himself sitting surrounded by strangers, talking and eating, drinking wine. Laurence shook his head in disbelief over this vision. No, that all seemed too foreign, too intrusive; he wasn't going to any dinner party.

161

The Queen Anne Branch and the downtown Central Library were also open until 6 PM on Saturday afternoon, but he preferred Ballard and the #18 bus home at 6:36 PM. Queen Anne was on his Thursday schedule. Downtown was on Monday. The Queen Anne branch was in the old brick and mortar style, cozy to some, not that aesthetic to him, and too close to his apartment for a good bus ride. That made Thursday a good day to go grocery shopping after the library at any of the Queen Anne markets and catch the #13 bus for a quick ride home that wouldn't defrost any frozen items he might purchase. He enjoyed the travel around the city and crossing the bridges to get to the other branches. There was no reason to change the schedule. He liked the Ballard building, the light, the spacious feeling, not as splendid as the Downtown library, which was a real engineering feat, but a better choice on Saturday. Ballard was his favorite branch. Not just because it was the old neighborhood, which didn't resemble itself that much anymore; it was the design of the library, the slope of the green grass roof, the curves, the art created by the wind speed being captured on the roof.

He enjoyed the short walk to and from the bus stop at NW Market Street and Ballard Avenue NW. The old storefronts all had new tenants that sold goods for yuppies. He had no interest in the merchandise. It all seemed frivolous. It was the crowds on the sidewalks he enjoyed, the healthy, young people out shopping and having fun with friends, going to the movie theater. They were pleasant to look at, a refreshing change from the downtown streets, the Central library regulars and the drunks in Belltown and at the Kid Valley bus stop. He liked over hearing bits of conversation, and slang even if he wasn't sure what it meant. Sex talk you could always understand. He was living vicariously through young strangers who had lovers, friends, and family, just by walking along Market Street and Ballard Avenue. Ingrid had been his lover and his family. She had been his life. Together they seemed invincible. They needed no one else. They wanted no one else.

What he had said to Steve about Ingrid was true. She was better now because she was dead. Five years later, everything about her last few years still seemed bruised and raw. He felt he had spent the last years of her life in shifting sand, never liquefied enough to suck you completely down over your head, where you breathed mud in until you choked and died, but shifting enough so you never really got your balance. It felt like running in the dunes, wobbling, and not making much progress forward. You could fall or twist an ankle at any time. You got tired and sweaty, with sand in your mouth and eyes.

The nightmare quality to those memories included the distorted sense of time slowing down in the Intensive Care Unit. Sitting, watching, waiting for the next attendant to perform some task made a day feel like a week, a week felt like a month. Whereas time at home after being released from the ICU was a high-pitched, squeaky fast-forward that was out of focus. He had to struggle to see what the activity really was in the grainy film of events. Was it day or night? Administering the pills, pans, shots, and drip lines was a full-time job you couldn't keep up with no matter how efficiently you tried to manage the process. When there were no more surgeries, no more protocols to try, the final wasting away with hospice help seemed ICU slow. When it was over, he was so very tired. He thought he might sleep for a long time. In retrospect, he felt he had slept on his feet the first few years after her death. Now five years later, he was still tired, but he was awake and counting the minutes of his days. Half of him had been sliced off. He was alive but bleeding to death from his wounds.

As he approached the library building on 22nd Avenue, he admired the roofline and the curves of the metal wall across from the new park. He loved the logic

163

of a live roof that insulated while it used water that would be wasted in the storm drains. This building featured good design in every way.

He was proud of the anemometers on the roof measuring wind speeds. Aerospace engineers appreciated anemometers. The data were used to create art displayed by LED, which was interesting in concept, but it annoyed him the artist was inspired by weather and fishermen. Art was subjective. Weather affected everyone. Sometime he would research the data on the total number of local employees in aerospace versus fishing to confirm which subset was bigger. He noted a few skateboarders going back and forth in front of Bartell's and in the Ballard Commons Park jumping off the concrete wall edge of the skate bowl and landing loudly. Skateboarding was so noisy.

The crowd inside looked pretty typical for Saturday afternoon. The two tables over by the quiet room each had two people at them. They all seated four, but the unofficial rule was to leave some empty seats if at all possible. He recognized some of the faces. The eight computer chairs in the center were all taken with collegiate types. He looked for his favorite chair at the tables under the big windows on 57th Street, officially the Ian McKenzie Black Reading Area. Old Ian or his relatives had given a nice sum of money to have those big letters on the wall. Laurence said a silent thank you to them every time he sat down. His chair was open. Someone he recognized from the back in a red plaid shirt who looked like Santa from the front, with long white hair, big beard, and classic belly, was sitting in the chair opposite his facing the window. Laurence made a quick vow to get a haircut soon. Steve's hippie joke had gotten to him.

A fat, homeless drunk, who was asleep, occupied the adjacent table under the window. Laurence's favorite chair across from Santa faced toward the front entrance and the door to the meeting room. He could see whoever came in the front through the gaps in the children's shelves before they approached the librarians' curved desk. He didn't mind sharing a table with Santa, but there was a group of young creeps sitting in the next row of tables. They looked greasy and sweaty. He hated listening to those idiots talk. All they knew was obnoxious, pseudo tough guy talk that depended largely on the verb and adjective "fuck."

He might have to break down and buy earplugs to get some privacy. This generation would ruin their hearing with the steady blasting of music and showed a lack of intellectual rigor to need a constant soundtrack to buoy the emotions. Most of the music he heard spilling out from those earphones he wished he couldn't hear. Nothing harmonious or symphonic escaped any of the orifices of these unwholesome youth. Whether high on pot, heroin, or pills, they sounded moronic and seemed interested in nothing but the state of their intoxication and music. Were they brain damaged at birth or had it happened to them gradually with drug abuse?

Laurence picked up Popular Science magazine off the reading rack on his way and settled into his chair with his back to the window to study one of his favorite topics. His companion, reading the Seattle Daily Journal of Commerce, looked up and nodded. They knew each other, just not by name. He began reading about spatial operating environments and the new language of hand gestures and the interfaces that recognize them being developed for Boeing and others. Incredible to believe that an inventor created a concept for a movie, Minority Report, that has become an important new scientific field of innovation.

He envied the engineers working on this phase of the project. It would be very exciting, even intoxicating, to be part of the team. Laurence was having a hard time staying focused with the idiots' chat nearby. The security

165

guard came around to wake the drunk. Although the guard spoke in low tones he couldn't understand, the drunk's responses made it clear he'd been asked to leave before and wasn't allowed back in yet. He argued and pleaded innocent, but he got up and let the guard guide him to the front door.

Santa muttered, "This place is getting to be just like downtown."

Laurence nodded in agreement. He hoped the guard would be back to ask the creeps to stifle themselves.

The teenagers were oblivious to the looks they were getting from those seated nearby.

"The Aurora Bridge, dude, that's the primo way to go. It's almost two hundred feet high and takes three seconds to splat down. You won't feel a thing."

"You're stupid. That couldn't be true. Three seconds?"

"Actually, you're stupid, Seth, you can hardly read. Did you ever throw a rock over the bridge, like trying to hit a boat or someone? It goes fast."

"I've thrown lots of rocks at cars and boats. I once hit a guy driving a boat! I couldn't believe it and neither could he. He fell down and almost crashed his boat into someone coming the other way. The other guy could see me and gave me the finger. I laughed until I almost peed my pants."

"You'll fall faster than a rock because you weigh more. I read it in the paper."

"So you're a cool newspaper reader, huh?"

"Sure, making like a fuckin' patron while waiting to fuckin' score. It's also useful sometimes to know important stuff. If you read the paper, you'd know they plan to spend millions soon to make it impossible to get over the side of the bridge. You should learn to read. Oh well, I guess you don't have time."

That got Laurence's attention.

166

"Well, fuck you. I remember hearing about Bret jump because of Shelton."

"They're still talking about him, not because of what he did to go to Shelton, or because of Shelton, but because they want to fix the bridge so no one else can jump. Now it's easy to hop over the railing from the footpath—before we get caught. It won't be cool if you or me or we get picked up today or tomorrow. Then we are going to Shelton."

"I'm cool, too, and I am not going to get caught because I'm going straight to being famous. Definitely not going to Shelton. I think we should do a few more people before we jump, though. One isn't enough. Let's make it a big spree. Then we could be famous for that, too. How many more people do you think we'd need to do?"

"The problem is I don't think we have much time and it's Saturday. School's closed. That would be the best place to rack up the numbers. Do you want to know them when you pull the trigger?"

"Yeah, that's better for sure, although I did picture myself blasting away at Zesto's. That would make a movie wouldn't it? Who'll play me?"

"Dude, you're beyond bad, you're evil. Let's stop by later and see who's there."

"Definitely. Maybe I don't need to know them, just give them a few seconds to know what's going to happen to them. They can wonder who I am. Then we'll go to the Troll. That's the cool spot before the three-second hop. Sounds like a rap. Maybe we should write that on the Troll."

"Sure. Why not?"

"Three seconds. Tell me again how high it is."

"The same height as a fifteen-story building."

"Fuck, man, that's high. I wonder if it feels like fuckin' flying?"

167

"I bet it feels like that, just like fuckin' Superman for three seconds."

"How bad could that be?"

"Fuck, yeah. It's definitely the way to go."

Laurence tried to concentrate on the microwave weaponry destined for the Boeing stealth planes, but they were talking too loud. He felt like saying, *Do yourselves a favor, idiots, and be sure to walk at least halfway across the bridge before you jump so you'll hit water, not concrete.* Where was the security guard? He must have gone outside with the drunk.

It was so painful being forced to listen to blathering crackheads. They must be crackheads. A rancid smell was coming his way, too, from body odor and smoke. There was no point in asking them to lower their voices. Asking would just encourage them to be even louder and possibly provoke them into a situation he didn't want to deal with. He wondered what terrible things they'd done to be planning to commit suicide. He knew that in the local suicide demographics, young people were a small percentage. Nine youths, nineteen years or younger, had committed suicide each year recently. It was hard to imagine how life could have gone so wrong in such a short period of time. Nothing horrible had happened to them yet. They weren't old enough to know how hard life could be.

He could tell them a few things about disappointments, disasters, and failures. His own age group, sixty and above, which he was most interested in of course, consistently comprised about 20 percent of suicides or fifty-one seniors in 2009. Seniors were definitely experts on adversity. Only five of the fifty-one chose drugs or poison. Three chose to jump and four to hang. It surprised him more people didn't choose jumping and hanging because they were inexpensive, available all day, every day, and a good choice for the no-gun crowd. Those NRA guys could do themselves in anytime they wanted to and apparently did, given that guns were the choice of one hundred people of all ages. The liberal anti-gun group needed to study jumping, poisonous exhaust fumes, and strangulation. The car-less crowd could chose jumping. He had been surprised only fourteen adults used the carbon monoxide from cars to commit suicide when it seemed so many people had cars. Most kids chose hanging. These kids probably had guns, so why jump?

Laurence was starting to get nervous listening to this exchange. These kids were probably killers, not tortured youth. It was incredible to think that there were teenage killers in Seattle. What was the world coming to? Like the moron who killed the convenience store clerk a few days ago, just a few blocks from here. What had happened to that murderer? He couldn't remember what had happened. Was there an arrest? The public outcry was because the young clerk, an immigrant of course, had been such a hard-working, straight arrow. Laurence stood up and walked over to put his magazine back in the rack. He looked around to see if the thugs were watching him. They weren't looking at him. Good. A young woman pushed back the chair from a nearby computer. He quickly walked by the tables next to the quiet room and slid into her warm seat and caught her log in still running. So many people neglected to log off. He went straight to the Seattle Times and looked for recent articles about robbery and murder.

The first search result was the story he remembered reading. It was memorable because of the large, grainy black and white photo from the surveillance camera with what appeared to be a thin-faced man in a dark knit cap pulled down low to his neck, sunglasses and a bandana covering his mouth. The sweater and pants were dark, too, with no designer logos visible. Laurence stared into the faint eyes behind the glasses, trying to get some feeling out of them. Was this really the gaze of

169

someone with a gun in his hand pointed at another human being while asking for money? It was hard to tell. That's quite an outfit for a balmy August night. You'd think the clerk would have pushed the panic button the minute he saw the costume.

Of course, he couldn't tell if the loudmouth stupid kid sitting at the next table was the bandit/murderer or not. If it was, their conversation made sense now. If it was, that kid was in a whole lot of trouble. He probably was going to Shelton unless he jumped off the bridge. The stuff that happened in the library! He tried a number of searches but couldn't get a follow-up story. He went back to the security camera photo. That bad smell came his way again and he felt something too close to him. He hit the screen-saver key and turned around. His whole body flinched. The wannabe jumper was standing behind him.

"Jeez, kid, didn't anyone ever tell you not to sneak up on someone? If you want to use a computer, there's one over there."

"I don't want to use a fucking computer. I wanted to see what you were doing, old man."

"Catching up on my reading."

"What are you reading?"

"Custom spatial operating environments where gesture recognition interfaces are being developed for Boeing. I was an aerospace engineer for forty years. You know what an SOE is? Interested in engineering?"

"Nah, I'm not fucking interested in engineering." He ambled back toward his seat.

Laurence tried to manage the relief his whole body felt and not let it all out in one big breath. A few of the other seven computer users stared at him with annoyance. He mouthed the word sorry. Nothing worked like a focused scientific monologue to drive a kid with no attention span away. He'd used it at bus stops before as an effective weapon on bullies who thought he looked

170

like easy prey. Senior citizen survival skills for bus stops could be the title of an article he could write from recent experience. Who ever imagined life would come to moments like these? Now he was stuck. He didn't know what the punk had seen on the screen. His instincts were still pretty sharp, but a seventy-five-year-old versus a teenager was not a fair race, even if the youth had handicapped himself with drugs. The screen-saver hot key was fast. The computers were new when the libraries reopened. He'd learned the key sequence watching the kiddie porn fans play cat and mouse with the security guards at the library.

The security team at the downtown branch had surveillance cameras. They observed inside and outside the building as well as the computer users. Each user got ninety minutes a day that was regulated by an internal system. There were always people waiting for a computer. Security was watching for bad behavior and sleepers. If they caught you asleep, you had to go outside. Someone else got lucky and got your chair in front of the computer. Security was also watching for illegal porn involving kids and animals. Consenting adults were not illegal. If they caught anyone with illegal activities on the screen, they called the police, who made the arrest in the building and proceeded straight to jail. It's freedom to not filter out porn, but it's a violation of the rules of conduct of the library to view illegal pornography on library computers. The computer screens were close together, sometimes with a short privacy wall that was more about keeping your hands and accessories in your space. It was impossible not to see what your neighbors on both sides were viewing unless it was small text. Everyone kept their eyes focused on their screen and all senses on alert for someone coming up behind them. The regular users at the library had good instincts about someone too close or someone approaching. Laurence had had the wits scared out of him by a security guard who had successfully reached his back without him hearing anything while trying to catch someone beside him watching a kiddie porn video.

Should he call the police? Was he jumping to conclusions? Would he have to be a witness? Punks like this wouldn't hesitate to beat an old man like him about the face—or worse. He wanted to get out of the library and go somewhere safe, like the #18 bus home. He didn't want to be anywhere around these two kids who seemed so guilty of something, but what? He was afraid that approaching the security desk in the library now or trying to find a security guard patrolling the premises to explain his concerns might get their attention. They were watching him and talking about him, he could see that from across the room, maybe narcotic paranoia settling in, as their deliveryman had not shown. Laurence was catching their paranoia like a contact high. How was he going to make a smooth exit without them noticing?

He decided he couldn't do anything but be alert for an opportunity to exit when they were distracted. He felt trapped in the library, which was crazy. He should go talk to security here or he should go to the police. What in the world would he say? He suspected that the kids were the murderers of the convenience store clerk because of what? His experience with them wasn't evidence of anything. Also, the two kids seemed like a pair. The newspaper hadn't said anything about a second person, an accomplice. But it made sense that the two of them committed the crime together to bolster the courage to go through with it. This scenario didn't sound like much when repeated to a stranger. The security guard probably wanted to go home, not get involved with the local police when it was almost closing time. Laurence felt he was putting himself at risk to talk to the security guard. Why did he want to do that? Who cared if these kids jumped tonight or not? Society would be better off if they were dead. They likely already deserved long sentences

172

for murder and armed robbery. Maybe his best effort was to make sure they did jump. How could he influence that very personal action? He could say nothing and let them go ahead with whatever mayhem pleased them.

He looked subtly in the direction of the kids as though stretching his neck and shoulders. They had their eyes toward the door at a young man entering who looked like a kindred spirit of theirs. With them distracted, he got up and walked around to the study rooms and back again, considering what to do. He saw the security guard standing next to the men's restroom door, in the entryway before the front door, so he had his alibi. He couldn't believe how paranoid he was. He walked out the front door and paused in the open restroom doorway.

"You see those punks sitting over there in the reading area? They are up to no good. Crime and drugs, I think. You should keep an eye on them. They are talking crazy about a crime spree in the Zesto's parking lot. Maybe you could call the cops?"

The security guard said, "There is nothing I can do unless they break the law inside this building. If I catch them doing something illegal, then I can call the police to arrest them." He looked at his watch. "All I can do is keep an eye on them so they know they're not alone." He walked toward the shelves with CDs and DVDs for a better view of the young men.

Laurence went out of the library into the blue-sky summer afternoon and breathed deeply to regain his composure. He resented being frightened by this episode. He resented his afternoon being disrupted. He had a lot to think about and he had needed some hours of quiet to reflect on the information that had been exchanged at the bar in Ballard and that the news of his life to date was already ricocheting around King County. It wouldn't matter what time he jumped, as no one would hear about it anyway.

Chapter 16

Ben looked at the clock again. Time was creeping here. He had made no progress on the problem he was working on since he'd told Alexis that he was leaving soon.

He decided to hang it up for the day. He was getting out of here. Not one minute more could he sit at this desk in this room in this building. With any luck no one would be in the hallway and speak to him; if they did, he would ignore them, pretending he didn't hear. Feigning deafness and self-absorption were highly effective means of dealing with hallways and other conversations.

He was not thinking about this problem, office, or company for another second. He was moving on to music, martinis, and food. He planned to create a very loud wall of sound between him and this place to lock the door of his mind.

The hallway was empty. The stairwell was empty. This was good, a clean departure. He hated it when he ran into someone in the hallway with an inevitable, "Can I talk to you for just a minute about something?" There was no such thing as a one-minute conversation.

Outside the front door, the fresh air felt like a wall he burst through. It felt cold in his nose as he sucked it in. It was so good to be out of that toxic building. Walking to the parking lot under blue skies felt like freedom. Getting into the battered 1983 Volvo station wagon with 215,204 miles made his escape successful. The back seat was folded down and a hi-tech mountaineering megalite 30-degree sleeping bag, two old down pillows and a few empty beer cans welcomed him with a familiar stale aroma. In the middle of the night it seemed like heaven but right now, he was happy he was headed home to his own bed with cleaner sheets and a hot shower. He looked up at the bridge. No bodies falling from the sky today. The engine turned over on the first attempt. Good job! He riffled through the glove box for Iggy Pop's *Detroit Studio Outtakes* tape, found it, and cranked the volume up as loud as it would go. He coaxed the transmission into reverse, which was always suspenseful, but the car backed up on command. Thank you! Very gently with respect to the ancient transmission, he engaged first gear, yes, second gear, yes! He was out!

Safe inside his music machine, Ben drove deliberately, the speed limit or a little less on North 34th Street turning into North Pacific Street paralleling Lake Union, his favorite part of the drive home. Did he need to stop at Pete's to buy some wine for the party? What did he have at home he could take? Surely there was something left from the last trip to Walla Walla or something from California. He didn't want to take time for wine shopping. There probably was no time for a nap now. He needed at least a few minutes to relax, before going to Amy and Kevin's. Alexis would drive them to the party in her car. His last job of the day was to get safely home and then his brain could be off-duty. Ben could practically taste the vodka. He envisioned Alan shaking the shaker. Shaking the shaker. That should be a song title about an adroit barman.

Alan was a quick wit. It would be good to see him, always some laughs there. Ben anticipated, too, the way Alan smiled at Alexis like an old blue-eyed crooner working the crowd. Alexis would smile back at him or laugh like he had told the most hilarious story in the world. Imagine a woman as smart as Alexis being susceptible to old-fashioned manipulations. Alan, he felt

175

almost sure, was harmless, just amusing himself, but it was annoying how much Alexis enjoyed his attention. Never mind the flirting, Ben told himself, he was glad Alexis was getting out of the house tonight. It should improve her disposition.

Kevin was pretty funny, too, in a different way. His sense of humor was dry to the point it was hard to know sometimes with him when he was joking. Ben liked to say, "Hey, look me in the eye when you say that so I know you're lying—or not." What a poker face Kevin had. Too bad he was down on gambling because he would be good at it—or gun smuggling. Ben thought Kevin would look at home in the dark alleys in Belfast, quietly waiting for his prey or purchase. Ben was always aware of how alert Kevin was, keeping track of the whole room, ready for whatever might happen. The air of vigilance gave him an extra edge that was interesting. The music, too, would be interesting. Kevin always set up a little musical jeopardy game with a selection of obscure songs for Ben to guess who the band was, which he seldom ever missed, but Kevin kept trying. Ben looked forward to the repartee about music. The mystery of Kevin was the pretty wife. He didn't get them as a couple. She didn't seem his type. What was she interested in besides food and cooking? He couldn't think of anything he had ever talked to her about except that, which seemed so limiting to him. Why hadn't Kevin aligned himself with someone more versatile and cynical? What in the world did they talk about? Amy was always so upbeat and quick to smile. A steady diet of that would get on his nerves. But he was looing forward to seeing her tonight and eating, eating, eating. He was so hungry. All the food he had eaten in the last few days hadn't seem to make a dent in his hunger. Maybe Kevin wasn't as subversive as he appeared to be. All the tax crap was pure establishment. Who ever heard of a lefty tax guy?

176

The food tonight would be good, whatever it was. The menu was a theme from their vacation, but where had they gone? He couldn't remember the country, if he had ever heard her say it. She probably had told him and he wasn't paying attention, but pandanus was tropical. Amy would knock herself out on the food. Ben always liked what she cooked. He envisioned spicy and salty with lime as equatorial cuisine. Would it be fish or fowl? She often gave him Dungeness crab as a first bite. He loved it, but wouldn't bacalao taste good right now? He craved the salt and the unctuousness of the cod completely saturated with olive oil over the sweetness of the crab. She had given him that once. Cod wouldn't be on the menu, wrong ocean temperature, but some salted fish would be, and garlic couldn't be far behind with chilies and green herbs. How could that be bad? There would be plenty of alcohol, drinks before dinner and wine with dinner; maybe he and Kevin would drink some grappa afterwards to end on a high note. What a great way to end a crappy week. He would look for a good bottle of wine for his drinking buddy, Kevin and for Amy for this feast she was preparing for him, having no idea how much he deserved it.

He wished Alexis would knock herself out a little bit more, drink more Red Bull, and throw herself into something other than her very moody, on the verge of nihilistic art. She didn't want to go out with friends anymore. She routinely said no to any invitation to the movies, restaurant, or a bar. Bigger parties seemed to be all she was willing to do. She seemed to be less and less interested in everything: no opinion about anything. Withdrawn most of the time, or ready to take his head off without warning, he was never really sure which Alexis would be waiting for him at home. He didn't want to think about that, either. He was done for the day with deep thinking. *Alexis has got to get a grip by herself. Nothing I can do about it. It's her problem.* Whatever it was she needed,

177

she had to figure it out herself. He was done trying to fathom her melancholy or her malicious moods.

The traffic slowed to a creep in the transition from the University Bridge to Eastlake Avenue NE. The Stooges' outrage was invigorating. The futility of the engineering problem was slowly falling away from him. Tomorrow he would look again and try to find a solution. Right now he was entering into the fun zone, the let's think about me and nobody else zone.

Ben contemplated spending a few minutes admiring his last welding project to see how solid the joints were. He would take a long, hot shower. If there was enough time after his shower, he would burn a music compilation he had made recently that would be fun to take Kevin. Ben was sure Kevin wouldn't know those particular songs. Kevin would be impressed. Ha! What a pleasure it would be to see him stumped!

As he turned right onto East Louisa Street, just a few blocks from home, Ben resolved to be very patient with Alexis, whatever her mood. If necessary, he would try to cheer her up. He loved her and he wanted her to be pleased about as many things as possible, particularly his arrival home and being in the same room with him. That would be good. Maybe she would be in an agreeable frame of mind because she was looking forward to going out to dinner. He would try to help her enjoy herself and the evening. He would make a special effort to listen to what she was saying and respond so that she knew he had heard what she said. That was so hard sometimes. Often the topics didn't hold his attention and he was on to another thought while she was still talking. When she looked at him expecting him to speak back, he couldn't remember what she was talking about. He understood it made her mad, but she didn't understand how difficult it was to follow long passages of no interest to him, especially anything to do with plumbing or painting.

Alexis' piercing point of view and her ability to communicate made her a formidable adversary in the best of times. They both enjoyed a high-spirited discussion that was challenging intellectually. Lately, however, he was taking it personally when she vented and seemed out to maim him rather than advancing the debate.

The atmosphere in the house seemed volatile, causing sparks to fly too easily and then explode. It was hard to have a normal conversation about anything without it quickly deteriorating into short-tempered outbursts. If he wasn't so busy at the office, under pressure of more layoffs, suicide jumpers, and managing substandard production work, he might be able to do more to distract her from her worries. Worrying about him losing his job had been a constant for both of them for a few years. Job security was a thing of the past. You couldn't get away from that reality. The days of loving his job and taking pride in his engineering seemed a long time ago to him. It bothered her. It bothered him, too. He hated his job. Every day he hated it. That was his point. The conditions were now a given. Live with it. Everyone else was. His situation was not unique or special in this level of pressure. That was the part Alexis couldn't wrap her brain around. She wanted the pressure to go away.

They needed a break from where things had been for the last few months. It was nice to be invited tonight. It would be great not to be at home watching television or holed up in his office avoiding her. Maybe this evening would turn things around some between them.

He pulled up in the driveway and sat quietly for a few moments after parking, trying to swallow away apprehension about the first physical interaction of the day with Alexis. What kind of mood would she be in?

Chapter 17

Amy could see Thor was thrilled to be leashed up for the fresh-air tour before his dinner. His tale was wagging and he bounced down the porch steps more quickly than she could keep up. His happy energy was transferring to her, and she, too, was happy to be out in the fresh air and exploring any change from the previous walk.

Riley was working in his front garden across the street. Amy waved at him because he was looking at her. It seemed to her that he kept his eye on her front door and was ready to pounce whenever she came out. He was old, maybe ninety years old and lived alone, so she tried to be friendly, even when he was needy and annoying. She knew he had worn out his welcome with everyone else on the block. She and Thor walked across the street toward him.

"Hello, Riley. How are you?"

"Oh, I'm good. How are you?"

"Very well, thanks. Off for a fresh-air tour before dinner."

"Hello, little dog. Have you bitten anyone today?"

"No, not today, not for a long time."

Thor showed a little polite interest by smelling Riley's shoes and pants. Amy could see how half-hearted he was.

"See, he likes me." Riley bent down to pet the top of Thor's head. Thor moved out of his reach. "I guess he doesn't like me anymore. How's your garden?"

"Riley, it's very exciting. The cucumber plants seem to produce a new one every day, which I'm eating at lunchtime. The tomatoes are sweet but tiny. There are lots of them. I love being a container farmer. We've got to mush on. See you."

Amy and Thor headed toward the graveyard where old trees canopied over the street. She thought walking a few extra blocks would help Thor relax with the company tonight. She was trying to review in her mind the last steps before the company arrived. She wanted to turn on all the lights everywhere in the house. She would quote Alexandra Stoddard if Kevin said anything: "Don't worry about the electric bill—it's only pennies to run a light bulb. Turn on every light to make your house look its best."Amy knew from experience if she waited until the last moment, she wouldn't get around to turning them on and wouldn't notice until people left that all the lights weren't on in the living room or the bathrooms or the stairwell. The wall sconces in the bedrooms were critical as they gave a nice, soft light visible from the street through the shutters. She wanted all the lights on before Kevin had a chance to say it was too early to turn them on. He sometimes turned them off before people arrived, which was very irritating. She would like to know how much that extra hour or so might cost to make her case but had never gotten around to researching it.

What serving platter for the Dungeness crab? She tried to list possible choices on her spreadsheet for each dish, but sometimes she didn't get around to it, like today. She knew there was nothing on the list because she hadn't been able to think of it last week, either. As often as she served this and with a house full of china and sterling, it was crazy not to have the right size serving pieces that were a good color to set off the white crab and lettuce cups, crackers, or chips. She had a fabulous silver small round tray and bowl with a red glass liner that looked terrific at Christmas, but seemed over the top in August.

The white cabbage pattern she usually ended up using seemed too casual, too white and it was too big for the counter space. She would buy the next serving piece she saw that was right for crab, no matter what the cost. A small hand painted Italian ceramic bowl and plate might be perfect.

She liked to toss the crab with a little mayonnaise or crème fraîche, just enough for a soft mouth feel and to highlight the sweetness of the crab meat; then give it a squeeze of Meyer lemon juice, fleur de sel to taste, and India red or cayenne. Either chili added a red visual. The India red made anything taste brighter; it awakened natural flavors like a pinch of salt. The cayenne was hotter, a high-heat note with a bigger contrast. Because of the Malaysian theme tonight, she would press fresh ginger in the garlic press for a teaspoon of juice to sprinkle over the crab at the last minute to create an initial fragrance and flavor to set the tone.

The rojak salad needed to come up from the refrigerator downstairs. Should she put it on the table before the company arrived or wait until later? That could be a task for anyone who asked if they could help. It didn't need to be ice cold; it would have better flavors at room temperature.

Amy really didn't want anyone to help. She didn't need any help. It was hard to think of things for people to do. It was distracting when people wanted to get involved in the last-minute cooking or serving. She would lose her rhythm and flow. She wanted it all done if possible before anyone arrived so she wouldn't be at the stove with an audience. This was her studio, not her stage. She didn't like being watched while she cooked. The easy way to make that happen was to cook everything ahead, maybe days ahead, put it in the oven just before the company arrived, and set the oven to turn itself on at the right time and temperature so all would be hot when she planned to serve. Having a great stove with convenience features made such a big difference.

Her gas range was a source of pleasure every time she used it. She used the 17,000 BTU power burner almost exclusively. The two regular burners were seldom ever used. Once a week she made soup on the simmer burner, which was so dependable to keep the soup at a bare simmer, she'd retired the cast-iron flame tamer she'd purchased thirty years ago after reading Laurie Colwin's first book where she mentioned the flame tamer she totally trusted to mind the stove while she went out shopping in New York City! Amy had to have one immediately and try it out. She never left the house while using it but she felt fine about leaving the room and returning when a timer reminded her to stir the soup. Amy would never give up that cooking trophy with the sentimental value of the hundreds of pots of soup she had made trying to learn to make good soup. She did make good soup now. The secret was as simple as good stock. But for a long time she had hoped there was a way around making the stock. There wasn't.

She should hang the flame tamer decoratively as cook's art above her precious stove. It could be a decorative focal point for a small collection of cooking-related art, a shrine to the stove she loved. Beyond the mighty and the minimalist burner, she was inspired by the griddle in the center of the range top to make latkes or grilled cheese sandwiches, so perfect for breakfast when she was starving or for dinner with homemade tomato soup. The oval burner underneath the griddle was perfect for sautéing in the big braising pan or for steaming mussels in the Dutch oven. The warming drawer initially seemed such a luxury, but now she couldn't do without it for having truffled popcorn or other hot hors d'oeuvres at the ready or overflow warm storage for bread or vegetables. The oven was deep enough for a half-sheet pan and a casserole to be side by side. Some of the status ranges she had looked at weren't deep enough for that.

What else? She needed to cut some twists for the bar—or delegate to Alan. Kevin could do the rest of the setup to get him involved and have a task. Well, it was looking like an all-white cocktail hour counter. The white platter and bowl for the crab and lettuce cups, white bowl for the rice snacks, and a white dish for the olives and twists. Enjoy the symmetry of the using one color and ignore the fact of two very different styles of ceramics, modern and country. Done. There was nothing like fresh air and exercise to clear the brain. She'd shrugged off her gloom by focusing on her tasks. She felt steady.

Thor dashed up the front steps when she dropped the leash in the front yard. She was trying to get her keys out of her pocket when Kevin opened the front door and said, "Welcome back. I am ready to help you. What should I do first?"

She smiled at him, very pleased he was making himself available. "Thanks for asking. We're in really good shape here, you'll be glad to know. Please give Thor his dinner and set up the bar. Put out that small divided white dish with olives on one side and a whole lemon in the other for making twists. I need to figure out something festive to wear."

Chapter 18

Alan stepped out onto Fremont Avenue from Costas Opa and looked at the blue sky and the crowds on the sidewalk. The sun was still shining. Good. Saturday shoppers' rush hour was bad. Not leaving about two hours ago was very bad. Woody had gone off to his wife and family responsibilities. Alan was a stone's throw away from the dinner party that started in a couple of hours. He was known to show up early because of bus schedules, but this was too early. Even dear old Amy wouldn't be amused if he showed up in time for a nap before dinner. He'd really boxed himself in.

He pondered what to do between now and then? Take a taxi home to take a nap seemed like setting himself up to sleep through the party.

Should he walk to Queen Anne to sober up and enjoy the beautiful day? No, it was too steep. How about a stroll around the block for fresh air and try to find a friendly coffee shop? He decided to sip on a triple espresso and see what happened. A triple might cut through the fog and digest the after-lunch digestives. The grappa had tasted delicious after the ouzo and the fish. What he really needed was sleep to digest his lunch. Where could he have a rest?

He walked up 35th Street and turned right toward the bridge. Well, well, there was the red tile roof of the Fremont Library. What a perfect spot to stop and read a little bit. Alan entered the double doors and studied the two rows of comfy Stickley-style chairs in the center of room with wooden racks of periodicals behind them. The room was charming, and only two chairs were occupied, so he had six to choose from. He settled into the last chair on the left and opened his *Traveler* magazine he had been reading. What a lovely library and how amazing it wasn't very busy. He started reading where he had left off in the cruise reviews.

Someone spoke loudly and he looked up startled. His head almost hit the mouth of a security guard bent over to speak directly into in his ear.

"Sir, you'll have to leave now. No sleeping at the library."

"I didn't know I was asleep. I was just reading."

"It's a policy, you have to leave now."

"Gee, I'm sorry. I didn't know."

"Now you know."

"I really have to leave now? I'm awake now."

"Yes, sir, you have to leave now."

Alan put his magazine back in his pack and headed for the door without looking left or right to see who might have witnessed this humiliation. How embarrassing. How mortifying to be caught sleeping and thrown out of the library like a bum. At the sidewalk, he decided to keep walking around the block as planned. When he passed by Costas Opa's window, he thought fondly of his lunch, but he couldn't go back in there.

Scanning both sides of the avenue again for options, he decided Peet's Coffee & Tea directly across the street would be perfect for serious caffeine and a rest. There was no one waiting in line at the coffee shop. The barista just looked at him, waiting to hear his order. Alan responded with the most minimal order possible: triple espresso. The tattoos and piercings were already turning to the task when he finished ordering. He wondered if these kids realized they look so much alike with all the body art that it was hard to tell them apart or were they under the illusion that they each looked unique? The tattooed necks and heads were the most repulsive to him.

Getting tattooed was one of the few errors of youth he hadn't made. He eschewed the layered flannel shirts over T-shirts grunge look and stuck with classic dark slacks and ironed dress shirts on weekdays and ironed khakis on weekends. He wore a dark suit but no tie for dining or charity benefits. That was still a uniform but acceptable anywhere he went. His peer group that emulated scruffy youth with shaggy hair and ripped clothes were kidding themselves and looked like fools to the real youth.

Coffee cup in hand, his quarters clanging in the tip jar, he headed for the church pew seat facing the window overlooking the Fremont Bridge. At last, a nice quiet place to relax before taking a taxi to the party.

The action on the street and the caffeine were bound to start working on his brain, getting it ready for the next event where he would need it. The lunch had been surprisingly good, better than Alan had expected. Woody had enjoyed the prawns, too, and seemed pleased with everything he ordered. He got over not trying the sandwich place. Alan had adored all the Woody chat. Woody was his best conversationalist. He loved Woody. They spoke the same language. Woody's vocabulary and diction were flawless. He was funny. They egged each other on at every level and topic. It was sad they couldn't get together more often. Woody, with a wife, kids, and a girlfriend, had not a minute to himself. Everything was for others. His life was much tougher than Alan's, with no wife to try to manage him. Alan patted himself on the back for having a very good life.

Alan had been wifeless many more years now than he had been married and was likely to remain so. It hadn't taken him too long being alone to accept that it was not bad being single. In fact, he preferred it to his experience with marriage. He did what he wanted to do, ate what he wanted, when he wanted to eat it. All the negotiating and compromise that made you weary was eliminated.

Freedom had been odd at first, but then it became natural and easy. His social life was as busy as he wanted it to be. He got a lot of dinner invitations to balance a dinner table or be an extra man for a party when there were several single women invited. He was happy to be a good guest and enjoyed making the cocktails if the host wanted him to do that. He knew as many cocktail recipes as most bartenders. Some weeks he dined out with friends two or three times. He cooked elaborate meals for himself and regular dinner guests.

Living in Belltown made it very convenient to have happy hour at home with his women friends who wanted to be discreet. There were a few, but two he was particularly fond of came by after work every week or so to have a cocktail and sometimes more and still went home at a decent time. This was the most perfect arrangement for him and them. They were his age and good conversationalists. They appreciated the perfection in his cocktails and his cooking skills. He'd known them for a long time. He'd learned that his male peers, who were all husbands, didn't understand the complexities of middle-aged women like he did. He listened and sympathized. In return, he felt cared for and appreciated. There was enough love and affection in those hours that he never felt lonely. They felt very special to be his private muse. They didn't know about each other. Discretion was the key that made all this work smoothly.

Everyone teased him about his young girlfriends, but they were a very amusing and aesthetic window dressing on his social life and an important philosophical statement. Instead of driving a Porsche to flaunt his financial success like so many of his colleagues, he escorted the babes to receive envious looks from other men his age. The dependable reactions made him feel generous toward the girls. Whatever he spent on them, it would never surpass the maintenance on a Boxter model that he heard so much about at the office. He hated cars and thought they were ruining the planet and city life. He gave the girls memberships to different museums, so there would always be parties and fund-raisers to take them to where they could wear the new dresses he bought them. They all knew about each other, were friendly with each other. Sometimes he took two out at a time so everyone could go to the party and he would have one on each arm. It was so much fun to watch the eyes in the room turn his way. He didn't sleep with them. They thought he was too old to get in bed with—and he was.

When it came to conversation combined with sexual satisfaction, his two long-term girlfriends were all he could wish for. They knew each other's bodies so well. Pleasure was easy to achieve and very comfortable. Neither of them wanted to get married, which was fine with him. One of them already was married with no plans for divorce. She got along with the husband well enough and looked forward to retiring in style. Every other Tuesday was perfect for her and for Alan. The other woman was now a widow with an inheritance she had no intention of sharing with anyone except her grown children and grandchildren. Once a week she came in town from the Eastside, usually on Thursday or Saturday, depending on her invitations or his. They dined at his place or out. Sometimes she spent the night, sometimes she didn't. He loved her and her independence. It kept him on his toes. With all her money, she could have anyone she wanted, but she wanted him.

Friday night alone with no dinner plans was a pleasure to contemplate. He chose his book, his music, his menu, and his movie. He took special pride in the making of his cocktails. Grilled lamb chops or King salmon were frequent stars of the Friday night menu. Because of the ease of the preparation and cooking, he could throw himself into making a complicated vegetable side dish. He liked to use his mandolin to make almost translucent strips of vegetables for a raw salad or au

189

gratin. Beets and fennel were so appealing visually to him and combined easily with so many other vegetables it was fun to try a new mix with oranges, avocado, celeriac, shallots, or carrots. All were delicious with the barest splash of good olive oil and a crunchy finishing salt. With the Pike Market as his grocery store, he could have anything he wanted, whenever he wanted it. The locavore trend did not hold him hostage.

In the coffee shop looking out over the Fremont Bridge, he felt relaxed. The bruising week of the layoffs that had long been anticipated was now over. His product had been scuttled. There would be another product in his future, but for now he was officially unemployed and determined to enjoy every minute of it. He'd given it a good effort at lunch, maybe a little too much, but it had been fun.

Alan felt that this day should be over, but unfortunately it was not. He couldn't miss the big deal at Amy's tonight. He didn't want to disappoint her. Was the espresso hitting the system yet? He wasn't sure. The heat and aroma of the coffee was pleasurable. He inhaled with his nose deep in the cup searching for the individual notes of flavor. Was this African? What did they serve here? He couldn't remember where he was. This wasn't Starbucks or Tully's. He looked around the room, trying to get his bearings from the exposed bare wood and vaulted ceiling. Damn. All these new coffee shops looked the same to him. Maybe he hadn't been here before. Alan put the empty cup on the table and closed his eyes to relax.

Chapter 19

Amy stood in front of the open double doors of her closet and stared at the rack of clothes organized by color on hangers. She only had a few solid colors in her closet, so any blouse went with white jeans or blue jeans or black or grey trousers. She never bought anything that could be identified as this year's trendy color or cut so she could wear everything for years. Remembering when she had made some of these purchases Amy felt sure that she looked *last decade* to the clerks at Nordstrom. Those black wool pants might be thirty years old and she could still get in them, a good reason to keep them.

Trying to make a decision about an outfit for tonight, suddenly all she could think about was how many people she had pretended not to see. One instance she frequently remembered came to mind immediately. Years ago she had ignored a man on a crowded bus because she really didn't want to talk to him. It's so awkward to chat with everyone listening to you. The chat needs to be carefully edited or else barely audible. In this case, she didn't really like him. She'd been nice to him on other occasions, but she really didn't care and wished he'd get off soon. In the seat behind the back exit door, she kept her head down, looking at her book. She hoped he hadn't seen her, but he probably had. She didn't look up again or whenever he exited the back door without speaking to her.

He had returned the insult at the theater. She had walked by him sitting in the same row and he pretended not to know her. She was surprised. *So, the shoe was on the other foot now.* Not that she particularly wanted to speak to him then either, but the conscious snub stung. What comes around goes around. She'd deserved that one. When she'd told Alexis about it, she said, "Oh, that's good, it's done now. You don't ever have to speak to him again." She tried to see it that way, but still felt that if it hurt her feelings when she didn't even care about the person, clearly the rule should be one shouldn't ignore people at all.

Then she easily summoned up a few other instances where it had seemed justified. Once shopping at Nordstrom, she'd seen her boss across the way in gloves. Amy was barely able to keep a calm tone at the office; she really didn't want to engage in any awkward chat in the accessories department, so she turned around to look at scarves and ever so slowly worked her way to the exit by hosiery. On Monday her boss said, "I thought I saw you shopping on Saturday." Amy said, "Oh, really, where? I hit several sale racks and got lucky. Did you have any luck?"

She resolved to never ignore someone again. Yet, the next week, wading her way through an artisan vinegar stall at a farmer's market when her old friend she was shopping with said, "There's someone over there you used to work with, but I can't remember his name. Go look at that guy in the scarf getting ready to pay."

Amy turned, approached close enough to get a glimpse, whipped around, and walked quickly back to the vinegars, out of sight of the register, whispering, "That old lecher! He's practically a pedophile. I hate him! I absolutely won't speak to him." Then she smacked her face. She had promised herself she wasn't going to pretend not to see people anymore! The instinct to look away or run away was more powerful than her resolutions, but she was not going up to speak to him. She had absolutely no curiosity about his life and times,

192

nor wanted him to know about hers. So, it seemed not ignoring people was a *guideline*, not a policy.

Recently running into someone in a mall she hadn't seen in years, her middle-aged brain couldn't think of the name, so she walked on by not making eye contact. Five minutes later, she figured it out and did the right thing. She went back up the escalator and found her standing where she had been passing out samples and said, "Patty, is that you? It's Amy. How are you? It just came to me who you are."

Patty said, "You're better than I am. I thought you looked familiar, but I couldn't remember your name or where I knew you from." They ended up having a nice chat even though they weren't friends and Amy found her meandering conversation in the office annoying. She was so proud of herself to go back and talk to her and hoped this event would be reported to someone else, anyone else she hadn't seen in years who had been part of that hellhole.

Amy started moving the clothes hangers methodically to the left, inspecting each item as it went by. It was a good night for white jeans because she had six pairs of them and loved wearing them any time of year. A linen blouse would be perfect because the linen season was so short and she had only three to choose from. She went for the milk chocolate, a very flattering color, more sophisticated than pink or lime, layered over a brown tank that would highlight her abs and lack of muffin top. She choose very comfortable, expensive leather sandals, good for standing at the bar chatting. Dressy gold earrings from Kevin for a significant birthday would add appropriate sparkle. She freshened up her makeup she put on first thing every morning with a little blush, eyeliner and mascara. That was enough looking in the mirror.

Every time she looked in her magnified mirror she braced herself for horrifying new developments.

Hallelujah—the eye bags extended to her cheekbones and the skin seemed thin—but not dark and crêpey. There was a cream for that when she needed it. Now she knew why the really old women had drawn on eyebrows. Hers seemed to recede a bit more every day and needed more enhancements with shadows and pencils. The neck wattle was discouraging, but her chin wasn't double yet. Everything she read said a low-cut top revealing cleavage distracted people from staring at her neck, so she always unbuttoned as far as possible without being indecent. She gave herself a big spray of cologne on the back of her neck to compensate. It made her feel prettier, more prepared for company and the evening. The next people to embrace her would hopefully inhale a pleasant scent and feel a lift, too. She would leave this cloud of social failures behind in the bathroom mirror and not think of them again tonight.

Amy told herself to take inspiration from Rohani and be proud of what she had created. Tonight would be a great night because she had put her best effort and heart into making wonderful food to share with friends. They would feel appreciated because of her effort. She breathed in slowly and exhaled just as slowly, creating her new serene attitude for the evening. She was calm. She was competent. She was fearless. Amy smiled at herself in the mirror and said out loud, "You look fine," without the dreadful modifier *for your age.*

Looking around the bathroom with a guest's eyes, she put a clean hand towel on the rack by the sink. Changing the direction of the shutters for nighttime, she noticed Kevin down in the yard talking to their next-door neighbor Henry. *Great. True procrastination. The man who hates to speak to the neighbors is having a big chat instead of working on his list. What other unexpected things will wind up on my plate tonight?*

Chapter 20

Kevin didn't believe in speaking to the neighbors every time he saw them like Amy did. When she saw someone on the street, she'd say hello, whether she knew them or not. She said it was becoming a dog walker that made her speak to everyone. Kevin wished she wouldn't do it. It made him cringe. Taking out the garbage was not a gregarious move in his mind. Sweeping the walk or raking leaves was not an invitation to chat. Henry seemed to agree with him on that. They seldom chatted through or over the fence while taking out the garbage. They nodded, waved, or said hello. That was enough. Unless they passed on the sidewalk, Kevin liked to keep quiet.

But Thor had gone with Kevin to the garbage cans by the basement door and barked loudly when Henry came out to his garbage can on the other side of the fence. Kevin felt obligated to speak.

"Thor, be quiet, that's Henry. Sorry, Henry, I don't want him to annoy you."

"Oh, don't worry about it. He only barks half the time and it doesn't bother me. He's hearing but not smelling me. If I was a burglar, it would be good."

"Thanks. Enjoying the summer so far?"

"Oh, yeah. The Mariners aren't losing too badly. My son's in summer school, and my daughter is going to Europe on vacation."

"That's nice. Whereabouts?"

"England and Ireland for three weeks."

"That's really nice."

"Yeah."

"See you."

"Yeah."

Sweeping down the front steps to the path to the sidewalk, he saw Riley come out of his front door and wave. Kevin nodded at him and kept sweeping. Keeping his head down, watching the stone path, he hoped Riley wasn't on the way down his stairs to chat, but he didn't want to look up in case that might be the signal to approach. It was hard to tell with these old dudes whether they got the signal or not. Thor, standing at the gate of his dog yard, started softly growling to let him know Riley had entered the zone, covering the ground between them much more quickly than expected. He looked up and rested his hands together on his broom handle.

"Riley, how are you?"

"I'm okay. How are you?"

"Good, thanks," said Kevin.

"What's new?"

"Nothing. How about you?"

"Nothing. How's your son?"

"You mean my dog? He's good, too. Excited because we're having some friends over tonight. He takes his job as the doorman seriously, announcing the arrival, leading them in and showing them out."

"Ha. Ha. Your daughter tells me he hasn't bitten anyone in a long time."

"That's true. Everyone is getting smarter."

"I don't pet him much anymore. He used to like me. I don't know why that changed."

"He's a weird dog, Riley, don't take it personally. He likes you. He just doesn't like anyone to pet him—not me, not even the one he loves best."

"That's hard to understand. I've had a lot of dogs in my life. They all liked me."

"Yeah, well," Kevin couldn't think of anything else to say and turned away toward the gate to the dog yard. "I don't know. I need to get going."

"Okay." Riley continued standing there, watching him go inside.

Kevin put the broom in the cleaning closet in between the dining room and kitchen. The rack was so full of shopping bags and long-handled cleaning tools that it rattled and clanked. Someone should make it stop being so noisy, but nothing fell down when he closed the door and the interior light went off. He liked that light going off and on with the door opening and closing. He wished every closet in the house had that wiring. That should go on the home improvement list for next year.

He surveyed the sparkling wine glasses and silver, the white napkins on a brightly colored tablecloth. All the lamps and sconces were on in the living room so every corner was lit and his old art deco torch lamp from his first apartment beamed up to the ceiling and highlighted the box beam molding. Kevin looked around the living room and he was pleased. The decorative pillows on the couches were arranged, but the newspapers, books, and magazines on every surface needed straightening. It looked messy and there was no room to put down a drink. Someone might want to sit there, although he couldn't remember anyone doing it. Everyone stayed in the kitchen or dining room. Why did Amy think it wasn't necessary to clear off the tables? She said no one noticed. He noticed. Methodically he went from table to table, around the room, making straight edges out of the piles of reading materials. Now it looked better to him.

The big corner window looked out onto West McGraw, and through the sheers he could see dog walkers and shoppers, his hedge, yard, and one porch pillar. He leaned around the table behind Amy's couch to grab the curtain wands and pulled the curtains shut carefully so as not to knock over the antique Spanish lamp behind the coffee table cookbooks or jostle the arrangement of silk peonies in a wooden Chinese rice carrier. Now the room looked even more golden with the

197

yellow curtains against the yellow walls looking like a big floral painting where the yard and the street had been. It seemed very cozy and he wished he could sit down on his couch in front of the fire under the glow of a lamp and read a magazine, have a quiet dinner, and go to bed early. That would be the perfect evening.

Instead, he went into the kitchen to try to remember his last task. The bar was clean and shiny. Nothing cluttered the surface but the laptop, landline phone, and the jug of Absolut he had bought that afternoon. His job was now clear. He opened the glass door of the cabinet above the bar and took down five martini glasses and a wine glass for Alexis. From the refrigerator door he found the jar of Spanish olives stuffed with almonds and the Dolin vermouth. Inside the fruit drawer of the refrigerator he found the lemon. He arranged the glasses in a cluster next to the vodka and the lemon twister found in the big drawer of utensils. Just looking at the paraphernalia brought on a desire for a cold, powerful drink, he thought. What was the right plate for the olives that had been part of the project description? He looked around, hoping for a clue. He wanted it to be right when Amy came downstairs. The only thing out of the ordinary on any of the kitchen counters was a big white platter with a white bowl on the back counter by the standing mixer. Yes! White was the key word.

He opened the cabinet above the back counter and out of stacks of serving pieces selected a small white dish separated down the middle so the twists wouldn't touch the olives. Perfect. He added the dish to the setup, put the whole lemon on one side and spooned some olives into the other without spilling juice on the counter. The stainless steel shaker in the liquor cabinet under the bar joined the lineup. Amy's grandmother's silver ice bucket filled with ice from the ice machine was the finishing touch. It was starting to look festive at that end of the bar and ready for the platter of food in the center spot and the filled glasses in the hands of people surrounding it.

He never looked forward to these evenings, but now that they were ready, he decided it would probably be fun. Alan would be amusing wielding the cocktail shaker. Alexis was always an attractive audience. Ben would bring him a book or music that would be a complete surprise, an author he'd never heard of, or music he'd forgotten about. Ben kept up with an amazing amount of different topics. He heard Amy and Thor coming down the stairs and turned, ready to greet her. She walked right into his chest and hugged him, then looked around him at the bar set up.

"Good job."

"You smell fabulous."

She nodded and smiled at him instead of saying thanks. "I'm ready for a glass of wine while I set up the crab. How about you?"

"Nah, I'll wait for Alan's performance. I'll pour for you, though. Anything else I can do to help you?" He grabbed a bottle of wine from the second shelf of the refrigerator where two more just like were resting sideways. He opened it, got a white wine glass down from the cabinet full of glasses, poured it half full, and presented it.

Thanks. That's delicious," she said after sipping the wine. It was off dry but had a mineral element that gave it backbone.

"Shall I leave this out?"

"Good idea. Alexis or I will want it and we'll be ready. The clear glass wine bucket is on the table. Do you want to open all the red wines I put on the chest?"

He looked around the corner at all the bottles on the chest in the dining room. "Why don't I open two more and let's see what anyone brings we might want to open too."

199

After he opened them he said, "Thor, my man, it's almost show time. Let's play ball until the company comes." The dog followed him downstairs to the dog cave in the basement.

Chapter 21

She watched them go and choked up for a few seconds. She hoped it was because she loved them so, not because her hormones were raging and she could expect more tears at any time. The top pleasures in her life were her husband and dog. She felt very lucky to have them in her life. Swallowing and exhaling deeply, she pulled the rolled-up cotton dishtowel with the washed butter lettuce leaves inside out of the refrigerator vegetable bin and opened it up on the counter next to the stove where the white platter lay waiting. *This is not a good time to get emotional about the day or anything. Hang on to your calm; stay focused on the tasks at hand.* She studied the size of the lettuce leaves and took another sip of the white wine Kevin had poured. It was crisp, dry on the tongue with a touch of effervescence. What a great choice in riesling and perfect with the all the seafood tonight.

She studied the lettuce leaves and chose the two biggest to line the bottom of the ceramic bowl for the crab, slightly overlapping with a little overhang around the rim. She quickly surrounded the bowl with enough smaller curved leaves to cover the platter generously but not solidly. The smallest ones were perfect for a spoonful of crab, but every head came with big leaves, too, that needed using. Maybe somebody would wrap it around the crab to make a saam, Japanese style, whatever would be fine. She transferred the crab salad she had mixed up earlier from a plastic storage dish to the lettuce-lined bowl, plumping it up to look higher in the center, and took a little taste with the spoon. It needed just a little more seasoning. She sprinkled a pinch of sea salt for a top note of ocean breeze and a pinch of African cayenne for palate jazz and the red highlights. She found the tiny jar with ginger juice in it and sprinkled it over the mound of crab. She followed the aroma of ginger across the kitchen and put the platter on the center of the bar and patted herself on the back metaphorically. *That was really good crab. Nothing says I love you like crab.*

From the top drawer of the chest in the dining room she selected some white linen cocktail napkins and placed them near the martini glasses on the bar. She examined the bar setup for missing items. What else? She needed a small sterling serving spoon and fork for the crab and a bowl of rice crackers next to the crab platter. Done. Now she needed to complete the setup for cooking the rendang. She got the big red cast-iron casserole out of the refrigerator and put it into the oven. She turned on the warming drawer to high, set the oven temperature for three hundred twenty-five degrees and to start cooking at 7:00 PM. She set the microwave timer for 7:30 to put the otak-otak in the oven.

There was nothing left to do but respectfully wash the rice and get the rice cooker going over by the stove and mixer. Since the cooking class, she had been trying to wash the rice gently by hand, showing respect, as Rohani Jelani had demonstrated. After more than thirty years of cooking rice without respect, it was hard to remember to not throw it in a strainer and run water over it before dumping it in the rice cooker. Tonight she remembered and got out a mixing bowl and gently stirred the rice with her fingers while cold water ran over it.

The value was in the mind-set, the attitude of appreciation for having food, a thank you woven into the routine of cooking the rice. She was very lucky to have a nice life with a certain amount of ease. She didn't have to count her grains of rice and she seldom forgot that. Actually, it was her anxiety about losing that ease that was more likely to be present than appreciation. The *anxiety* was what she needed to lose.

Staring at the rice grains as she ran the water over them and scooped them into the cooker made her sigh and think, *Oh well, all this is good and the bad doesn't really matter.* Friendships wax and wane. Best buds today isn't always best friends for life. Best friends in elementary or high school hadn't lasted much beyond graduation. Best friends at work usurped best friends in college. Neighbors became friends and then moved away. *Moved away* should be the category of lost friends after *awful husbands.* Amy felt quietly resigned to life's ups and downs.

She plugged in the rice cooker and turned it on to cook and sat down on a bar chairs. There would always be people she would miss, but Natalie, probably not too long.

"Well, look at the hostess drinking wine at her own bar and relaxing before her party."

"Oh, Kevin, I take it as a compliment that I'm sitting right this minute and we still have a few before show time. Come sit with me. It feels divine to be ready and sipping this fine wine."

"Have you recovered from the shock on Western Avenue?"

She sighed. "That sounds like a good title for a disaster flick. I think I've got a grip on it, but I'm still pretty amazed that's the way it played."

"Don't forget, she is the one that changed. We were all friends. I was there, too. People drift apart. That's why lifelong friends are so rare."

"Why do I care so much and you don't? Aren't your feelings hurt?"

"It just doesn't seem like a huge loss to me. We haven't even seen them in years. I've forgotten about them."

"Well, women can't live by husbands alone. Women need girlfriends!"

"Honey, men are different. A man with girl friends is probably in big trouble with his wife." He grinned at her, trying to get her to smile.

"Well, there's always that queasy feeling that I did something horrible and don't know what it is."

"Stop blaming yourself. It's not your fault—things change—roll with it."

She looked at him and smiled. "I might get seasick."

"That's my sailor! Good riddance to Natalie. Let's drink to the top of the ex-friends list, Ellen!" He raised his imaginary glass toward her.

"To the original shrill castigating bitch," Amy said.

"Do you miss her?"

"No! Actually, that's not true. Sometimes when I think about some of the fun we had, I do. She could be fun, but most of the time, no. I remember how many times I swore I'd never spend another weekend with her. Do you miss her?"

"Sure. She provided endless amounts of material for me."

"I'd like myself a lot more if I had screamed back at her even once, 'You don't have the right to speak to me or anyone else in that tone of voice.' But I will do it if anyone else ever insults me the way she frequently did."

"I'm trying to visualize you old and cranky. Will you have gray hair?"

"Never. I will have blonde hair until the day I die."

Chapter 22

Laurence walked quickly down 22nd Avenue toward Market Street, where shoppers and a happy-hour crowd would be developing. He couldn't believe what a relief it was to be outdoors and away from the library, his refuge. Those kids had gotten to him. Crossing over Market Street when the pedestrian walk signaled, he looked around and continued walking along Market toward Ballard Avenue, unable to shake the feeling of someone behind him, and thought he might stroll down the avenue back to Hattie's Hat, which was beckoning him like a safe harbor. He still had cash because Steve had picked up the check earlier and figured the kids were getting high behind a bush at the library or had gone back to the adult-free house where they lived. He wanted distance between them and him. One thing they weren't doing right now was getting exercise and fresh air. They also wouldn't be going to a bar, as they were not old enough to drink. His money was begging to be spent. He'd have a beer now and bask in the tavern glow of prosperity and well-being.

Laurence wrestled with himself as he passed by the Sunset Tavern. Too bad that wasn't open yet. He'd like to see what it looked like inside these days. In the 1970s after moving into her parents' house in Sunset Hill, he and Ingrid frequently went out Saturday evenings after dinner to hear music at the Melody, now called the Tractor Tavern, just past Hattie's. It had been exciting to upgrade to a nice house in a better neighborhood with good bars close by. Those were great years. If he went out by himself to meet Steve or other guys from work at Honeywell in the afternoon, they liked Hattie's and the Owl, now called Conor Byrne Pub. The Honeywell days before going to Boeing seemed like another century. They'd all been young engineering graduates ready to change the world. No danger today of seeing anyone he knew after all these years. Afterwards he could walk back up to Market and Ballard Avenue to catch the #18 Downtown at 6:36 or 7:07. That would be a quick ride home.

When he reached the door of the Conor Byrne Pub, he couldn't resist opening it to look inside to see the changes of the latest owner. The bar was busy, only one seat left. He settled in and ordered a Rainier on draft, the local cheap beer for people who hadn't embraced expensive brew-pub beers. It was cold and light-bodied in his mouth. It felt good to be sitting in a busy tavern with men and women surrounding him who looked clean and like they were having fun. It had been so long since he had been out at happy hour he'd forgotten what a festive crowd looked like. Very different looking than the lunch crowd that had to go back to work or those that had decided they weren't going back to work.

He suddenly felt hungry and remembered he hadn't eaten in a long time. Did he want to spend money on eating or just wait until he got home? He'd wait to eat until he got home. The forced frugality of never eating out was an important way to always have a little money in reserve. Undoubtedly, roast chicken with vegetables was waiting for him at home.

No one paid him any attention, but he felt part of the crowd and that was a nice feeling. He sipped the beer very slowly. The bartender was his hired friend here, and that was okay with him; he wasn't there to chat, just to be in the space. When the beer was gone and he indicated no more to the bartender, his mug was taken away. He'd save the rest of the beer money for another time. He was ready to go home for dinner. He was really hungry now.

Ballard Avenue was busier than when he'd gone inside. Still blue sky and daylight but the evening crowd was picking up. He noted the ages and the costumes parading on the sidewalk. He looked in the shop windows at expensive clothes and shoes for young people as he walked up Ballard Avenue. Waiting to cross Vernon Street in front of the Athletic Club, he saw the creeps from the library approaching the sidewalk from the vacant lot by the Hotel Ballard. He could not believe his bad luck to run into them again. He hoped they would not turn left or look his way. He backed up a few steps and into the old vestibule of the hotel turned into an athletic club. He could see them through the glass window. They turned left in front of the hotel. He hoped he blended into the sidewalk crowd, suddenly not seeming as busy as it had before he saw them. He was afraid to move for fear of attracting their attention. They turned left on Vernon, heading toward Leary Way. Whew. That was a near miss. He shook his head.

He crossed Vernon and walked as fast as possible up Ballard Avenue toward his bus stop at Market Street. Those two long blocks seemed a mile. *Let's see how lucky I am with metro. Anybody who rides the buses a lot knows they are frequently not on time and sometimes don't come at all.* He silently wished the #18 to be waiting for him to board when he reached the stop. A small crowd had gathered at the bus stop when he arrived. He tried to stand in the middle of it and not feel like a sitting duck. He had to leave room for the shoppers passing by with baby strollers and skateboarders. Luck was with him. The downtown bus was coming! The crowd lined up to board the bus with him at the end of it.

He had his wallet open to the ORCA card encased in plastic in his right hand for scanning when it was his turn to climb aboard. He felt a sharp shove

207

against his right shoulder and rib cage. He hit the sidewalk with a thud on his left hip and face. He heard running feet but couldn't move his left cheek off the sidewalk to look toward the running sound. His left hip hurt where he had landed on it. People were bending around him and trying to talk to him. "You okay? Are you hurt?" He looked up and the bus door was still open with the driver coming down the steps. "You want me to call the medics or the police?"

Laurence let the people help him stand up. "What happened?" he said. He wasn't sure if he was okay or not. He seemed to be able to stand, but he didn't want to. He felt his face for damage and couldn't feel any wetness, so he was just bruised. His face stung. His hip hurt. He was embarrassed and angry.

The bus driver said, "I'm not sure, but I think two kids pushed you down just as you were getting on and they ran off with your wallet. You could press charges, if someone can catch them. Anybody else see anything? Want me to call 911? You don't look too good."

"I'm fine. What I need is a cop." The driver got back in his bus and called his supervisor.

Laurence thanked the people, a young man and a woman, who had helped him up and now were helping him sit down on the bus stop bench made vacant after he said he'd prefer sitting. Standing made him dizzy and it seemed much safer sitting on the bench. He tried to think of something to say to these people but couldn't think of anything. How awkward to have strangers on either side of him seemingly in charge of him now. Damn those kids. All his efforts to stay hale and hearty wiped out in a second by some lowlifes. If he was really hurt, he was going to be so mad. Hospitals and insurance claims were always a nightmare to deal with. What a way to ruin the day. Oh, for a chance to kick the kids back. How embarrassing. How humiliating to be sprawled on the sidewalk, a pathetic spectacle for the Ballard evening crowd. Another old person falls and breaks in two or more pieces. Another bus came and left, depositing new people on the street. More people arrived. He encouraged the couple who had helped him to the bench to go on and thanked them for their time and kindness. They insisted they would wait for help to arrive. The siren of an emergency vehicle startled him. His head jerked forward and bounced against the wall of the bus stop shelter. Aaaah! God, that hurt. Add it to the list. Maybe he would die today after all, but banging his head against a Plexiglas wall had never been on his preferred list of methods. A patrol car parked a few feet away and the officer approached him.

Laurence was quick to call out to him, "Officer, I want to report a crime. The punks that knocked me down have stolen my wallet. We need to find them quickly. They're on the way to the Troll under the Aurora Bridge. I can help you find them so you can arrest them."

The EMS vehicle noisily made its approach to the sidewalk, clearing a space by force. The medics got out and began the routine questions like name and date of birth, and checked his pulse.

"I don't need to go to the hospital."

The medics were nodding their heads yes at the officer.

"Sir, these gentlemen think you need to go to the hospital. Give me your name and number and a description of the suspects. I'll take a look for them and check on you at the hospital later. Did anyone else here see anything?"

The crowd that might have seen something, if they had been paying attention to anything but cell phones, was gone on the last bus that had stopped. The current crowd waiting for the next bus didn't know anything about the incident. Even the couple who helped him stand up was ahead of him in line to get on the bus. They had only heard Laurence fall down.

"Officer, these punks are violent and have already committed crimes. It's important to find them immediately before they do more harm. Let me help you find them." Laurence said with all the gravity he could muster in his voice and delivery. He was afraid he sounded shaky.

The policeman shook his head and Laurence could see he was disappointed that there were no witnesses who knew anything except one senior victim who might not know everything.

Chapter 23

Thor suddenly got up and ran to the front door.

"Here's the first guest now. Who will it be?" Kevin asked.

"Alan, no doubt."

The doorbell rang. Thor barked so loudly Amy flinched. Kevin went to open the door, talking to both sides.

"That's our friend, Alan. It's okay. Alan, my man, how are you?"

"I'm not early am I?" said Alan with a little bow to Kevin.

"You are perfect. Come on in and don't forget, don't pet the dog."

"I know, don't pet the monster. Believe me, I won't," Alan said.

"I want to hear all about living the life of leisure," Kevin said, ushering him through the living room and dining room into the kitchen.

"It's only been a week and I love being unemployed. If I had the choice, I would never work again."

"Hey," Amy said, getting up to give him a hug. "I feel like the first one in the unchartered waters figuring it all out so the rest of you can follow my path later. What I've learned so far is that it takes special talent to *not* work. Not everyone can do it."

"Well, I think I might have what it takes." Alan studied the tools set out for him for a moment and said,

"Good to go here with the drink du jour. Who wants a martini?"

Alan methodically began the task, first putting ice in each of the glasses set out to chill them while he worked on assembling all the ingredients in a big cocktail shaker: ice, six jiggers of Absolut, and a splash of vermouth. He put the top on tightly and shook it with rhythm. Then he poured exactly equal amounts into three glasses with a flourish. Each glass was garnished with care, an olive for Kevin and twists for Amy and himself, rubbed around the rim of the glass and squeezed to make the citrus oil squirt on the top of the vodka forming a floating pattern, a good oil spill, spreading to the edges of the glass.

Amy sat on the opposite side of the bar facing Alan. She loved sitting on this side, looking at her kitchen. While she watched him perform the martini ritual, she had helped herself to a spoonful of crab on a lettuce leaf, enjoying the aroma of ginger and just as pleased with the second bite of the sweet Dungeness flavor and the contrast of the texture of the lettuce. A success. The first sip of cold Absolut was bracing, straightening her posture and breathing through the nose. An invigorating combination of sensory awareness is what made a good pairing.

"Where is your girlfriend?" Amy asked.

"My girlfriend?" Alan looked mystified.

"The one that you invited to come with you to dinner tonight." Amy looked at him.

"Ah, yes, that woman, not exactly a girlfriend. She's just a friend and she has a car. She's driving here. I gave her the address. I didn't talk to her today as I've been away all day." Alan busied himself with arranging the cloth napkins next to each glass, not looking Amy in the eyes. *Oh, crap I totally forgot about her. She was going to pick me up and drive us here. I hope this won't be a big problem.*

"Where's your cell phone?"

212

"I had it surgically removed from my hip my first day of unemployment and don't plan to have it reattached until absolutely necessary."

"I imagine she would have called you several times today already. Do you want to call and see if there is a message from her or call her directly? The phone is right here," Amy said, pointing at the cordless phone on the stand next to her glass.

"Let's give her a few minutes." Alan smiled at Amy and did not say, *She's left more like ten or twenty messages by now and I sure don't want to talk to her. She will be calmer tomorrow when we can go shopping.*

This didn't comfort Amy at all, but she shrugged her shoulders to signal okay. She vowed it was not going to distract her or upset her tonight. She would be calm and patient and remind him again in about twenty minutes.

Alan and Kevin took up the current status of the war in the Middle East that they predicted would never be over in their lifetimes and were going back and forth with zeal, but as they were on the same side, she didn't pay attention to the words. *I hate thinking about this war. I wish they'd talk about music. Look at Alan's hands shake. It's quivering, not in a good way.*

"Alan, enough blather about the insanity of U.S. policy in the Middle East—tell me what you think of the crab." She watched his hand reach over for the lettuce leaf and clumsily spoon some crab in it, almost dropping it before it got to his mouth.

"Stupendous. Dungeness is the best. I like the crackers, too," he said, putting a few in his mouth after he said it.

Thor suddenly was up and running for the door.

"Marvelous to have the doorman on duty. I'll be right back." She walked off through the dining room, reaching the front door as the bell rang. Thor barked and jumped at the door. "Thor, it's our friends, Alexis and

213

Ben." She opened the door, and he ran out on the porch, circling them and brushing against their legs.

"Hello, how nice to see you. Alexis, you look terrific. I love your hair. It's practically Raggedy Ann red, so perfect with the electric blue dress," Amy said.

Alexis gave her an air kiss and a hug. "Thanks. I was feeling very festive when I selected the color today. You always open the door so fast, like you're standing there waiting for the bell."

"It's my assistant here, the doorman. He let me know you had arrived."

"Hello, assistant." Alexis gave Thor a sniff of her closed fist. Ben handed Amy a bottle of Pine Ridge Charmstone with a grin.

"Thanks for the fancy wine. We'll open this immediately. Come on in. We didn't wait for you to have a drink, so you have Alan's undivided attention."

Amy went back to her bar chair by the French doors and motioned for Alexis to sit beside her. Alexis hugged and air-kissed Kevin and Alan, who both eyed the blue dress up and down approvingly before she took the seat next to Amy.

Kevin said, "Alexis, that's quite a dress!"

"Thanks, Kevin," Alexis said with a smile and a pout.

"Alexis, my lovely, what will you have?" Alan said.

"I'd like wine, please. Amy, your table looks beautiful and it smells so good in here." Alexis inhaled the aroma of curry while looking around the kitchen at all the stainless steel appliances gleaming and the dark stone counter shining. The hardwood floors looked freshly mopped. She was so glad to be here with these people around this nice bar in this nice house with nothing but fun ahead. She leaned back in her chair to be waited on. This felt great. She smiled at Alan. Alan smiled back. He was so reliably charming.

"Ben, how about you?" Alan inquired, looking away from Alexis.

"Bludgeon me." Ben grinned at him.

Kevin looked Ben up and down and said, "Damn, Ben, you look terrible as usual."

"Well, thanks. I spent a long time picking out this T-shirt and it's clean." He stretched out the lower hem for Kevin's inspection and then turned his elbow out to best show the big hole in the flannel shirt he wore unbuttoned over the T-shirt. "This delightful plaid has only been slept in once and that was indoors."

Kevin nodded approvingly at Ben and poured Alexis a glass of white wine from the open bottle in the wine bucket, while Alan began the martini ritual with fresh ice in the stainless steel shaker, a few drops of vermouth, and three jiggers of Absolut.

Ben said, "Yes, you understand about my week." as the third jigger went in.

"Thank you so much for inviting us tonight." Alexis raised her glass to everyone.

Shake, shake, shake. The ring of the ice banging on metal and the gushing sound of the cold liquid pouring into the long-stemmed glass had everyone's attention. Kevin could see Alan's hands in motion reflected in Ben's glasses. What a home video that would make; a martini being made in someone's glasses.

Ben felt like one of Pavlov's dogs in training. Alan seemed to move so slowly. Was he being dramatic on purpose? Ben dove immediately into the crab and lettuce cups to pass the time. Good crab! He nodded at Amy to make sure she saw his first response to the Dungeness. The flick of the wrist at the end of the pour from the shaker seemed theatrical. Ben gave Alan a salute on the handover, took the first big gulp, and focused on the slide down the gullet, whooee. Cold, almost a brain freeze, and a little herbal taste and aroma from the French vermouth rising from the smooth vodka. Ben made his own melodramatic pause through pursed lips, with wide eyes, and pronounced the martini excellent and worth waiting for. He turned to toast Alexis, who gave him the tiniest bit of an *I told you so* smirk and resumed waiting for Alan's next remark. He smirked back at her, *You're making a fool of yourself with that fawning look*, but she wasn't paying attention to him. Relaxing back in his bar chair like a magician giving his audience a false hand to follow, Ben pulled a CD out of his pocket with a grand gesture. "Ah ha. Guess what this is?" he asked Kevin.

"Lux and Ivy influences?" Kevin laughed at his own swift choice of an esoteric music compilation habit by a few serious fans of a long-defunct band.

"No, guess again."

"Steve Goodman?" Kevin now seemed in earnest.

"I wish I could have found some of that for you—believe me, I've looked."

Alan couldn't resist, "You old fools are making me sick with your reverence for the demented and the dead."

Ben gave him the finger and said, "Focus on your craft. I'll be ready for another in a minute."

Thor suddenly was up and running for the door. "I hope that's Alan's friend." Amy got up from her bar chair and followed him and opened the door before the bell rang.

It was Riley, with his finger poised close to the bell. He looked freshly pressed and shampooed with wet hair slicked back with hair product. He smiled at her. She paused briefly, "Hi, Riley. What's up with you?"

"It's a party, isn't it?" He smiled more with his blue eyes staring deeply into hers. "I saw everybody else come in."

She looked right back at him, not smiling, sighed, and nodded. "Yes, we have some friends visiting. Would you like to come in and have a drink with us?"

She and Thor led him through the dining room and living room into the kitchen where everyone looked up expectantly but said nothing. Kevin's eyebrows raised in the question *What's he doing here?* Amy repeated the move back to Kevin with a shrug, trying to telegraph, *He's old and lonely.*

"This is our neighbor, Riley. He's come to have a drink with us. He prefers white wine," Amy said, looking at Alan. "This is Alan, the bartender, and our friends, Alexis and Ben."

Riley stood at the end of the bar between Alan and Kevin. "Nice to meet you all. I love a party. Especially when you can just walk across the street."

"Well, Riley, what's new with you?" Kevin said, trying to be a good host and not display his annoyance with this party crashing.

Alan poured him a glass of white wine and handed it to him with a nod and bow.

"Not too much, enjoying the nice weather. I visited my brother in Oregon for a few days."

"Oh yeah, where in Oregon?"

"Not far from Portland. He doesn't drive anymore, so I go there to see him."

Amy resumed her bar chair, spooned some crab on a lettuce leaf, and handed it to Alexis, who put it in her mouth in two bites. They agreed it was good and perfect with the wine. Alexis and Ben seemed relaxed and enjoying themselves. Amy was going to enjoy herself, too, no matter what. She sipped her icy martini, which really was a treat she didn't have that often. She smiled at Kevin, who looked a bit peeved. She understood. She winked at him and handed him a small leaf with crab on it. Amy knew the hostess has to sell the hors d'oeuvres and the guest always appreciates personal service, particularly when it is the husband. Hopefully, it would help him not be so annoyed with the uninvited guest.

217

Riley turned to Alan and said, "Great to have a bartender. That's a real party. So, where do you work when you're not here?"

"Downtown at the Mayflower, plus occasional moonlighting at the Fairmont."

"I don't drink martinis anymore."

"I may quit myself soon."

"Where do you come from, Ben?"

"Eastlake."

"I built some houses there a long time ago. I used to be a developer, but I went broke in the 1980s. I live across the street now in one of my houses that never sold."

"Riley, you should tell them about the famous mansion you deconstructed in the Highlands," Amy said.

"Well, it was a really good deal. That's what made me buy it." He made eye contact with everyone, warming up the audience for the story. "The family fortune was lost." Smiling, with a twinkle in his eye, he said, "The house was custom, custom with details from all over the world, marble, antique wood, and massive carved doors. The light fixtures alone were worth a fortune. The property was acres and acres. I bought it for almost nothing and subdivided it." He gestured with his right hand, indicating the size of the property, and leaned into the bar like a podium. "The house was so big, with huge rooms that no one needs anymore like a fifty-foot-long living room and an equally big dining room. So I cut it in two and sold half the house to someone who moved it in pieces to another piece of property. Then for years I lived by selling off the artifacts. It was going to fall down anyway; they hadn't been able to take care of it for a while, so no need for all that marble and carved doors to be wasted . . ."

Everyone listened intently. He was articulate and told his story well. It held their attention, and they encouraged him with questions for more details about the house. The imagery of the abandoned mansion being deconstructed enthralled everyone along with the perversity of his living in it and off of it simultaneously. It was always a good story with some new details or some omitted. Amy always asked him to describe the old mansion because he was sketchy on more recent events, names, and relationships. The truth might be he had lived alone for a long time and there wasn't much to report. He was estranged from his family and had never said why. After some years of being neighbors and impromptu visits any time she sat on her porch, he referred to her as Kevin's daughter and to Thor as his son. His glass was empty.

"Riley, want some more wine?" Amy said, looking in his blue eyes with the hostess's power of telepathy. She told him the answer to her question without saying anything.

"No, thanks. I think it's time for me to go now. Thanks for inviting me."

"We're so glad you could come. Let me walk you to the door."

She rolled her eyes and smiled when she returned. "Well, isn't our neighbor, Riley, a charming old dude?"

"You're so nice to take in old drunks off the street," Alan said.

"Well, you are clever and amusing so I'll take you in at any age, but I have a soft spot for old dudes. Be kind to others and maybe someone will be kind to you when you're ancient. And my dog bit him. How about a glass of wine for me, please."

Kevin leaned into the end of the bar. "That bite is Riley's insurance policy at this bar." He shrugged, "I guess we're lucky. Alan, tell us, about your new friend."

Alan poured Amy a glass of white wine and handed it to her. "She's interested in art and loves the Frye."

"We guessed that part, tell us something else." Kevin and Alan exchanged a look, but Alan didn't seem ready to take the bait.

"Have you seen the new exhibit there?" Alexis leaned forward for Alan's response.

Ben noted the distance between their noses and looked away, shaking his head.

The dog took off again for the front door. Everyone looked at Amy.

"Hurrah! Must be Alan's date," she said, getting up and heading through the living room for the front door. She opened the door and there was Drew, with a big bouquet of flowers in his hand. She opened her mouth and no words came out.

"Oh jeez. You didn't get my message did you? I can tell you didn't."

She smiled at him and shook her head. "I got Julie's message about being out of town."

"Well, I wasn't part of that trip and I did email you, but when I didn't hear back I wondered if you'd gotten the message."

"For heaven's sake, come in. I'm glad to see you, Drew. It's no problem. You can be Alan's date. I think he's going to need one tonight." Leading the way back to the bar, she said, "Look everybody, Alan's date is here at last!"

Alan embraced Drew with a hug and a European kiss on each cheek. "My dear, you look enchanting. Care for a cocktail?"

"I'll have what everybody's having, please," Drew said, as he shook Kevin's outstretched hand.

"Good to see you, buddy. Glad you could make it." Kevin moved over toward Alan to make room for Drew at the end of the bar and looked sideways at Amy. She nodded that his arrival was fine with her and started making the introductions over the noise Alan was making putting the ice cubes in the stainless steel container.

"Alexis, Ben, this is Drew, an old buddy of Alan's and a new friend of ours. He really was invited, along with his fabulous woman, Julie, but she's traveling."

Alexis looked at Drew. He was grinning at her. All she could think was *No, please no, not him.*

"Alexis, it is you. You've given up your blue hair. You haven't given up the art life have you?" He didn't put out his hand to shake across the bar, he had put it in his pocket and the left hand held the bouquet of flowers. He just stood there looking at her, waiting for a response with a small smile.

Alan stopped mixing the drink and looked at Drew.

"Hummm, the blue hair days. That's a while ago. Let me guess who you used to be." Alexis showed no emotion at all and appeared to be thinking very slowly while studying him.

Ben looked at Alexis with raised eyebrows. "Blue hair? I recall many hues, pink, purple, orange, yellow, but I don't remember blue."

Drew tilted his head, looking at Alexis expectantly, waiting for her next move. He wasn't going to supply any hints. He thought she was stalling to come up with a humorous put-down but couldn't think of a good one yet.

Kevin, Amy, and Alan said nothing, but they all closed their mouths that had been hanging open and watched carefully.

Alexis returned Drew's gaze and said, "You must have been a student in one of Michael Dailey's acrylic classes. Did you go on to become an artist?"

"Ouch," said Drew. "You haven't lost any of your bite. Actually I own a gallery these days. You must not get out much if you haven't heard of it or me, same name."

"Sorry, I don't recall you. It's true I don't get out much. I work alone and stay pretty busy."

221

No one said anything in response to that. Amy decided this situation needed a hostess intervention. "Drew, let me have those gorgeous flowers and I'll put them in water."

Drew passed the flowers to Amy, still keeping his eyes on Alexis.

Kevin said, "Drew, please have a seat," indicating the empty stool at the end of the bar close to where he was standing.

Alan finished mixing and handed Drew the martini, and everyone held up their glasses and did the silent clink. Everyone took a sip except Amy who was dealing with the bouquet. Alan alternated taking a look at Alexis to see if her face had changed and then at Drew. How fascinating that his old buddy knew Alexis.

Amy turned away from the group, opened a high cabinet, reached for a vase she could touch but not see, and then set it on the counter by the sink. She tapped Kevin on the back of his ankle with the toe of her sandal, "Honey, would you please get me another vase?"

Ben looked at Drew and said, "I'm her husband. I seldom ever meet anyone from the old days when Alexis was a full-time painter. Where's your gallery?"

Amy filled the first vase half full with water thinking, *Thank you, Ben, for your concise summary of the situation.*

Kevin turned around and easily grabbed a vase off the top shelf and put it down by the sink and refocused on his guests and this very interesting conversation.

Drew took a slow sip of his drink, still looking at Alexis and Ben sitting on the bar stools on the side with one empty next to Ben, "I'm located in Sodo, curating and representing the newest of the not-quite-yet-famous, and I host performance art in the space some weekend nights. It's an interesting combination of talent, visitors, and patrons. The weekend crowd is quite lively."

Amy was listening carefully, trying to appear casual as she slipped off the plastic sleeve and unwrapped the wet newspaper from the flower stems. She was working on a good hostess jump into this conversation that might lighten it up a little. She was astonished at Alexis's icy response to Drew. *Daggers might be more accurate. She definitely knew him and was giving him some serious payback. What could he have done for her to still be so mad? Old boyfriend? Old boss? Old business?* Deftly dividing the bundle in half, she stuffed the stems in the prepared vases without spilling any water and placed one of the vases on the bar in between Alexis and Alan, making them both have to adjust their posture to see each other. "Kevin and I attended one of the weekend happenings recently and all I can say is that the current exhibit is so unusual I couldn't describe it to you. I didn't love it or hate it. I was baffled by it." She smiled at Ben and took the other vase of flowers into the dining room and put it on the painted chest.

Drew, sipping again on his martini during that report, seemed very pleased with the description and nodded affirmatively. "Thank you! I appreciate you both coming and your open mind to a new experience. Looking around and being baffled is a good thing. Sometimes people leave after two minutes, obviously not our crowd."

After disposing of the floral debris in the garbage under the sink, Amy picked up her wine glass. "Kevin, sit over there by Ben and tell him what you thought about the performance," she said, motioning to her previous seat. "The artist was Canadian and took her bows practically naked except for a lot of red paint! Alexis, bring your glass of wine and come sit with me on the deck for a minute. I have got to tell you about the shock on Western Avenue today."

Amy and Alexis went through the French doors and sat in the two chairs under the flowering clematis

223

vine in the back corner of the deck. They put their glasses down on a small tile table between the chairs. It felt very private to be out of the sight of everyone sitting around the bar. They could hear the murmur of banter inside, but the music muffled the sound. The deck was enclosed on two sides by clematis-covered walls made of a metal grid above a wooden railing. The summer night sky was still daylight, but strings of soft lights in mini bamboo shades along the top of the clematis sparkled. The neighbors' lights on both sides shone through the clematis as additional mood lighting.

"What shock? I didn't know we had an earthquake. I didn't feel anything."

"It was my personal earthquake, an 6.5 with the epicenter at the Spanish Table."

When the unmistakable electronic clanging of the timer went off in the kitchen a few minutes later, Amy and Alexis came in from the deck. Alexis stood by Ben, who was in a dialogue about music with Kevin. Amy, after checking on everyone at the bar, went to work in the kitchen to take the hot rendang out of the oven and put it in the warming drawer and reset the temperature to 375 degrees for the fish custards. The amazing gas range would be up to the new temperature in minutes. She got the ramekins out of the refrigerator and put them in a large, deep baking pan. She slowly filled the pan half full from the hot water dispenser, careful not to splash water in the ramekins, as she had done more than once before. She put the pan in the oven and set the timer on the microwave for twenty-five minutes.

"Kevin, I want you to show everybody a few pictures of Malaysia."

"No, let's wait until after dinner."

"No, now is perfect. It's musical chairs time. Ben, let Kevin sit there so he can be in the middle. I promise we have edited this down to the best fifty and they are really good. No bad music either, like I usually put on my movies, but Kevin's personal narration. I'll get the empty crab dish out of the way."

Alan took the seat at the end of the bar with another full drink in front of him, waving everyone away from him. "I've already seen the photos."

Kevin looked resigned to his fate, saluted Amy silently, *Yes ma'am,* and stood up to facilitate switching places with Ben to move over to the center bar stool. He dragged the laptop to the center of the bar in front of him. Alexis resumed her seat next to Kevin at the other end by the French door.

Ben moved over a little clumsily to sit on the other side of Kevin. It was the first time he'd stood up since he sat down upon arrival and he felt stiff already. He was sorry to see the crab dish go and had hoped it was going to be refilled. He gently moved his martini glass with Alan's last effort full to the rim to be safely on his left side where no drops could be inadvertently spilled into the keyboard or get in anyone else's mouth by mistake. He tried to get Amy's attention to bring him some more crackers or something, but she was already busy greasing a hot griddle, with what smelled like sweet butter, and didn't look at him. He thought about asking Alexis to get him something because she would know how hungry he was but decided that wasn't a good idea. Kevin was busy and probably wouldn't know where more food was anyway. So he helped himself to an olive stuffed with almonds and then pulled the dish of olives over by his glass. They were really good olives and would have to hold him during the photos. He hoped dinner would be ready soon. He was so hungry and whatever had just come out of the oven and into the warming drawer smelled awesome.

Drew stood behind Alexis and Kevin, holding his glass up in his right hand with his elbow resting on his left hand. Amy looked over at him after pouring the first batch of batter for the small crepes on the griddle and bet he frequently assumed that pose with his pointer finger on his cheek instead of the glass as he looked at art. The pose seemed so natural to him, the casual but expensive clothes on his slim body and the carefully trimmed short white hair and short partial beard. He really was a nice-looking guy in his total presentation. Of course, anybody in the art world had to have a look and he had probably been working on his look all his life. She wondered how Alexis was enjoying being so close to him.

The first photo of a man's hairy legs, no clothes or torso showing, in a big fish tank with tiny fish swarming around the man's legs made them all gasp. Kevin now had the stage. Astonishment over the fish pedicure was unanimous. No one had seen or heard of it before. Kevin felt pleased his choice of the first photo was successful at getting the attention of his audience of three and a half people. Ben had immediately focused hard on the laptop. Kevin was always impressed with how fast Ben switched gears. Alexis and Drew seemed to be paying attention; they were making noises anyway like they were. Amy was listening but busy making the roti jala. Alan had zoned out. He wondered if Alexis was enjoying the proximity of the man she couldn't remember. Ha! He didn't believe that for a minute. He would ask Amy to spill the details on that the minute everyone left. This was turning out to be an interesting evening.

"What's going on here, torture or pleasure? Who paid whom for this? Some people report that the fish pedicure tickles. Others say it hurts as the fish nibble your dead skin, but some people like it when it hurts. Everyone agrees your feet will be clean when the fish are done." Kevin smiled deviously at his audience.

Alexis squealed. Ben grimaced. Drew shivered. Amy laughed. "It's so creepy it's funny."

Kevin advanced his next slide of a sculpture attached to the roof of a building. "Can anyone name the famous blue-skinned flute player and his white cow? You're right, Drew; it's Krishna, the young Hindu heartthrob god. Why is he blue? Because it's cool and no one else is." He showed a few slides of the same building to illustrate the walls and the roof were packed with brightly painted three-dimensional figures like the statue of blue boy and his cow. Inside the building, the decorations of every surface were just as dense. The colors were riotous.

Amy paused in her preparations for a moment and leaned on the granite counter next to Alan, sipping her wine and enjoying watching the faces. She loved watching Kevin give a show. She had to push him to get him to do it, but once he got going, he was so good at it, very funny, and subversive. Why was it such an effort to get him to do it?

Kevin succinctly explained how the ancient cultures of Malaysia melded with the European and Asian invasions into a shockingly flamboyant background that is charming and captivating. His photos showed vibrant blue Portuguese tiles, multicolored Indian murals in Hindu temples, dark geometric designs on mosques, red Chinese temples, pink Dutch forts, and green British cricket fields. In between all the astonishing religious edifices, traditional two- and three-story beige stucco buildings with worn red tile roofs, palm trees, and shady patios indicated the tropical climate.

As amazing as the Indian temples were, the Chinese temples competed for attention with equally outrageous roof ornaments that drew you into the entrance courtyard crowded with commerce and fire. Kevin felt the chaos of it all was Felliniesque. Vendors sold five-foot-long red joss sticks, flowers, and food items to use as offerings to the ancestors. Flames and black smoke poured out of big ceramic or metal ovens as people threw the joss sticks in to complete the ritual. Add the beating white wings of small birds around your face as they were sold and then released from cages. Watch where you walk as visitors often prostrated themselves on the floors indoors or outside in the fervor of the moment.

He told them about the old shops with big windows and shutters that had once opened to the street to do business from had been the homes of the merchants with living quarters on the upper floors. The ground floors now housed restaurants and reflexology studios. At night, every restaurant put tables outside on the narrow sidewalks and the street, creating a bustling scene. "Look, there's Amy eating dumplings. There's Amy drinking gin and tonic."

In the new Kuala Lumpur, strikingly modern mosques and skyscrapers surrounded the iconic Petronas Towers that looked like Angkor Watt and Blade Runner at the same time. In the old Kuala Lumpur, beautiful young Muslim girls lounged, bored and provocative on bales of multicolored textiles, which made everyone watching the slideshow in Seattle ooh and ah. The monks, adolescent and younger, in saffron robes were photogenic posed against plain stone buildings and green garden backgrounds. Next, he jolted them out of the cultural montage with a close-up of a giant white male foot, with a dozen red, swollen, oozing bites. Everyone gasped and then laughed when he confessed it was his own foot, hideous not from hiking through the rain forest on Langkawi Island, but inflicted mysteriously while eating breakfast with his sandals on in an outdoor dining room of a beach hotel. Then they all laughed in relief and sympathized about the hazards of dining al fresco.

Alexis couldn't stop giggling about his foot and patted him on the shoulder in support of suffering while traveling and appreciation of his show. He patted her knee affectionately in response and was pleased he had succeeded in relaxing her and distracting her from the warm body behind her that seemed to bump into them more than was necessary, leaning over to take a closer look at some of the photos.

At the beginning of Kevin's show, Alexis didn't know how she was going to endure it with Drew hovering behind her, but Kevin had been very amusing and she felt comfortable on her own turf with her friends. She was determined to stick with her story that she didn't remember him. That would be the ultimate insult to one of the world's biggest egos with no visible evidence to support his self-anointed status as a great art critic and somewhat good painter.

Kevin showed a few photos of the night markets' plastic dining tables obscured by plates of food with three or four generations of family squeezed in elbow to elbow in red plastic chairs. Kevin described how he selected his fish for dinner, still swimming in a washtub full of fish, based on size and eye contact with the fish.

"Slow down, zoom in, and name the foods on the plates! I want to see it better," Ben said. He was very aware of the cooking smells coming his way, the curry and the pancakes and something else he couldn't quite identify. He was getting hungrier by the minute. He took the last sip of his drink and looked at Alan next to him to see if there was a chance of another before dinner. Alan looked like he was asleep. Was it too much trouble to get up and walk around the bar to make himself one? No. He stood up and tested his feet by lifting them up and down.

Kevin paused over the juxtaposition of bikinis and burkas on the beach to look at Ben. Ben held up his empty glass.

"Please help yourself. There are only three photos left. You don't need to look at them, you can hear about them. This is a ridiculous fashion item, a Muslim woman's swimsuit. It looks like she will drown with all that fabric flowing to the ground, but she can see through some eye slits so she didn't fall down or get swept away by a wave. This is her husband in Ralph Lauren pretending he is not an Arab. This photo will prove to you what a sport I am if you had any doubt: Here's my wife and the Omar Sharif of Georgetown with the Indian Ocean behind them. Amy was so hot she was wilting, so I bought her a tour of the island in his air-conditioned taxi, which included a thousand years of history, global politics, and a Chinese lunch on a beach. He was so good we thought about hiring him to take us around the rest of the trip. And yes, he plays bridge, too."

The closing shot was the supreme religious leader in a pink silk brocade jacket with a black pill box hat, delivering a television lecture on the evils of alcohol with Kevin's bottle of Malaysian gin standing next to the flat screen television in their hotel room. "I love watching television in foreign countries."

"That was great!" Alexis was enthusiastic.

"More," Drew said.

"No, no encore," Kevin said. "It must be time to eat." He looked over at Amy. "More? Well, I guess we can do an encore with Amy's slideshow, staring Amy, doing guess what, cooking! Halfway around the world on vacation, she can't take a rest. This movie needs no narration, thank goodness—it has a soundtrack and runs itself. I am now tired and thirsty. Ben, fix me up while you're standing there." He pushed his empty glass toward Ben, who had finished making himself a drink. He looked over his shoulder at Drew. "How about you?" Drew shook his head no.

Kevin slid a CD into the laptop and watched while Ben put ice cubes in his martini glass, poured vodka over them to the rim, no vermouth, no garnish, and pushed it back to him. "Thanks, pal, I love them ice cold like that."

When Ben got seated again beside him, Kevin clicked the start icon. With a loud percussion boom, tropical music accompanied a big tour bus in primary colors filling the screen and zipping past the coconut palm trees on the highway to Kuala Lumpur. In seconds, it seemed to drive by the big metal towers to the kitchen of the cooking class with the petite teacher with the big glasses and forehead. Alexis, Drew, and Ben appeared mesmerized again; they were smiling, making some comments and questions. Kevin was glad to sit there, sip his new cocktail, and give brief answers. He watched Amy pause from moving rapidly around her stove to give him a big thumbs-up for the show. They exchanged a look that said she was pleased with him and he acknowledged that he'd done it (and got his points). Her movie stopped playing as suddenly as it had begun. The room seemed very quiet after all the music and conversation.

Amy used that as her cue to pick up the pandan leaf basting brush she had made earlier and the roti jail cup and walked over to the bar, waving them around in the air to get their attention. "Look everybody, tools from the cooking class in Kuala Lumpur. Swish the green brush around in melted butter in a hot pan for instant, *free* sweet vanilla flavoring. You will taste it in the little crepes you will be eating soon. This copper cup is the tool that dispenses the batter and creates the lacy pattern of the crepes. Just imagine the hundreds of years of culinary history in these souvenirs."

ROTI JALA by Rohani Jelani

Makes about 30 pieces *

10.5 ounces all-purpose flour

1 teaspoon salt

1/4 teaspoon ground turmeric

1/2 cup thick coconut milk

3/4 cup water

3 large eggs

1-1/4 cup water, divided

2 tablespoons light vegetable oil

A little oil for greasing the pan

Sift flour, salt, and turmeric into a medium-sized mixing bowl. Combine the thick coconut milk and 3/4 cup water. Make a well in the center and into this, pour in coconut milk mixture, eggs, one half of the additional water and the oil. Using a wooden spoon or balloon whisk, gradually incorporate the flour into the liquid, to make a smooth, thick batter free from lumps. Do not beat too vigorously!

Stir in the remaining water and strain batter (important) through a fine sieve. (This removes any lumps that would otherwise clog the spouts in the roti jala cup.) Cover bowl with cling wrap and set aside 20–30 minutes to rest. One hour is better.

Heat a heavy iron griddle or non-stick pan over medium heat and brush surface lightly with oil.

Stir batter, dip the roti jala cup into it, filling it about half full. Move in steady concentric circles to form fine, lacy pancakes. (See tips below.)

232

Once roti jala is lightly colored, remove it with a spatula and place it, top side facing down, on a plate. There is no need to cook both sides. Either fold the pancake into wedges or from them into small, neat rolls.

TIPS

Always strain batter.

Do not over fill roti jala cup, as the batter will then flow out too fast, causing thick strands. After experimenting a few times, you should be able to fill up your cup with just enough batter to make one pancake without having to refill.

Rotate the cup about 3-4 inches above the pan, working in smooth, concentric circles. Avoid going over the same area too many times or you will end up with thick, untidy pancakes.

* The roti jala cup is a small copper cup with a handle and five pointed tips on the bottom with tiny openings to dispense the batter in thin threads. Filling it about half full with batter is about 1/3 cup of batter. The flavor is the same without the lacey look created by the cup. One way, albeit tedious, to imitate the lace without having the official cup is to use a plastic ketchup or garnish dispenser to squirt the batter into swirls in the hot pan trying to make consistent, small crepes.

Note about metric conversions: Weighing flour is a good habit as it is much more accurate than using a measuring cup. The original recipe specified 300 grams of flour or 10.5 ounces or about 3 cups.

Chapter 24

Laurence woke up strapped to a gurney and couldn't move his head enough to get a complete view of the room or who was moaning and groaning. He knew immediately where he was. How long had he been asleep? The sight and smell and sounds brought all his senses to instant alert. Any hospital was unpleasant to him, but this one was toxic. No offense to the staff, but this had been his home away from home for years while Ingrid was sick. He had vowed never to visit here again, which had seemed easy to keep if he didn't dial 911, yet here he was.

The Emergency Department was crowded with people waiting in chairs and milling around the admissions desk. Obviously, he was not in the worst shape here tonight. He hurt but not enough to make any noise. The novelty of being on a gurney instead of standing next to it was infuriating. He couldn't believe this was happening, being a patient in an emergency room, waiting for god knows how long to learn if he was hurt or not. How long had he been here? He was beginning to think he wasn't hurt very badly. He was bruised and humiliated but not broken anywhere. He wanted to go home. He tried to get the attention of staff passing by. His "excuse me" wasn't working in the din of the crowd or someone with a clipboard said it would be his turn soon. He fumbled with the restraints, finally freeing his arms. Then someone returned to tell him it would be a few more minutes before a transporter would deliver him to the examining room.

"I've changed my mind," he said. "I'm feeling fine having had this rest. I want to go. I don't need to stay."

"Sorry, sir, you have to stay. You're in the process now. It won't be long."

"Let me get up. I want to stand up."

"In a few minutes you can stand up, sir."

Laurence silently cursed his luck, watching the medical people move around the room in no discernible pattern. This was ridiculous. Stuck. Bound. Helpless. Next, he was sure, would be indignities. He was suddenly determined that it was not his fate to lie here and wait for whatever happened next. He was not ill and he was no longer tired. He wanted to get out of this hospital and go find his wallet. He undid the restraint on his chest so he could sit up and look around. He sat up on the gurney slowly as though doing a slow-motion sit-up, just in case he might be dizzy. No problem. All that daily practice paid off. Now there were just his feet to free.

A policeman entered his view. Laurence called out to him. "Officer, I need to report a crime."

"Are you Laurence Hansen?"

"I am. Are you looking for me?"

"You reported a crime to me earlier this evening. I looked for the suspects but didn't see them. I'm checking on you like I said I would."

"Sorry, I didn't recognize you at first, different lighting. This is perfect timing. I'm ready to leave now. If you could give me a hand with this," he said, pulling at the restraints on his feet. "I'd rather tell you all about it sitting in your patrol car."

"Are you sure you're okay?"

"Oh, yeah, they can't find a wheelchair. It's a rule, or a rather guideline, that you need to leave by wheelchair, but I'm ready to go without one."

"You weren't here very long."

"It seemed quite long enough to me. They say I'm fine, no problem, but whomever was to set me free went to phone about the wheelchair and disappeared." He swung his legs over the side, rotated his ankles, stretched his hands over his head, and dropped nimbly to the floor. "See, no problem at all," he said, as he walked deliberately toward the door without looking back.

The policeman followed him toward the patrol car parked on the street near the entrance of the semicircular drive.

"Can I get in? No, I don't mind sitting in the back." Laurence walked around the far side of the car and got in the backseat behind the officer so he would be in the shadow if anyone came out of the hospital looking for him. It looked like a prison built for two in the backseat of the car with metal mesh covering the windows and the partition between the front and back seats.

"Officer, around 5:30 PM, I alerted the security guard at the Ballard Library that those young men, who knocked me down and stole my wallet at the bus stop on Market Street, were up to no good, waiting for a drug dealer. What I didn't tell him is that I think one or both of them are involved in the recent murder of a convenience store clerk.

"What makes you think that?"

"I overheard them talking about being on a crime spree, one murder so far, before they get famous jumping off the Aurora bridge. Jumping is their plan to avoid going to prison in Shelton. Apparently Shelton has quite a reputation. But the fame associated with jumping seems to be an incentive also."

"Why did they push you down?"

"They are punks. I think what they wanted was to hurt me or frighten me. That makes them feel powerful. It's easy to steal a wallet from someone who is holding it out in plain sight. Believe me, they are not much richer for taking it."

"You want to report a stolen wallet with no money in it?"

"Twenty dollars is not much, but yes. I want to report them for assault and robbery. They have caused

236

me pain and inconvenience today. Replacing the contents of the wallet will take a week of dealing with city government and banks. It's not just the driver's license; it's the library card, my senior gold card, my insurance card, and my ORCA card. You have to pay to replace the ORCA and the library card. How will I get home tonight without my ORCA? Not many dollars, but all valuable, particularly if they use my ORCA card, which has at least $20 on it. That's cash, too! Is there a minimum dollar loss to report? If it needs to be $50 or more, I can make it be that easily. Don't forget my debit and credit cards. They could be out charging up thousands of dollars right now. I will be standing in line all over town replacing this stuff. I'd like to get it back before they jump. Okay? That would be a big help to me. Let's go immediately to the bridge so you can arrest them and get my wallet."

"Yeah, yeah, yeah, I hear you about the cards and lines. We'll make sure you get home. But what exactly happened at the library?"

"Do you know the Ballard Library? We were sitting in the same area. I was reading. They were talking, waiting for someone. I couldn't help hearing what they were saying. They talk loudly as though their hearing is bad. It's the conversation of idiots, but the references to the murder, being worried about being caught, how famous jumping would make them, all that stuff began to make sense. So I moved away from them and looked up online the newspaper story I remembered reading about a robbery and murder from a few days ago. It featured a big, grainy security camera photo of someone in a ski hat. Remember that? One of them came up behind me. We had some words. They must have seen me at the bus stop. Believe me, I was hoping to never see them again."

"Would you be able to identify them?"

"Absolutely. Two of them, sweaty, greasy, smelly. Crackheads. Young. The third one that came with the drugs, not so sure he'll still be with them. They don't even look old enough to drive. The security guard will be able to identify them as well."

"How did you become an authority on drugs?"

"I live in the city. I wait at bus stops for public transportation. How could I not know what's for sale and who buys it?"

"You say they are going to the Troll?"

"Yes, the Troll under the Aurora Bridge. Behind it is a place to do drugs. They agreed as soon as 'the dude with the drugs' came they were headed for the bridge, with a last stop at the Troll. That's where we'll find them."

"Well, that's where I looked for them after the EMS picked you up in Ballard. I didn't see anyone like that on the way or behind the Troll, or up on the deck of the bridge."

Laurence looked perplexed for a moment, reviewing the conversation at the library. What was he forgetting? *'You're evil.'* "Zesto's. I forgot they were going to Zesto's first and shoot 'em up in the parking lot or some nonsense. Guns or needles? It's hard to know sometimes what these young idiots are talking about. We know they have at least one gun. You know Zesto's over by the high school, right?"

"Yes, no matter what you have heard, that location is well known to me."

The officer communicated with someone, "About the teenagers I spoke to on 60th Street NW earlier, we're now ready to *stop and identify*. I have a citizen with me who wants to press assault and theft charges. I'm going to try to find them again at Zesto's by the high school."

Laurence looked back as they pulled away into the traffic passing the semicircular entrance to the hospital. A hospital employee with a clipboard was looking around the Emergency entrance, shrugging his shoulders. Whew. What a relief to be away from there. This was quite a day he was having. He was feeling invigorated by the events,

238

even feisty. If he got a chance, he would chase those kids and show off his aerobic fitness from climbing stairs. That would be very satisfying.

The officer drove straight up 15th Avenue to 65th Street. Rounding the corner, the flashing lights of EMS vehicles and police squad cars told them it was an incident, a crime scene. The officer parked the patrol car and said, "Stay inside. Do not get out."

Laurence watched his policeman join his colleagues in a huddle. The EMS workers were busy with three stretchers with bodies on the ground in the parking lot. A crowd inside Zesto's pressed against the big window overlooking the parking lot, watching the action. More people watched from the sidewalk. He couldn't see what looked like anybody being held by the policemen or locked in the back of any of the other squad cars. The kids weren't there. They had done whatever they had done and run. He felt it was a waste of time to be sitting here when they should be on the way to the bridge looking for them.

Sitting in the back of the patrol car waiting for the officer to finish with his comrades, he tried not to think about how hungry he was. The exhaust fan at Zesto's was broadcasting *french fries* loud and clear. It had been so long since Laurence had had a french fry, which made the deep fat fryer oil smell ambrosial. He could smell the beef fat from the burgers dripping into the broiler pan. He had eaten burgers and fries there when they were considered nutritious food, when he was a teenager. These days, Zesto's was all-American junk food for modern teenagers from the high school a block away and a parking lot to hang out in. The glamour of celebrities like Elvis and Governor Rossolini dining there in the 1950s was of little interest to anybody and certainly not the local youth.

The whole sad situation with these juvenile criminals made him shudder at the quantity of human beings who never had a chance to make a positive contribution. The world was likely to end up no good at all with so many wasted possibilities. How many productive minds were necessary to compensate for all the minds that accomplished nothing or reversed the progress of intelligence?

Laurence felt curiously light. Trying to methodically examine this odd sensation, he decided that his personal despair had evaporated into the summer night. The black cloud he had lived with for so long didn't seem to be overhead. His early morning complaints seemed like small potatoes in life's potential for horrors, certainly not enough reasons for feeling sorry for himself. He'd been lucky with Ingrid and the good years of being part of aerospace. He'd had fun with friends like Steve. He wasn't going to become homeless. He wouldn't starve. The slow death at home alone was possible, but maybe he'd get lucky on that, too. Maybe he'd die in his sleep in his own bed that he had made as a young man.

That *lucky* feeling was certainly an indication that something had changed with him. He hadn't felt lucky in a long time. Right now, he was feeling that he was looking forward to sticking to his schedule. He liked his schedule. Creating it to satisfy certain criteria for goals in learning and diversity in daily settings had proved out the model over time. Who knew what might come of his new skills? Things could get *exciting* again. He definitely was feeling different. How long did a man have to fast before visions came to him easily? Surely one long day without eating wasn't enough to explain his odd thoughts and feelings. He wished the policeman would hurry up. He wanted to chase the punks.

Laurence's feet started to cramp, and he decided to stretch his legs and see if opening the door would be enough to get the officer's attention. As soon as he stood up next to the car, stamping his feet and arching his back and neck, sure enough his policeman looked over at him and shook his head no. Laurence took that to mean don't move away from the car, so he continued standing there because it felt good. He kept watching from the far side of the squad car. He wished he could hear what they were saying. Now all the policemen looked at him. He waved at them. His guy was shaking his head again but not at him, probably about him. This chat was taking way too long. They weren't going to catch them standing around here.

Chapter 25

Kevin stood up and said, "The chef says we're ready to move to the table. Follow me."

Kevin took Alexis by the elbow and directed her to a chair next to his at the end of the table. He motioned Ben to the chair next to Alexis. From the painted chest, he picked up the bottle of red wine Ben had brought and one of the white wines he had opened earlier and started pouring wine, giving everyone a sample of a red and a white.

Amy took her seat at the other end of the table, double-checking all the place settings as she waited for everyone to get settled. The aroma of the six portions of otak-otak created a cloud of fresh-baked fish with citrus over the table. The porcelain ramekins with a gold rim were beautiful and the perfect size for a first course, however, next time she would use the aubergine individual casseroles with lids to keep the scent a secret until the cover was lifted. If everyone lifted the lids simultaneously, it would create a powerful display of heat and Asian herbs rising. She touched the side and confirmed the ramekin was maintaining the heat.

She knew what the riesling tasted like having sipped it earlier and was eager to try the elite bottle from California. She stuck her nose deeply into the glass of the Charmstone. Bordeaux blends were one of her favorite styles of wine and this one was hand crafted in the Napa Valley with mostly cabernet sauvignon. It was luscious and fruity, a wine that lived up to its surely lofty price, whatever that was. It would be delicious with anything but was probably better equipped to stand up with the rendang than the fish custard. Ben had shared a bottle with them before at a dinner he had cooked and it was every bit as good as she remembered it. All good!

Drew had Alan's elbow, looking at Amy for guidance even though the only two empty seats were to her right. She was a peach. She wasn't mad a bit. He was glad he had decided to come. The evening so far was fun except for Alan, who was listing badly. Drew followed her signal and seated Alan adroitly in the chair on Amy's right. Old Alan probably shouldn't have had that last round. Drew predicted he would be an early casualty. Alan intelligently put his hand over his wine glasses in the no signal when Kevin paused by him.

Drew took his seat between Alan and Kevin, directly across from Alexis. He was happy there was a seat for him at this table shining with sterling silver. He appreciated the attention to detail on the table. Smart hostess to set up whatever was coming for the best possible reaction. He smiled at Alexis, who was still pretending she didn't know him. He would find a moment to apologize to her privately and try to de-fang her hostility. He was glad Julie wasn't here, as she would have bitten into the blue hair thing like a pit bull when no one here seemed inclined to make a big deal about it. What a mellow crowd this was, obviously old friends. He was happy to play along at being someone who was forgettable. That was a riot! He was enjoying himself more than he thought he might. He'd really only come because he didn't have anything else to do. Other plans had fallen through, and he wasn't in the mood for staying home with takeout or sitting in a restaurant by himself. He had guessed there would be plenty of food and a warm welcome for a *somewhat* invited guest. It sure was a pleasant change to be sitting at a well-set table. He liked all the old school style and comfort.

243

He thought Kevin had done a good job editing the photos. The quantity was perfect for a little entertainment. They were decent photos, not commercial quality, but above-average tourist snapshots with a point-and-shoot digital camera. Drew was excited about trying the food. He didn't think he'd ever had Malaysian food. He considered himself a sophisticated eater who enjoyed being wined and dined, particularly by clients. The location of the new gallery wasn't working that well for his Eastside patrons, who had been the most generous with dinner invitations. Maybe he'd have to open something closer to the 520 bridge to keep those contacts active. He definitely planned to work on this couple. He sensed they could be buyers of smaller things that work in a small house like this one.

As the otak-otak began wafting from little cups toward him, the first note was lime and then lemon as in Thai food. Drew had anticipated a Chinese influence on the food Amy had talked about as his reference point. He snuck a quick bite while Kevin was still pouring wine. Ah, it was salty and fishy with sweet garlic. He liked it.

Kevin put the white bottle in the crystal bucket by Amy's place setting and put the red on the wine coaster in front of his plate where he could reach it easily. Surveying the table after taking his seat with all the eyes looking at him, he appreciated the aesthetics of the scene and smiled, raising his glass. "I thank you all for coming and my beautiful wife for sharing her cooking class with us."

Cheers and *ching-ching* all around the table as everyone raised their glass and touched the glasses near them. Amy beamed at Kevin. It was a very festive noise, Drew thought.

"Tell me the truth, Alan. Which one of your lovelies was supposed to be in this chair tonight?" Drew asked.

"I can't remember now, I have so many."

244

"The mystery girl is going to remain mysterious," Kevin said. "Too bad, not enough twenty-three-year-olds pass through this door, but you have your charms, Drew. Nice goatee to go with the short cut. Is that the boho Sodo look? Am I behind the times with my haircut?"

"Mine is definitely boho, as well as the I haven't got quite as much as I used to look. With all the hair you have, I'd say you can flaunt it anyway you want."

Kevin touched his graying temples and looked up as though to confirm how much hair he had on the top of his head. Yep, it was all still there.

Amy looked at Ben and smiled. "I hope you're not crushed, too, being deprived of a youthful visual?"

"Only semi-crushed. I recover quickly from disappointment, particularly where youth is concerned. We have some at the office so I'm up to date on the user experience."

"I agree. Give me an accomplished, worldly woman who knows how to cook like this. That's what I like." Drew put another bite in his mouth and winked at Amy.

"You're welcome, Drew. I'm so glad you came tonight." Amy raised her glass and said, "We all need to taste this amazing red wine that seldom comes through our door and thank Ben for sharing his wine club bounty from California. You can't buy this at retail."

Everyone took a sip or a gulp and nodded their appreciation toward Ben.

He shrugged, "Our pleasure," and dug into the otak-otak, which was still hot and steaming, noting the green shiso leaf garnish for its color and perfect size on the small dish. He was savoring the creaminess and the fermented fish on his tongue. His nose caught the kaffir lime and the lemongrass, but he didn't taste either of them in a pronounced way.

Amy admired the table and the faces around it in the soft lighting. Kevin was immersed in quiet conversation with Alexis. Everyone looked happy and animated. They had really enjoyed the photos. She was so pleased about everything.

After a generous first mouthful of the Milbrandt riesling, Ben put down his glass. He looked at her and nodded. "Quite nice. I think the texture of the custard is perfect. I get the lime and lemon aroma, while I taste the umami, that shrimp paste you were telling me about, but everything is so integrated, I need more details about it. What else is in it beside garlic and chilies?"

"You are such a good taster! I think you got it all but two pieces of the puzzle that were new to me, too. Galangal is subtler than ginger and paired with lemongrass in Malaysian recipes. Fresh turmeric, which I'd never seen before, seems to tie things together like the base note of the shrimp paste, but it can make things bitter if you use too much. I've read it's more about being a rose fragrance, gold color, and preservative, but I personally don't get the fragrance at all. That could be the quality of the product here."

"Uwajamaya has the galangal and the turmeric?"

"Yes. Who knew? What do you think about the wine with it? I'm trying to break out of my sauvignon blanc world. I thought about a viognier, but there's so much local riesling out there to try."

"I like the peachy, effervescent quality to it. I think it's great with the fish that's been seduced by golden cream." Ben stuck his nose back in the glass and sipped again pleased with his description.

Amy looked at Alan on her right side to see if he was following the conversation. Actually, Alan looked a little wobbly upon closer look.

"Alan, tell everyone how you are enjoying being unemployed."

"I wish never to work again. This respite has shown me my true calling."

"Did I tell you yet tonight that I hate my job?" Ben was grinning at Alan.

"Yes, even I can recall you saying that."

"How did I miss it?" said Drew.

"You weren't here when I got here. I try to fit it into the conversation right away, just in case anyone forgot from the last time."

Drew raised his wine glass. "To all who love their job."

"Yow! Drew, we don't have anyone here who can drink to that." Amy looked down the table making eye contact with Kevin.

"OK. I'll take it. My job beats daytime TV. It provides me with a place to go every day. It pays for a few things, too, not enough, but the essentials."

"That's weak. Is that the best you can do?"

That's love in my book." Kevin raised and lowered his glass to Drew.

"I love Kevin's job!" said Amy, raising her wine glass to him.

"No fair," said Drew. You can't like it for him. What about your own?"

"I don't go to the snake pit anymore. I'm reinventing myself as a 'nonworking spouse,' one of those odd situations the feminists, like me, hate, but other people envy."

"Well, what are you doing to juggle the mixed emotions?" Drew looked at her while she composed her answer.

"Working hard at my new responsibilities as the FLM, family lifestyle manager. I have already achieved positive results from new policies. Kevin, tell Drew how much you enjoy the royal welcome you get now when you come home, plus fifty-nine minutes of uninterrupted listening."

Kevin shook his head no, he wasn't commenting.

"I didn't use to be so sympathetic to the stresses in his day. Does Julie have a limit on nightly sympathy?"

"I'd say about two minutes." Drew grinned.

"Alexis, how sympathetic are you?" Amy asked.

Ben gave Alexis an uplifted eyebrow as if daring her. "Tell the truth."

"Well, I'd say somewhere in between two and fifty-nine minutes, but no royal welcome." Alexis laughed and looked at Ben.

Ben shook his head smiling. "She means between two and five minutes. Numbers aren't her strong suit."

"Amy, would you call me a taxi, please?" Alan said.

"Are we boring you already? It's your turn next to tell them again how much you love not working. You don't want to eat anything else?" Amy looked at his half-eaten otak-otak.

"No, I've had plenty. It was delicious. Would you call me a taxi, please?"

She looked him in the eye and he nodded and she nodded back and got up and went into the kitchen, silently cursing this ridiculous turn of events. Shaking her head, she thought, *How annoying*, while scrolling for the number in the auto dial menu. With it ringing in her ear, she stood in front of the refrigerator out of the sight of Kevin at the end of the table and Alexis if she should turn around. *These people had better be on the ball tonight, answer the phone, and have a taxi ready.* Lately they had not, and listening to the stupid automated answer saying she was third in line didn't make her feel she was valued at all.

"Would you call me a taxi, please?"

Alan was standing two inches away from her face, bathing her in the not-unpleasant aroma of vodka and otak-otak. That might be a better pairing than the riesling. "I'm doing it right now," she said, waving the phone at him. "We're waiting for the next available operator."

248

She maneuvered him back into the corner of the countertop with the phone still pressed in between her ear and shoulder to prop him up and stay out of sight. He wobbled as she moved away, so she leaned against him to keep him in place. He put his arms around her waist to hold her to him or just to hold on. There was no break in the conversation at the table. She wanted to keep this quiet and not disrupt the dinner. Her two bites of the fish had melted in her mouth, the fresh fish flavor just what she had hoped for, and she wished she could surreptitiously grab the ramekin and finish eating it while it was hot. She was hungry. Drat, there was no glass or bottle in reach, either. The rendang smelled delicious, which meant to her it was ready. She opened the warming drawer with the end of her sandal and toes to look inside. It was bubbling gently at the sides of the casserole dish, the indication it was maintaining the heat throughout. At last, a human voice broke through the recorded music. She closed the drawer with the side of her foot.

"I need a taxi right now, please," she said firmly and gave her phone number. "An hour! Are you serious? That's terrible service. Okay, what choice do I have?" She hung up the phone and turned around and put her hand on his elbow.

"Alan, it's going to be an hour. Why don't you have a nap in the guest room?"

"Sure. If that's okay with you."

"It's no problem." They walked together into the guest room off the dining room. She turned on the light and pulled back the down comforter embroidered with pink rosebuds and pushed the decorative pillows to the side.

Alan politely kicked off his shoes and promptly sprawled out diagonally. "This is a great bed. I should sleep here more often."

Amy turned off the light, closed the door, and stood behind Kevin's chair with her hands on his

249

shoulders, looking at everyone's empty dishes. "Sweetheart, if we're ready to serve the next course, will you clear and offer more red wine? I have two interesting choices to go with the next course that are thought to go well with bold flavors. Let's put both on the table for everyone to try. I'd like to know if you agree."

She went in the kitchen, grabbed the potholders to remove the rendang from the warming drawer, and transferred the rice from the rice cooker into a ceramic bowl. Reentering the dining room, she put the rice down close to Alexis and came back with the casserole dish securely in two hands with potholders.

She presented the rendang to Alexis. "Please serve yourself. This is chicken rendang and the dish is too hot to handle, but the rice is not. We'll pass the rice." As she walked around the table she told them about the Australian grenache-shiraz blend and a California zinfandel, both she thought were food friendly and big enough to work nicely with the rendang. If anyone didn't enjoy those combinations, and thought the wines were too big, there was a California sangiovese to fall back on that was an excellent supporting player.

Amy took her seat when everyone was served. Regrettably, the last of her otak-otak had gone cold and been cleared away before she could finish it, but the exotic aroma of the rendang was rising up around the table and from her plate, requiring her complete attention now. She tasted the rendang. The time in the warming drawer had not hurt the sauce. It was still moist and not the least bit dry looking. She sighed in relief. Let's add warming drawers to the great inventions list right after refrigerators and Novocain. It tasted just as she remembered it from this afternoon, maybe better. The browned coconut was working its magic with nutty flavor and richness on top of the spicy but not too spicy curry. The chicken was tender. She had forgotten to scatter the chopped cilantro on top, which would have added bright green to the gold dish, freshness, and a sweet fragrance, but no one would notice. She looked around at the group all busy eating and sipping. No one reached for the salt dish or the pepper grinder. Ben's wine tasted elegant. She wondered how much the extra time in the glass might have improved what was good to begin with. Wouldn't it be nice if Kevin would join this wine club to have a bottle in the cellar for special occasions!

She was aggravated with Alan for not being his usual self, but she would not dwell on it now. After the odd bump with Alexis when Drew arrived, everything else was going well. Surely Alexis would tell her about him later or tomorrow. Amy was glad to see Drew. He was being a very good guest, paying attention to her and telling her something funny about his employees running cheap vodka through a Brita filter to make expensive vodka for parties at the gallery. Amy and Ben were ready to begin experimenting tomorrow. Infusions with ginger and lemons would be a great project for a vat of cheap vodka.

Alexis felt she was enjoying herself for what seemed like the first time in ages. Kevin was being very attentive to her while engaging Ben in a discussion about the music Ben had brought him on the CD. She felt thin and glad she had selected the blue silk dress, which had received positive reviews from every man here when she had arrived. Although Drew hadn't said a word about the dress, that's probably what reminded him of the blue hair. She knew he had noticed it as part of studying her, assessing the differences since he had last seen her. No question he thought she was still attractive after all these years. That almost made up for his obnoxious presence.

She loved being in the middle of the three men. She felt like the center of the action even though neither Ben nor Drew was speaking to her directly about anything. She was relishing watching Drew tiptoe around her, being deferential to her and to everyone. He was conducting himself in a very polished way. This is how the bullshit artist works: He listens carefully and responds appropriately. He knew what they were talking about and made himself appear to easily fit into the group. He was the same smoothie she remembered, all charm and guile, with no morals whatsoever. The opening exchange with him had revved her adrenalin and made her feel sharp and awake. She had shown him she wasn't to be trifled with. He knew that she knew exactly who he was and he was showing respect not to push it any further because these were her friends and he was probably after them for business. Everybody else seemed to believe her and accepted the painting class as some long ago event the two of them participated in. Nobody had said another word about it. Tomorrow she forecasted an animated conversation with Ben about the blue hair period, which he wasn't going to learn much about, as it was so brief and unmemorable in tomorrow's version. That's why she couldn't remember Drew. Ben wouldn't push it tonight. He had common sense about privacy in public and was too busy eating and drinking everything he could get his hands on. After dinner, he would sleep soundly for about twelve hours, a good thing after his wretched week, and then he would be ready to roll again.

She wondered what Drew's wife was like and if she knew the truth about him. Where was she tonight? Amy had said traveling, but had she said where? She probably wasn't a wife. Amy had said "woman." Marriage and Drew seemed incongruous.

The wine was a pleasure, too, particularly the red one they had brought. It felt like velvet in her mouth and was perfectly balanced between fruit and acidity. It tasted expensive. That bottle had been consumed promptly after being poured into five glasses. She was glad Ben had decided to bring a really good bottle that showed their appreciation of Amy cooking for them. The food, so far, was top notch. She'd loved the cold crab starter that Amy frequently served and the hot custard thing, whatever it was. The funny name escaped her. It was curry-like, but not like Indian curry, more subtle. She felt there was a delicacy to these dishes she had not encountered in Indian, Chinese, or Thai food. The chicken dish seemed very substantial compared with the custard. The sauce was so hearty and so bold it could be beef or pork and she wouldn't know. The crepes were light with a whiff of vanilla from the rustic brush made with green leaves. Amy was all fired up about this cooking class and she could see why. All the flavors were different but not too weird or too hot and spicy. Amy was a chili head and sometimes went overboard with heat. Kevin was being so affable tonight. Sometimes he seemed so reserved, but not tonight. She could see it in their faces they had really had a good time on vacation. She and Ben would have to come up with something splendid to reciprocate in the winter.

The photos of their trip had made her want to cry that she wasn't going anywhere any time soon. They weren't spending any money until she found a new job and Ben felt more confident he wasn't going to be fired or laid off. It could be a long time before they went even to the East Coast to visit family. Malaysia was colorful in the way Mexican markets were with bright stacks of textiles in stalls and dark-haired beauties taking the money. What would be the Malaysian equivalents of margaritas and mole? This rendang could be the mole. She would ask Kevin about the tourists' favorite cocktail.

She was disappointed Alan had flaked out so early. She had been looking forward to chatting with him on the way home. He seemed a little off his game during cocktails, not as sharp as usual, a little blurry. She wasn't completely surprised when he got up so suddenly, but she pretended not to notice. A good hostess takes care of these things quietly, just like Amy did, shuttling him to the guest room. There was no reason to disturb the party.

253

It was totally his loss. Amy should be mad at him for missing the party.

Alexis was really impressed with how smoothly Amy was hosting this evening, considering the shock on Western Avenue and all the surprise guests. She seemed to be shrugging that insult off quickly. That might be a first for Amy, who could be a drama queen about odd things most people wouldn't worry about. Alexis knew she might not have been as gracious as Amy was about the unexpected guest, Drew, even if she liked him. The uninvited guest and the no-show were ridiculous. That wouldn't happen at her house. Alexis would never have let that old man in the front door and she would have insisted Alan call his friend the minute he arrived without her. Natalie dissing Amy was so high school. People did things like that to feel superior, assuming they'd get away with it, and of course, deny it, if ever confronted. "Oh no, I didn't see her." It was another example of why it made no sense to be too close to anyone. There's no pain if you keep a little distance. Care too much and you'll eventually be tortured. She was a believer in staying back out of the zone where people think they have you. That was Amy's mistake again and again. She threw herself into people and activities—and got burned.

Alexis tried to make little of these events that upset Amy, shrugging her shoulders and shaking her head, slightly sympathetic but not much response. "Why do you care? That woman is an idiot." It was her way of trying to make Amy feel like it wasn't that big a deal, whether it was or not. The irony was the complaints she had had to listen to about Amy, who was capable of delivering some insults herself that she seemed totally unaware of. Amy would be astonished if she knew that every time she said no it caused a ripple. First, it surprised people when she declined invitations. Then they thought she was snobby. Then they got mad. Amy didn't realize how invincible she looked to people who didn't know her well. Alexis had a similar response for those people as the one she gave Amy. "Why do you care? Aim higher." Amy wasn't super smart. She hadn't been to a good school. She was harmless at the office. What Alexis really thought was Amy's charm was that she was fun. You never had to worry about her boring you to death.

So why did Natalie feel like she needed to stick it to her? The surprising thing about this Natalie event was it sure had looked like they were good friends. Natalie seemed to be such a cool operator. She seemed to thrive on being overbooked or was she just bragging about her calendar? Alexis had watched her at parties at Amy's. She and Ben had been invited to her house once. It was high style in every way, Lake Washington views, flowers all over the place, and every surface styled for a photo shoot with boxes, bowls, and frames. It was a nice party with lots of laughs, but she had never invited them to her house. She didn't want to be on those terms with Natalie and her husband. It wasn't that it could get tricky trying to be friends of friends, which Alexis usually but not always avoided; they were a little too freshly dressed and coiffed for her. Alexis liked a more random approach to her decor, as though the furniture had been rearranged at a party last night and not yet put back in place, but that was a *look,* too, she knew. Her costume tonight gave the air of simplicity, one intense color, no accessories except her hair and skin, just a powerful dress that she might have thrown on without much deliberation but in fact had taken quite a while to decide on. As they used to say in college, "It takes the Brown girls a remarkably long time to look like they haven't spent any time getting ready."

She loved her old college friends who lived on the East Coast and would be friends until they died—because she didn't see them often enough to foul it up or wear it out. They exchanged long letters or phone calls once or twice a year. That was enough for her. The in-town

255

friends they tried to see only once or twice a year and that was perfect as there would be plenty to talk about. If you saw anyone more than that, they knew all the details and they started feeling like you owed them something.

What were the odds of running into Drew here tonight after all these years? She seldom thought of him, and it had been a long time since she worried about running into him. But obviously, she was still angry about how he had treated her. The immediate venom that surfaced from within her had taken her by surprise. She hadn't felt like scratching someone's eyes out in recent memory and was glad to know she still had that lifesaving instinct. He was disrupting her attempts at focusing on being receptive for new inspiration. Blast Alan for not being available to chat on the way home. She had planned to ask him a few questions about his old friend Drew, who he had never mentioned before. Why was that?

Chapter 26

Finally, his policeman headed back to the patrol car. Laurence waited for him to explain the situation. The facts were few. Three injured. No sign of whoever did the shooting. Vague, inconsistent descriptions of the shooters were all the police had gleaned from the parking lot witnesses. It had happened really fast. They looked like ordinary students from the high school, but no one knew their names. They had run off while everyone stood around dumbfounded.

"What's the plan?" Laurence asked when he thought no more information was coming.

"Your suggestion of the bridge will be followed up on. One car will go there quickly and wait. Another will go looking for them on foot."

"Well, it could take them an hour to walk there even if they used small streets and backyards. They wouldn't walk on 65th or Leary Way, where it would be easy to see them. Are we going quickly or slowly?"

"You're not going."

"Who can identify them better than I can?"

"We'll bring you down to the station when we have them in custody."

"I know you have your protocols and instructions. But I think we need to hurry if you want to catch them alive. They may very well have jumped on the #28 bus. It goes by within a block of here every thirty minutes, and they might have been lucky to see one when they were running. They have my ORCA card, remember. If so, they could already be at the bridge as long as we have been here." Laurence's irritation with the police speed and the strategy was showing through even though he was trying to be calm and even. He didn't want to appear to be challenging the policeman's plan.

"I'm going to take you home now, sir, and we'll call you when we need you."

"That's very inefficient since I'm here now and can point them out in a crowd. Let me go to the bridge with you, the quickest possible way, and if we don't see them en route or at the bridge, then you can take me home. But I don't have a telephone, so if you need me later you'll have no way to contact me and will have further to go to pick me up."

The policeman shook his head at that last bit of information. "Get in the car." He turned on his flashing lights but not the siren and pulled out onto 64th heading east.

Laurence watched both sides of the street carefully, hoping they would get lucky on the way to the bridge. It would be so great to see them, grab them, and get his wallet back before anything else could happen. The shooting in the parking lot gave him the creeps. They were worse human beings than he had imagined. Who knew what unlucky person would cross their path next?

The squad car stopped in front of the troll, and the officer got out with the engine and lights running and another instruction to Laurence to stay inside. He ran up the small hill to take a look behind the statue and came right back.

"Nobody back there." He got back in the car and drove around the block to jockey back into position for approaching the bridge from Fremont Way North, which ran one way the direction he needed. He stopped the car in front of the last bus stop before the bridge. Laurence looked at the people waiting for a bus and saw how they were looking at him. They wondered what he had done. Wouldn't they be surprised to know he was being chauffeured, not arrested? While he watched, the policeman spoke with them about whom they had seen. They all shook their heads. Nobody had noticed two teenagers get off a bus or run up or run away. Back in the car, the policeman drove up onto the bridge slowly enough to force the Saturday night traffic to follow him at a leisurely pace. Who wants to pass a police car with the lights flashing? Laurence watched the pedestrian path on his right. He couldn't see the other side clearly because the pedestrian safety wall blocked his view.

As they approached the Queen Anne U-turn, the officer said, "This is the end of the road for you. What's the quickest way to your place from here?"

"Why not use the U-turn and take a good look at the other pedestrian walkway?"

"No, they are not here. Who knows where they are or when they might show up here, if they do at all. I have to get back to work, and I can't do that until I deposit you some place safe and out of the way."

"I still think I am your best chance of finding them. Let me help you. I'll stay in the car."

"No. You have done all you can do to help, and now it's time for you to say goodnight. I'm giving you a free ride at the taxpayers' expense. What's the address?"

"I beg your pardon. I am an aerospace engineer, a taxpayer, and have been all my life." He could feel his last chance to get his wallet back and make sure these kids were caught alive sliding out of his reach over a stupid telephone. Who had a phone he could use? He really didn't know any of his neighbors well enough to know if they had a phone. He'd never been in any of the apartments of the people he saw in the hallways.

"What's the address?"

"West McGraw by Ken's Market."

"That's close by."

When the squad car pulled up in front, he said, "Nice digs. You fooled me with the no phone."

259

"It's not my house, but they have a phone, so you can call me as soon as you think you see them. Taking them into custody may not be an option. I'll wait here for your call. That's the most efficient way. I was invited to eat dinner here, so I know they are at home."

"Whatever you say, sir."

Chapter 27

Ben helped himself to another serving of the rendang and the rice. This was a good party! The martinis had worked like magic. The office had disappeared from his thoughts. The food and wine were stimulating his nose, lips, mouth, and all the way down his throat. What an adventure in flavor this food was and full of surprises. He felt like his whole head was tingling from the spices, not from hot chili but the combinations of citrus and cream, the ginger and garlic, the salty and the sweet. Amy would send him the recipes tomorrow. He would make some experiments with the spices and herbs. Heat, particularly slow heat, versus fast high heat was one aspect of developing and accentuating flavors. Some Chinese food depended on the high heat of the wok to char smokiness into the food. But this had none of that element. It was slowed cooked at low temperatures. He was sure of that but had confirmed it by asking her. He loved Amy's idea of braising a five-blade roast with the Belacan shrimp paste as the main seasoning as a test of the power of the ingredient. She felt the fermented shrimp paste was the central and essential Malaysian base flavor. He would try the otak-otak without the Belacan. He might try it also with his favorite brand of anchovies and see what happened when east meets Italy. Deconstructing the recipes and trying the ingredients individually with and without cooking would be illuminating. He didn't know any better way to test new flavors.

The table was overflowing with dishes and glasses, as was his plate with the generous portions he intended to consume to the last bite. All his senses were gratified. He agreed with everyone the small crepes were perfect with this food. His very special bottle of wine had been well received, drunk quickly, and followed by an Australian blend that was not in the same league but pleasing. More to try was already open. He wished he could think of that Maugham quote about "excess," maybe it would come to him later. Nothing could be more appropriate about this meal than that quote.

Alexis seemed relaxed and happy. What a relief. The odd man out was okay, too. The blue hair remark seemed to make Alexis sharpen her weapons, but he had backed down, which was smart of him. Alexis did not always fight fair. He would ask her about him tomorrow. He must be part of the timeline when she had decided to embrace a full-time corporate job with a salary and health benefits and become a part-time painter. She still didn't appreciate what a smart decision that had been. She saw the decision as a materialistic sell-out and it wasn't. It was realistic. Money and benefits were important, especially if you enjoyed spending it as much as Alexis did. She spent more money on a stick of butter than some people did on a bottle of wine. She was creative at her job and had never stopped painting as so many wannabe artists did after taking a paying job. *That* would have been a failure to be sad about. He was curious what role this gallery guy had in it. Maybe he was one of the ones who said she wasn't good. Who wouldn't hold a grudge about that uninformed critique? Ben thought Alexis was a very good painter and loved the art of hers they had selected to hang in the house, although he hoped some of the recent pieces stayed down in her studio forever. Ben would go by himself some time to see this man's gallery, just to see how unusual and eclectic it was. Amy and Kevin weren't necessarily the arbiters of art.

It certainly hadn't bothered him that Alan had passed out. He hadn't contributed that much humor tonight. Alexis had had her little flirtation and should be happy about the short drive home. The hostess was enjoying her party. He liked it when that happened. Actually, that was one of Amy's talents; she thoroughly enjoyed herself. Even the host at the other end of the table, who usually kept on a face to go with his dry wit, seemed to be pleased, almost jolly, as he should be. This evening was outstanding on all scores.

"This is amazing stuff. What other meats might be used?" Ben asked Amy in between bites and sips.

"Anything, I think. Rohani specified chicken or beef, that shows how versatile the sauce is, but why not pork? The Muslims don't eat it, but the Chinese sure do."

"Well, it really is fun to see the photos and then eat the food. It's made an impression on me that's almost like going, call it virtual travel, but a lot less hassle. I would hate the plane ride."

"Thanks. I think in this economy we all have to travel vicariously through each other. Sometimes I doubt I'll ever see Europe again. I suppose vacationing in South America and Asia is a high-end problem to have."

Ben smiled in agreement and caught Kevin's eye. "Keep your wife in high-end problems, okay. She's doing good work here. More cooking classes!"

Kevin nodded at him. "That's my goal. Glad you're enjoying the food. You can see why we were happy about the trip. It was interesting every day."

Kevin was pleased about the evening he hadn't been looking forward to at all. Everyone was enjoying themselves and appreciating his spare-no-expense attitude. The food was exceptional. It tasted to him just as good as what they had eaten in Malaysia. Whatever the secrets were to this cuisine, she seemed to have them in her control. Amy looked thrilled. She made him feel like a lucky man to have the job of providing the castle. He was

263

sure Ben and Drew were envious of him tonight and wondering how he deserved all this lifestyle. He wasn't sure himself, but he did work hard at maintaining it. Right now, he was glad to be sharing his largesse, and they all seemed worthy of it. Oh, the marvelous sense of well-being and humor from good food and drink. Tomorrow he knew he would be content with a frugal, quiet day with no interactions or interruptions from the world except Amy going on about all the details of the evening. That would require no effort from him. He could listen, enjoy her pleasure in her success, relax, and then go see that documentary.

Thor bolted for the front door. Amy looked up at the ceiling and around the table in disbelief. "Who could that be now?" She was headed for the door as the doorbell rang. She peered through the security view and opened the door wide, letting Thor dance around the two men standing there, a policeman and Laurence. She stared at them and said, "Well, hello, gentlemen, what can I do for you?"

The officer took charge, introducing himself and explaining that Mr. Hansen had requested to come to this location because it had a telephone and he had been invited to dinner. Amy kind of resented him for inferring that the telephone and invitation might not be true.

"Of course, Officer. We have a phone, and Laurence was invited to dinner, twice actually, weeks ago and no later than this morning. I didn't think he was coming. That's why I was so surprised to see you. Is there a problem?"

"Do you mind giving me your phone number in the event we need to speak to him later this evening?"

"Of course not." She gave him the number. "Anything else I can help you with?"

"No, thank you. I'll be leaving now and I guess he is staying." He looked at Amy expectantly.

"Oh, yes," she said finally getting his cue, "please come in, Laurence. Good night, Officer."

She led Laurence into the dining room to stand with her by her place at the end of the table where every eye was on them and no one was saying a word. Kevin, she was appreciative, was on his feet, waiting, ready to do whatever might be required of the host. "This is Laurence Hansen, a friend from the library I told you about, who didn't think he would be able to come for dinner tonight, but has had a change of plans. This is my husband, Kevin." Kevin came over and shook his hand. Everyone else stayed seated. Amy said the name of each person beginning with Alexis, who smiled and said hello. Ben and Drew just nodded at Laurence.

"Please sit here," she said, indicating Alan's chair. The place setting looked like it was ready for him with nothing missing except for the salad fork Alan had used for the otak-otak. He'd never even taken his napkin out of the ring. The new guest would not know there had been a previous occupant.

Laurence had nodded to each person as introduced and continued standing behind the empty chair considering his response to the welcome. "My apologies for arriving so late and somewhat unexpectedly. It's nice to meet you." With that politeness out of the way, he sat down.

"Would you like a glass of wine or a cocktail?" Amy asked.

He looked around the table at what everyone else had and said, "Red wine, please, thank you."

Kevin said, "I'll pour you some wine." He grabbed the closest bottle and walked around the table to pour wine generously in the red wine glass Alan had declined. No point in *tasting* at this time of night. Kevin couldn't wait to hear how Amy was going to integrate the Kindle guy into the group. *This should be good.*

Laurence sat uneasily and watched the wine being poured. He didn't seem to know what else to do or say and everyone was watching him quietly.

Amy was still standing by her chair, watching Kevin and contemplating her next move. *Let's put some traction on this welcome.* When the wine was poured, she picked up her glass and said, "Cheers, Laurence, we're so glad you could make it after all. I told everyone about the electric reader you were developing before you retired from Boeing. They were all fascinated. Ben is an engineer, too, and would love to know more about it. I'm going to warm up the dinner for you." She smiled at Ben, thinking, *You're IT, Ben!*

Ben looked at Amy as she walked around the table to pick up the serving dishes of rendang and rice and disappear into the kitchen. He looked at Laurence and paused for what seemed like a long time to everyone else at the table before he said, "There are always inventors who don't get credit. Did you know any of the guys who are listed on the patent filed in 2006?"

Laurence took a sip of his wine and took as long to answer, as Ben had to formulate his question. "No. I have no idea who is on the patent. Unfortunately I didn't know anyone working on the idea either. No one in my group was working on it with me, although they were interested. I corresponded for a while with a Boeing electrical engineer in southern California. He thought it was a promising idea, but he had no solution at the time for the lighting issues and he died before I retired. It was just my hobby at the office. Everyone in those days had something on the side."

"I'm an electrical engineer from MIT. I know all about those office hobbies and have helped a few friends and professors with projects. All those guys had hobbies at home, too. What did you pursue at home?" Ben asked as though he knew the answer would be interesting.

"I'm a UW man, in aeronautics. At home I worked with wood, mostly to build furniture. Baking was a hobby, too."

Ben laughed. "I told you, Alexis, every engineer has alternate energies! I, too, have kitchen skills, but I'm currently involved in recycling scrap metal into cold smokers for fish. The welding process is my new passion. Functional art I call it. What sort of baking do you do?"

"Sweets, mostly for good causes. My wife and I were known for our Scandinavian pastries like Lefse and Fattigman to sell at the holiday Yulefest to raise money at the Swedish Cultural Center. We made Krumkake for ice cream for children's events. Are you familiar?"

"Would that be three examples of dough rolled so thin you can practically see through it?"

Laurence smiled ever so slightly and nodded. "The first two certainly fit that description. The Krumkake needs only to be poured scantily to get the perfect thinness and crispness but be strong enough to hold the scoop of ice cream without breaking."

"You must be a pasta maker also?"

"Of course." Laurence spoke quietly but confidently. He sipped his wine and looked around the table to see they were all looking at him, but now it didn't feel stressful. They were listening to him. He was the center of attention. That was a heady feeling.

Amy returned with a dinner plate heaped with rendang and rice to place in front of Laurence. "Here you have the main event, a traditional dish, all the way from Kuala Lumpur. Is there any of my thick, heavy roti left?" Amy tried to make a joke. "No, well, that's good. I'll give you a rain check on my roti jala when I've practiced a few more times." She sat down and took a sip of her wine to watch his reaction to the food.

Everyone watched Laurence take a small bite and chew carefully. He looked up and seeing the audience paused before he said, "I always eat slowly, but this habit also provides an opportunity to observe the ingredients. This is a very nice curry made from shallots, garlic, chilies, lemongrass, kaffir lime, and coconut. But I do not recognize the other ingredients. I haven't had any curry in a while."

Amy looked at him, bedazzled. "Oh, my god, that's a parlor trick! Laurence, I knew you were good, but you amaze me. Ben, are you impressed?"

"Yes." Ben was nodding his head, plenty impressed. "Well, Laurence, you get the prize for naming the most ingredients, and you didn't see the photos of the flora and fauna, but you were stumped by the same I was stumped by, the fresh turmeric and galangal, a softer ginger."

Laurence shook his head as he finished another bite. "I have never seen or eaten fresh turmeric, but I get it now, not like powdered. I should have known by the gold color. I didn't taste any ginger."

Kevin said, "Thank you, Laurence, for joining us in this Malaysian extravaganza. It means a lot to the chef that you enjoy it and understand it."

Drew said, "I am so glad to meet you. I'd like to invite you to a pasta contest that I'm organizing. It's for a good cause, and you can be a judge."

"Oh, no, I don't think I could do that." Laurence shook his head and looked at Drew.

"You absolutely could do it better than anyone I know in town who fancies himself a pasta maker. I'll forward you the information to review and you can see who's involved." He pulled out his iPhone. "What's your email?"

Laurence, stunned to be asked, and so forcefully, to do anything by a complete stranger, gave him his gmail account, without any extra information and went back to eating the piquant curry. How pleasurable were the citrus aromas and flavors as bright accents on the rich coconut cream that coated his tongue. He could taste the toasted coconut in the cream, what a great double emphasis that was. He had been so hungry and the more he ate, the more it seemed like he wanted to eat. The portion was twice as much as he normally had, and he felt like he would finish it all easily. The wine tasted sublime. He couldn't remember when he'd last had nice red wine, or any wine, and what a big glassful the husband had poured him as though he knew he was thirsty. He was relieved he'd been asked for an email, not a phone number, which would have begun a predictable reaction around the table about his lack of telephone at home. The gmail account stored research information on his projects that he sent to himself from the library databases. No one here would know he checked his mail at the library. He didn't want to appear indigent in front of this crowd, which was proving to be more interesting than he imagined it might. In fact, they all seemed quite intelligent and capable of listening, two attributes not necessarily bound together.

Amy couldn't stop watching Laurence eat. He seemed to be relishing every bite as though he was famished. His arrival had given her a moment of panic, but she could see it was all going to work out just fine. She looked at Kevin and silently acknowledged that all was well and more stimulating than she ever thought the evening could be. The unexpected guests were earning their dinner. First Drew and now Laurence had really perked the crowd up. They had been having a good time, but now it was fascinating. Amy felt a surge of pride in her idea of creating the party and being aware of how much everyone was enjoying the food and each other. The thrill she was feeling at the moment was what kept a hostess coming back to the planning stage again and again. This evening was her unique performance art not to be re-created anywhere else in the world, ever. She could host a dozen Malaysia night events and no two would be alike. How could anyone not think this was fun?

Kevin watched Amy from the other end of the table and could see her satisfaction in herself as she watched Laurence eat. He loved watching her enjoy herself. She worked so hard to make it be fun for everyone and she had succeeded again. He never doubted her ability and wondered why she ever doubted herself. Ben and Drew were chatting now about photography software programs. Alexis was listening quietly, not participating but seemed to be relaxed. Amy and Laurence were discussing the curry paste technique in different cuisines.

"Kevin, I was thinking about those stone buildings you said were the British government offices, that this was the place where Somerset Maugham hung out in colonial times, and wrote *Rain* and *the Outstation*, is that right?" asked Ben.

"You bet. I haven't read them, though; they were listed in the guidebook, along with Maugham's favorite bar and anecdotes about what a bad drunk he was most of the time," Kevin said and sat forward in his seat.

Drew pounced on the small break. "Have you seen the Gloria Swanson silent film *Sadie Thompson*? That's the classic Maugham in Malaysia story to me."

"Yes, I have and that's exactly what I am talking about. It was made from the short story 'Miss Thompson' and then again as the movie with sound titled *Rain*," Ben said, looking around for more wine. "Getting low here, boss," he added, looking at Kevin.

Kevin handed the bottle in front of him to Alexis to pass to Ben. "Laurence, please help yourself to more wine. Ben doesn't mind sharing." After Laurence nodded at him he looked at Drew and said, "I love Gloria Swanson's silent films. I think Malaysia is more famous as a setting for Joseph Conrad. *Lord Jim* and *Victory* have sort of a Malaysian location and both have been made into movies several times."

270

"Too bad Alan isn't here to get the facts straight. I bet he's read the whole genre," Drew said.

Kevin looked at him and smiled, "Well, you think my facts are slippery? I think they are pretty accurate, but you're right that Alan always has something to add. He particularly likes coming behind me."

Amy said, "I'm sure you're both right. Yes, it is too bad he's missing this dandy conversation, but Laurence, now that you've had something to eat, will you tell us how you happened to catch a ride here tonight with the police?"

"No, I don't mind, I apologize for not explaining earlier. I was just so hungry I couldn't do anything but eat. I had a situation with some young punks today, and they stole my wallet. I hoped to get it back from them intact if the police arrested them quickly, but no luck so far. I'm the only one who can identify them. I want to be close by when the police call."

"Why will they be close by here?" Amy asked.

"Well, it's a little complicated, but they are in the midst of a crime spree and intend to end it, literally, by jumping off the Aurora Bridge."

"What do you mean by crime spree?" asked Ben.

"The usual, robbery and murder."

"Good grief!" Amy said, looking very alarmed.

Alexis said, "Who is dead?"

"To the best of my knowledge, a convenience store clerk and possibly three people who had the misfortune to be in Zesto's parking lot earlier today."

"Oh dear," sighed Amy.

Kevin said, "They did the robbery and murder just a few days ago?"

Laurence nodded. "Yes, it seems so."

Shaking his head in disbelief, Drew said, "How did you get in the middle of this?"

"Minding my own business reading at the Ballard library, I overheard them plotting their next move and they must have noticed me listening. They definitely noticed when I foolishly went online to look up the news story and found the security camera photograph from the convenience store. That got the attention of the young man who did the shooting. Shortly thereafter, they saw me getting ready to board the bus with my wallet out to swipe the Orca card. I was an easy target because I wasn't paying attention to my surroundings. It's my own fault."

"You're the victim of a crime today. It's not your fault there are creeps ready to take advantage when ever they can," Kevin said.

"Laurence, that's just awful. What a terrible day you've had and it's not over yet. How about dessert before anything else happens?" Amy looked at Kevin and said, "Sweetheart, are you ready to serve the dessert?"

"Yes, when Laurence is ready. We're in no hurry." Kevin looked at Laurence and his almost empty plate and got the signal he was finished. He stood up and said, "Dessert is on the way." Kevin began picking up the dinner plates on the far side of the table from Drew and Laurence.

Alexis got up to help him clear, taking Amy's and Ben's plates into the kitchen and started putting them in the dishwasher.

When Alexis reappeared, she delivered Amy and Ben yellow hibiscus-shaped dessert plates with a scoop of pale orange mango sherbet garnished with the planned grated coconut and chopped mint. Amy eyed the third, unplanned garnish, a thin pretzel stick inserted in the top of the scoop of sherbet. When all the plates were served, she held up her glass.

"Let's toast the artist of the dessert course. New textures and flavors just for you. I bet no one in Malaysia, or anywhere else in the world, is eating salt in sherbet. Kevin, what inspired you?"

"Alexis and I inspired each other."

Amy welcomed the coldness of the sherbet in her mouth. It was refreshing after the heat and spice of the rendang. Not overly sweet, but the ripe mango flavor came through almost as though it was fresh fruit with cream poured on top. She liked the crunch of the coconut as the menthol of the mint hit her nose. Even the silly looking pretzel added a second level of crunch and salty contrast with the sweetness. Roasted peanuts would have worked well too for that effect. Garnishes were worth all the effort. It was so easy to be lazy and not prepare them, or more likely for her, to forget to serve them.

"Good job, Kevin and Alexis," Ben said. "I'm never serving plain ice cream again."

Alexis smiled at the compliment to herself. All was going so well she had forgotten about Drew being a flaw in her evening. "We have those giant pretzels for watching football games. What do you say we throw them in the food processor or beat them with a hammer in a dishtowel and make a nut mix? It would make a great garnish for ice cream, soup, or salad."

"What nuts were you thinking about?" Ben was serious now.

"Cashews or almonds."

"Not peanuts?"

"No, that would be a cliché." Alexis took another bite of mango sherbet and slowly chewed the garnishes. She liked the aroma of the mint but envisioned in her new garnish recipe a different herb flavor.

"Oh, Ben, how about chopped rosemary? That would be so cool with the salt and the nuts and such a surprise to be used with a sweet instead of savory."

"We can try it when we get home." Ben was excited about a late-night experiment.

"Sounds like a nice after-party shaping up in Eastlake. If it's a big success, don't call, send me an email in the morning," Amy said, glad she hadn't voiced her peanut idea.

"Please help yourself to more wine. Do we need to open something different? I'm sure there is some late harvest something if anybody wants it. Ben?"

"I never say no. My inspiration is none other than Maugham himself; 'Excess on occasion is exhilarating. It prevents moderation from acquiring the deadening effect of a habit.' How about that?"

"Brilliant," laughed Drew.

"I am impressed," said Alexis.

"Me too!" Amy chuckled and clapped her hands.

"Is there anything else in my house you would like?" Kevin got up again to get small after dinner drink glasses from the cabinet in the kitchen and get the dessert wine out of the refrigerator. "We're giving it all away to our friends tonight. We have some sterling silver. How about my Brutarian collection or a classic recording of Maria Callas? Don't be shy, Ben."

"I'd like some tax advice."

"That's never freely given. My meter is at the office, so you'll have to pay me a call."

Alexis said, "Ha, ha. Very funny. Take what you can get, Ben."

Drew looked at Kevin, puzzled. "Are you really a tax guy? I thought that was a joke."

"For better or worse, it keeps the cash flow going."

"How long have you been in that business?" Drew still wasn't sure if he was being duped somehow.

"Since I had to go to law school because I couldn't think of anything else to do and once there gave careful thought to business cycles. The advisors assured me taxes were recession-proof."

"You were a cynic in the 1970s! I thought we were supposed to choose something we had a passion for: art, rock n' roll, or the perfect loaf of bread. It's passion that keeps me crazy and almost broke."

"My passion is avoiding hard times," Kevin said.

274

"Earlier you said you loved it. What do you really do?" Drew said again, not willing to give up easily on learning the details about the profession of a potential client.

"More importantly, do you hate to go to work every day? Did I tell you that I hate to go to work every day?" Ben threw in.

"No, Ben, you haven't mentioned it in at least thirty minutes. I don't love to go, but I don't hate to go, either. The tax law I practice is probably not what you think it is. I don't prepare taxes or go to court. As a rookie tax lawyer from Willamette University, I got a job at the IRS trying to make cases against corporate tax evaders. In that role, I learned about our local and state tax laws, which are not well understood, and that specialty knowledge later got me a job in a big firm and ultimately to starting my own practice with one partner. What I really do is figure out how to best structure or restructure entities to take advantage of the laws that encourage companies to do business here. Washington competes with the world to entice employers. We are generous with all sorts of tax credits. Our clients want to make sure they haven't missed any opportunity to save on taxes."

Kevin looked at Amy at the end of the table and they exchanged a small glance. He knew she was thinking of a compliment about his expertise but wouldn't say it out loud as it made him uncomfortable. This wasn't meant to be a bragging session, just clarifying the situation. He was happy she was enjoying herself.

Drew said, "I actually think I understood what you said. The best current example is our illustrious, local hero of commerce, Amazon, not collecting sales tax in some states, even where it has a warehouse, correct?"

"Boeing, Microsoft and Nike also make the news fairly often because they are big and the tax incentives they receive add up to some big numbers, but all

275

businesses are entitled. You just don't hear much about the smaller companies."

Drew continued, "I hear you. So you all went to college together in Salem?"

"Alan, Amy, and I lived the good Oregon life for six years." Kevin looked at Ben, who he could see was preparing to launch into a well-known rant.

"While I was killing myself studying in the gritty city Boston was then, you were lying around a cow pasture smoking dope and reading Beowulf!"

"That's about right, Ben," Kevin said drolly.

"I'm still killing myself, but for underage slave drivers who don't know as much as I do about anything." No one laughed. Ben seemed angry, not amused.

"Oh, buddy, I think you're taking it all too seriously. Work is work and nothing more. It's not personal." Kevin's attempt to diminish the tone of Ben's emotion backfired.

"Nothing personal about my body being in the same chair sixty to eighty hours a week with the whip cracker nearby and noisy?" Now Ben was incredulous.

Kevin shook his head at him but said nothing. There was no point in continuing, as he knew from experience where the discussion went.

Disappointed, Ben turned his focus to refilling his wine glass, uncertain which way to go if Kevin wasn't going to play along. He looked at Drew and Laurence to see if either of them would pick up the thread.

Laurence had listened carefully about the opposing views of passion and dispassion in careers but said nothing. As a student he had embraced aeronautics as the most exciting career imaginable. He suspected Ben had been a passionate student. Looking back now, it seemed that the trajectory of passion inevitably led downwards, as conditions never stayed the same. Kevin may never have been as thrilled in his detachment, but he imagined there was satisfaction for him in designing effective solutions for complicated businesses. The media loved to throw sand at the public occasionally with articles on how little taxes Boeing paid. Laurence completely understood the business value of incentives and credits. That type of knowledge was a career at Boeing.

Alexis had had enough of Ben's rants and intervened to change the subject. "Amy, anything new at the library?"

"I think the best line of the week was in response to a woman railing at me about all the service cats and dogs in the building. An Afghan vet in line behind her told her to come back next week when he was bringing his PTSD-trained rattlesnake wrapped around his neck. It strikes before he does." She laughed.

"Aren't people incredible?" Alexis asked Laurence.

Laurence looked like he didn't understand the question and said nothing.

"I mean aren't you amazed by the variety of people you run into at the library?" Alexis focused on his eyes, watching him prepare his response and thinking, *No quick answers from this guy.*

"Yes, I suppose so, particularly if you consider the range of topics being studied. That's probably the most interesting aspect. There is digital art hanging above the reference desk that displays the topics being checked out numerically and in words. Have you seen it Drew?"

"Yes, I have and met the artist at one of the events related to the opening. I think he is a talent and he is also a professor of interactive media in the UC system."

"Amy, why do you like volunteering at the library?" Laurence said to direct some attention to the hostess.

"It's a good job for me. I help the tourists, who are happy because they are on vacation. I'm the expert on the location of the restrooms and the next attraction.

They are appreciative. It's fun to be an expert at something. The architecture buffs are a pleasure to deal with because they are so excited about the building and usually want a restaurant recommendation. The regulars I deal with are mostly people I am glad to see every week, like you, Laurence."

"Thank you. I find all the staff at the library to be high quality."

Amy invited everyone to tour the building, assuring them that every week she had locals visit who had had it on their list since it opened in 2004. Alexis was tepid as the parking was so awful. She wasn't sure if Ben was being humorous when he said he wasn't coming.

"Fremont is the center of the universe. I don't need downtown. All the cool people hang out in Fremont. Most of the homeless guys you see are ex-engineers. I'll probably be one of them soon, but I'm lucky; I've got my trusty 1983 Volvo to sleep in on rainy nights after I smoke crack."

"Ben, where are the dog and I staying if you go live with your buds on the street?" Alexis got some laughs around the table.

"You can tell our banker I jumped off the bridge and you need a widow's break on the mortgage payments until you sell the house and move in with your boyfriend." Now Ben was enjoying himself again.

Kevin said, "Alexis, you didn't tell me about your boyfriend. Is he in a recession-proof industry?"

"Kevin, my dog is my only boyfriend. I'm done with the two-legged kind. Four legs is the new perfect for me. We'll go keep house for my parents quick before any of my siblings beat me to it. They're recession-proof; they're on Social Security in a rent controlled apartment."

The phone in the kitchen rang. Everybody looked at each other. Kevin as usual shook his head that he was not answering it. Amy got up, moving toward the ringing sound in the kitchen. She answered and paused for a few

278

seconds, then held out the phone. "Laurence, it's for you."

He got up, walked over to her in the kitchen to take it from her hand, and went around the corner out of the view of the dining table.

He was listening and then speaking so softly no one could understand what he was saying. He returned to stand by the table near Kevin and Alexis. "That was the police. They are coming to pick me up right now as they think the suspects are on the bridge. Thank you very much for the hospitality. I enjoyed meeting you all. Amy, your dinner was wonderful. I will wait outside. Please don't get up."

Laurence walked toward the front door followed by Thor, and they heard the chime when he opened it and then the door closing. He moved efficiently with no extra motion or sound. His departure happened so fast everyone at the table was silently staring in the direction he had taken, in the space he had once filled. Thor returned to sit under the table by Amy.

Amy looked around at everyone at the table who appeared as stunned by his exit as she was. She smiled. "He's pretty cool isn't he?"

Kevin nodded in agreement. Ben said, "It's always good to have another engineer around, particularly when he is older than I am."

"He looks like the future to me, for all of us. We should probably take notes."

Drew gave Amy a thumbs up. "He looks great, good posture and energy. He exudes credibility. A haircut and a nice dress shirt will be all he needs. He's going to be very helpful to my pasta event and me. I think he'll be a crowd pleaser. He could have a new career as a judge in the fund-raising circuit."

Alexis said, "The way things are going tonight, who knows what might happen next?"

Ben stood up. "The standard protocol these days is to close the bridge so no one can heckle the jumpers. That should make for a good traffic jam on Saturday night. We can probably watch it all online. So much for keeping suicides out of the news."

Ben pulled his iPhone out of his pocket and began, scrolling. "Already the tweets say they have blocked both sides of the bridge to traffic. Haven't been able to get a picture yet, but the traffic alerts show the bridge is closed. Someone should have a phone camera in soon to give us a visual—or one of the neighbors with a view of the bridge and a telescope will help out. I love technology in a disaster. Yo, Kevin, crank up your laptop so we can watch the movie."

Kevin got up and went over to the bar to open the laptop and set up several searches looking for the unofficial news. Someone wanting to cross the bridge should be venting their aggravation online soon so everyone could know how they felt. Drew and Ben moved over to bar chairs with their fingers flying over the smart phones' screens, calling out promising locations. "Try myballard.com, queenanneview.com, or public911.com."

"Oh, Alexis, this is like rubbernecking isn't it?" Amy twirled her half glass of wine, looking around at the table debris of unused silver, dirty dessert plates, glasses, and the empty chairs.

"Yeah, I think so, but it's hard not to do it."

"Let's don't. Let's go sit outside and talk about something fun."

Amy grabbed a partially full bottle of wine from the dining table and her wine glass and headed through the French doors back to the little tile table and chairs in the dark corner of the deck.

"How's the job hunt going?" Amy asked after she settled in and refreshed both their wine glasses.

"It sucks in that it's not going. There's very little out there and what is out there isn't interested in me." Alexis shook her head. "I don't think Macy's would hire me now to paste up newspaper ads. I'm afraid it shows on the outside that I don't take instruction well."

"Ha! That's why I quit looking, too. Kevin is so mean, he said I had to stop saying I was *unemployed* and start saying I was *retired* when I hadn't applied to anything for a long time. As you noticed tonight, I don't say *retired*—I hate that word—I have a new job description. You can't kill an old marketing manager."

"I think it's nothing but age discrimination. No one wants to hire anyone who is fifty-something. We're just a liability for health and retirement benefits, plus what young manager wants an old woman working for him who earns more than he does and might know more than he does?"

"Alexis you have special skills, in my case, I think it's easy for them to find someone younger and cheaper."

"Don't sell yourself short. Your experience across product lines is valuable. You know about so many different things."

"I don't know. I think I'm too general; you need to be more specific these days. I was kicking myself the other day for choosing marketing instead of going to law school. It seems to me that lawyers can work until the day they die—and I hope Kevin does. But I chatted with a friend I haven't seen in ages who has almost thirty years as a lawyer with the government and she's desperate to change departments or agencies. She says no one will hire her. I said what about all your prosecuting experience, isn't it valuable? She said no, for exactly the reason you just said, she knows too much."

Alexis nodded. "That reminds me, when I was about forty I hired someone who was almost sixty and overqualified for the job. I felt bad for her. She turned out to be a backstabbing, undermining bitch. She caused me so much trouble. If I ever run into her again I might be rude!"

"I can picture that," Amy laughed.

"The worst part is I hate not having my own money!"

Amy nodded in agreement. "I requested a monthly line item titled *FLM Expenses* so I wouldn't have to ask for money and he can't ask me for receipts."

"Amy, that is a great idea. I'll ask for one tomorrow. What could I call mine? How about *Ambiance Expenses* as in, no more free ambiance around here?"

"That sounds like a good deal for Ben."

"Have you got any good cottage industry ideas?"

"I think about it every day. I still love my idea for a recipe app with a personal database to use at the grocery store when you see a good deal but can't think of a recipe or remember what else is in it. I need an engineer to write the code, of course. The lime pickles in Malaysia were to die for and could become a force in the condiment aisle. My best idea today is gourmet dog treats. You want to be partners in something?"

"Do you really have a good dog recipe?" Alexis looked at her.

"You bet I do. All organic and Thor loves them. I eat them, too. Plain tasting to me without salt, but the crunch is very satisfying. The base recipe can be flavored with herbs, vegetables or protein. You could start out with four varieties. Thor loves the cheese and rosemary best. Carrot and parsley would be easy. Got to have a fish flavor. What else?"

"I love the idea of doing anything but software! Food would be so refreshing. We could have fun with shapes and packaging. I have cookie cutters shaped like a squirrel and a cat. What do you think?"

"I am so glad you think it sounds worth pursuing. There's the big dog, small dog angle. Maybe we could even add some nutrition or teeth cleaning ingredient to make them seem more important." Amy raised her wine glass in Alexis's direction.

"Let's make a list of pet-supply stores tomorrow to visit and see what the competition is."

"We could start with a table at a farmer's market for testing consumer reaction to the product and pricing. That would give us time to look into the local regulations on production facilities. Home kitchens are usually not allowed. They should change that rule. A backup idea might be Alexis's All-Purpose Pretzel Topper. That sounded good to me at dinner."

"Let's try dog biscuits first. Fewer critics," Alexis said, already visualizing packaging ideas for small, medium, and large dogs.

"Do you really think you have the energy to start something new from scratch? It's a lot of hard work," Amy said, looking at Alexis. "I'm not sure I do."

"I have to! I can't do without my own money for ten more years. If I don't get some new cash flow going, I'll be the next one jumping off the bridge."

"I know what you mean. It's also frightening to think that whatever we've done so far is all that we're doing. Maybe that fear will motivate us."

Alexis nodded. "Desperation could be what's needed—or terror—middle-aged woman terror, to get us in high gear ready to ignore adversity, rejection, and young competitors. How much money do you think we'll need?"

"I haven't pushed a pencil on this idea, but I have some money and an empty credit card I would be willing to invest if our test results are promising." Amy felt brave volunteering financing. She wanted to encourage Alexis to really think about it. Having a partner might make all the difference to Amy in summoning up the courage to try a new venture. Alexis as that partner would add an aggressive edge; it wouldn't be a hobby. They would have to talk seriously about how they had worked well together in the past and what they could do to give themselves the best chance to succeed.

"Amy, I can see you're really thinking about this. Is there anyone else you'd thought of partnering with?"

"We've got KIRO on the bridge!" Kevin called out to them through the open French door and was motioning for them to come inside.

"Oh, my god. Shall we go see what has happened?" Alexis stood up.

"No, let's don't, stay here." Amy was pleading, but Alexis was already moving to the bar with the men and the assortment of screens, leaving her alone in the dark. She was unhappy about the gathering in the kitchen right now, but all in all, she was delighted about the connections made tonight. Amy toasted herself for the successful food. Every dish had been what she wanted it to be and achieved the reactions she had hoped for. Everyone here now loved Malaysian food and wanted more of it. Watching Laurence eat and interact had been thrilling. Drew inviting him to be a pasta judge was beyond thrilling. A potential partnership with Alexis was invigorating. Kevin looking so pleased all night was wonderful, too.

Sitting in the center seat of the bar with Drew and Ben on either side of him massaging their phones, Kevin kept a close watch on the laptop screen positioned so they could all view the helicopter film footage of patrol cars and unmarked cars parked to block both entrances to the bridge. Police sawhorses and orange tape divided the center span of the west edge of the Aurora Bridge. All the crime scene activity generated by disaster and mayhem was in progress. With all his inside information, Kevin felt so superior to the reporter trying to make compelling news with no details of why traffic was backed up for miles. The reporter was free-associating speculations about what the incident on the bridge might be: a bomb threat, a murder, or perhaps a man attempting to jump.

Whatever the activity, there was no information yet on who the person might be. There appeared to be plainclothes and uniformed experts involved at the scene, while more uniformed police kept the vigil at the barricades in the center and at both entrances to the bridge. Kevin gave the reporter credit for his ability to spin something out of nothing. He either had politics or stand-up as a background before TV news reporting.

Kevin turned down the volume on the laptop so he could report the visual he was seeing as the broadcast wasn't interesting to him. "The action is on the west side of the bridge, the southbound traffic side, but there's still no close-up to see how many people are involved."

Kevin turned to Alexis. "Look at the crowd gathered by the pedestrian walkway! Who are these night owls? Amy, come see this."

Amy refused to stand up and called out to him instead, "No, thanks. I'll read about it in the morning paper."

Kevin was getting more animated. "Where do these people work? Where do they live?"

Drew and Ben were now speculating on what the crowd had been doing to be so close by the bridge.

The KIRO spokesperson on the Fremont edge of the barricade was interviewing anyone who would talk to him, trying to create some news, asking what anyone had seen or heard—just in case it turned out to be newsworthy—so far the first twenty bystanders had not been. He gave them no screen time, blocking their bodies from the camera with his own while he talked to the microphone.

"Look, it's Laurence!" Drew shouted.

Kevin turned up the volume. "Amy, look quick, it's Laurence!"

"What!" She jumped up from the porch chair and came inside to stand beside Kevin to be able to see the laptop.

"Who are you, sir, and how do you happen to be here right now?" The reporter held the microphone out for his response.

"My name is Laurence Hansen. I've been following or followed by those teenage punks since late in the afternoon."

"Do you mean you know who they are?"

"The names, no, but from what I overheard them say, they've been on a crime spree and intend to jump off the bridge to become famous and to avoid going to jail."

"What sort of crimes?" asked the reporter.

"Robbery and murder," he said.

"Have you talked to the police?"

"Yes. I have filed a report for robbery and assault." Laurence looked so calm and dignified.

The interviewer continued, "You personally were assaulted and robbed by the person or people who are attempting to jump off the bridge right now?"

"Yes. Two teenagers."

"Who have they murdered?"

"I don't know for sure, but perhaps a convenience store clerk, perhaps some people at Zesto's."

"Breaking news here on the Aurora Bridge, which is closed due to potential suicide jumpers who have been on a crime spree to become famous. The bridge is closed to traffic in both directions. This is an exclusive report live on the Aurora Bridge."

"He'll be well known tomorrow," said Drew. "This is going to be great for my pasta contest! I will take him first thing in the morning to my hair stylist and then Nordstrom for a shirt. I can give him some media coaching on the way or maybe take him to the gallery for some practice sessions."

"You aren't kidding around, are you, Drew! This gets better and better." Ben was bouncing up and down.

286

Chapter 28

Kevin, Drew, Ben, and Alexis were standing huddled around the bar talking simultaneously. Kevin was searching on the laptop. Drew, Alexis, and Ben stroked their iPhones looking for tweets, blogs, and phone photos from people standing in the crowd on the bridge or underneath it, calling out the location of each new find. Ben was doing a monologue to no one in particular about teenage crime sprees—theorizing maybe this was Columbine in Seattle.

Amy sat on a bar chair twirling the wine in her glass, feeling a little sick at heart. The speed with which bad news traveled was disheartening. Why did everyone rally around tragedies and car wrecks but seldom around anything else? She would have been so happy to get a good night's sleep and read about this in the morning. If they were criminals, she was glad they had jumped. If they were teenage murderers, she was glad they had jumped, too. She didn't think that total disrespect for human life could be instilled or reinstilled by a lifetime in prison.

She felt bad about the two young men whose short lives were so filled with depravity that they had embraced it as a culture. How is a place like Seattle, the green, the clean, the politically correct, the well-read, caffeinated city of technology able to generate atrocities, even on a small scale? What cruel and illegal things are for sale here that are not also for sale in Moscow or Mumbai? How much did an exponentially larger standard of living in the U.S. prevent inhumanities?

287

What would Laurence do with his few minutes of fame after being on television? Hopefully, it would bring some attention to him that was useful—not just invasive media harassment. He was such an intelligent, gentle soul. She was so glad he felt he could come to her house tonight—not just to use the phone—but because he felt he would be welcomed. He had enjoyed himself, she was sure of it. He had fit in just by being himself. She would ask him to something else sometime.

The media blitz going on around her bar was annoying and not fun at all to her. All the conversations before these dumb teenagers had hijacked the party had been amusing, interesting, and good interactions that everybody participated in. Now they might as well have Game Boys in their hands, every eye locked on a screen, mouthing single syllables, hoping something sensational would happen next. The party was a big deal to her, a celebration of a great vacation and an amazing cooking class. The class had created a reason to get together with these people. Had it changed her life? Not exactly, but Rohani had certainly inspired her to try to stop worrying, particularly about aging, and accept that her life was fine, not perfect, but nothing to complain about. She was trying to enjoy that she looked pretty good and not wait for twenty years to appreciate how good. She was trying to embrace all the positives about where she was in life. Her cooking skills, which were such a source of pleasure to her, were a good example of something that could only be acquired through many years of practice. She had lost the youthful desire to be like somebody else or different than what she was. She was trying to remember to respect the rice.

The insult on Western Avenue today had been put into perspective and hadn't ruined the day. It hurt her feelings, but she had shrugged it off instead of closing the curtains, getting in bed, and pulling the covers over her head. She was proud of that. She had moved forward

288

through her day and put the finishing touches on the special meal she'd prepared for her friends here tonight. Everyone had enjoyed each other's company and interests. It didn't matter that they didn't get together that often. They were friends. It had been this way for years and it had bothered her for years that it wasn't quite right or quite enough. Tonight she turned that over and could see that it was just fine.

The guest bedroom door opened and out came a disheveled Alan. "I thought I went home."

She got up and gave him a hug. "No, you were having too much fun and enjoying the delicious dinner. We'll just charge you a half-night rate for the room."

Drew got up and offered his seat to Alan. "Hear all about it. I'm going out for some fresh air." He walked out through the French doors to the deck and disappeared in the dark.

"Really? Oh, good. What's all the hubbub?" He eyed everyone with electronics in their hands who were now eyeing him as he took Drew's seat.

"Our party was commandeered by some jumpers on the Aurora Bridge. We're trying to get the latest on who they are. What can I get you, Alan? Does anyone want coffee?" Amy looked around for interest and got no takers.

"I'd like a gallon of water, please, with ice," Alan said.

Ben looked up. "What happened to the grappa?"

"I don't want any grappa," said Alan.

Kevin shook his head at Ben and Alan. "The late harvest didn't do it for you, Ben? Well, I agree it's a little floral as they say. I'll be right back with a very manly grappa that hasn't been infused with anything sweet. Amy, you help Alan with the gallon of water." He got up and headed for the wine cellar.

Alexis could smell irresistible cigarette smoke out on the deck and took it as a sign she should indulge herself and force him into action.

Drew got his pack out as he saw her approaching in the dark and offered her one, which he lit quickly and quietly.

"Thanks," Alexis said, dragging and exhaling deeply. She looked at him without emotion, waiting for him to make the move, whatever it would be. He had obviously been thinking about it, as it didn't take him too long.

"I am sorry I was such a jerk when I had the chance to be with you. I truly apologize for all the crappy things I did to make you hate me as much as you do. I'm not quite as horrible these days as I used to be. I don't expect you to forgive me, but I'd like to be able to see you without rancor now that it seems we all know the same people."

They stood quietly for a while just smoking while Alexis considered his speech and how much sincerity was in it. Probably not much, but she gave him a few points for delivery. "Okay. You're insufferable and I am glad you know it. I accept your apology. It doesn't mean we're friends. You won't be seeing me at your gallery. We can be civil now that we know each other."

"Is this going to be a problem with your husband?"

Alexis put out her cigarette in the ashtray on the table, "No. He doesn't know anything about you and me."

"He won't ask?"

"He will tomorrow, but I will tell him that you're an egomaniac from a painting class thirty years ago who thinks everyone who took the class with him should remember him. He'll believe me."

Drew looked at her, absorbing the words before responding. "I agree with you, honesty is not always the best policy."

"What's not true about that?" She shook her head with disdain and turned around to walk back inside and join the group at the bar.

Drew studied the sky thinking, *Alexis was still something! No change or mellowing at all.* He was glad that he had had a chance to apologize. It had been so long since he had seen her, he didn't think of her too often, mainly when he had the opportunity to try to make amends with another wronged woman. Then he always thought, *Oh, I hope I run into Alexis so I can use that line again. That would be perfect for her.* He liked apologizing about old fuck-ups. He thought his choice of words sounded meaningful and relevant to her even though he'd used them a few times before. It made him feel that he was a better human being and the women were always appreciative. He had deeply, or as deeply as he could, regretted screwing things up with Alexis. She really was special. She stood out in the small group who had had the gumption to walk out on him when his behavior was egregious. There was no question that he had been in love with her when she was the voluptuous model with the blue hair for the painting classes. She still had world-class skin and a very good figure, remarkable for her age, he thought. A small inspiration to paint came to him. He could visualize himself doing a new portrait of her, but he didn't paint anymore. The important point here tonight was that it would be good to have this crowd on his mailing list. He was even curious what she was doing these days art wise, though he wasn't going to ask to see it. He was also a little smarter than he used to be. He went back into the kitchen to see if anyone had jumped yet.

Grappa in one hand and iPhone in the other, Ben read aloud the latest news from under the bridge. "They say only one jumped and is DOA. The police have the

291

other one in custody. No one's sure who he is, but he appears to be a teenager."

Alexis looked at Amy and smiled. "We had another great time. Thanks for having us. I'll call you tomorrow. Maybe you can get a spreadsheet going for our project."

"It was our pleasure. Tomorrow afternoon is wide open for me. We could meet at Voxx or Starbucks by you. What are you liking these days?"

"Let's decide when we get up. I imagine I'll be serving breakfast in the early afternoon." Alexis patted Ben's shoulder. "Ben, time to drink up. We need to go home. Alan, can we give you a ride?"

"That would be lovely. I hate calling a taxi at this time of night. Drew lives near me; maybe he'd like a ride, too."

Alexis looked over her shoulder at him and said, "Drew, what about you?"

"I had planned to take the bus, which should be coming soon, but if you have room, I'll get out at Alan's."

"You might as well ride with us then."

"Thanks. That's very nice of you to offer."

Kevin took Alexis by the elbow and began escorting her to the door with Thor running ahead and Amy close behind holding Alan's elbow. Kevin and Amy stopped at the top of the steps on the front porch to say their goodbyes.

Alexis and Alan paused at the sidewalk by her car, chatting after she unlocked the doors with her remote and watching Ben and Drew say goodnight on the porch. "Hmmm, what are we going to talk about with two awake guys in the backseat?"

"No worries. I can always think of something that's not about them and Drew is unlikely to be silent," said Alan.

Drew shook Kevin's hand and kissed Amy on the cheek. "Thank you both so much for the evening. The

292

food and the company were extraordinary. I hope to see you again soon."

Ben air-kissed Amy's cheek and high-fived Kevin. "Next time, buddy." He looked down at the two waiting for him by the car. "Alan, you riding shotgun?"

Alexis nodded and said, "Yes." She walked around the front of the car and got in the driver's seat. Alan opened the passenger's door and got in beside her.

"Come on, Drew. This limo is leaving." Ben and Drew walked down the steps together headed for the car.

As he got in the backseat behind Alexis, Drew thought, *My, what a surprising end to the evening this drive home will be with my old and new friends. Wonder what would happen if I asked them all to come up for a nightcap, just to be friendly and appreciative of the ride home? Alexis and Ben might enjoy seeing my collection.*

Chapter 29

Laurence couldn't believe he was sitting in the back of the patrol car again waiting for the officer talking with his colleagues. At least this time he wasn't hungry. The food at Amy's had been substantial and such a treat to eat something different. He realized what a rut he had been in with his roast chicken. The rendang dish had been chicken, too, but you would hardly have noticed that aspect of it because there were so many other aromas and flavors clamoring for attention. The fresh turmeric was very intriguing to him. He wanted to investigate it and would go to Uwajamaya soon and wander around. He made a shopping list in his mind and put the kaffir lime leaf on it too, so he could reproduce that sweet citrus fragrance that he remembered from a once popular Indian restaurant Ingrid liked that he doubted existed anymore. Making a curry paste was really not that much effort. He might just make a batch of the curry paste cooked to the ready point and keep it refrigerated as a condiment. A spoonful could be used to season most any vegetable. He planned to do some research into Malaysian recipes. Learning more about the cuisine and ingredients would be a good new topic for his schedule. Mondays might be the day to do it since the culinary collection at the downtown library was much larger than at the branches. Coming home for dinner would have extra appeal with a new menu occasionally.

Sadly, he accepted how much he had enjoyed sitting around the table and listening to the conversation. He had even been amused by a few comments. Not knowing the people hadn't made any difference in appreciating or comprehending their thoughts as he had imagined it would when the invitation was first extended. The idea of him sitting down with a group of strangers to eat had seemed absurd, absolutely out of the question. He thought he was past caring about or enjoying being social in any way. Evidently, his solitary life was not enough. Acknowledging this was somewhat embarrassing to him. It seemed like weakness in his self-sufficiency. He would have to think about it and how he might manage it. Maybe Steve would be interested in coming to town again. How would Steve get in touch with him? He had been so sure he would be the one jumping off the bridge tonight instead of the imbecile that he hadn't given him his email address. Laurence would have to be the one to call him. Oh, he didn't want to do that again right away. He'd wait a few weeks and see how he felt.

The bridge was still cordoned off to traffic. It was weird to see it empty except for the police presence. It looked much bigger than it did from the bus window. The patrol car seemed small, almost vulnerable traveling on the wrong side of the road. Identifying the kids standing in the pedestrian walkway in the middle of the bridge had been easy, even from inside the police car as it drove slowly by. The clothes, the posture, the dirty hair were unmistakable. He had rolled down his window to get the clearest look at them and felt the breeze on his face. It was windy. When he had studied the pedestrian path on the bridge, this was exactly the spot he had chosen as the perfect place to jump from. Laurence asked the officer to stop the car for a better look. Again, he was given the warning not to get out of the car and the added instruction not to say a word.

Laurence looked over at the boys horsing around and some official person talking to them over the guard railing, foolishly thinking it was possible to talk sense into them. He thought about getting out of the car quickly to get a word with them before the policemen could drag him back. He wanted to ask for his wallet and say something else to them. He wanted to talk to them, make them look him in the eye, recognize who he was in this drama today. Their obliviousness to everyone and everything infuriated him. He wanted to scream *Wake-up!* He also wanted to be there with them for a moment and think back on the many times he had envisioned himself standing where they were standing to try to get his mind wrapped around what were the commonalities, what were the differences that brought them all to this place on this night. It was troubling to him that he shared with them deliberate steps to avoid pain and skip ahead to the desired end spot. Living a law-abiding life did not make him exactly a polar opposite of them but something else oddly off balance that permitted him to think he was entitled in some way, as they felt entitled in some way. He had mixed emotions about everything that had happened today. He had been so sure this morning that today was the day to free himself of all his difficulties. The change in him tonight was that jumping no longer looked like a practical solution to the problem; it looked like the route for the spineless. He would have to deal with the inevitable, just like every one else.

But it would be so easy to get out of the police car and vault himself forcefully over the low railing to startle the kids and scare the wits out of them. He was strong enough to do that and would enjoy giving them a fright. He could beat them to the jump. He could say, *Follow me* as his last words. Would they? Or would the sight of an old man beating them to the bottom make them hesitate and reevaluate their plan? Why not make his exit after a nice meal and good wine? Right now was the perfect opportunity. He was so close. He could probably succeed before any of the law enforcement could stop him. Last chance.

He must have tensed up his shoulders at that thought as though preparing to open the door. The policeman said sharply, "Well? Are those the ones you saw at the library that took your wallet?"

Once he said he was certain, the officer parked the car closer to the end of the bridge on the Fremont side where a few other patrol cars were forming an additional blockade behind the yellow tape. He looked at Laurence in the back seat and said, "You know what to do, right?"

Laurence nodded at him and said, "Stay."

The crowd gathering on the other side of the yellow tape seemed almost festive, talking amongst themselves, some with paper cups and beer cans, some were taking photos with their telephones. Once the media arrived and started interviewing everyone, the crowd got livelier. Laurence finally couldn't restrain himself and had to get out and walk toward the bright lights to join the crowd. His policeman was involved elsewhere and wouldn't notice. Why would he care anyway if Laurence waited on the other side of the yellow tape with everyone else? The man with the microphone seemed to be motioning to him. He couldn't resist walking over to him, looking into the camera lens as he walked. He felt like he had something to say about all this. He wanted to be recognized.

Chapter 30

Kevin, Amy, and Thor watched from the porch as the car drove away. When there was nothing left to see, they went back inside and started the postmortem on the party while clearing the remaining glasses and silverware from the dining table and loading the dishwasher. Thor patrolled the floor close to the food-fall zone.

"What a night. In the hostess diaries, this one will stand out. Am I unflappable or what?"

"I thought you were amazing. Your food was great. Nothing wrong there."

"Thanks. I thought it was good, too. I'm proud of myself to have powered on through Riley, the mystery woman, and Drew. Oh, then Alan and Laurence. Maybe we have a new friend in the making with Laurence." She looked at him to see him considering that idea without any immediate response. "Actually, the media frenzy around the bar was the worst part for me, and the best part was your performance. I thought you were hilarious with the photos. Everyone loved them."

"Oh, god, don't remind me. I had already forgotten about that."

"Say, thank you, for the compliment."

Kevin ignored her request and busied himself putting dessert plates in the dishwasher.

"So, what did Alexis tell you about Drew when you were out on the deck?"

"Nothing. I didn't ask her. I was waiting for her to bring it up and we talked about Natalie."

"That was showing self-control above and beyond necessary. Now I'll be awake all night wondering what happened between them."

The phone rang. He looked up at her as usual and shook his head no he was not answering it.

"I can't help myself, I have to know who this is now." She grabbed the phone on the bar, "Hello?" She smiled at Kevin. "No, we don't need the taxi anymore. We got tired of waiting for it and he took the bus. Good night." She laughed as she put the phone back down. "How do these people stay in business?"

Kevin shook his head. "Speaking of business—I never got a chance to tell you that I nailed that defaulted building problem today at the office and have a wrap-up meeting with the client Monday afternoon."

"Wow! That's great. I didn't know you went to the office today."

"It's been kind of busy around here since I got home."

"That's true. Sorry for hogging the stage. Tell me how you figured it out and when you think he'll pay."

"It was genius striking at 3:30 AM while listening to you and Thor snore and the world news on the radio. I just needed to rethink it. We are going to reorganize the ownership entity and entitle him to a hefty tax refund from previous years. He'll pay right away he is so happy to have a big check coming his way."

"You're so smart. I'm so proud of you. What do you think about a new slipcover for the chaise upstairs? It would be so great to have a winter look, maybe a really plush gold chenille."

"Whatever you think is fine with me. Do we need to wash the serving dishes or just soak them?" He looked at her for the answer but could see she was already swept up in fabric ideas. "Amy, I am so glad you took the cooking class."

She turned and looked at him surprised. "Really? Why are you glad?"

"You came away inspired about yourself as well as Malaysian cuisine. You put all that into the evening and that made it more than just another night with the old crowd."

"Oh, thank you for seeing that. I felt it all night. Everyone got something extra out of the evening. I think about the cooking class every day and it reminds me of my goal to be comfortable in my sagging skin. I'm not saying I'm going to let my hair go gray or announce my age at parties, but I've been feeling quite competent— because of my age. You should probably sit down before I tell you Alexis and I are talking about a cottage industry to beat the unemployment blues."

He stared at her. "I'm still standing, but I felt a tremor. Should I hide my wallet? What are you two selling?"

"Organic dog treats." She held her head high and looked him in the eye.

Thor heard the two magic words and sat at her feet.

Kevin looked at her and nodded his head slightly, taking his time with the response. "Well, that would certainly put you in the kitchen and not in a cubicle. Nothing makes you happier than cooking, and I know there is no limit to what a dog lover will pay for a treat."

"So, you don't think we're crazy?"

"No. I think you're both smart and are excellent marketers."

"It's funny to me how devastated I was not to get to take the cooking class at the Oriental Hotel in Bangkok. Now I'm so glad that didn't work out."

"I remember having drinks there overlooking the Chao Phraya River. I think we ate something crunchy and hot as hell."

"Ikan bilis? I remember that too, those little dried, fried anchovies, spiced to the upper limits of salt and chili. I saw them packaged recently at that Filipino market at South Center. The salt content made my hand shake as I put them back on the shelf. Maybe we should cook some fresh anchovies and spice them up for a healthier version." Amy looked over at the refrigerator. "Anchovies will be great tomorrow with oh, my god, the rojak salad! I forgot to serve it tonight. We have enough for a week—or another party."

"Don't even think about sharing it with anyone. I want it for my lunch. We'll go to Chinatown tomorrow for the anchovies. Why were you devastated to be overlooking one of the most important river views in the world?"

"I realized as we sat there that I was never going to take the cooking class at the Oriental Hotel. I never looked into the details, like five nights in the five-star hotel! The all important details I'm usually so good at my job, but not my personal life."

"That might be the only detail you ever missed. How come I don't remember hearing about this?"

"You know I'm not a complainer. When Malaysia became our destination, I started looking for a cooking school just to be able to say *I went to it*—and I wanted you to figure out something to do while I was busy, for a change. I walked out of Rohani's class knowing how I *ought* to feel about my age and my life—confident, competent, and content with what I have. I think I'll feel it every time I make one of these recipes. That's so much better than a travel status symbol. It's not world peace," she raised her eyebrows, "but it seems to make people feel good." She stopped wiping off the counters and focused on his gaze and grin. "You didn't forget, did you?"

He put his arms around her, pulling her close to him, and whispered in her ear, "You think I don't listen, but I do."

Thor took advantage of the moment and rubbed against both their legs to share in whatever good was in the air.

BLACK STICKY RICE PUDDING by Rohani Jelani

1 cup black sticky rice *
1 quart water
2 pandan leaves, tied into a knot, or vanilla to taste **
1 handful dried longans, or raisins ***
1/4 – 1/2 cup sugar

Coconut Cream Topping

1/2 cup coconut milk
1/4 cup water
1/4 teaspoon salt

Pick rice over for husks and foreign objects and wash in several changes of water. Add 1 quart fresh water and bring to a boil. Turn down heat, add pandan leaves, and simmer for 30–40 minutes, stirring occasionally, until rice is soft and creamy. If needed, add more water as mixture cooks.

Add dried longans and continue simmering another 15 minutes. Add sugar to taste, take pan off the heat.

To make coconut cream topping, place coconut milk, water, and salt in a small pan. Heat gently, stirring all the time, until mixture comes to a boil. Take pan off the heat and transfer coconut milk into a small jug or bowl to serve at the table.

Serve (hot) rice pudding in small bowls drizzled with a little coconut cream.

* black sticky rice or black glutinous rice is sold at Asian markets, some specialty markets and online. It may be labeled Thai or Indonesian black sticky rice. Using Chinese black rice will not give the same result in texture.

** substitute vanilla bean or vanilla extract to taste

*** dimocarpus longan is sweet, juicy and used fresh, dried or canned in syrup. Longan (sometimes called dragon eye because of the eyeball shape) is sold at Asian markets, some specialty markets and online.

The End

Acknowledgements

I feel very lucky to have met Rohani Jelani, BayaIndah.com, a multi-talented food professional, who was the inspiration for a novel about trying to get okay with aging. I also feel fortunate to have worked with Debra Ginsberg, debraginsberg.com, a great editor, who always says what's working well first and is a great writer and baker to boot.

My thanks to the artists who have worked with me to present the book to you:

Cover art by Ryan Hobson, RyanHobson.com

Design services by Jennifer Rogers, jenniferrogersdesign.co

Cover photography by Steve MacAulay, SteveMacAulayPhotography.com

My shaggy muse, Grady, will never know how much he helped me by sharing the office space. He is well fed for his loyalty and discretion.

My wonderful husband, who chooses to stay off the grid, deserves a standing ovation for being encouraging and supportive every step of the way.